Ten weeks on the New York Times *best-seller list!*

"He eats hobbits for breakfast and makes Sauron look like a harmless little muppet. The star of The Dark Elf Trilogy, Drizzt Do'Urden is back in this latest tale. . . . If you haven't had the chance to read The Dark Elf Trilogy yet, run out and do so immediately. It ranks right up there with The Lord of the Rings as one of the best fantasy tales ever conceived, and this new chapter only expands upon its brilliance."

—Game Informer

"The author breathes . . . new life into the stereotypical creatures of the milieu. . . . Salvatore has long used his dark elf protagonist to reflect on issues of racial prejudice . . . and this novel is no exception."

—School Library Journal

"Drow Elf Drizzt Do'Urden and friends return for another rousing tale of derring-do and harrowing escapes."

—Publishers Weekly

FORGOTTEN REALMS® NOVELS BY

R.A. SALVATORE

FORGOTTEN REALMS

R·A·SALVATORE

THE THOUSAND ORCS

THE HUNTER'S BLADES TRILOGY
BOOK I

Wizards OF THE COAST

The Hunter's Blades Trilogy, Book I
THE THOUSAND ORCS

©2002 Wizards of the Coast, Inc.

Cover art by Todd Lockwood
Cartography by Dennis Kauth
First Printing: October 2002
Library of Congress Catalog Card Number: 2002114363

9 8 7 6 5

ISBN: 978-0-7869-2980-1
620-17974-001-EN

U.S., CANADA,
ASIA, PACIFIC, & LATIN AMERICA
Wizards of the Coast, Inc.
P.O. Box 707
Renton, WA 98057-0707
+1-800-324-6496

EUROPEAN HEADQUARTERS
Hasbro UK Ltd.
Caswell Way
Newport, Gwent NP9 0YH
GREAT BRITAIN
Save this address for your records.

Visit our web site at **www.wizards.com**

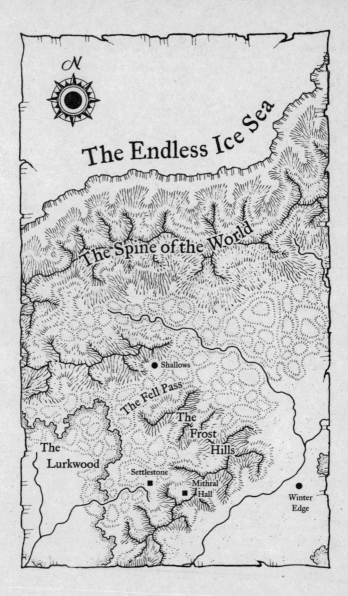

"Oh, well ye got to be pullin' harder than that!" Tred McKnuckles yelled to his team of two horses and three dwarves. "I'm hoping to be making Shallows afore the summer sun shines on me balding head!"

His voice echoed off the stone around them, a bellow befitting one of Tred's stature. He was stout, even as dwarves go, with a body that could take a beating and lumpy arms that could dish one out. He wore his yellow beard long, often tucked into the front of his huge belt, and kept a throwing hammer—commonly called "a dwarven arrow"—strapped on the back of each shoulder, ready for launch.

"It'd be easier if ye didn't have th' other horse sitting in the back o' the wagon, ye blasted fool!" one of the pulling dwarves yelled back.

Tred responded by giving him a crack on the rump with the whip.

The dwarf stopped, or tried to, but the fact that the wagon kept on rolling, and he was strapped into the yoke, convinced him that maybe it would be a good idea to continue moving his strong and stubby legs.

"Don't ye doubt that I'll be payin' ye back for that one!" he growled at Tred, but the other dwarves pulling, and the three others still sitting up on the wagon beside the boss dwarf, all just laughed at him.

They had been making fine progress since leaving Citadel Felbarr two tendays earlier, chancing the north run along the western face of the Rauvin Mountains. Breaking through to the flat ground, the group had done some minor trading and re-supplying at a large settlement of the Black Lion barbarian tribe. Named Beorunna's Well, it, along with Sundabar, Silverymoon, and Quaervarr, was a favored trading locale for the seven thousand dwarves of Citadel Felbarr. Typically, the dwarves' caravans would run to Beorunna's Well, swap their wares, then turn back to the south, to the mountains and their home, but this particular group had surprised the leaders of the barbarian settlement and had pressed on to the west-northwest.

Tred was determined to open up Shallows and the other smaller towns along the River Surbrin, running the western edge of the Spine of the World, for trade. Rumors had it that Mithral Hall had for some unknown reason slowed its trade of late with the towns upriver, and Tred, ever the opportunist, wanted Felbarr to fill that void. Other rumors, after all, said that some pretty amazing gems and even a few ancient artifacts, thought to be dwarven, were being pulled from the shallow mines on the western edges of the Spine of the World.

The late winter weather had been quite favorable for the fifty mile run, and the wagon had rolled along without incident past the northern tip of the Moonwood and right to the foothills of the Spine of the World. The dwarves had gone a bit too far to the north, however, and so had turned south, keeping the mountains on their right. Still, the temperatures had remained relatively warm, but not so warm that they would destroy the integrity of the snow sheets and thus rain avalanches all about the trails. That same morning, though, an abscess had reared its ugly head on the hoof of one of the horses, and while the handy dwarves had been able to extract the stone the horse had picked up and drain the abscess, the horse was not yet ready to pull the laden wagon. It wasn't even walking very comfortably, so Tred had the team put the horse up on the back of the large wagon, then he split the other six dwarves into two teams of three.

They were quite good at it, and for a long time, the wagon had kept up its previous pace, but as the second team neared the end of its second shift, they were starting to drag.

"When're ye thinking we'll get that horse back in the harness?" asked Duggan McKnuckles, Tred's younger brother, whose yellow beard barely reached the middle of his chest.

"Bah, she'll be trotting along tomorrow," Tred answered with confidence, and all the others nodded.

None knew horses better than Tred, after all. In addition to being one of the finest blacksmiths in all of Citadel Felbarr, he was also the place's most prominent farrier. Whenever merchant caravans rolled into the dwarf stronghold, Tred would inevitably be called upon, usually by King Emerus Warcrown himself, to shoe all the horses.

"Might be that we should be putting up for the night then," said one of the dwarves pulling along in front. "Set a camp, eat us a good stew, and lighten that load we got by a keg o' ale!"

"Ho ho!" several of the others roared in agreement, as dwarves usually did when the possibility of consuming ale was mentioned.

"Bah, ye've all gone soft on me!" Tred pouted.

"Ye're just wanting to beat Smig to Shallows!" Duggan declared.

Tred spat and waved his hands. It was too obvious a protest. Everyone there knew it was true enough. Smig was Tred's greatest rival, two friends who pretended to hate each other, but who, in truth, only lived to outdo each other. Both knew that the small town of Shallows, with its trademark tower and renowned wizard, had seen an influx of people right before the winter—frontiersmen who would need fine weapons, armor, and horseshoes—and both had heard King Warcrown's proclamation that he would be pleased to establish trading routes along the Spine of the World. Since the recapture of the dwarven citadel, which had been in orc hands for three centuries, the area west of Felbarr had calmed considerably, with the mountainous region to the east still buzzing with monstrous activity. There was an Underdark route to Mithral Hall, but none had been discovered thus far to open the lands north of Clan Battlehammer's stronghold. All of those accompanying Tred—his workers, including his brother Duggan, Nikwillig the cobbler, and the opportunistic brothers, Bokkum and Stokkum, who were carrying essential goods (mostly ale) for other Felbarr tradesmen—had eagerly signed on. The first caravan would be the most profitable one, taking their pick of the treasures garnered by the frontiersmen. Even more important than that, the first caravan would carry bragging rights and the favor of King Warcrown.

Right before the departure, Tred had engaged Smiggly "Smig" Stumpin in a good-natured drinking game, but not before he had paid one of the Moradin priests well for a potion that defeated the effects of alcohol. Tred figured that he and his had been out of Citadel Felbarr for a day and more before poor Smig had even awakened, and another day before the dwarf could shrink his head enough to get out the citadel's front door.

Tred would be damned if he'd let a little thing like an abscessed horse hoof slow them down enough for Smig to have a chance of catching up.

"Ye put up a trot for three more miles and we'll call it a good day," Tred offered.

Groans erupted all about him, even from Bokkum, who stood to lose the most profits by an early camp, and hence, more ale consumed and less to sell—though the betting was that he wouldn't end up selling it in Shallows anyway, and that he'd take it back for the celebration on the return journey.

"*Two* miles, then!" Tred barked. "Are ye wanting to share a camp this night with Smig and his boys?"

"Bah, Smig ain't even out yet," Stokkum said.

"And if he is, he and his got slowed plenty by the rock-fall we dropped in the path behind us," Nikwillig added.

"Two more miles!" Tred roared.

He cracked the whip again, and poor Nikwillig stood up very straight and managed to turn about enough to put a glower over the rugged driver.

"Ye hit me again and I'll be making ye a pair o' shoes ye won't soon be forgetting!" Nikwillig blustered.

His feet were digging little trenches as he got dragged along, and that only made Tred and the others laugh all the louder. Before Nikwillig could start his grumping again, Duggan kicked up a song about a mythical dwarven utopia, a great town in a deep mine that would please Moradin himself.

"Climb that trail!" Duggan crooned, and several looked at him, not sure if he was singing or ordering them around. "Break down that door!" Duggan went on, prompting Stokkum to yell out, "What door?"

But Duggan only continued, "Find that tunnel and run some more!"

"Ah, Upsen Downs!" Stokkum yelled, and the whole crew, even surly Nikwillig, couldn't resist, and broke into a rowdy, back-slapping song.

"Climb that trail
Break down that door
Find that tunnel
and run some more

"Cross the bridge of fiery glow
Running deeper down below
Make some smiles from those frowns
Ye've found the town of Upsen Downs!

"Upsen Downs! Upsen Downs!
Ye've found the town of Upsen Downs!
Upsen Downs! Upsen Downs!
Make some smiles from those frowns.

"Ye've found the place o' the finest ale
With arm-sized pretzels that're never stale!
With big Chef Muglump and his coney stew
And Master Bumble with his forty brews!

"And in the holes ye can break the rock
and haul it up with yer tackle and block
Smelt it down and ye'll get it sold
Upsen Downs's got the finest gold!

"Upsen Downs! Upsen Downs!
Ye've found the town of Upsen Downs!
Upsen Downs! Upsen Downs!
Make some smiles from those frowns.

It went on for many verses, and when the seven dwarves ran out of the formal lines of the old song, they just improvised, as they always did, with each piping in his own wants from such a remarkable place as Upsen Downs. That was the fun of the dwarven song, after all, and also a fairly subtle way for any perceptive dwarf to take a good measure of a potential friend or a potential foe.

Also, the song was a fine distraction, mostly for the three tugging the wagon along, backs bent and straining. They made fine progress through those minutes, bouncing along the rocky ground, the mountains rising up to their right as they moved south along the trail.

In the driver's seat, Tred called out names in order, bellowing for each to add the next verse. It went on smoothly, until he called out to his little brother Duggan.

The other five kept humming, providing the background, but they went through almost an entire verse, and there was still no response from Duggan.

"Well?" Tred asked, turning to regard his little brother and seeing a very confused look on Duggan's face. "Ye got to sing in, boy!"

Duggan looked at him curiously, confusedly, for a long moment, then quietly said, "I think I be hurt."

Only then did Tred look past that puzzled expression, moving his head back and taking a wider view of Duggan. Only then did Tred notice the spear sticking out of Duggan's side!

He gave a shriek, and the humming behind him stopped, with the two sitting in the back of the wagon turning to regard the slumping Duggan. Up front it quieted, too, but not completely, until a huge boulder whistled down, slamming the path right beside the three surprised dwarves and bouncing over them, clipping Nikwillig on the shoulder and knocking him silly.

The terrified horses broke into a gallop, and both the injured horse and poor Stokkum broke free of the rig, with Stokkum tumbling out onto the stony ground. Tred grabbed the reins hard, trying to slow the beasts, for his poor kinsmen up front were being tugged and dragged along, especially Nikwillig, who seemed unconscious.

Another boulder smashed down right behind the bouncing wagon, and a third hit the ground before the charging team. The horses veered wildly to the left, then tried to turn back to the trail on the right, putting the wagon up on two wheels.

"Move right!" Tred ordered, but even as he spoke the command, the wagon's left wheels buckled and the cart crashed down and flipped.

The horses broke free, then, taking the harness and the three strapped dwarves on a dead run down the rocky trail.

The two dwarves behind Tred went flying away—and Duggan was hardly aware of it—and Tred would have, too, except that his leg got hooked under the wagon seat. He felt the crunch of bone as the wagon came down atop him, then he got smacked on the head, and hard. He thought he had erupted into a bloody mess for a moment as the wagon continued its sidelong roll, but he had the fleeting notion that it was ale washing over him.

Luck alone extracted the dwarf from the crunching catastrophe, for he somehow wound up inside that decapitated keg. He went bounding and rolling away down the slope of the foothills. A rock stopped him abruptly, shattering the keg, and Tred went into a weird twisting somersault.

Tough as the stone around him, the dwarf struggled to his feet. One of his legs gave out under him, so he fell forward against the stone, stubbornly propping himself up on his elbows.

He saw them then, dozens and dozens of orcs, waving spears, clubs, and swords, swarming over the destroyed wagon and fallen dwarves. A pair of giants followed them down from the higher ground—not hill giants, as Tred would have expected, but larger, blue-skinned frost giants. He knew then that this was no ordinary band of raiders.

Slipping from consciousness, Tred kept enough of his wits about him to throw himself backward, falling into a roll down another slope, ending hard against another rock beneath a tangle of brambles. He tried to stand again but then tasted bloody dirt in his mouth.

Tred knew no more.

"Well, are ye alive, or ain't ye?" came a distant, gravelly voice.

Tred opened one eye, caked with blood, and through a haze saw the battered form of Nikwillig, crouched before the brambles and staring in at him.

"Good, so ye are," said Nikwillig and he slipped his arm in, offering

Tred a hand. "Keep your arse low or the pickers'll be skinning it good."

Tred took that hand and squeezed it tightly but did not start out of the tangle.

"Where're the others?" he asked. "Where's me brother?"

"The orcs killed 'em all to death in battle," came the grim response, "and the pigs're not too far away. Damned horses dragged me a mile an' more."

Tred didn't let go, but neither did he start forward.

"Come on, ye dolt," Nikwillig scolded. "We got to get to Shallows and get the word spreadin' back to King Warcrown."

"Ye run on," Tred replied. "Me leg's all broke. I'll slow ye down."

"Bah, ye're talking like the fool I always knowed ye was!"

Nikwillig gave a great tug, dragging Tred right out from under the brambles.

"Bah, yerself!" Tred growled at him.

"And so ye'd be leaving me if it was th' other way around?"

That question hit home. "Get me a stick, ye stubborn old fool!"

Soon after, arm in arm, with Tred leaning on both Nikwillig and a stick, the two hardy dwarves ambled off toward Shallows, already plotting their revenge on the ambushing orc band.

They didn't know that another hundred such bands were out of their mountain holes and roaming the countryside.

PART ONE | A LONGER ROAD THAN EXPECTED

When Thibbledorf Pwent and his small army of battleragers arrived in Icewind Dale with news that Gandalug Battlehammer, the First King and Ninth King of Mithral Hall, had died, I knew that Bruenor would have no choice but to return to his ancestral home and take again the mantle of leadership. His duties to the clan would demand no less, and for Bruenor, as with most dwarves, duties to king and clan usurp everything.

I recognized the sadness on Bruenor's face as he heard the news, though, and knew that little of it was in grieving for the former king. Gandalug had lived a long and amazing life, more so than any dwarf could ever hope. So while he was sad at losing this ancestor he had barely known, that wasn't the source of Bruenor's long look. No, what most troubled Bruenor, I knew, was the duty calling him to return to a settled existence.

I knew at once that I would accompany him, but I knew, too, that I would not remain for long in the safe confines of Mithral Hall. I am a creature of the road, of adventure. I came to know this after the battle against the drow, when Gandalug was returned to Clan Battlehammer. Finally, it seemed, peace had found our little troupe, but that, I knew so quickly, would prove a double-edged sword.

And so I found myself sailing the Sword Coast with Captain Deudermont and his pirate-chasing crew aboard Sea Sprite, with Catti-brie at my side.

It is strange, and somewhat unsettling, to come to the real-ization that no place will hold me for long, that no "home" will ever truly suffice. I wonder if I am running toward something or away from something. Am I driven, as were the misguided Entreri and Ellifain? These questions reverberate within my heart and soul. Why do I feel the need to keep moving? For what am I searching? Acceptance? Some wider reputation that will somehow grant me a renewed assurance that I had chosen well in leaving Menzoberranzan?

These questions rise up about me, and sometimes bring distress, but it is not a lasting thing. For in looking at them rationally, I understand their ridiculousness.

With Pwent's arrival in Icewind Dale, the prospect of settling in the security and comforts of Mithral Hall loomed before us all once more, and it is not a life I feel I can accept. My fear was for Catti-brie and the relationship we have forged. How would it change? Would Catti-brie desire to make a home and family of her own? Would she see the return to the dwarven stronghold as a signal that she had reached the end of her adventurous road?

And if so, then what would that mean for me?

Thus, we all took the news brought by Pwent with mixed feelings and more than a little trepidation.

Bruenor's conflicted attitude didn't hold for long, though. A young and fiery dwarf named Dagnabbit, one who had been instrumental in freeing Mithral Hall from the duergar those years ago, and son of the famous General Dagna, the esteemed commander of Mithral Hall's military arm, had accompanied Pwent to Icewind Dale. After Bruenor held a private meeting with Dagnabbit, my friend had come out as full of excitement as I had ever seen him, practically hopping with eagerness to be on the road home. And to the surprise of everyone, Bruenor had immediately put forth a special advisement—not a direct order, but a heavy-handed suggestion—that all of Mithral Hall's dwarves who had settled beneath the shadows of Kelvin's Cairn in Icewind Dale return with him.

When I asked Bruenor about this apparent change in attitude, he merely winked and assured me that I'd soon know "the greatest adventure" of my life—no small promise!

He still won't talk about the specifics, or even the general goal he has in mind, and Dagnabbit is as tight-lipped as my irascible friend.

But in truth, the specifics are not so important to me. What is important is the assurance that my life will continue to hold adventure, purpose, and goals. That is the secret, I believe. To continually reach higher is to live; to always strive to be a better person or to make the world around you a better place or to enrich your life or the lives of those you love is the secret to that most elusive of goals: a sense of accomplishment.

For some, that can be achieved by creating order and security or a sense of home. For some, including many dwarves, it can be achieved by the accumulation of wealth or the crafting of a magnificent item.

For me, I'll use my scimitars.

And so my feet were light when again we departed Icewind Dale, a hearty caravan of hundreds of dwarves, a grumbling (but far from miserable) halfling, an adventurous woman, a mighty barbarian warrior, along with his wife and child, and me, a pleasantly misguided dark elf who keeps a panther as a friend.

Let the snows fall deep, the rain drive down, and the wind buffet my cloak. I care not, for I've a road worth walking!

—Drizzt Do'Urden

1

ALLIANCE

He wore his masterwork plated armor as if it was an extension of his tough skin. Not a piece of the interlocking black metal was flat and unadorned, with flowing designs and overlapping bas-reliefs. A pair of great curving spikes extended from each upper arm plate, and each joint cover had a sharpened and tri-pointed edge to it. The armor itself could be used as a weapon, though King Obould Many-Arrows preferred the greatsword he always kept strapped to his back, a magnificent weapon that could burst into flame at his command.

Yes, the strong and cunning orc loved fire, loved the way it indiscriminately ate everything in its path. He wore a black iron crown, set with four brilliant and enchanted rubies, each of which could bring about a mighty fireball.

He was a walking weapon, stout and strong, the kind of creature that one wouldn't punch, figuring that doing so would do more damage to the attacker than to the attacked. Many rivals had been slaughtered by Obould as they stood there, hesitating, pondering how in the world they might begin to hurt this king among orcs.

Of all his weapons, though, Obould's greatest was his mind. He knew how to exploit a weakness. He knew how to shape a battlefield, and most of all, he knew how to inspire those serving him.

And so, unlike so many of his kin, Obould walked into Shining

White, the ice and rock caverns of the mighty frost giantess, Gerti Orels-dottr, with his eyes up and straight, his head held high. He had come in as a potential partner, not as a lesser.

Taking his lead, Obould's entourage, including his most promising son Urlgen Threefist (so named because of the ridged headpiece he wore, which allowed him to head-butt as if he had a third fist), walked with a proud and confident gait, though the ceilings of Shining White were far from comfortably low, and many of the blue-skinned guards they passed were well more than twice their height and several times their weight.

Even Obould's indomitable nature took a bit of a hit, though, when the frost giant escort led him and his band through a huge set of iron-banded doors into a freezing chamber that was much more ice than stone. Against the wall to the right of the doors, before a throne fashioned of black stone and blue cloth, capped in blue ice, stood the giantess, the heir apparent of the Jarl, leader of the frost giant tribes of the Spine of the World.

Gerti was beautiful by the measure of almost any race. She stood more than a dozen feet tall, her blue-skinned body shapely and muscled. Her eyes, a darker shade of blue, focused sharp enough to cut ice, it seemed, and her long fingers appeared both delicate and sensitive, and strong enough to crush rock. She wore her golden hair long—as long as Obould was tall. Her cloak, fashioned of silver wolf fur, was held together by a gem-studded ring, large enough for a grown elf to wear as a belt, and a collar of huge, pointed teeth adorned her neck. She wore a dress of brown, distressed leather, covering her ample bosom, then cut to a small flap on one side to reveal her muscled belly, and slit up high on her shapely legs, giving her freedom of movement. Her boots were high and topped with the same silvery fur—and were also magical, or so said every tale. It was said they allowed the giantess to quicken her long strides and cover more ground across the mountainous terrain than any but avian creatures.

"Well met, Gerti," Obould said, speaking nearly flawless frost giant. He bowed low, his plated armor creaking.

"You will address me as Dame Orelsdottr," the giantess replied curtly, her voice resonant and strong, echoing off the stone and ice.

"Dame Orelsdottr," Obould corrected with another bow. "You have heard of the success of our raid, yes?"

"You killed a few dwarves," Gerti said with a snicker, and her assembled guards responded in kind.

"I have brought you a gift of that significant victory."

"Significant?" the giantess said with dripping sarcasm.

"Significant not in the number of enemies slain, but in the first success of our joined peoples," Obould quickly explained.

Gerti's frown showed that she considered the description of them as "joined peoples" a bit premature, at least, which hardly surprised or dismayed Obould.

"The tactics work well," Obould went on, undaunted. He turned and motioned to Urlgen. The orc, taller than his father but not as thick of limb and torso, stepped forward and pulled a large sack off his back, bringing it around and spilling its gruesome contents onto the floor.

Five dwarf heads rolled out, including those of the brothers Stokkum and Bokkum, and Duggan McKnuckles.

Gerti crinkled her face and looked away.

"I would hardly call these gifts," she said.

"Symbols of victory," Obould replied, seeming a bit off-balance for the first time in the meeting.

"I have little interest in placing the heads of lesser races upon my walls as trophies," Gerti remarked. "I prefer objects of beauty, and dwarves hardly qualify."

Obould stared at her hard for a moment, understanding well that she could easily and honestly have included orcs in that last statement. He kept his wits about him, though, and motioned for his son to gather up the heads and put them back away.

"Bring me the head of Emerus Warcrown of Felbarr," Gerti said. "There is a trophy worthy of keeping."

Obould narrowed his eyes and bit back his response. Gerti was playing him and hard. King Obould Many Arrows had once ruled the former Citadel Felbarr, until a few years previous, when Emerus Warcrown had returned, expelling Obould and his clan. It remained a bitter loss to

Obould, what he considered his greatest error, for he and his clan had been battling another orc tribe at the time, leaving Warcrown and his dwarves an opportunity to retake Felbarr.

Obould wanted Felbarr back, dearly so, but Felbarr's strength had grown considerably over the past few years, swelling to nearly seven thousand dwarves, and those in halls of stone fashioned for defense.

The orc king fought back his anger with tremendous discipline, not wanting Gerti to see the sting produced by her sharp words.

"Or bring me the head of the King of Mithral Hall," Gerti went on. "Whether Gandalug Battlehammer, or as rumors now say, the beast Bruenor once again. Or perhaps, the Marchion of Mirabar—yes, his fat head and fuzzy red beard would make a fine trophy! And bring me Mirabar's Sceptrana, as well. Isn't she a pretty thing?"

The giantess paused for a moment and looked around at her amused warriors, a wicked grin spreading wide on her fine-featured face.

"You wish to deliver a trophy suitable for Dame Orelsdottr?" she asked slyly. "Then fetch me the pretty head of Lady Alustriel of Silverymoon. Yes, Obould—"

"*King* Obould," the proud orc corrected, drawing a hush from the frost giant soldiers and a gasp from his sorely out-powered entourage.

Gerti looked at him hard then nodded her approval.

They let their banter go at that, for both understood the preposterous level it had reached. Lady Alustriel of Silverymoon was a target far beyond them. Neither would put her and her enchanted city off the extended list of potential enemies, though. Silverymoon was the jewel of the region.

Both Gerti Orelsdottr and Obould Many Arrows coveted jewels.

"I am planning the next assault," Obould said after the pause, again, speaking slowly in the strange language, forcing his diction and enunciation to perfection.

"Its scope?"

Obould shrugged and shook his head. "Nothing major. Caravan or a town. The scope will depend upon our escorting artillery," he ended with a sly grin.

"A handful of giants are worth a thousand orcs," Gerti replied, taking the cue a bit further than Obould would have preferred.

Still, the cunning orc allowed her that boast without refute, well aware of her superior attitude and not really concerned about it at that time. He needed the frost giants behind his soldiers for diplomatic reasons more than for practical gain.

"My warriors did enjoy plunking the dwarves with their boulders," Gerti admitted, and the giant to the side of the throne dais, who had been on the raid, nodded and smiled his agreement. "Very well, King Obould, I will spare you four giants for the next fight. Send your emissary when you are ready for them."

Obould bowed, ducking his head as he did, not wanting Gerti to see his wide grin, not wanting her to know how important her additions would truly be to him and his cause.

He came up straight again and stomped his right boot, his signal to his entourage to form up behind him as he turned and left.

* * *

"They are your pawns," Donnia Soldou said to Gerti soon after Obould and his orc entourage had departed.

The female dark elf, dressed head to toe in deep shades of gray and black, moved easily among the frost giants, ignoring the threatening scowls many of them assumed whenever she was about. Donnia walked with the confidence of the dark elves, and with the knowledge that her subtle threats to Gerti concerning bringing an army to wipe out every living creature in the Spine of the World who opposed her had not fallen on deaf ears. Such were the often true tactics and pleasures of the dark elves.

Of course, Donnia had nothing at all to back up the claim. She was a rogue, part of a band that included only four members. So when she threw back her cowl and shook her long and thick white hair into its customary place, thrown to the side so that the tresses covered half her face, including her right eye, she did so with an air of absolute certainty.

Gerti didn't have to know that.

"They are orcs," Gerti Orelsdottr replied with obvious disdain.

17

"They are pawns to any who need to make them so. It is not easy to resist the urge to squash Obould into the rock, simply for being so ugly, simply for being so stupid . . . simply for the pleasure of it!"

"Obould's designs strengthen your own," Donnia said. "His minions are numerous. Numerous enough to wreak havoc among the dwarf and human communities of the region, but not so overwhelming as to engage the legions of the greater cities, like Silverymoon."

"He wants Felbarr, so that he can rename it the Citadel of Many Arrows. Do you believe that he can take so prosperous a stronghold and not invoke the wrath of Lady Alustriel?"

"Did Silverymoon get involved when Obould's kin sacked Felbarr the last time?" Donnia gave a chuckle. "The Lady and her advisors have enough to keep them concerned within their own borders. Felbarr will be isolated, eventually. Perhaps Mithral Hall or even Citadel Adbar will choose to send aid, but it will not be substantial if we create chaos in the neighboring mountain ranges and out of the Trollmoors."

"I have little desire to do battle with dwarves in their tiny tunnels," the frost giant remarked.

"That is why you have Obould and his thousands."

"The dwarves will slaughter them."

Donnia smiled and shrugged, as if that notion hardly bothered her.

Gerti started to respond, but just nodded her agreement.

Donnia held her smile, thinking that this was going quite well. Donnia and her companions had stumbled upon the situation at exactly the right time. The old Grayhand, Jarl Orel of the frost giants, was very near death, by all accounts, and his daughter was anxious to assume his mantle. Gerti was possessed of tremendous hubris, for herself and her race. She considered frost giants the greatest race of Faerûn, destined to dominate. Her pride and racism exceeded even that Donnia had seen from the matron mothers of her home city, Ched Nasad.

That made Gerti an easy mark indeed.

"How fares the Grayhand?" Donnia asked, wanting to keep Gerti's appetite whetted.

"He cannot speak, nor would he make any sense if he did. His reign is at its end in all ways but formal."

"But you are ready," Donnia assured the already self-assured giantess. "You, Dame Gerti Orelsdottr, will bring your tribes to the pinnacle of their glory, and woe to all of those who stand against you."

Gerti finally sat down upon her carved throne, resting back, but with her chin thrust high and strong, a pose of supreme pride.

Donnia kept her smile to herself.

"I hate them damn giants as much as I hate them damn dwarves," Urlgen proclaimed when he and the others were out of Gerti's caves. "I'd spit in Gerti's face, if I could reach it!"

"You keeps you words to youself," Obould scolded. "You said them giants helped in you's raid—didn't you like their bouncing boulders? Think it'll be easier like going after dwarf towers without those boulders softening them up?"

"Then why is we fighting the damn dwarves?" another of the group dared to ask.

Obould spun and punched him in the face, laying him low. So much for that debate.

"Well, let's see how much them giants'll be helping us then," Urlgen pressed. "Let's get them all out on a raid and flatten the buildings aboveground at Mirabar!"

A couple of the others bristled and nodded eagerly at that thought.

"Need I remind you of the course we have chosen?" came a voice from the side, very different from the guttural grunting of the orcs, more melodic and musical, though hardly less firm. The group turned to see Ad'non Kareese step out of the shadows, and many had to blink to even recognize how completely the drow had been hidden just a moment before.

"Well met, Sneak," said Obould.

Ad'non bowed, taking the compliment in stride.

"We met the big witch," Obould started to explain.

"So I heard," said the drow, and before Obould could begin to elaborate, Ad'non added, "All of it."

The orc king gave a chortle. "Course you's did, Sneak. Can get anywhere you wants, can't you?"

"Anywhere and anytime," the drow replied with all confidence.

Once he had been among the finest scouts of Ched Nasad, a thief and assassin with a growing reputation. Of course, that distinction had eventually led him to an ill-fated assassination attempt upon a rather powerful priestess, and the resulting fallout had put Ad'non on the road out of the city and out of the Underdark.

Over the past twenty years, he and his Ched Nasad associates, fellow assassin Donnia Soldou, the priestess Kaer'lic Suun Wett, and the newcomer, a clever fellow named Tos'un Armgo sent astray in the disastrous Menzoberranzan raid on Mithral Hall, had found more fun and games on the surface than ever they had known in their respective cities and more freedom.

In Ched Nasad and in Menzoberranzan, the four had been hire-ons and pawns for the greater powers, except for Kaer'lic who had been fashioning a mighty reputation among the priestesses of the Spider Queen before disaster had blocked her path. Up among the lesser races, the four acted with impunity, ever with the threat that they were the advance for great drow armies, ready to sweep in and eliminate all foes. Even proud Obould and prouder Gerti Orelsdottr would shift uncomfortably in their respective seats at the slightest hint of that catastrophe.

"So we push up that course a bit," Urlgen argued against the drow. "Choice ain't you'ses, Sneak. Choice is Obould's."

"And Gerti's," the drow reminded.

"Bah, we can fool the witch easy enough!" Urlgen declared, and the others nodded and grunted their agreement.

"Fool her into bringing about complete destruction for her designs and for your father's," the drow calmly replied, ending the cheering session. Ad'non looked at Obould as he continued, "Small forays alone, for a long while. You asked my opinion, and I have not wavered on it for a moment. Small forays and with restraint. We draw them out, little by little."

"That might be taking years!" Urlgen protested.

Ad'non nodded, conceding the point.

"The minor skirmishes are expected and even accepted as an unavoidable by-product of the environment by all the folk of the region," he explained, as he had so often in the past. "A caravan intercepted here, a village sacked there, and none will get overly excited, for none will understand the scope of it. You can tickle the gold sacks of the dwarves, but prod your spear too deeply, move them beyond a reasonable response, and you will unite the tribes."

He stared hard at Obould and continued, "You will awaken the beast. Think of the three dwarf strongholds joined in alliance, supplying each other with goods, weapons and even soldiers through their connecting tunnels. Think of the battle you will face in reclaiming the Citadel of Many Arrows if Adbar lends them several thousand shield dwarves and Mithral Hall outfits them all in the finest of metals. Why, Mithral Hall is the smallest of the three, yet she fended the army of Menzoberranzan!"

His emphasis on that last word, a name to strike terror into the hearts of any who were not of Menzoberranzan—and in the hearts of a good many who *were* of the city—had a couple of the orcs shuddering visibly.

"And through it all, we must take care, wise Obould, not to invoke the wrath of Silverymoon, whose Lady is a friend to Mithral Hall," the drow advisor went on. "And we must never allow an alliance to form between Mithral Hall and Mirabar."

"Bah, Mirabar hates them newcomers!"

"True enough, but they do not fear the newcomer dwarves in any but economic ways," Ad'non explained. "They will fear you and Gerti with their very lives, and such fear makes for unexpected alliances."

"Like the one between me and Gerti?"

Ad'non considered that for a moment, then shook his head.

"No, you and Gerti understand that you'll both move closer to your goals by allying. You are not afraid, of course."

"Course not!"

"Nor should you be. Play the game as we've discussed, as you and I have planned it all along, my friend Obould." He moved closer and whispered so that only the orc king could hear. "Show why you are above the others of your race, why you alone might gather a strong enough alliance to reclaim your rightful citadel."

Obould straightened and nodded, then turned to his kinfolk and recited the litany that Ad'non had taught him for months and months.

"Patience . . ."

"I'll not even bother to ask how your parlay with Obould progressed," priestess Kaer'lic Suun Wett remarked when Ad'non finally arrived at the comfortable, richly adorned chamber off a deep, deep tunnel below the southernmost spurs of the Spine of the World, not far from the caverns of Shining White, though much deeper.

Kaer'lic was the most striking member of the group. Heavyset, which was very unusual for a dark elf, and with broad shoulders, Kaer'lic had lost her right eye in a battle when she was a young priestess nearly a century before. Rather than have the orb magically restored, the stubborn Kaer'lic had replaced it with a black, many-chambered eye pried from the carcass of a giant spider. She claimed the orb was functional and allowed her to see things that others could not, but her three friends knew the truth of it. Many times, Ad'non and Donnia had sneaked up on Kaer'lic's right side, completely undetected, for no better reason than to tease her.

Still, the two assassins had gone along with Kaer'lic's ruse to their newest companion for many tendays. Spiders, after all, made quite an impact on dark elves from Menzoberranzan, and Tos'un Armgo had remained suitably impressed for a long time, until Ad'non had finally let him in on the ruse—and that, only after the three long-term friends had come to understand that Tos'un was one who could be trusted.

Ad'non shrugged in response to Kaer'lic's remarks, telling the other three that it had gone exactly as they would all expect when dealing with an orc. Indeed, Obould was more cunning than his kind, but that wasn't really saying much by drow standards.

"Dame Gerti holds the course, as well," Donnia added. "She

believes it to be her destiny to rule the Spine of the World and will follow any course that may lead her to that place."

"She might be right," Tos'un put in. "Gerti Orelsdottr is a smart one, and between Obould's masses and the stirring trolls from the moors, enough chaos might be created for Gerti to step forward."

"And we will be ready to profit, in material and in pleasure, whatever the outcome," Donnia said with a wry grin, one that was matched by her three friends.

'It amazes me that I ever considered returning to Menzoberranzan," Tos'un Armgo remarked, and the others laughed.

Donnia and Ad'non were staring rather intently at each other when that laughter abated. The lovers had been apart for several days, after all, and both of them found such talk of conquest, chaos and profit quite stimulating.

They practically ran out of the chamber to their private room.

Kaer'lic howled with renewed laughter as they departed, shaking her head. She was always more pragmatic about such needs, never reducing them to overpowering levels, as the two assassins often did.

"They will die in each others' arms," she remarked to Tos'un, "coupling and oblivious to the threat."

"There are worse ways to go, I suppose," the son of House Barrison Del'Armgo replied, and Kaer'lic laughed again.

These two were part-time lovers as well, but only part time, and not for a long, long time. Kaer'lic wasn't really interested in a partner, in truth, far preferring a slave to use as a toy.

"We should expand these raids to the Moonwood," she remarked lewdly. "Perhaps we could convince Obould to capture us a couple of young moon elves."

"A couple?" Tos'un said skeptically. "A handful would be more fun."

Kaer'lic laughed yet again.

Tos'un leaned back into the thick furs of his divan, wondering again how he could have ever even considered returning to the dangers discomforts and subjugation that he, as a male, could not avoid, along the dark avenues of Menzoberranzan.

NOT WELCOME

The wind howled down at them from the peaks to the north, the towering snow-capped Spine of the World Mountains. Just a bit farther to the south, along the roads out of Luskan, spring was in full bloom, fast approaching summer, but at the higher elevations, the wind was rarely warm, and the going rarely easy.

Yet it was precisely this course that Bruenor Battlehammer had chosen as the route back to Mithral Hall, walking east within the shadow of the mountains. They had left Icewind Dale without incident, for none of the highwaymen or solitary monsters that often roamed the treacherous roads would challenge an army of nearly five hundred dwarves! A storm had caught them in the pass through the mountains, but Bruenor's hearty people had trudged on, turning east even as Drizzt and his other unsuspecting friends were expecting to soon see the towers of Luskan in the south before them.

Drizzt had asked Bruenor about the unexpected course change, for though this was a more direct route, it certainly wouldn't be much quicker and certainly not less hazardous.

In reply to the logical question, Bruenor had merely snorted, "Ye'll see soon enough, elf!"

The days blended into tendays and the raucous band put more than a hundred and fifty difficult miles behind them. Their days were full of dwarven marching songs, their nights full of dwarven partying songs.

To the surprise of Drizzt, Catti-brie, and Wulfgar, Bruenor moved Regis by his side soon after the eastward turn. The dwarf was constantly leaning in and talking to the halfling, while Regis bobbed his head in reply.

"What's the little one know that we don't?" Catti-brie asked the drow as they flanked the caravan to the north, looking back on the third wagon, Bruenor's wagon, to see Bruenor and Regis engaged in one such discussion.

Drizzt just shook his head, not really sure of how to read Regis at all anymore.

"Well, I'm thinking we should find out," Catti-brie added, seeing no response forthcoming.

"When Bruenor wants us to know all the details, he will tell us," Drizzt assured her, but her smirk made it fairly clear that she wasn't buying into that theory.

"We've turned the both of them from more than one ill-aimed scheme," she reminded. "Are ye hoping to find out right before the cataclysm?"

The logic was simple enough, and in considering the pair on the wagon, and the fact that raucous and none-too-brilliant Thibbledorf Pwent was also serving Bruenor in an advisory position, the drow could only chuckle.

"And what are we to do?"

"Well, hot pokers won't get Bruenor talking, even against a birthday surprise," Catti-brie reasoned, "but I'm thinking that Regis has a bit lower tolerance."

"For pain?" Drizzt asked incredulously.

"Or for tricks, or for drink, or for whatever else might work," the woman explained. "Think I'll be getting Wulfgar to carry the little rat to us when Bruenor's off about other business tonight."

Drizzt gave a helpless laugh, understanding well the perils that awaited poor Regis, and glad that Bruenor had taken the halfling into his confidence and not him.

As with most nights, Drizzt and Catti-brie set a camp off to the side of the gathering of dwarves, keeping watch, and even more than that, keeping a bit of their sanity aside from Thibbledorf Pwent's antics and the Gutbuster's training. Pwent did come over and join the pair this night, though, walking right in and plopping down on a boulder to the side of their fire.

He looked at Catti-brie, even reached up to touch her long auburn hair.

"Ah, ye're looking good, girl," he said, and he dropped a sack of some muddy compound at her feet. "Ye be putting that on yer face each night afore ye go to sleep."

Catti-brie looked down at the sack and its slimy contents, then up at Drizzt, who was sitting on a log and resting back against a rock facing, his hands tucked behind his head, brushing wide his thick shock of white hair so that it framed his black-skinned face and his purple eyes. Clearly, the battlerager amused him.

"On me face?" Catti-brie asked, and Pwent's head bobbed eagerly. "Let me guess. It will make me grow a beard."

"Good and thick one," said Pwent. "Red to match yer hair, I'm hoping. Oh, a fiery one ye'll be!"

Catti-brie's eyes narrowed as she looked over at Drizzt once more, to see him choking back a chuckle.

"Make sure ye're not putting it up too high on yer cheeks, girl," the battlerager went on, and now Drizzt did laugh out loud. "Ye'll look like that durned Harpell werewolf critter!"

As he finished the thought, Pwent sighed and rolled his eyes longingly. It was well known that the battlerager had begged Bidderdoo Harpell, the werewolf, to bite him so that he too might be afflicted by the ferocious disease. The Harpell had wisely refused.

Before the wild dwarf could continue, the trio heard a movement to the side, and a huge form appeared. It was Wulfgar the barbarian, nearly seven feet tall, with a broad and muscled chest. He was wearing a beard to match his blond hair, but it was neatly trimmed, showing the renewed signs of care that had given all the friends hope that Wulfgar had at last overcome his inner demons. He carried a large sack over one shoulder, and something inside of it was squirming.

"Hey, what'cha got there, boy?" Pwent howled, hopping up and bending in curiously.

"Dinner," Wulfgar replied. The creature in the sack moaned and squirmed more furiously.

Pwent rubbed his hands together eagerly and licked his lips.

"Only enough for us," Wulfgar said to him. "Sorry."

"Bah, ye can spare me a leg!"

"Just enough for us," Wulfgar said again, putting his hand on Pwent's forehead and pushing the dwarf back to arm's length. "And for me to bring some leftovers to my wife and child. You will have to go and dine with your kin, I fear."

"Bah!" the battlerager snorted. "Ye ain't even kilt it right!"

With that, he stepped up and balled his fist, retracting his arm for a devastating punch.

"No!" Drizzt, Wulfgar, and Catti-brie all yelled together.

The woman and the drow leaped up and rushed in to intercept. Wulfgar, spinning aside, put himself between the battlerager and the sack. As he did, though, the sack swung out wide and bounced off the rock facing, drawing another groan from within.

"We're wanting it fresh," Catti-brie explained to the befuddled battlerager.

"Fresh? It's still kicking!"

Catti-brie rubbed her hands together eagerly and licked her lips, mimicking Pwent's initial reaction.

"It is indeed!" she said happily.

Pwent backed off a step and put his hands firmly on his hips, staring hard at the woman, then he exploded into laughter.

"Ye'll make a good dwarf, girl!" he howled.

He slapped his hands against his thighs and bounded away, back down the slope toward the main encampment.

As soon as he was gone, Wulfgar swung the sack over his shoulder and bent low, gently spilling its contents: one very irate, slightly overweight halfling dressed in fine traveling clothes, a red shirt, brown vest, and breeches.

Regis rolled on the ground, quickly regained his footing, and frantically brushed himself off.

"Your pardon," Wulfgar offered as graciously as he could while stifling a laugh.

Regis glared up at him then hopped over and kicked him hard in the shin—which of course hurt Regis's bare toes more than it affected the mighty barbarian.

"Relax, my friend," Drizzt bade him, stepping over and draping his arm over the halfling's shoulder. "We needed to speak with you, that is all."

"And asking is beyond your comprehension?" Regis was quick to point out.

Drizzt shrugged. "It had to be done secretly," he explained. Even as the words left his mouth Regis began to shrink back, apparently catching on.

"Ye been talking a lot with Bruenor of late," Catti-brie piped in, and Regis shrank back even more. "We're thinking that ye should be sharing some of his words with us."

"Oh, no," Regis replied, patting his hands in the air before him, warding them away. "Bruenor's got his plans spinning, and he will tell you when he wants you to know."

"Then there is something?" Drizzt reasoned.

"He is returning to Mithral Hall to become the king," the halfling replied. "That is something, indeed!"

"Something more than that," said Drizzt. "I see it clearly in his eyes, in the bounce of his step."

Regis shrugged. "He's glad to be going home."

"Oh, is that where we're going?" Catti-brie asked.

"You are. I am going farther," the halfling admitted. "To the Herald's Holdfast," he explained, referring to a renowned library tower located east of Mithral Hall and northwest of Silverymoon, a place the friends had visited years before, when they were trying to locate Mithral Hall so that Bruenor could reclaim the place. "Bruenor has asked me to gather some information for him."

"About what?" asked the drow.

"Gandalug and Gandalug's time, mostly," Regis answered, and while it seemed to the other three that he was speaking truthfully, they also sensed that he was speaking incompletely.

"And what might Bruenor be needing that for?" asked Catti-brie.

"I'm thinking that's a question ye should be asking Bruenor," came the gruff reply of a familiar voice, and all four turned to see Bruenor stride into the firelight. "Ye go grabbing Rumblebelly there, when all ye had to do was ask meself."

"And ye'd be telling us?" Catti-brie asked.

"No," said the dwarf, and three sets of eyes narrowed immediately. "Bah!" Bruenor recanted. "Hoping to surprise ye three is hoping for the impossible!"

"Surprise us with what?" asked Wulfgar.

"An adventure, boy!" the dwarf howled. "As great an adventure as ye've ever knowed."

"I've known a few," Drizzt warned, and Bruenor howled.

"Sit yerselfs down," the dwarf bade them, motioning to the fire, and all five sat in a circle about the blaze.

Bruenor pulled a bulging pack off his back. After dropping it to the ground he pulled it open to reveal packets of food and bottles of ale and wine.

"Though ye're fancying fresher food," he said with a wink to Catti-brie, "I was thinking this'd do for now."

They sorted out the meal, and Bruenor hardly waited for them to begin eating before he launched into his tale, telling them that he was truly glad they had pressed the issue, for it was a tale, a promise of adventure, that he desperately wanted to share.

"We'll be making the mouth o' the Valley of Khedrun tomorrow," he explained. "Then we're turning south across the vale, to the River Mirabar, and to Mirabar herself."

"Mirabar?" Catti-brie and Drizzt echoed in unison, and with equal skepticism.

It was hardly a secret that the mining city of Mirabar was no supporter of Mithral Hall, which threatened their business interests.

"Ye're knowing Dagnabbit?" Bruenor asked, and the friends all nodded. "Well, he's a few friends there who'll be giving us some information that we're wanting to hear."

The dwarf paused and hopped up, glancing all around into the darkness as if searching for spies

"Ye got yer cat about, elf?" the red-bearded dwarf asked.

Drizzt shook his head.

"Well, get her here, if ye can," Bruenor bade him. "Send her out about and tell her to drag in any who might overhear."

Drizzt looked to Catti-brie and to Wulfgar, then reached into his belt pouch and brought forth an onyx figurine of a panther.

"Guenhwyvar," he called softly. "Come to me, friend."

A gray mist began to swirl around the figurine, growing and thickening, gradually mirroring the shape of the idol. The mist solidified quickly, and the huge black panther Guenhwyvar stood there, quietly and patiently waiting for Drizzt's instructions.

The drow bent low and whispered into the panther's ear, and Guenhwyvar bounded away, disappearing into the blackness.

Bruenor nodded. "Them Mirabar boys're mad about Mithral Hall," he said, which wasn't news to any of them. "They're looking for a way to get back an advantage in the mining trade."

The dwarf looked around again, then bent in very close, motioning for a huddle.

"They're looking for Gauntlgrym," he whispered.

"What is that?" Wulfgar asked.

Catti-brie looked equally perplexed, though Drizzt was nodding as if it was all perfectly logical.

"The ancient stronghold of the dwarves," Bruenor explained. "Back afore Mithral Hall, Citadel Felbarr, and Citadel Adbar. Back when we were one big clan, back when we named ourselves the Delzoun."

"Gauntlgrym was lost centuries ago," Drizzt put in. "Many centuries ago. Beyond the memory of any living dwarves."

"True enough," Bruenor said with a wink. "Now that Gandalug's gone to the Halls of Moradin."

Drizzt's eyes widened—so did those of Catti-brie and Wulfgar.

"Gandalug knew of Gauntlgrym?" the drow asked.

"Never saw it, for it fell afore he was born," Bruenor explained.

"But," he added quickly, as the hopeful smiles began to fade, "when he was a lad the tales of Gauntlgrym were fresher in the mouths o' dwarves." He looked at each of his friends in turn, nodding knowingly.

"Them Mirabar boys're looking for it under the Crags to the south. They're looking in the wrong place."

"How much did Gandalug know?" Catti-brie asked.

"Not much more than I knew about Mithral Hall when first we went a' lookin'," Bruenor admitted with a snort. "Less even. But it'll be an adventure worth making if we're finding the city. O, the treasures, I tell ye! And metal as good as anything ye've e'er seen!"

He went on and on about the legendary crafted pieces of the Gauntlgrym dwarves, about weapons of great power, armor that could turn any blade, and shields that could stop dragonfire.

Drizzt wasn't really listening to the specifics, though he was watching every movement from the fiery dwarf. By the drow's estimation, the adventure would be well worth the risks and hardships whether or not they ever found Gauntlgrym. He hadn't seen Bruenor this animated and excited in years, not since the first foray to find Mithral Hall.

As he looked around at the others, he saw the eager gleam in Catti-brie's green eyes and the sparkle in Wulfgar's icy blue orbs—further confirmation to him that his barbarian friend was well on the road to recovery from the trauma of spending six years at the clawed hands of the demon Errtu. The fact that Wulfgar had taken on the responsibilities of husband and father, Delly and the baby never far from him even in their present camp, was all the more reassuring. Even Regis, who had no doubt heard this tale many times already along the road, leaned in, drawn to the dwarf's tales of dungeons deep and treasures magical.

It occurred to Drizzt that he should ask Bruenor why they all had to go to Mirabar, where they wouldn't likely be welcomed. Couldn't Dagnabbit go in alone or with a small group, less conspicuously? The drow held his thoughts, though, understanding it well enough. He hadn't been with Bruenor in Icewind Dale when the first reports of antagonism from Mirabar had been sent to him from King Gandalug. He and Catti-brie had been sailing the Sword Coast at that time, but when they had found Bruenor back in Icewind Dale, the dwarf had pointed it out more than once, a simmering source of anger.

Openly, the Council of Sparkling Stones, the ruling council of Mirabar, comprised of dwarves and men, spoke warmly of Mithral Hall, welcoming their brothers of Clan Battlehammer back to the region. Privately, though, Bruenor had heard over the years many reports of more subtle derogatory comments from sources close to the Council of Sparkling Stones and Elastul, the Marchion of Mirabar. Some of the plots that had caused Gandalug headaches had been traced back to Mirabar.

Bruenor was going there for no better reason than to look some of the folk of Mirabar straight in the eye, to make a proclamation that the Eighth King of Mithral Hall had returned as the Tenth King, and he was one a bit more clued in to the subterfuge of the present day politics of the wild north.

Drizzt just sat back and watched his friends' continuing huddle. The adventure had begun, it seemed, and it was one the drow believed he would truly enjoy.

Or would he?

For something else occurred to Drizzt then, a memory quite unexpected. He recalled his first visit to the surface, a supposed great adventure alongside his fellow dark elves. Images of the slaughter of the surface elves swirled through his thoughts, culminating in the memory of a little elf girl he had smeared with her own mother's blood, to make it appear as if she too had been mortally wounded. He had saved her that terrible day, and that massacre had, in truth, been the first real steps for Drizzt away from his vile kinfolk.

And, all these years later, he had killed that same elf child. He winced as he saw Ellifain again, across the room in the pirate cavern complex, mortally wounded and pleased by the thought that in sacrificing herself, she had taken Drizzt with her. On a logical level, the drow could surely understand that nothing that had happened that day was his fault, that he could not have foreseen the torment that would follow that rescued child all these decades.

But on another level, a deeper level, the fateful fight with the anguished Ellifain had struck a deep chord within Drizzt Do'Urden. He had left Icewind Dale full of anticipation for the open road, and indeed, he was glad to be with his friends, traveling the wilds, full of adventure and excitement.

But the keen edge of a purpose beyond material gain, beyond finding ancient kingdoms and ancient treasure, had been dulled. Drizzt had never fancied himself a major player in the events of the wider world. He had contented himself in the knowledge that his actions served those around him in a positive way. From his earliest days in Menzoberranzan, he had held an innate understanding of the fundamental differences between good and evil, and he had always believed that he was a player for the side of justice and goodness.

But what of Ellifain?

He continued to listen to the excited talk around him and held fast his consenting smile, assuring himself that he would indeed enjoy this newest adventure.

He had to believe that.

There was nothing pretty about the open air city of Mirabar. Squat stone buildings and a few towers sat inside a square stone wall. Everything about the place spoke of efficiency and control, a no-nonsense approach to getting their work done.

To the sensibilities of a dwarf like Bruenor, that made Mirabar a place to be admired to a point, but to Drizzt and Catti-brie as they approached the city's northern gate, Mirabar seemed an unadorned blotch, uninteresting and unremarkable.

"Give me Silverymoon," Drizzt remarked to the woman as they walked along to the left of the dwarven caravan.

"Even Menzoberranzan's a prettier sight," Catti-brie replied, and Drizzt could only agree.

The guards at the north gate seemed an apt reflection of Mirabar's dour attitude. Four humans stood in pairs on opposite ends of sturdy metallic doors, halberds set on the ground and held vertically before them, silver armor gleaming in the early morning sun. Bruenor recognized the crest emblazoned on their tower shields, the royal badge of Mirabar, a deep red double-bladed axe with a pointed haft and a flaring, flat base, set on a black field. The approach of a huge caravan of dwarves, a veritable army, surely shook them all, but to their credit, they held their posture perfect, eyes straight ahead, faces impassive.

Bruenor brought his wagon around, moving to the front of the caravan, Pwent's Gutbusters running to keep their protective guard to either flank.

"Bring her right up afore 'em," Bruenor instructed his driver, Dagnabbit.

The younger, yellow-bearded dwarf gave a gap-toothed grin and urged his team on faster, but the Mirabar guards didn't blink.

The wagon skidded to a stop short of the closed doors and Bruenor stood up tall (relatively speaking) and put his hands on his hips.

"State your business. State your name," came a curt instruction from the inner guard on the right.

"Me business is with yer Council o' Sparkling Stones," Bruenor answered. "I'll be tellin' it to them alone."

"You will answer the appointed gate guard of Mirabar, visitor," the inner guard on the left hand side of the doors demanded.

"Ye think?" Bruenor asked. "And ye're wantin' me name? Bruenor Battlehammer's the name, ye durned fool. *King* Bruenor Battlehammer. Now ye go and run that name to yer council and we'll be seeing if they're to talk to me or not."

The guards tried to hold their posture and calm demeanor, but they did glance over at each other, hastily.

"Ye heared o' me?" Bruenor asked them. "Ye heared o' Mithral Hall?"

A moment later, one of the guards turned to the guard standing beside him and nodded, and that man produced a small horn from his belt and blew a series of short, sharp notes. A few moments later, a smaller hatch cunningly cut into the large portals, banged open and a tough-looking, many-scarred dwarf wearing a full suit of battered plate mail, ambled out. He too wore the badge of the city, emblazoned on his breastplate, as he carried no shield.

"Ah, now we're getting somewhere," Bruenor remarked. "And it does me old heart good to see that ye've a dwarf for a boss. Might be that ye're not as stupid as ye look."

"Well met, King Bruenor," the dwarf said. "Torgar Delzoun

Hammerstriker at yer service." He bowed low, his black beard sweeping the ground.

"Well met, Torgar," Bruenor replied, offering a gracious bow of his own, something that he, as head of a nearby kingdom, was certainly not required to do. "Yer guards here serve ye well at blocking the way and better as fodder!"

"Trained 'em meself," Torgar responded.

Bruenor bowed again. "We're tired and dirty, though the last part ain't so bad, and looking for a night's stay. Might ye be opening the doors for us?"

Torgar leaned to one side and the other, taking a good look at the caravan, shaking his head doubtfully. His eyes went wide and he shook his head more vehemently when he glanced to his right, to see a human woman standing off to the side beside a drow elf.

"That ain't gonna happen!" the dwarf cried, pointing a stubby finger Drizzt's way.

"Bah, ye heared o' that one, and ye know ye have," Bruenor scolded. "The name Drizzt ringing any bells in yer thick skull?"

"It is or it ain't, and it ain't making no difference anyway," Torgar argued. "No damned drow elf's walkin' into me city. Not while I'm the Topside Commander of the Axe of Mirabar!"

Bruenor glanced over at Drizzt, who merely smiled and bowed deferentially.

"Not fair, but fair enough, so he's stayin' out," Bruenor agreed. "What about me and me kin?"

"Where're we to put five hunnerd o' ye?" Torgar asked sincerely, correctly estimating the force's size. He held his large hands out helplessly to the side. "Could send a bunch to the mines, if we let anyone into the mines. And that we don't!"

"Fair enough," Bruenor replied. "How many can ye take?"

"Twenty, yerself included," Torgar answered.

"Then twenty it'll be." Bruenor glanced at Thibbledorf Pwent and nodded. "Just three o' yers," he ordered, "and me and Dagnabbit makes five, and we'll be adding Rumblebelly . . ." He paused and looked at Torgar. "Ye got any arguing to do about me bringing a halfling?"

Torgar shrugged and shook his head.

"Then Rumblebelly makes six," Bruenor said to Dagnabbit and Pwent. "Tell th' others to pick fourteen merchants wanting to go in with some goods."

"Better to take me whole brigade," Pwent argued, but Bruenor was hearing none of it.

The last thing Bruenor wanted in this already tenuous circumstance was to turn a group of Gutbuster battleragers loose on Mirabar. In that event Mithral Hall and Mirabar would likely be at open war before the sun set.

"Ye pick the two goin' with ye, if ye're planning on going," Bruenor explained to Pwent, "and be quick about it."

A short while later, Torgar Delzoun Hammerstriker led the twenty dwarves through Mirabar's strong gate. Bruenor walked at the front of the column, right beside Torgar, looking every bit the road-wise, adventure-hardened King of Mithral Hall spoken of throughout the land. He kept his many-notched, single-bladed axe strapped on his back, but prominently displayed atop the foaming mug shield that was also strapped there. He wore his helmet, with one horn broken away, like a badge of courage. He was a king, but a dwarf king, a creature of pragmatism and action, not a flowered and prettily dressed ruler like those common among the humans and elves.

"So who's yer marchion these days?" he asked Torgar as they crossed into the city.

Torgar's eyes widened. "Elastul Raurym," he replied, "though it's no name ye need be thinking of."

"Ye tell him I'm wanting to talk with him," Bruenor explained, and Torgar's eyes widened even more.

"He's fillin' his meetings for the spring in the fall, for the summer in the winter," Torgar explained. "Ye can't just walk in and get an audience . . ."

Bruenor fixed the dwarf with a strong, stern gaze. "I'm not *gettin'* an audience," he corrected. "I'm *granting* one. Now, ye go and get a message to the marchion that I'm here for the talking if he's got anything worth hearing."

The sudden change in Bruenor's demeanor, now that the gates were behind him, clearly unsettled Torgar. His off-balance surprise fast shifted to a grim posture, eyes narrowing and staring hard at his fellow dwarf.

Bruenor matched that stare—more than matched it.

"Ye go an' tell him," he said calmly. "And ye tell yer council and that fool Sceptrana that I told ye to tell him."

"Protocol . . ."

"Is for humans, elves, and gnomes," Bruenor interrupted, his voice stern. "I ain't no human, I sure ain't no elf, and I'm no bearded gnome. Dwarf to dwarf, I'm talking here. If yerself came to me Mithral Hall and said ye needed to see me, ye'd be seeing me, don't ye doubt."

He finished with a nod, and dropped his hand hard on Torgar's shoulder. That little gesture, more than anything previous, seemed to put the sturdy warrior at ease. He nodded, his expression grim, as if he had just been reminded of something very important.

"I'll be telling him," he agreed, "or at least, I'll be tellin' his Hammers to be tellin' him."

Bruenor smirked at that, and Torgar shuffled. Against the obvious disdain of the dwarf King of Mithral Hall, the inaccessibility of the Marchion of Mirabar to one of his trusted shield dwarf commanders did indeed seem a bit trite.

"I'll be tellin' him," Torgar said again, with a bit more conviction.

He led the twenty visitors away then to a place where they could stay the night, a large and unremarkable stone house with several sparsely furnished rooms.

"Ye can set up yer wagons and goods right outside," Torgar explained. "Many'll be comin' to see ye, I'm sure, 'specially for them little white trinkets ye got."

He pointed to one of the three wagons that had come in with the visitors, its side panels tinkling with many trinkets as it bounced along the rough ground.

"Scrimshaw," Bruenor explained. "Carved from knucklehead trout. Me little friend here's good at it."

He motioned to Regis, who blushed and nodded.

"Ye make any of the stuff on the wagon?" Torgar asked the halfling, and the dwarf seemed genuinely interested.

"A few pieces."

"Ye show me in the morning," Torgar asked. "Might that I'll buy a few."

With that, he nodded and left them, heading off to deliver Bruenor's invitation to the marchion.

"You turned him over quite well," Regis remarked.

Bruenor looked at him.

"He was ready for a fight when we first arrived," the halfling observed. "Now I believe he's thinking of leaving with us when we go."

It was an exaggeration, of course, but not ridiculously so.

Bruenor just smiled. He had heard from Dagnabbit of many curses and threats being hurled against Mithral Hall from Mirabar, and surprisingly (or not so, when he thought about it), more seemed to be coming from the dwarves of Mirabar than from the humans. That was why Bruenor had insisted on coming to this city where so many of his kinfolk were living in conditions and climate much more fitting to human sensibilities than to a dwarf's. Let them see a true dwarf king, a legend of their people come to life. Let them hear the words and ways of Mithral Hall. Maybe then, many of Mirabar's dwarves would stop whispering curses against Mithral Hall. Maybe then, the dwarves of Mirabar would remember their heritage.

"It's troubling ye that they wouldn't let ye in," Catti-brie remarked to Drizzt a short time later, the two of them on a high bluff to the east of the remaining dwarves and the caravan, overlooking the city of Mirabar.

Drizzt turned to regard her curiously, and saw sympathy etched on his dear friend's face. He realized that Catti-brie was reacting to his own wistful expression.

"No," he assured her. "There are some things I know I can never change, and so I accept them as they are."

"Yer face is saying different."

Drizzt forced a smile. "Not so," he said—convincingly, he thought.

But Catti-brie's returning look showed him that she saw better. The woman stepped back and nodded, catching on.

"Ye're thinking of the elf," she reasoned.

Drizzt looked away, back toward Mirabar, and said, "I wish we could have saved her."

"We're all wishing that."

"I wish you had given the potion to her and not to me."

"Aye, and Bruenor would've killed me," Catti-brie said. She grabbed the drow and made him look back at her, a smile widening on her pretty face. "Is that what ye're hoping?"

Drizzt couldn't resist her charm and the much-needed levity.

"It is just difficult," he explained. "There are times when I so wish that things could be different, that tidy and acceptable endings could find every tale."

"So ye keep trying to make them endings acceptable," Catti-brie said to him. "It's all ye can do."

True enough, Drizzt admitted to himself. He gave a great sigh and looked back to Mirabar and thought again of Ellifain.

Dagnabbit went out later that afternoon, the sun setting and a cold wind kicking up through the streets of the city. He didn't return until right before the dawn, and spent the day inside with Bruenor, discussing the political intrigue of the city and the implications to Mithral Hall, while the merchants and Regis worked their wagons outside.

Not many came to those wagons—a few dwarves and fewer humans—and most of those who did bargained for deals so poor that the Clan Battlehammer dwarves ultimately refused. The lone exception arrived soon after highsun.

"Well, show me yer work, halfling," Torgar bade Regis.

A dozen heads, those of Torgar's friends, bobbed eagerly behind him.

"Regis," the halfling explained, extending his hand, which Torgar took in a firm and friendly shake.

"Show me, Regis," the dwarf said. "Me and me friends'll need a bit o' convincing to be spendin' our gold pieces on anything ye can't drink!"

That brought a laugh from all the dwarves, Battlehammer and Mirabarran alike, and from Regis. The halfling was wondering if he should consider using his enchanted ruby necklace, with its magical powers of persuasion, to "convince" the dwarves of a good deal. He dismissed that thought almost immediately, though, reminding himself of how stubborn some dwarves could be against any kind of magic. Regis also considered the implications on the relationship between Mithral Hall and Mirabar should he get caught.

Still, soon enough it became apparent to Regis that he wouldn't need the pendant's influence. The dwarves had come well stocked with coin, and many of their friends joined them. The goods on the wagons, Regis's work and many other items, began to disappear.

From the window of the house, Bruenor and Dagnabbit watched the bazaar with growing satisfaction as dozens and dozens of new patrons, almost exclusively dwarves, followed Torgar's lead. They also noted, with a mixture of apprehension and hope, the grim faces of those others nearby, humans mostly, looking upon the eager and animated trading with open disdain.

"I'm thinking that ye've knocked a wedge down the middle o' Mirabar by coming here," Dagnabbit observed. "Might be that fewer curses'll flow from the lips o' the dwarfs here when we're on the road out."

"And more curses than ever'll be flowing from the mouths o' the humans," Bruenor added, and he seemed quite pleased by that prospect.

Quite pleased indeed.

A short while later, Torgar, carrying a bag full of purchases, knocked on the door.

"Ye're coming to tell me that yer marchion's too busy," Bruenor said as he answered the knock, pulling the door open wide.

"He's got his own business, it seems," Torgar confirmed.

"Bet he didn't answer yer knock," Dagnabbit remarked from behind Bruenor.

Torgar shrugged helplessly.

"How about yerself?" Bruenor asked. "And yer boys? Ye got yer own business, or ye got time to come in and share some drink?"

"Got no coins left."

"Didn't ask for none."

Torgar chewed his lip a bit.

"I can't be speaking as a representative o' Mirabar," he explained.

"Who asked ye to?" Bruenor was quick to reply. "A good dwarf's putting more into his mouth than he's spilling out. Ye got some tales to tell that I ain't heared, to be sure. That's more than worth the price o' some ale."

And so, with Torgar's agreement, they had a party that night in the unremarkable stone house on the windswept streets of Mirabar. More than a hundred Mirabarran dwarves made an appearance, with most staying for some time, and many sleeping right there on the floor.

Bruenor wasn't surprised to find the house surrounded by armed, grim-faced soldiers—humans, not dwarves—when daylight broke.

It was time for Bruenor and his friends to go.

Torgar and his buddies would find a bit of trouble over this, no doubt, but when Bruenor looked back at him with concern, the tough old veteran merely winked and grinned.

"Ye find yer way to Mithral Hall, Torgar Delzoun Hammerstriker!" Bruenor called back to him as the wagons began to roll back out the gates. "Ye bring all the friends ye want, and all the tales ye can tell! We'll find enough food and drink to make ye belch, and a warm bed for as long as ye want to warm yer butt in it!"

No one on the caravan from Icewind Dale missed the scowls the human guards offered at those dangerous remarks.

"You do like to cause trouble, don't you," Regis said to Bruenor.

"The marchion was too busy for me, eh?" Bruenor replied with a smirk. "He'll be wishing he met with me, don't ye doubt."

Drizzt, Catti-brie, and Wulfgar linked up with Bruenor's wagon when it and the others had rejoined the bigger caravan outside the city gates.

"What happened in there?" the dark elf asked.

"A bit o' intrigue, a bit o' fun," Bruenor replied, "and a bit o' insurance that if Mirabar e'er decides to openly fight against Mithral Hall, they'll be missing a few hunnerd o' their shorter warriors."

3

RETREAT INTO VICTORY

"Ye gotta keep running!" Nikwillig scolded Tred.

The wounded dwarf was slumped against a boulder, sweat pouring down his forehead and cheek, a grimace of pain on his face as he favored his torn leg.

"Got me in the knee," Tred explained, gasping between every syllable. "She's not holding me up no more. Ye run on and I'll give them puppies reason to pause!"

Nikwillig nodded, not in agreement of the whole proposal, but in determination concerning the last part. "Ye can't run, then we'll stop and fight," he answered.

"Bah!" Tred snorted at him. "Bunch o' worgs coming."

"Bunch o' dead worgs, then," Nikwillig answered with as much grit and determination as Tred had ever witnessed from him.

Nikwillig was a merchant more than a warrior, but now he was "showing his dwarf," as the old expression went. And in viewing this transformation, despite their desperate situation, Tred couldn't help but smile. Certainly if the situation had been reversed, with Nikwillig favoring a torn leg, Tred would never have considered leaving him.

"We're needin' a plan, then," said Tred.

"One using fire," Nikwillig agreed, and as he finished, a not-so-distant howl split the air and was answered several times. Still, in

that chorus, both dwarves found a bit of hope.

"They're not coming in all together," Tred reasoned.

"Scattered," Nikwillig agreed.

An hour later, with the howling much closer, Tred sat beside a roaring fire, his burly arms crossed before him, his single-bladed, pointy-tipped axe set across his lap. His leg was glad of the reprieve, and his tapping foot alone betrayed his patient posture as he waited for the first of the worgs to make its appearance.

Off to the side, in the shadows behind a pile of boulders, an occasional crackle sounded. Tred winced and bit his bottom lip, hoping the rope held long enough against the weight of the withered but not yet felled pine.

When the first red eyes appeared across the way, Tred began to whistle. He reached to the side and scooped up a large pail of water, dumping it over himself.

"Ye likin' yer meat wet, puppies?" he called to the worgs.

As the huge wolves leaped into sight, he kicked at the closest edge of the fire, sending sparks and burning brands their way, momentarily stopping them. The action brought a cry of pain from the dwarf, as well. His torn leg could not hold him as he kicked out with the good one, and he went tumbling down to the side.

The chopped, dead tree came tumbling too, along the line the cunning dwarves had planned. The dried out old pine fell into the blazing fire, the wind of its descent sending sparks and dry needles rushing out to the side. More than one stung poor Tred, even igniting his beard a bit. He slapped the flickers out, stubbornly growled against his agony, and forced himself into a defensive posture.

Across the way, the rushing flames bit at the handful of worgs that had stepped into the clearing, sending them yelping and scrambling away, biting at sparking bits of fur. More came on, some even getting bit by the frenzy of their companions.

The dried pine went up in a fiery blaze between Tred and the wolves, but not before several dark forms leaped across or circumvented it.

Hands low on the handle, Tred slashed his axe across, batting aside the first flying wolf and sending it spinning to the ground. He reversed quickly, sliding his lead hand up the axe handle and setting it against his belt. As the second wolf leaped at him, it skewered itself on the axe's pointy tip. Tred didn't even try to slow that momentum, just held the flying wolf up high, guiding it over him. He brought his axe back at once, a ferocious downward chop that got the third charging worg right atop the head, smashing and splitting its skull, driving its front end down to the stone with its forelegs splaying out wide.

Nikwillig was beside him, sword in hand. When the next two worgs approached, one from either side, the dwarves turned back to back and fended the attacks.

Frustrated, the worgs circled. Nikwillig pulled a dagger from his belt and sent it flying into one worg's flank. The creature yelped and rushed off into the shadows.

Its companion quickly followed.

"First round's ours," Tred said, shying back as the heat from the burning tree became more intense.

"That pack's not wanting more of a fight," Nikwillig reasoned, "but more'll be catching us, don't ye doubt!"

He started away, pulling Tred along. Just out of the clearing, though, Tred stood taller and held his companion back.

"Unless we're catching them first," Tred said into Nikwillig's puzzled expression, when the merchant turned back to regard him. "Orcs're guiding the worgs," Tred reasoned. "No more orcs, no more worgs."

Nikwillig considered his friend for a few moments, looking mostly at Tred's torn leg, a clear indication that the pair could not hope to out-distance their pursuit. That seemed to leave only two choices before them.

And the first, leaving Tred behind, simply was not an option.

"Let's go find us some orcs," Nikwillig offered.

His smile was genuine.

So was Tred's.

They moved along as swiftly as they could, backtracking in a roundabout manner through the dark trees and rocky outcroppings, scrambling over uneven ground when they could find no trail. More often than not, Nikwillig was practically carrying Tred, but neither dwarf complained. The sound of worgs echoed all around them, but their diversion had worked, it seemed, throwing the pursuit off the scent and making more than a few of the creatures think twice about continuing their pursuit.

Sometime later, from a high vantage point, the dwarves spotted a few small campfires in the distance. Not one large encampment, it seemed, but several smaller groups.

"Their mistake," Tred remarked, and Nikwillig thoroughly agreed.

With a new goal in sight, the dwarves moved along at an even swifter pace. When his leg locked up on him, Tred merely hopped, and if he fell to the stone, which he often did, the tough dwarf merely pulled himself up, spat in his hand to clean off the new scrape, and scrambled forward. Down along one clear patch of ground, they encountered another wolf, but even as it bared its teeth and hunched its back in a threatening posture, Tred launched his axe into its flank, laying it low. Nikwillig was quick to the spot, finishing the beast before its yelps could alert the orc camp, which wasn't far away.

Soon after, and with the eastern sky brightening in the first signs of dawn, the pair crept up a small dirt banking and peered through the gap between a tree trunk and a boulder. A small campfire burned beyond, with a trio of orcs sitting around it and several more sleeping nearby. A single, injured worg sat beside the trio, snarling, growling, licking its wounds, and turning a hateful eye upon one of the orcs whenever it offered a berating curse at the inability of the worg and its companions to catch the fleeing dwarves.

Nikwillig put a finger to his pursed lips and motioned for Tred to stay put. He slipped off to the side, taking full advantage of the obvious fact that the confident orcs weren't expecting any unannounced visitors.

Tred watched his progress with a nod and a grin as Nikwillig bellycrawled to the edge of the encampment, putting his knife to fast work on one, then a second, sleeping orc. The observant dwarf saw the worg's head come up fast, though, and so he knew the game was up. With all the strength he could muster, Tred pulled himself up between the boulder and the tree.

"Well, ye wanted me, and so ye found me!" he roared.

The trio of orcs, and the worg, leaped up and gave a shout. Their third sleeping companion similarly started, but Nikwillig was already beside it, laying it low before it could even begin to respond.

The closest orc brandished a huge axe and charged headlong at Tred, coming in with a fancy, spinning maneuver that showed the creature was no novice with the weapon. But neither was he a profound thinker, obviously, for when Tred lifted his hand and hurled the stone he had picked up when he had announced himself, the orc was caught completely by surprise, and taken right in the face. The stunned orc stumbled forward, and Tred's swinging battle-axe promptly swatted it aside.

The other two orcs glanced around, only then realizing the devious work of Nikwillig, and the presence of the second dwarf.

"Two against two," Nikwillig said to them in the grunting Orcish tongue.

"We got wolfie!" one started to respond, but the battered worg apparently didn't agree, for it darted out of the camp and ran yelping along the dark trails.

One of the orcs tried to take the same course, leaping off to the side. Tred didn't hesitate, launching his axe at the fleeing creature. The spinning weapon didn't miss, but neither did it fully connect, tripping up the orc and slowing it as the handle tangled between its legs, but not hurting it much at all.

The second orc, seeing the obviously wounded dwarf standing there, apparently unarmed, howled and lifted its jagged sword. It charged in hard.

Nikwillig knew he couldn't get to Tred in time, so he went for the fallen orc first. Leaping upon the creature even as it started to rise, he bore it to the ground beneath his heavy boots. Nikwillig stomped and stabbed with his sword, trading a stinging hit from the orc's spear as it came around in exchange for a clear opening at the creature's chest. Nikwillig's shoulder stung from the stab, to be sure, but his sword opened the orc from breast to belly.

He heard Tred crying out for his brother then, with grunts between each shout. Nikwillig turned, expecting to see his friend in dire straits.

He let his weapon slide low, for Tred had the situation, and the orc, well in hand. He gripped the orc by the wrists, holding the creature's arms up high and out wide, and after every cry for his lost brother, Tred snapped his head forward and yanked the orc's arms out wider, the pair connecting forehead to face with each jolt.

The first few belts sounded loud and solid, bone on bone, but each succeeding smash made a crunchier sound, as if Tred was driving his forehead into a pile of dry twigs.

"I think ye can put it down now," Nikwillig remarked dryly after a few more thumps, the orc having long gone limp.

Tred grabbed the battered, dying creature by the collar with one hand and slapped his other hand hard into the orc's groin. A heave and a twist had the orc high over the powerful dwarf's head. With another call for his lost brother, Tred launched the orc down the bank behind him, to crash hard against a rock below.

"Lots of supplies," Nikwillig remarked, hopping about the camp.

"Damn orc sticked me," Tred replied.

Only then did his companion notice a new wound on the sturdy dwarf, a bright line of blood running from the side of Tred's chest. Nikwillig started for his companion, but Tred waved him back.

"Ye gather the supplies and we'll get going," he explained. "I'll dress it meself."

He did just that, and the pair were on their way soon after, Tred grunting in pain with every step, but otherwise offering not the slightest complaint.

He had lost a bucket of blood or more, and every time his foot slipped on a loose rock, the resulting lurch opened his newest wound anew, moistening his side with fresh blood. Still Tred didn't complain, nor did he slow Nikwillig's brisk pace. Their turn and attack had daunted the pursuit, it seemed, for few howls came rolling out to them on the night winds, and none of those were very close.

When Tred and Nikwillig crested a high ridge and looked far down upon a distant village—just a cluster of houses, really—they looked to each other with concern.

"We go in there and we might bring a horde o' orcs and wolfies on 'em," Tred reasoned.

"And if we don't go in, ye're gonna slow, and slow some more," Nikwillig replied. "We'll not be making Mithral Hall anytime soon, if we can even find our way to the place."

"Ye think they're knowin' how to fight?" Tred asked, looking back to the village.

"They're living in the wild mountains, ain't they?"

Simple enough, and true enough, and so Tred just gave a shrug and followed Nikwillig along the descending trail.

A wall of piled stones as tall as a man surrounded the cluster of houses, but it wasn't until the pair got very close that they noted any sentries. Even the two humans—a man and a woman—who finally peeked over the wall to call out to them didn't seem as if they were formal sentries. It was as if they simply happened to be walking by and noticed the dwarves.

"What are you two about?" came the woman's call.

"We'd be about to fall, I'd be guessin'," Nikwillig answered. He propped Tred up a bit to accentuate his point. "Ye got a warm bed and a bit o' hot stew for me injured kinfolk here?"

As if all of his energy had been given in the march, and his stubborn mind finally allowed his body the chance to rest, Tred fell limp and collapsed to the ground. Nikwillig guided him down as softly as possible.

There was no gate on that side of the village, but the woman and man came right out, scrambling over the wall and rushing to the dwarves. They, particularly the woman, went to work inspecting the injured dwarf, but they also both looked past the two dwarves, as if they expected an army of enemies to be chasing the battered duo in.

"You from Mithral Hall?" the man asked.

"Felbarr," Nikwillig answered. "We was headin' for Shallows when we got hit."

"Shallows?" the woman echoed. "Long way."

"Long chase."

"What hit you? Orcs?" asked the man.

"Orcs an' giants."

"Giants? Haven't seen any hill giants about in a long time."

"Not hill giants. Blue-skinned dogs. Lookin' pretty and hittin' ugly. Frost giants."

Both the man and woman looked up at him in concern, their eyes going wide. The folk of this region were not unfamiliar with trouble concerning frost giants. The old Grayhand, Jarl Orel, hadn't always kept his mighty people deep within the mountains over the decades, though thankfully, the frost giant forays hadn't been numerous. Still, any fight in any part of the area that included frost giants, perhaps the most formidable enemy in all the region next to the very occasional dragon, became news, dire news, the stuff of fireside tales and nightmares.

"Let's get him inside," the woman offered. "He's needing a bed and a hot meal. I can't believe he's even alive!"

"Bah, Tred's too ugly to die," Nikwillig remarked.

Tred opened a weary eye and slowly lifted his hand toward his friend's face, as if to pat him thankfully.

But as he got close, he pressed his index finger under his thumb, and flicked Nikwillig under the nose. Nikwillig fell back, grabbing his nose, and Tred settled back down, closing his eyes, a slight smile spreading on his crusty, pale face.

The folk of the small village, Clicking Heels, multiplied their guarding duties many times over, with a third of the two hundred sturdy folk working at a time as sentries and scouts in eight hour shifts. After two days recuperating, Nikwillig joined in those duties, bolstering the line, and even helping to direct the construction of some additional fortification.

Tred, though, was in no position to take part in anything. The dwarf slept through the night and through the day. Even after a couple of days, he woke only long enough to devour a huge meal the good folk of Clicking Heels were kind enough to supply. There was one cleric in the town, as well, but he wasn't very skilled at the magical part of his vocation and his healing skills, though he piled them on Tred, did little more good than the rest.

By the fifth day, Tred was up and about and starting to look and sound like his surly old self once more. By the end of a tenday, and still with no pursuit—giant, orc or worg—in sight, Tred was anxious to get moving.

"We're off to Mithral Hall," Nikwillig announced one morning, and the folk of Clicking Heels, humans all, seemed genuinely sorry to see the dwarves off. "We'll get King Gandalug to send some warriors up to check in on ye."

"King Bruenor, you mean," one of the villagers replied. "If he's returned to his folk from far off Icewind Dale."

"That right?"

"So we've heard."

Nikwillig nodded, offering a sigh for the loss of Gandalug before returning to his typically determined expression.

"King Bruenor then, as fair a dwarf as e'er there's been."

"I'm not sure he'll comply and send his soldiers, nor am I convinced that we need them," the man went on.

"Well, we'll tell him what's about and let him make up his own mind, then," Tred interjected. "That's why he's the king, after all."

That same morning, Tred and Nikwillig walked out of Clicking Heels, their steps strong once more, their packs full of supplies—good and tasty food and drink, not the slop they had stolen from the orcs. The folk had given them detailed directions to Mithral Hall as well, and so the dwarves were hopeful that they would find the end of this part of their journey soon enough. They intended to go to Mithral Hall, warn King Bruenor, or whomever it was leading their bearded kin, then get an escort from there through the connecting tunnels of the upper Underdark, back to their homes in Citadel Felbarr.

Even that wouldn't be the end of the road for Tred at least, for the tough dwarf had every intention of raising a band of warriors to head back out and avenge his brother and the others.

First things first, though, and that meant finding their way to Mithral Hall. Despite the directions, the dwarves found that no easy task in the winding and confusing mountain trails. A wrong turn along the narrow channels running through the stone often meant a long and difficult backtrack.

"It's the wrong damn stream," Tred grumbled one morning, the pair moving along steadily, but going south and east, whereas Mithral Hall was southwest of Clicking Heels.

"It'll wind back," Nikwillig assured him.

"Bah!" Tred snorted, shaking a fist at his companion.

They were lost and he knew it, and so did Nikwillig, whether he'd admit it or not. They didn't turn back, though. The road along the river had led them down a pair of very difficult descents that promised to be even more difficult climbs. To turn around after having gone so far seemed foolish.

They continued on, and when the stream took another unexpected dive over a waterfall, Tred grunted, grumbled, and climbed down the rocks to the side.

"Might be that it's time to think about going th' other way," Nikwillig offered.

"Bah!" was all that stubborn Tred would reply, and that grunt was exaggerated, for Tred hit an especially slick stone as he had waved his hand in a dismissive manner at Nikwillig.

He got down to the bottom faster at least.

They went on in silence after that and were looking about for a place to set camp when they crested one outcropping of huge cracked boulders to see the land fall away, wide and low before them, a huge valley running east and west.

"Big pass," Nikwillig remarked.

"One caravans might be using to get to Mithral Hall," Tred reasoned. "West it is!"

Nikwillig nodded, standing beside his companion, glad, as was Tred, to see that the going might be much easier the next day.

Of course, neither knew that they were standing on the northern rim of Fell Pass, the site of a great battle of old, where the very real and very dangerous ghosts of the vanquished lingered in great numbers.

4

CONFLICTING LOYALTIES

The dwarf councilor, Agrathan Hardhammer, shifted uneasily in his seat as the volume around him increased along with the agitation of the others, all human, in the room.

"Perhaps you should have granted him an audience," said Shoudra Stargleam, the sceptrana of the city.

Shoudra's bright blue eyes flashed as she spoke, and she shook her head, as she always seemed to be doing, letting her long dark hair fly wide to either side. Her hair was often the subject of gossip among the women of the city, for though Shoudra was in her thirties and had lived for all her life in the harsh, windblown climate of Mirabar, it held the luster and shine that one might expect on the head of a girl half Shoudra's age. In all respects, the sceptrana was a beautiful creature, tall and lithe, yet with deceptively delicate features. Deceptive, because though she was ultimately feminine, Shoudra Stargleam was possessed of a solidity, a formidability, that rivaled the strongest of Mirabar's men.

The fat man sitting on the cushioned throne, the Marchion of Mirabar, smirked at her and waved his hands in disgust.

"I had, and have, more important matters to attend to than to see to the needs of an unannounced visitor," the marchion said, staring hard at Agrathan as he spoke, "even if that visitor is the King of Mithral Hall.

Besides, is it not your duty, and not mine own, to negotiate trade agreements?"

"King Bruenor did not come here for any such purpose, by any reports," Shoudra protested, drawing another wave of Marchion Elastul's thick hands.

Elastul shook his head and looked about at his Hammers, his principal attendants, scarred old warriors all.

"Might that she should've met with Bruenor anyway," Djaffar, the leader of the group, remarked. He nudged the marchion's shoulder. "Shoudra's got a trick or two that could soften even a dwarf!"

The other three soldier-advisors and Marchion Elastul burst out in snickers at that. Shoudra Stargleam narrowed her blue eyes and assumed a defiant pose, crossing her arms over her chest.

To the side, Agrathan shifted again. He knew Shoudra could handle herself, and that she, like all the folk of Mirabar who had any access to Elastul, was used to the liberties of protocol often taken by the vulgar Hammers and by the marchion himself. His was an inherited position, unlike the elected councilors and sceptrana.

"He asked to see you, Marchion, not me and not the council," Shoudra reminded curtly, ending the snickers.

"And what am I to do with the likes of Bruenor Battlehammer?" Elastul replied. "Dine with him? Cater to him, and quietly explain to him that he will soon be irrelevant?"

Shoudra looked over at Agrathan plaintively, and the dwarf cleared his throat, drawing the marchion's attention.

"Ye wouldn't be doing well to underestimate Bruenor," Agrathan advised. "His boys're good at what they do."

"Irrelevant," Elastul said again, settling back comfortably. "That curiosity piece Gandalug is dead, may the stones powder his bones, and Bruenor is inheriting a kingdom on the decline."

Again, Shoudra looked over at Agrathan, this time wearing a doubting smirk, for she and the dwarf knew what was coming.

"More than two dozen metallurgists and alchemists." Elastul boasted. "I'm paying them well, and they'll be showing results soon enough!"

Agrathan lowered his eyes so that Elastul wouldn't see his doubting expression as the marchion went on to describe the most recent promises of those folks he had hired in an effort to strengthen the metal produced by Mirabar's mines. The metallurgists had been promising from the day they arrived, several years before, combinations of strength and flexibility beyond anything anyone in all the world could produce. Grand, and as far as Agrathan believed, empty claims all.

Agrathan hadn't worked the mines in over a century—since he had turned to the practice of preaching the word of Dumathoin—but as a priest of that dwarf god, a deity who was known as the Keeper of Secrets Under the Mountain, Agrathan firmly believed that the claims of the hired alchemists and metallurgists were not among those secrets. To Agrathan, if some magical way to enhance any metal wasn't among the secrets of Dumathoin, then it simply didn't exist.

The hired group was very good at what it did. What it did, as far as Agrathan was concerned, was keep the marchion curious and intrigued enough to keep the gold flowing, and that was all that was flowing. Mirabar boasted less than half the dwarves of Mithral Hall, just over two thousand, and several hundred of those were busy serving in the Axe, keeping the mines clear of monsters. The thousand who worked the mines could barely meet the quotas set out by the Council of Sparkling Stones each year and that from existing veins. Little exploration was being done at the deeper levels, where the dangers were greater, but so too were the true promises of better quality in the form of better ore.

The simple fact was that Mirabar couldn't afford to cut production long enough to seek out those better veins, so the marchion had fallen into the scam of these supposed specialists—with not a dwarf among them—who claimed to understand metals so well. Besides, to Agrathan's thinking, if there were such processes as the marchion believed, why hadn't they been put in practice centuries before? Why hadn't these metallurgists and alchemists reduced the dwarves of Mithral Hall, the dwarves of all the world, to positions of providing base material alone? They promised weapons, armor, and other metal goods strong enough to outshine anything Bruenor's folk might produce, and yet, if they knew of such secrets, if there were such secrets, then why weren't there weapons of legend that had been produced through such processes?

"Even if your specialists deliver their promises, we will still be far from making King Bruenor and Mithral Hall 'irrelevant'," Shoudra Stargleam replied, and Agrathan was glad that she was taking the lead. "They are out-producing us in volume more than three-to-two."

The marchion waved his hands at her. "There was nothing for me to say to Bruenor Battlehammer anyway. Why did he come here? Who invited him? Who asked . . ." He ended with a derisive snort.

"Perhaps we should not have allowed him entrance," Shoudra remarked.

Agrathan looked up at Elastul, guessing correctly the dangerous glare the marchion would be offering to Shoudra at that moment. When word that King Bruenor was at Mirabar's gate had been passed along, it had been Elastul's decision to let Bruenor and the others in. None on the council, or the sceptrana, had even been informed until the Clan Battlehammer dwarves had already set up their carts on Mirabar's streets.

"Yes, perhaps my faith in the loyalty of my citizens was misplaced," the marchion countered, harsh words aimed more at Agrathan, the dwarf knew, than at Shoudra. "I expected King Bruenor to find greater embarrassment than rejection by the ruler of the city. I expected the folk of Mirabar to know enough to not even bother with our guests."

Agrathan glanced over to see that the marchion was indeed staring directly at him as he spoke. No humans, after all, had gone to do business with Clan Battlehammer, only dwarves, and Agrathan was the highest-ranking dwarf in the city, the unofficial leader and voice of Mirabar's two thousand.

"Have you spoken with Master Hammerstriker?"

"What would ye have me say?" Agrathan asked.

While he was the accepted voice for the dwarves among the human leaders, that wasn't always the case among the Mirabarran dwarves themselves.

"I would have you remind Master Hammerstriker where his loyalties lie," the marchion replied. "Or where they *should* lie."

Agrathan worked hard to keep his expression placid, to hide the sudden storm welling inside of him. The loyalty of Torgar Delzoun Hammerstriker could not be questioned. The crusty old warrior had served the marchion, and the marchion before him, and before him, and before him, and before him, and before him, for longer than any human in the city could remember, longer than the long dead parents of the dead parents of any human in the city could have remembered. Torgar had been among the leading soldiers charging along the tunnels of the upper Underdark against monsters more foul than anything any of the marchion's Hammers—those elite advisors selected supposedly because of their glorious veteran warrior status—had ever known. When the orc hordes attacked Mirabar, a hundred and seventeen years past, Torgar and a very few other dwarves had held the eastern wall strong against the assault, fending off the hordes while the bulk of Mirabar's warriors had been engaged on the western wall, against what had proven to be no more than a feint by the enemy. In scars, wounds, and cunning victories, Torgar Delzoun Hammerstriker had earned his position as a leader among the Axe.

But even to Agrathan the marchion's words rang with a bit of truth. It wasn't a question of loyalty, as far as Agrathan was concerned, but rather one of judgment. Torgar and his fellows had not understood the implications of trading with their rivals from Mithral Hall or from subsequently socializing with them.

With that, Agrathan and Shoudra left the agitated marchion, walking side by side along the outer corridors of the palace and out into the pale sunlight of the late afternoon. A chill breeze was blowing, a reminder to the pair that in Mirabar, winter was never far away.

"You will approach Torgar with a bit more gentleness than Marchion Elastul showed?" Shoudra asked the dwarf, her smile one of genuine amusement.

As sceptrana, Shoudra was involved in signing trade agreements. With the rise of Mithral Hall, she too had suffered, or at least her work had. Shoudra Stargleam had taken it more in stride than many others in the city, though, including many of the dwarves. To her, the way to beat Mithral Hall was to increase production and find better ore for better product. To her, the rise of a trading rival should be the catalyst to make Mirabar stronger.

"I'll tell Torgar and his boys what I can, but ye know that one, and know that not many can be telling Torgar anything."

"He is loyal to Mirabar," Shoudra stated, and though Agrathan nodded, the expression on his face showed that he wasn't so certain of that anymore.

Shoudra Starglean caught that look and stopped, and put her hand on Agrathan's shoulder to stop him as well.

"Is he loyal to city or to race?" she asked. "Does he consider the marchion his true leader or King Bruenor of Mithral Hall?"

"Torgar's fought well for every marchion since before yer parents were born, girl," Agrathan reminded her.

Shoudra nodded, but like Agrathan a moment earlier, she didn't seem overly convinced.

"They should not have gone to trade and drink with the visiting dwarves," Shoudra remarked.

She bustled her cloak in front of her and started on her way.

"Mighty temptations there. Good trade, good drink, and better stories. Are ye thinking that my folk aren't wanting to hear the Battle of Keeper's Dale? Are ye thinking that your own world would be a better place if the damn drow invaders had won at Mithral Hall?"

"Well, perhaps if the dark elves had inflicted a bit more damage before they had been chased off. . . ." Shoudra replied.

Agrathan snapped a scowl over her, but it was quickly defeated, for the woman was grinning mischievously even as she spoke the words.

"Bah!" Agrathan snorted.

"So by your reasoning, Mirabar owes a debt to Mithral Hall for their victory against the dark elves?" Shoudra asked.

Agrathan paused for a moment and thought long and hard on that one. In the end, he shrugged, not willing to make a commitment.

Shoudra grinned again and nodded, for it was obvious that the dwarf's heart was giving one answer and his pragmatic head, the part that owed loyalty to Marchion Elastul and Mirabar, was giving another. It wasn't a laughing matter, though. In fact, the notion that Agrathan, a major voice on the Council of Sparkling Stones, was apparently holding mixed feelings concerning Mithral Hall incited more than a little trepidation in the sceptrana. Agrathan had been one of the strongest voices of opposition to Mithral Hall, often relating the words of his more vocal dwarf constituents who wanted covert action to be taken against Clan Battlehammer. Agrathan had once outlined a plan for infiltrating the neighboring kingdom and slipping cooler-burning charcoal into their stores, weakening their smelting and shaping work.

Many times during council meetings Agrathan Hardhammer had himself exploded in tirades against the dwarves of Clan Battlehammer, but having seen them face-to-face, Shoudra was seeing the true depth of his, and his people's, resolve.

"Tell me, Agrathan, was that famous drow elf accompanying King Bruenor's caravan?"

"Drizzt Do'Urden? Yes, he was there, but they didn't let him into the city."

Shoudra looked at him curiously. Drizzt had made quite a reputation for himself in the North, even before his actions against his own people when they had attacked Mithral Hall. By all accounts, he was a hero.

"The Axe weren't about to let a cursed dark elf walk the streets, whatever his name," Agrathan said firmly, "but he was there. Torgar and some others saw him and that human girl that Bruenor is calling his own, along with that human boy that Bruenor is calling his own, off to the side, watching it all."

"Was he as handsome as they say?" Shoudra asked.

Agrathan turned an even bigger scowl over her, twisted into an expression of skepticism.

"He's a drow, ye damned fool!"

Shoudra Stargleam merely laughed, and Agrathan shook his hairy head.

They stopped their walk then, for they had come to Undercity Square, an open area between three buildings, one of them a large sectioned building where Shoudra kept her apartment. In the center of the triangular area was a descending stairway, which led to the most heavily guarded room in all of Mirabar, the main entrance to the Undercity— the real city as far as Agrathan and his kin were concerned—where the real work went on.

Shoudra bid the dwarf farewell and entered her house. Agrathan stood at the top of the stairway for a long, long while, more uncomfortable than he had ever been before entering the domain of Mirabar's two thousand dwarves. It was his solemn duty to go and deliver the marchion's message to Torgar and the others, but Agrathan knew his kin well enough to understand that the words would cause more than a little anger and division among the dwarves. Their emotions ran the gamut concerning Mithral Hall. Many of the Mirabarran dwarves had even called for confiscation of any Mithral Hall caravan moving west of Clan Battlehammer's domain, knowing full well that such an action might mean open warfare between the two cities. Others quietly remarked that their ancestors had lived in Mithral Hall with King Bruenor's predecessors, and that it had been a good life, as good a life as any dwarf could ever want.

Agrathan snorted—a "dwarven sigh," he called it—and thumped his way down the stairs, brushing past the many human guards in the upper chamber as he made his way to the lift. He waved away the attendant and worked the heavy ropes himself, lowering himself down hundreds of feet to a second well-guarded room, with all exits blocked by external portcullises and iron-bound doors. The guards there were all dwarves, some of the toughest of all the Axe.

"Ye go and put the word to all our kin in all the holes," Agrathan instructed them, "and to them working the walls up top. We're meeting after sunset in the Hall of All Fires, and I want every one of my boys there. Everyone!"

The guards opened one of the exits for Agrathan and he exited, head down and murmuring to himself, trying to discern the best way to handle this most delicate of situations.

Though he was more tactful than most, as was evidenced by his rank in a city that was dominated by humans, Agrathan was still a dwarf, and subtlety had never been his strong point.

The scene was never controlled and quiet in the Hall of All Fires when a significant number of Mirabar's dwarves were assembled, but that night, with nearly all of the city's two thousand in attendance and with the subject so controversial, the place was in absolute chaos.

"So now ye're to tell me whose story I can hear, and whose I can't?" Torgar Hammerstriker roared back at Agrathan. "It was a good bit o' ale, and a finer bit o' tales!"

Many of the dwarves who had accompanied Torgar to the Icewind Dale bazaar and later to the Clan Battlehammer reception shouted their agreement. One or two held up beautiful pieces of scrimshaw they had purchased from the traders, wonderful pieces gotten at better prices.

"I can resell this in Nesmé for ten times what I paid!" one industrious, red-bearded fellow declared. He jumped high onto a dark furnace, holding up his small statue—a scrimshaw depiction of a shapely barbarian woman—for all to see. "Ye tellin' me I can't be making good deals, priest?"

Agrathan slumped back a bit, not surprised by the reaction.

"I have come to deliver the words of Marchion Elastul, a reminder—and yes, a stern one—to us all that the dwarves of Clan Battlehammer are not friends to Mirabar. They take our trade—"

"Is there a one of us here who can rightly say that he's livin' better since they opened Mithral Hall again?" another dwarf cut the priest off. "Even wit' yer pretty statue, fat Bullwhip, ye're not to have a good year in the matter o' yer purse, now are ye?"

Many dwarves seconded that, cheering the agitated speaker on.

"We had better lives and bigger coins afore the damn Battlehammers came back in! And who invited them?"

"Bah! Ye're talking the part of a fool!" Torgar lashed out.

"Says the dwarf who looked to other councilors for a loan!" the fiery one shot back. "Ye needin' coin now, Torgar? Will King Bruenor's stories fill yer belly?"

Torgar climbed up to the raised area at the north end of the hall to stand beside Agrathan. He paused for a long while, looking to and fro, commanding everyone's attention.

"What I'm hearing here is jealous talk, plain and simple," he said, very calmly. "Ye're talking about Clan Battlehammer as if they've declared war upon us, when all they've done is open up mines that've been there, and been theirs, since afore Mirabar was Mirabar. They've a right to their homeland and a right to make it work. We're sittin' here making plans to bring 'em down, when it's seemin' to me that we should be making plans to bring ourselfs up!"

"They been stealin' our business!" someone yelled from the crowd. "Ye forgetting that part?"

"They been beatin' us," Torgar pointedly, and immediately, corrected. "They got better mines an' better metal, and they built themselves a strong reputation one dead orc, duergar, and stinkin' drow elf at a time. Ye can't be blamin' King Bruenor and his boys for working hard and fighting harder!"

The shouts erupted from every corner, many in agreement and many in dissent. A couple of fistfights broke out in various corners of the hall.

Up on the raised platform, Torgar and Agrathan stared hard at each other, and though neither had fully embraced the other's viewpoint on this matter only a few days before, their respective visions were crystallizing.

There came a shout from somewhere in the crowd, "Hey priestie, ye taking the side o' the humans over that o' yer kinfolk dwarfs?"

Both Torgar and Agrathan turned at once, and many others did as well. All the great meeting chamber went silent, dwarves stopping their fighting in mid-swing, for there it was, spelled out simply and to the point.

For Torgar, it was a moment of confusion and self-examination. Was it actually coming down to this, a choice between his dwarven kin of Mithral Hall and the joint community of Mirabar?

For Agrathan, leading member of the Council of Sparkling Stones, the choice was less fuzzy, for indeed, if that was the way that some of his kin chose to view things, then so be it. Agrathan's loyalties lay to Mirabar and to Mirabar alone, but when he looked at his counterpart, he saw that the marchion's remarks, which Agrathan had considered insulting, toward Torgar Delzoun Hammerstriker were not without merit.

Agrathan's faith in his community was a bit shaken a moment later, when the great gates of the Hall of All Fires swung wide and a large contingent of the Axe of Mirabar swept in, wading into the confused throng in a wedge formation, then forcefully widening their stance so that a huge triangular area of the room was quickly secured. In marched the marchion and several of the more stern councilors, along with the sceptrana.

"This is not the behavior the human folk of Mirabar expects from their dwarf comrades," Elastul scolded.

He should have left it at that, a quiet and calm reminder that the city had enough enemies without to worry about such squabbles within.

"Accept that Torgar Hammerstriker and those who accompanied him to the carts of Clan Battlehammer, and to the liars . . . er, the *bards* of the same clan erred, and badly, in their judgment," Elastul bluntly warned. "Beware, Master Hammerstriker, lest you lose your position in the Axe. For the rest of you, lured by ale and this creature, this false legend, who is Bruenor Battlehammer, remind yourselves where your loyalties lie, and remind yourselves as well that Clan Battlehammer threatens our city."

Elastul swiveled his head slowly, taking in all the gathering, trying to wilt them under his stern gaze. But these were dwarves, after all, and few wilted, and few of those who agreed with the marchion wagged their heads.

Many of those who disagreed stood a bit straighter and a bit taller, and in looking at his counterpart on the stage, Agrathan seriously wondered if Torgar was going to peel off his Axe insignia then and there and throw it at Elastul's feet.

"Disperse, I command you!" Marchion Elastul roared. "Back to your work, and back to your lives."

The dwarves did disperse then, and the marchion and his entourage, including the human soldiers, departed, with the sole exception of Shoudra Stargleam who stayed to speak with Agrathan.

"Well, ain't them the words of a true king," Torgar muttered as he walked past Agrathan, and he spat at the priest's feet.

"The marchion was ill-advised to be coming here like that now," Agrathan remarked to Shoudra when they were alone.

"Many of your peers on the council pressed him to action,"

Shoudra explained. "They feared that the visit of King Bruenor might be having an adverse affect on our dwarf citizens."

"It was," Agrathan said glumly, "and it is. Even more now."

Agrathan meant every word. He watched the remaining dwarves departing the hall or going back to stoke the furnaces that lined it. He noted their expressions, their deep-set scowls and angry eyes. Torgar's misjudgment had brought a rift in the clan, had put a wedge into the solid community.

Agrathan couldn't help but think that the marchion had just taken a sledge and smashed that wedge hard.

5

WHERE GHOSTS ROAM

The troupe crossed the bridge to the south of Mirabar, then followed the River Mirar to the east of the city for a tenday of easy marching. South of them loomed the tall trees of Lurkwood, a forest known to harbor many orc tribes and other unpleasant neighbors. To the north stood the towering mountains of the Spine of the World, their tops holding defiantly white against the coming summer season.

The grass grew tall around them, and dandelions dotted the rolling fields of the Valley of Khedrun, but the ever-vigilant dwarves were not lulled by the peaceful season and scenery. This far to the north, anywhere outside of a city had to be considered untamed land, so they doubled their guard every night, circled their wagons, and kept Drizzt, Catti-brie, and Wulfgar working the flanks. Guenhwyvar joined the trio in their scouting whenever Drizzt was able to summon her.

At the eastern end of the valley, with nearly a hundred miles between them and Mirabar, the River Mirar bent to the north, flowing from the foothills of the Spine of the World. The Lurkwood, meanwhile, also bent to the north, following the line of the river as if shadowing the water, several miles to the south.

"Ground's gonna get tougher," Bruenor warned them all as they set camp that night. "We'll be back in the foothills tomorrow by midday, and moving tight under the shadows o' the forest."

He looked around at his clan, to see every head nodding stoically.

"Next days'll be tougher," Bruenor told them, and not a one batted an eye.

They broke their gathering, and went back to their posts.

"The road's not so bad, by my measurin'," Delly Curtie said to Wulfgar when he joined her and Colson, their young daughter, at the small lean-to Delly had set beside a wagon. "No meaner than Luskan's streets."

"We've been fortunate so far," Wulfgar replied, holding his arms out to take Colson, whom Delly gladly gave over.

Wulfgar looked down at the tiny girl, the daughter of Meralda Feringal, the Lady of Auckney, a small town nestled in the Spine of the World not far to the west of the pass that had brought the troupe out of Icewind Dale. Wulfgar had rescued Colson from the trials of Lord Feringal and his tyrannical sister, retribution against the bastard child since Colson was not Feringal's daughter. The Lord of Auckney had thought Wulfgar the father, for Meralda had concocted a lie to protect the man's honor, claiming that she had been raped on the road.

But Wulfgar was not the father, had never known Meralda in that manner. Looking at Colson, though, at the tiny creature who had become so precious to him, he wished that he was. He looked up from Colson to see Delly staring at him lovingly, and he knew that he was a lucky man indeed.

"Ye going out with Drizzt and Catti-brie tonight?" Delly asked.

Wulfgar shook his head. "We're too close to the Lurkwood. Drizzt and Catti-brie can keep the watch well enough without me."

"Ye're staying close because ye're afraid for me and Colson," Delly reasoned, and Wulfgar didn't disagree.

The woman reached to take the baby back, but Wulfgar rolled his shoulder to block her hands, grinning at her all the time.

"Ye cannot be forsaking yer duties for me own sake," Delly complained, and Wulfgar laughed at her.

"This," he said, presenting the baby, then pulling her back in close when Delly reached for her, "is my duty, first and foremost. Drizzt and Catti-brie know it, too. We are close to the Lurkwood now, and that means close to orcs. You might be thinking that Luskan's streets are meaner than the wilds because you've not yet truly seen the wilds. If the orcs come upon us in numbers, the blood will flow. Orc blood, mostly, but with dwarf blood mixed in. You've never witnessed a battle, my love, and I hope it stays like that, but out here. . . ."

He let it go at that, shaking his head.

"And if the orcs come for us, ye'll be there keeping them off me and Colson," Delly reasoned.

Wulfgar, determined, looked at her then down at Colson who was sleeping angelically in his arms. His smile widened.

"No orc, no giant, no dragon will harm you," he promised the babe, lifting his eyes to include Delly as well.

Delly started to respond, and Wulfgar was sure she meant to offer one of her typically sarcastic remarks, but she didn't. She stopped short and just stood there staring at him, even offering a little nod to show that she did not doubt him.

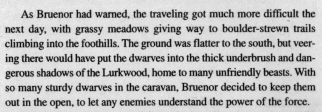

As Bruenor had warned, the traveling got much more difficult the next day, with grassy meadows giving way to boulder-strewn trails climbing into the foothills. The ground was flatter to the south, but veering there would have put the dwarves into the thick underbrush and dangerous shadows of the Lurkwood, home to many unfriendly beasts. With so many sturdy dwarves in the caravan, Bruenor decided to keep them out in the open, to let any enemies understand the power of the force.

The dwarves did not complain, and when they came upon a gully or a particularly broken stretch over which the wagons could not roll, a host of dwarves moved up beside each cart, lifting it in their strong hands and carrying it across. That was their way, an attitude of logical stoicism and pragmatism that cut long tunnels through hard rock, one inch at a time.

Watching them at their march, Drizzt understood well the kind of determination and long-range thinking that had produced such beautiful and marvelous places as Mithral Hall. It was the same patience that had allowed one such as Bruenor to create Aegis-fang, to deliberately engrave perfect representations of the trio of dwarf gods on the hammer's head, where one errant scratch would have ruined the whole process.

Soon after the second day out of Khedrun Pass, with the trees of the Lurkwood so near that the group could hear birds singing in the boughs, a cry from the front confirmed Bruenor's other fear.

"Orcs outta the woods!"

"Form yer battle groups!" Bruenor called.

"Group One Left, make yer wedge!" Dagnabbit shouted. "One Right, square up!"

To the left, farthest from the woods, Drizzt and Catti-brie watched the precision of the veteran dwarf warriors and saw the small band of orcs rushing out of the forest, making for the lead wagons.

The orcs hadn't scouted their intended target properly, it seemed, for once they cleared the brush and saw the scope of the force allayed before them, they skidded to a stop and fell all over each other in fast retreat.

How different were their movements from those of the calm, skilled dwarves—well, almost all of the dwarves. Ignoring the calls of Bruenor and Dagnabbit, Thibbledorf Pwent and his Gutbusters assembled into their own formation, unique to their tactics. They called it a charge, but to Drizzt and Catti-brie it more resembled an avalanche. Pwent and his boys whooped, hollered, and scrambled headlong into the darkness of the forest shadows in pursuit of the orcs, leaping through the first line of brush with gleeful abandon.

"The orcs may have set a trap," Catti-brie warned, "showing us but a small part o' their force to drag us into their webs."

Cries resounded within the boughs, just south of the caravan, and flora and fauna, and orc body parts, began to fly wildly all about the area the Gutbusters had entered.

"Stupid orcs, then," Drizzt replied.

He started down from the higher ground, Catti-brie in tow, to join Bruenor. When they reached the king, they found him standing on his wagon bench, hands on his hips, and with groups of properly arrayed dwarves in tight formations all around him. One wedge of warriors passed skillfully by the defensive squares two others had assembled.

"Ain't ye going to join the fun?" Bruenor asked.

Drizzt looked back at the forest, at the continuing tumult, a volcano come to life, and shook his head.

"Too dangerous," the drow explained.

"Damn Pwent makes it hard to see the point o' discipline," Bruenor grumbled to his friends.

He winced, and so did Drizzt and Catti-Brie, and Regis who was standing near to Bruenor, when an orc came flying out of the underbrush to land face down on the clearer ground in front of the dwarves. Before any of Bruenor's boys could react, they heard a wild roar from back within the boughs, up high, and stared in blank amazement as Thibbledorf Pwent, high up in a tree, ran out to the end of one branch and leaped out long and far.

The orc was just beginning to rise when Pwent landed on its back, blasting it back down to the ground. Likely it was already dead, but the wild battlerager, with broken branches and leaves stuck all about his ridged armor, went into his devastating body shake, turning the orc into a bloody mess.

Pwent hopped up, then hopped all around.

"Ye can get 'em moving again, me king!" he yelled back to Bruenor. "We'll be done here soon enough."

"And the Lurkwood will never be the same," Drizzt mumbled.

"If I was a squirrel anywhere around here, I'd be thinking of making meself a new home," Catti-brie concurred.

"I'd pay a big bird to fly me far away," Regis added.

"Should we hold the positions?" Dagnabbit called to Bruenor.

"Nah, get the wagons moving," the dwarf king replied with a wave of his hand. "We stay here and we'll all get splattered."

Pwent and his boys, some hurt but hardly caring, rejoined their fellows a short while later, singing songs of victory and battle. Nothing serious emanated from this group. Their songs sounded more like the joyful rhymes of children at play.

"Watching Pwent makes me wonder if I wasted my youth with all that training," Drizzt said to Catti-brie later on, the pair patrolling with Guenhwyvar along the northern foothills again.

"Yeah, ye could've just whiled away the hours banging yer head against a stone wall, like Pwent and his boys did."

"Without a helmet?"

"Aye," the woman confirmed, keeping a straight face. "Though I'm thinking that Bruenor made him armor the poor wall. Protecting the structural integrity of the realm."

"Ah," said Drizzt, nodding, then just shaking his head helplessly.

No more orc bands made any appearances against the caravan throughout the rest of that day, nor over the next few. The going was difficult and slow, but still, not a dwarf complained, even when they had to spend the better part of a rainy day moving the remnants of an old rockslide from the trail.

As the days wore on, though, more and more rumbles began to filter through the line of wagons, for it became obvious to them all that Bruenor wasn't planning a turn to the south anytime soon.

"Orcs," Catti-brie remarked, examining the partial footprint in the dirt of a high trail. The woman looked up and all around, as if gauging the wind and the air. "Few days, maybe."

"At least a few," replied Drizzt, who was a short distance away, leaning on a boulder with his arms crossed over his chest, scrutinizing the woman's work as if he knew something that she did not.

"What?" the woman asked, catching the non-verbal cue.

"Perhaps I have a wider picture of it," Drizzt answered.

Catti-brie narrowed her eyes as she stared hard at the drow, matching his mischievous grin with a thin-lipped one of her own. She started to say something less than complimentary, but then caught on that perhaps the drow was speaking literally. She stood up and stepped back, taking in the area of the footprint from a wider viewpoint. Only then did she realize that the orc print was beside the mark of a much larger boot.

Much larger.

"Orc was here first," she stated without hesitation.

"How do you know that?" Drizzt wasn't playing the part of instructor here, but rather, he seemed genuinely curious as to how the woman had come to that.

"Giant might be chasin' the orc, but I'm doubting that the orc's chasing the giant."

"How do you know they weren't traveling together?"

Catti-brie looked back to the tracks. "Not a hill giant," she explained, for it was well known that hill giants often allied with orcs. "Too big."

"Mountain giant, perhaps," said Drizzt. "Larger version of the same creature."

Catti-brie shook her head doubtfully. Most mountain giants typically didn't even wear boots, covering their feet with skin wraps, if at all. The sharp definitions of the giant heel print made her believe that this particular boot was well made. Even more telling, the foot was narrow, relatively speaking, whereas mountain giants were known to have huge, wide feet.

"Stone giants might be wearin' boots," the woman reasoned, "and frost giants always do."

"So you think the giant was chasing the orc?"

The woman looked over at Drizzt again and shrugged. With it put so plainly—Drizzt apparently wasn't questioning her—she realized just how shaky that theory truly was.

"Could be," she said, "or they might've just passed this way independent of each other. Or they might be workin' together."

"A frost giant and an orc?" came the skeptical question.

"A woman and a drow?" came the snide response, and Drizzt laughed.

The pair moved on without much concern. The tracks were not fresh, and even if it was an orc or a group of orcs, and a giant or two besides, they'd think twice before attacking an army of five hundred dwarves.

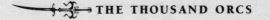

It was slow and it was hot and it was dry, but no more monsters showed themselves to the force as the dwarves stubbornly made their way to the east. They climbed up one dusty trail, the sun hot on their backs, but when they crested the ridge and started down the backside, all the world seemed to change.

A vast, rocky vale loomed before them, with towering mountains both north and south. Shadows dotted the valley, and even in those places where there seemed no obstacle to block the sunlight, the ground appeared dull, dour, and somehow mysterious. Wisps of fog flitted about the valley, though there was no obvious water source, and little dew-catching grass could be seen.

Bruenor, Regis, Dagnabbit, and Wulfgar and his family led the way down the backside of the ridge to find Drizzt and Catti-brie waiting for their wagon.

"You're not likin' what ye're seein'?" Bruenor asked Drizzt, noticing a disconcerted expression on the face of the normally cool drow.

Drizzt shook his head, as if he couldn't put it into words.

"A strange feeling," he explained, or tried to.

He looked back toward the gloomy vale and shook his head again.

"I'm feelin' it too," Catti-brie chimed in. "Like we're bein' looked at."

"Ye probably are," Bruenor said.

He cracked the whip and sent his team, which also seemed more than a little skittish, moving down the trail. The dwarf gave a laugh, but those around him didn't seem so comfortable, particularly Wulfgar, who kept looking back at Delly and Colson.

"Your wagon should not be in the front," Drizzt reminded Bruenor.

"As I been telling him," Dagnabbit agreed.

Bruenor only snorted and drove the team on, calling back to the next wagons in line and to the soldiers flanking them.

"Bah, they're all hesitating," Bruenor complained.

"Can ye not feel it?" Dagnabbit asked.

"Feel it? I'm swimmin' in it, shortbeard! We'll put up right down there," he conceded, pointing to a flat, open area just below, about a third of the way down the side of the ridge, "then ye get 'em all about and I'll give them the tale."

"The tale?" Catti-brie asked, the same question that all the others were about to voice.

"The tale o' the pass," Bruenor explained. "The Fell Pass."

It was a name that meant little to Bruenor's Icewind Dale non-dwarf companions, but Dagnabbit blanched at the mention—as much as the others had ever seen a dwarf blanch. Still, Dagnabbit performed as instructed, and with typical efficiency, bringing the wagons in line from the ridge top to the plateau Bruenor had indicated. When the dwarves had finished their bustling and jostling, setting their teams in place and finding acceptable vantage points to hear the words of their leader, Bruenor climbed up on a wagon and called out to them all.

"Ye're smellin' ghosts, and that's what's got ye itching," he explained. "And ye should be smellin' ghosts, for the valley here is thick with them. Ghosts o' Delzoun dwarves, long dead, killed in battle by orcs." He swept his arm out to the east, to the wide pass opening before them. "And what a battle she was! Hunnerds o' yer ancestors died here, me boys, and thousands and thousands o' their enemies. But ye keep yerselfs strong in heart. We won the Battle o' Fell Pass, and so if ye're seeing any o' them ghosts down there on our way through, ye taunt it if it's an orc and ye bow to it if it's a dwarf!"

The other friends from Icewind Dale watched Bruenor with sincere admiration, noting how he added just the right inflections to his voice, and emphasis on key words to hold his clan in deep attention. He was acknowledging that there might be supernatural things down in the reputedly haunted valley, yet if there was an ounce of fear in Bruenor Battlehammer, he did not show it.

"Now we could've gone further south," he went on. "Coulda swung along the northern edge o' the Trollmoors and into Nesmé."

He paused and shook his head, then gave a great, "Bah!"

Drizzt and the others surveyed the audience, noting that many, many bearded heads were bobbing in agreement with that dismissive sentiment.

"But I knowed me boys'd have little trouble walking among the dead heroes of old," Bruenor finished. "Ye won't embarrass Clan Battlehammer. Now ye get yer teams moving. We'll bring the wagons in a tight double line across the pass, and if ye're seeing a dwarf of old, ye be remembering yer manners!"

The army swung into precise action, sorting the wagons and moving them along the trail, down to the floor of the wide pass. They tightened their ranks, as Bruenor had instructed, and rolled along two-by-two. Before the last of the wagons had even begun moving, one of the dwarves struck up a marching song, a heroic tale of an ancient battle not unlike the one that had taken place in Fell Pass. In moments, all the line had joined in the song, their voices strong and steady, defeating the chilling atmosphere of the haunted place.

"Even if there are ghosts about," Drizzt whispered to Catti-brie, "they'll be too afraid to come out and bother this group."

Just to the side of them, Delly was equally at ease with Wulfgar.

"And ye keep telling me how ugly the road can be," she scolded. "And here I was, all afraid."

Wulfgar gave her a concerned look.

"I never known a better place to be," Delly said to him. "And how ye could e'er have thought o' giving up this life for one in the miserable city, I'm not for knowing!"

"Nor are we," Catti-brie agreed, drawing a surprised look from the barbarian. She returned Wulfgar's stare with a disarming smile. "Nor are we."

The wind moaned—perhaps it was the wind, perhaps something else—but the sound seemed like a fitting accompaniment to the continuing song. Many white stones covered the area—or at least, the dwarves thought they were stones at first, until one of them looked closer and realized that they were bones. Orc bones and dwarf bones, skulls and femurs, some laying out in the open, others half-buried. Scattered about them were pieces of rusted metal, broken swords, and rotted armor. It seemed like the former owners, of both bones and armor, might still be about as well, for sometimes the wisps of strange fog seemed to take on definitive shapes—that of a dwarf, perhaps, or an orc.

Clan Battlehammer, lost in the rousing song and following their unshakable leader, merely saluted the former and sang all the louder, growled away the latter and sang all the louder.

They set their camp that night, wagons circled, nervous horses brought right into the center, with a ring of torches all around the tight perimeter. Still the dwarves sang, to ward off the ghosts that might be lurking nearby.

"Ye don't go out this night," Bruenor instructed Drizzt and Catti-brie, "and don't bring up yer stupid cat, elf."

That brought him a couple of puzzled expressions.

"No plane-shifting around here," Bruenor explained. "And that's what yer cat does."

"You fear that Guenhwyvar will open a portal that unwelcome visitors might also use?"

"Talked to me priests and we're all agreein' it's better not to find out."

Drizzt nodded and settled back.

"All the more reason for me and Drizzt to go out and keep a scouting perimeter," Catti-brie reasoned.

"I ain't suggesting that."

"Why?"

"What do you know, Bruenor?" Drizzt prompted.

He moved in closer, and so did Catti-brie, and so did Regis, who was nearby and eavesdropping.

"She's a haunted pass, to be sure," Bruenor confided, after taking a moment to look all around.

"Full o' yer ancestors," said Catti-brie.

"Full o' worse than that," said Bruenor. "We're to be fine—too many of us for even them ghosts to be playing with, I'm guessing."

"Guessing?" Regis echoed skeptically.

Bruenor only shrugged and turned back to Drizzt.

"We're needin' to get an idea o' all the land about," he explained.

"You think that Gauntlgrym is near?"

Another shrug. "Doubtin' that—it'd be more toward Mirabar—but we're likely to find some clues here. That fight them centuries ago was going the orcs' way—a bad time for me ancestors—but then the dwarves outsmarted them . . . not a tough thing to do! There's tunnels all about this pass, and deep caves, some natural, others cut by the Delzoun. Me ancient kin interlocked them all and used them to supply, to bind their wounds, and to fix their weapons—and for surprise, for the dwarfs lured them stupid orcs in on what looked like a small group, and when them ugly beasts came charging, their tongues flapping outside their ugly mouths, the Delzoun popped up from trapdoors all about them, within their ranks.

'Was still a fierce fight. Them orcs can hit hard, no one's doubting, and many, many o' me ancestors died here, but me kin won out. Killed most o' them orcs and sent the others running back to their holes in the deeper mountains. Them caves are likely still down there, holding secrets I mean to learn."

"And holding nasties of many shapes and sizes," Catti-brie added.

"Someone's gotta clear them nasties away," Bruenor agreed. "Might as well be me."

"You mean *us*," Regis corrected.

Bruenor gave him a sly smile.

"You plan to find a way down there and take the army underground?" Drizzt asked.

"Nah. I'm plannin' on passing through, as I said. We'll go back to Mithral Hall and get through with the formalities, then we'll decide how many we should be bringing back out after the next winter blows past. We'll see what we can find."

"Then why go through here now?"

"Think about it, elf," Bruenor answered, looking around at the encampment, which seemed fairly calm and at ease, despite their location. "Ye look danger right in the face, at its worst—or what ye're thinking to be its worst—right up front, and ye're not to be caught off yer guard by fear no more."

Indeed, in looking around at the settled camp, Drizzt understood exactly what Bruenor was driving at.

The night was not completely restful, and more than once, a sentry team cried out, "Ghost!" and the dwarves and others scrambled.

There were sightings and shrieks from unseen sources out in the darkness. Despite their weariness from the road, the clan did not get a good night's sleep, but they were back on the move in the morning, singing their songs, denying fear as only a dwarf could.

"Dreadmont and Skyfire," Bruenor explained to his friends the next day, pointing out two mountains, one to the south and one to the north. "Markin' the pass. Ye take in every landmark, elf. I'll be needing yer ranger nose if we're finding a place worth a return visit."

That day went uneventfully, and the troupe passed another fitful, but not overly so, night and were back on the road before the dawn.

At mid-morning, they were rolling along at a brisk pace, singing their songs from front to back, the battleragers and other soldiers trotting along easily.

But then the wagon beside Bruenor's lurched suddenly, its back right wheel dropping, and its front left coming right off the ground. The horses reared and whinnied, and the poor drivers fought hard to hold it steady. Dwarves rushed in from the side, grabbing on, some trying to catch the cargo that was sliding off the back, sliding into a gaping hole that was opening in the ground like a hungry mouth.

Drizzt rushed across in front of Bruenor's wagon and darted back behind the frightened, rearing horses, who were being dragged back with the rest of the wagon. His scimitars flashed repeatedly, cutting loose the harness, saving the team.

Catti-brie ran past the drow, heading for the drivers, and Wulfgar leaped from Bruenor's wagon to join her.

The wagon fell backward into the hole, taking the two struggling dwarves and the woman who had rushed to rescue them into the darkness.

Without even hesitating, Wulfgar dived down to his chest at the lip of the hole and reached out, catching the remains of the horse harness in his powerful hands. The wagon wasn't falling free. If it had been, Wulfgar would have disappeared along with it. Rather, it was slipping down along a rocky shaft, and enough of its weight was supported from below so that Wulfgar somehow managed to tentatively secure it.

The growling barbarian nearly let go in shock when a diminutive figure ran past him and leaped headlong into the hole, and behind him, Drizzt did cry out for Regis. Then both noticed that the halfling was tethered, and with Bruenor standing secure on his wagon, holding the other end of the line.

"Got them!" came a cry from below.

Dagnabbit and several other dwarves joined Bruenor, taking up the line and locking it in place.

Catti-brie was the first to climb out along the lifeline, followed in short order by the two shaken and bruised but not badly hurt drivers.

"Rumblebelly?" Bruenor called when the other three were out with no sign of the halfling.

"Lots of tunnels down here!" came Regis's cry, cut short by a shriek.

That was all the dwarf team had to hear, and they began pumping their powerful arms, hoisting a very shaken Regis from the hole. Wulfgar could hold the wagon no longer. It went crashing down, disappearing from view, until the clatter of its descent became a distant thing.

"What'd ye see?" Bruenor and many others yelled at Regis, who was as white as an autumn cloud.

Regis shook his head, his eyes wide and unblinking. "I thought it was you," he said to one of the drivers. "I . . . I went to hand you the rope. It went right through . . . I mean, it didn't touch . . . I mean."

"Easy, Rumblebelly," Bruenor said, patting the halfling on the shoulder. "Ye're safe enough here and now."

Regis nodded but didn't seem convinced.

Off to the side, Delly gave Wulfgar a huge hug and kiss.

"Ye done good," she whispered to him. "If ye hadn't caught the wagon, then all three would've crashed down to their deaths."

Wulfgar looked past her to Catti-brie, who was standing comfortably in Drizzt's embrace but was looking Wulfgar's way and nodding appreciatively.

Surveying the scene, recognizing that many were thoroughly shaken, Bruenor Battlehammer walked over to the edge of the hole, put his hands on his hips, and yelled down, "Hey, ye damned ghosties! Ye got nothing more about ye than a wisp of smoke?"

A chorus of moans rolled out of the hole, and dwarves scrambled away.

Not Bruenor, though. "Oo, ye got me shaking in me boots now!" he taunted. "Well, if ye got something to say, then get up here and say it. Otherwise, shut yer traps!"

The moans stopped, and for a short, uncomfortable moment, not a dwarf moved or made the slightest sound, all of them wondering if Bruenor's challenge was about to be met by a wave of attacking ghosts.

As the seconds slipped by and nothing ominous crawled out of the hole, the troupe settled back.

"Ye get Pwent and his boys tethered together on long lines and out in front, stomping the ground as they go," Bruenor instructed Dagnabbit. "Don't want to be losin' any more wagons."

The team went back into action, and Drizzt moved near his dwarf friend.

"Challenging the dead?" he asked.

"Bah, they don't mean nothing with their booing and floating about. Probably don't even know they're dead."

"True enough."

"Mark well this spot, elf," Bruenor instructed. "I'm thinking that it might be a good place to start our hunt for Gauntlgrym."

With that, the unshakable Bruenor moved back to his wagon, patted Regis on the shoulder one more time, then led the clan forward as if nothing had happened.

"Roll on, Bruenor Battlehammer," Drizzt whispered.

"Don't he always?" Catti-brie asked, moving beside the drow and wrapping her arm comfortably around his waist.

It took them three days to cross the broken ground of the Fell Pass. The ghosts hovered around them every step of the way and the wind did not cease its mournful song. Some areas were relatively clear, but others were thick with remnants of that long-ago battle. The signs weren't always physical, often just a general feeling of loss and pain, a thick, tangible aura of a land haunted by many lost souls.

Late that third day, up high on one ridge, Catti-brie spotted a distant, welcomed sight, a silvery river running through the land to the east like a giant snake.

"The Surbrin," Bruenor said with a smile when she told him, and all heads about began to bob in recognition, for the great River Surbrin passed only a few miles to the east of Mithral Hall, and the dwarves had actually opened an eastern gate right along its banks. "Couple o' days and we'll be home," the dwarf explained, and a great cheer went up for King Bruenor, who had conquered the Fell Pass.

"I'm still not figuring why ye took us this way, if ye're just meaning to go home anyway," Catti-brie confided to the dwarf as the excitement continued around them.

"Because I'm coming back out here, and so're yerself, the elf, Rumblebelly, and Wulfgar if he's wanting it. And so're Dagnabbit and some o' me best shield dwarves. Now we're knowing the ground, and we learned it under the protection of an army. Now we can start our looking."

"Ye think the leaders in Mithral Hall are to let ye go out and run free?" Catti-brie asked. "Ye're their king, ye might be remembering."

"Are they to *let* me? Well, I'm their king, ye might be remembering," Bruenor shot back. "I'm not thinking that I'm needing anyone's permission, girl, and so what makes ye think I'm to be askin'?"

There wasn't really much that Catti-brie could say against that.

"Ain't ye supposed to be out hunting with Drizzt?" Bruenor asked.

"He took Regis with him today," Catti-brie answered, and she looked to the north, as if she expected to spot the pair running along a distant ridgeline.

"The halfling howl about going?"

"No. He asked if he could go."

"Still wonderin' what's got into Rumblebelly," Bruenor admitted with a shake of his hairy head.

Regis, once the lover of comfort, did indeed seem transformed. He had pressed on through the bitter cold of winter in the Spine of the World without complaint, indeed even lending rousing words for his friends. In every action, the halfling had tried to get involved, to somehow help out, whereas the Regis of old seemed amazingly adept at finding an out of the way shadow.

The change was somehow unsettling to Bruenor and to all the others, a shifting of the sand beneath the world as they had known it. At least it seemed to be shifting in a positive direction.

Not so far away, Wulfgar came upon Delly as she watched Catti-brie and Bruenor in their private discussion. The barbarian noted that his wife was focusing almost exclusively on Catti-brie, as if taking a measure of the woman. He walked up behind her and wrapped his huge arms around her waist.

"She is a fine companion," he said.

"I can see why ye loved her."

Wulfgar gently turned Delly around to face him. "I did not . . ."

"Oh, sure ye did, and stop trying to save me feelings!"

Wulfgar stammered over a couple of responses, not knowing how he should respond.

"She is a companion to me, on the road, in battle . . ."

"And in all yer life," Delly finished.

"No," Wulfgar insisted. "Once I thought that I desired such a joining, but now I see the world differently. Now I see you, and Colson, and know that I am complete."

"Who said ye weren't?"

"You just said . . ."

"I said that yer Catti-brie was a companion in all yer life, and so she is, and so ye're better off for it," Delly corrected. "Ye don't be puttin' her back from yerself for me own sake!"

"I do not wish to hurt you."

Delly turned around to regard Catti-brie.

"Nor does she. She's yer friend, and I'm liking it that way." She pulled away from Wulfgar but stood back and stared at him, a sincere smile wide on her pretty face. "To be sure, there's a part o' me fearing that ye'll want her for more than friendship. I can't be helping that, but I'm not to be giving in to it. I trust ye and trust in what me and ye have started here, but don't ye be putting Catti-brie away from yerself in trying to protect me, because that's not where she belongs. Most folks-s'd be glad to have a friend like her."

"And I am," Wulfgar admitted. He looked curiously at Delly. "Why are you saying this now?"

Delly couldn't suppress her telling grin.

"Bruenor's talking about coming back out here. He's hoping that ye'll be joining him."

"My place is with you and Colson."

Delly was shaking her head even as he started that predictable response.

"Yer place is with me and our girl when yer life permits. Yer place is on the road with Bruenor and Drizzt and Catti-brie and Regis. I'm knowing that, and it makes me love ye all the more!"

"Their road is a dangerous one," Wulfgar reminded.

"Then more the reason for ye to help them along it."

"They're dwarfs!" Nikwillig exclaimed, his voice breaking with excitement and relief.

Tred, who had not climbed the last part of the steep boulder tumble and so could not see the huge caravan rolling along the flat ground to the south, leaned back against a rock and put his head in his hands. His left leg was swollen and would not bend. He hadn't realized how badly it had been torn during their respite in the small village, and he knew that he would not be able to go on for much longer without some proper tending, maybe even some divine intervention, courtesy of a cleric.

Of course, Tred hadn't complained at all and had fought with every ounce of his strength to keep up with Nikwillig in their flight. It had been a strong and valiant run, but both dwarves knew they were nearing the end of their endurance. They needed a break, and apparently, one had found them.

"We can catch them if we angle out to the southeast," Nikwillig explained. "Ye up for one more run?"

"We need to make the run, we make the run," Tred said. "Ain't come this far to lay down and die."

Nikwillig nodded and turned around, gingerly beginning the steep descent. He stopped, though, freezing in place, his eyes locked across the way. Tred noted that look and followed that gaze to see a huge panther, black as the night sky, crouched on a ledge not so far away—not far enough away!

"Don't ye move," Nikwillig whispered.

Tred didn't even bother to answer, thinking exactly the same thing, though he understood that the great cat knew exactly where they were. He pondered what he might do if the cat sprang his way. How could he even begin to hurt that mass of muscle and claws?

Well, he decided, if it comes on, it goes away bloody.

The seconds slipped past, neither the cat nor the dwarves moving an inch.

With a growl that seemed a challenge, Tred pushed out from the wall to stand straight and strong and put his heavy axe up at the ready beside him.

The great panther looked his way but not threateningly. In fact, the cat seemed almost bored.

"Please don't throw that at her," came a voice from below and to the side, and the two dwarves glanced down to see a brown-haired halfling moving out onto an open, flat stone. "When Guenhwyvar gets an invitation to play, it's hard to stop her."

"That yer cat?" Tred asked.

"Not mine, no," the halfling answered. "She a friend and mastered by a friend, if you get my meaning."

Tred nodded. "Well, who are ye then?"

"I could be asking you the same question," the halfling answered. "In fact, I believe that I will."

"And ye'll be getting yer answer after we're getting ours."

The halfling bowed low. "Regis of Mithral Hall," he said. "Friend to King Bruenor Battlehammer, and scout for the caravan your friend sees below. Returning from Icewind Dale."

Tred relaxed, and so did Nikwillig.

"The King o' Mithral Hall keeps strange company," Tred remarked.

"Stranger than you would ever believe," Regis was quick to answer.

He glanced to the side, and so did both dwarves, to see a second dark figure, this one not feline, but a drow elf.

Tred nearly fell over. Above him, Nikwillig did slip a bit, barely catching a hold before he tumbled from the climb.

"You still have not told me your name," Regis reminded, "and I am guessing that you're not from around here if you've not heard of Drizzt Do'Urden and his panther Guenhwyvar."

"Wait, I heared o' him!" Nikwillig said from above Tred, and Tred looked up. "Bruenor's friend drow. Yeah, we heared o' that!"

"And pray tell us where you were when you heard," Drizzt prompted.

Nikwillig moved down fast, dropping beside Tred, and both dwarves set themselves more presentably, with Nikwillig brushing some of the road dust from his weathered tunic.

"Tred McKnuckles's me name," Tred announced, "and this's me friend Nikwillig, outta Citadel Felbarr and the kingdom o' Emerus Warcrown."

"Long way from home," Drizzt observed.

"Longer than ye're thinking," Tred answered. "Been a road o' orcs and giants, and one wrong trail leading to another wrong trail."

"A tale well worth hearing, I am sure," Drizzt replied, "but not here and not now. Let us get you down to Bruenor and the others."

"Bruenor's in that caravan?" Nikwillig asked.

"Returning from Icewind Dale to assume the throne of Mithral Hall, for word reached us that Gandalug Battlehammer is dead."

"Moradin put him to work at his anvil," said Tred, a customary blessing for dead dwarves.

Drizzt nodded. "Indeed. And may Moradin guide Bruenor well."

"And may Moradin, or whatever good god is listening, guide us well, back to the caravan," Regis reminded.

When Drizzt and the others regarded the halfling, they saw that he was looking around nervously, as if he expected that Tred and Nikwillig had led a host of giants to the ridge, giants that were preparing to rain stones on the five of them.

"Keep scouting, Guenhwyvar," Drizzt instructed, and he started toward the dwarves.

Both of the bearded fellows instinctively stiffened and the perceptive drow stopped his approach.

"Regis, you accompany them to Bruenor," Drizzt decided. "I will keep the perimeter with Guenhwyvar." He saluted the dwarves and slipped away, and both Tred and Nikwillig visibly relaxed.

"We're safe with Drizzt and Guenhwyvar flanking us," Regis assured the dwarves as he approached. "Safer than you can imagine."

Tred and Nikwillig looked at each other, then back at the halfling, and nodded, though neither seemed overly confident in Regis's words.

"Don't worry," the halfling said, offering an understanding wink. "You'll get used to him."

6

SMARTER THAN
AN ORC OUGHT

The arrival of the two dwarves brought much excitement to the village of Clicking Heels, and that deep into the wilds of the Spine of the World, excitement was not usually welcomed. After the two dwarves had gone on their way, the villagers settled back from the initial fear that they would be attacked and began to savor the story. Excitement within a larger cocoon of safety was always welcomed.

Still, the villagers of Clicking Heels were seasoned enough to not fall too deeply into that cocoon. They limited their out-of-town travel over the next few days and doubled the daytime watch and tripled the nighttime watch.

All through the nights, at short, regular intervals, the sentries would call out, "All clear!" from one checkpoint to another. Everyone kept his eyes peeled to the cleared ground around the village walls with that special vigilance that could only be learned through harsh experience.

Even toward the end of the first tenday after the dwarves' departure, the watch held strong and steady, with no slacking, no sleeping or even dozing along the wall.

Carelman Twopennies, one of the sentries that particular night seven days after Nikwillig and Tred had gone on their way, was tired, and so he wouldn't even lean against a pole for fear that he would nod off.

Every time he heard the all clear call circling along the wall to his right, the man shook his head briskly and strained his eyes toward the dark field beyond his section of wall, ready for his turn to yell out.

Soon after midnight, the calls circling, Carelman did just that, and peering into the emptiness beyond, he was fairly certain that his impending call would be an honest one. When it came to his turn, he yelled out, or started to, "All clear!"

He heard a rush of air above him as the words began to leave his mouth, though, and was merely unfortunate enough to be standing in the way of the giant-thrown boulder, and so his "All clear!" came out as "All clea—*ugh!*"

He felt the explosion, for just an instant, then he was dead, lying on the ground beneath the rubble of the wooden parapet and the heavy stone.

Carelman Twopennies didn't hear the cries erupting around him or the subsequent explosions as heavy boulders smashed through the walls and buildings, softening the defenses of the small village. He didn't hear the shouts of alarm after that as a horde of orcs, many riding fierce worgs, swept down upon the battered town.

He didn't hear the deaths of his family, his friends, his home.

Marchion Elastul stroked his wild red whiskers, a movement that many dwarves took as a proud gesture, one used for showing off one's beard. Of course, Torgar wasn't overly impressed by the red whiskers of the human marchion, for no human could grow a beard to match the worst of dwarf beards.

"What am I to do with you, Torgar Hammerstriker?" Elastul asked.

Behind him, his four guardsmen, the Hammers, bristled and whispered amongst themselves.

"Didn't think ye was to do anything with me, your honorness," the dwarf answered. "Been going about me business in Mirabar since before ye was born and before yer daddy was born. I'm not needing ye to do much."

The marchion's sour look showed that he was not overly impressed with the statement or the not-so-subtle reminder that Torgar had been in service to Mirabar for a long, long time.

"It is just that heritage that brings me a quandary," Elastul explained.

"Quandary?" Torgar asked, and he scratched his own beard. "That a place where ye get both rocks and milk?"

The marchion's face screwed up with confusion.

"A dilemma," he explained.

"What is?" asked the dwarf.

Torgar worked hard to hide his grin. One thing he knew about humans was that they carried an internal superiority belief, and playing dumb was the easiest way a dwarf could deflect ire.

"What is what?" the marchion replied.

"Yeah, that."

"Enough!" the marchion cried. He was visibly trembling, to which Torgar only shrugged, as if he understood none of it. "Your actions present me with a dilemma."

"How's that?"

"The people of Mirabar look up to you. You're one of the most trusted commanders in the Axe, a dwarf of fine reputation and honor."

"Bah, Marchion Elastul, ye're bringing a blush to me bearded cheeks and to me other ones, as well." He finished the sentence by twisting to look over his shoulder. "Though I'm guessing them nether ones're becoming about as hairy as old age begins to set in."

Elastul looked as if he wanted to slap himself across the face, which pleased Torgar greatly.

The man gave a great sigh and started to respond, but the door to the audience chamber banged open and Sceptrana Shoudra Stargleam entered.

"Marchion," she greeted with a bow.

"We are discussing whether or not I should have you melt the Axe symbol off of Torgar's armor," the marchion replied, throwing aside Torgar's distracting remarks.

"We are?" the dwarf asked innocently.

"Enough!" Elastul scolded again. "You know well enough that we are, and you know well enough why I have summoned you here. To think that you, of all dwarves, would go consorting with our enemies."

Torgar held up his stubby-fingered hands, his expression going suddenly grim.

"Ye take care on who ye're calling our enemies," he warned Elastul.

"Need I remind you of the wealth that Bruenor Battlehammer and his dwarves have stolen from us?"

"Bah, they've stolen not a thing! I made me a couple o' pretty deals from where I'm looking."

"Not their caravan! Their mines to the east. Need I remind you of the drop in business since Mithral Hall's forges began to burn once more? Ask Shoudra there. She above all others can tell you of the difficulty in renewing contracts and attracting new buyers."

"True enough," the woman added. "Since the return of Mithral Hall, my job has become far more difficult."

"As have all of our jobs," Torgar agreed. "And that'll make us better, from where I'm looking."

"Clan Battlehammer is no friend of Mirabar!" Elastul declared.

"Nor are they our enemy," Torgar replied, "and ye should be careful afore ye go callin' them such."

The marchion came forward in his chair so suddenly that Torgar reflexively brought a hand up by his right shoulder, near to the hilt of the large axe he always kept strapped across his back, and that movement, in turn, made the marchion and his four Hammers start and widen their eyes.

"King Bruenor came in as a friend," Torgar remarked when things had settled a bit. "He came here on his way through, as a friend, and he was let in as a friend."

"Or to take a measure of his greatest rivals," Shoudra remarked, but Torgar just shrugged that thought away.

"And if ye're letting a dwarf legend into yer city, then how can ye be sayin' the dwarves o' yer city can't go and sit with him?"

"Many of the dwarves of my city are among the loudest voices for espionage against King Bruenor's Mithral Hall," Elastul reminded. "You have heard their calls for spies to go into Mithral Hall and find some way to shut down the forges, or to flood some of the more promising tunnels, or to place cheaper goods in among the armor and weapons Clan Battlehammer is sending out to market."

Torgar couldn't deny the truth of the marchion's words, nor the fact that he, himself, had uttered similar curses against Mithral Hall in the past, but that seemed different to him than this personal visit, a rant against a faceless rival. Torgar might not wish Clan Battlehammer well with their merchandising, but if an enemy came against Bruenor and his clan, Torgar would gladly lead a charge to assist them.

"Ye ever think that we might be going against Clan Battlehammer in the wrong way?" the dwarf asked. The marchion and Shoudra exchanged curious looks. "Ye ever think that we might be using their strengths and our own strength together to the benefit of us all?"

"What do you mean?" Elastul asked.

"They got the ore—better ore than we'll be findin' here if we dig a hunnerd miles down—and they got some great craftsmen, don't ye doubt, but so do we. Might that our best and their best could work with their good ore to make great pieces, while our apprentices and their apprentices, or a few who're too old to see it right or lift the hammer well enough, could work with the lesser ore in making the lesser pieces—railings and cart wheels instead o' swords and breastplates, if ye see me meaning."

The marchion's eyes went wide indeed, but not because he was the least bit intrigued by the suggestion of cooperation. Torgar saw that immediately and knew that he had crossed a line.

Trembling so badly that he seemed as if he might vibrate right out of his chair, Elastul forced himself, with great effort, to settle back. He shook his head, seeming too enraged to even speak a denial.

"Just a thought," Torgar remarked.

"A thought? Here is a thought—why don't we have Shoudra burn that axe from your breastplate? Why don't I have you dragged out and flogged publicly, perhaps even tried for treason against Mirabar? How dare you lead so many into the embrace of King Bruenor Battlehammer! How dare you bring comfort to our principle rival, a dwarf who leads a clan that has cost us piles of gold! How dare you represent any prospect of friendship between Mithral Hall and Mirabar, and how dare you suggest such a thing to me!"

Shoudra Stargleam came forward to the side of the marchion's throne. She put her hand on Elastul's arm, obviously trying to calm him. She looked to Torgar as she did and nodded toward the door to the room, motioning for him to make a fast exit.

But Torgar wasn't ready to leave just yet, not before he had the last word.

"Ye might be hatin' Bruenor and his boys, and ye might have reason," he said, "but I'm seein' it more as our own weakness than anything Bruenor and his boys did to us."

Marchion Elastul started to respond with another "how dare you," but Torgar kept on rolling.

"That's the way I'm seein' it," the dwarf stated flatly. "Ye want to take me Axe emblem, then take it, but if ye're thinking o' flogging me, then ye should be looking more closely at me kin."

With that threat hanging in the air, Torgar Delzoun Hammerstriker turned and stormed from the room.

"I will have his head on a pike!"

"Then you'll have two thousand shield dwarves running wild in Mirabar," Shoudra explained. She was still holding the man's arm and firmly. "I don't completely disagree with any of the things you say about Mithral Hall, good Elastul, but given the response from Torgar and many others, I wonder the wisdom of holding our present course of open animosity."

Elastul shot her an angry and threatening glower, the look alone reminding her that few on the Council of Sparkling Stones would side with her reasoning.

So Shoudra let him go and stepped back, bowing her head deferentially, while silently wondering how destabilizing King Bruenor's visit had truly been to Mirabar. If the marchion kept pushing this hard, the result could be disastrous for the ancient mining city.

Shoudra also silently applauded King Bruenor for his shrewd move of even showing up where he knew he would not be welcomed, but where he would neither be flatly rebuked. Yes, it was a cunning maneuver, and it seemed to the Sceptrana of Mirabar that her boss was playing right into Bruenor's hands.

"Prisoners?" Obould asked his son as they stood overlooking the ruins of Clicking Heels.

"Few left," Urlgen said with an evil grin.

"Ye're interrogating?"

Urlgen straightened, as if the thought hadn't occurred to him.

Obould gave a growl and slapped Urlgen on the back of his head.

"What we need to know?" the confused Urlgen asked.

"Whatever they can tell us to help us," Obould explained, speaking slowly and articulating each word carefully, as if he was addressing a toddler.

Urlgen snarled but didn't voice his displeasure. The insult had been earned, after all.

"Ye know how to interrogate?" Obould asked, and his son looked at him as if the question was purely ridiculous. "Just like torture," Obould explained anyway, "except ye ask them questions while ye play."

Urlgen's lips curled into a perfectly evil smile, and with a nod, he headed back into the village, where many of his warriors were already at play on the few unfortunate villagers who had not died in the attack.

An hour later, Urlgen caught up to his father, finding Obould at parlay with the giants who had helped in the raid, playing the political angles as always.

"Not all them dwarfs got killed when we hit them," Urlgen remarked, his tone a mixture of excitement for the chase, and disappointment.

"Dwarfs? There were dwarfs in that stupid little town?"

Urlgen seemed confused. "Not them dwarfs," he said. "Weren't none of them dwarfs."

Now Obould and the giants seemed confused.

"No dwarfs in the town," Urlgen stated clearly, trying to end the circular confusion. "When we hit them dwarfs a tenday ago, two got away."

It wasn't completely surprising to Obould, for they knew that some dwarves, at least, were running around the region. A band of orcs had been slaughtered not too far from this town, with tactics indicating a dwarven ambush.

"They come in there, and hurt," Urlgen explained.

"And they died in there?"

"Nope, kept runnin', looking for Mithral Hall, and were gone before we hit."

"How long?"

"Not long."

Obould wore an excited expression. "A fun hunt?" he asked the giants, and as one the great blue-skinned behemoths nodded.

But Obould's expression quickly changed as he remembered the warnings of Ad'non Kareese. "Small forays, and with restraint. We draw them out, little by little," the drow had said. Chasing these dwarves to the south would bring the force dangerously close to Mithral Hall, perhaps, and might incite a battle far beyond what Obould wanted.

"Nah, let 'em go," the orc king decided, and while the giants seemed to accept that readily enough, Urlgen's eyes popped open so wide that they seemed as if they would fall right out of his ugly head.

"Ye can't be . . ." the younger and rasher orc started to argue.

"I can be," Obould interrupted. "Ye let 'em make the hall, with their tales o' death and destruction, and the dwarfs there'll send out a force to investigate. That'd be a bigger and better fight."

Urlgen's smile began to widen once more, and Obould let him in on the rest of the reasoning, just for prudence. After all, any mention of Mithral Hall might send the young warriors charging headlong to the south.

"We get too close and start that fight, and some o' them dwarfs might get back home, and all the stinkin' Mithral Hall'll empty out on us, and that's a fight we're not wantin'!"

Despite the nods of agreement, even from sour Urlgen, Obould felt obliged to add, "Not yet."

THE TRAPPINGS
OF ROYALTY

Bruenor purposely excluded Thibbledorf Pwent from the meeting with the two dwarves of Citadel Felbarr, knowing the gist of their story beforehand from Regis, and knowing that the battlerager would likely charge right off into the mountains to avenge their fallen Felbarr kin. And so Nikwillig and Tred recounted their adventures to a group that was comprised more of non-dwarves—Drizzt, Catti-brie, Wulfgar, and Regis—than dwarves.

"A fine escape," Bruenor congratulated when the pair had finished. "Ye done Emerus Warcrown proud."

Both Tred and Nikwillig puffed up a bit at the compliment from the dwarf king.

"What're ye thinking?" Bruenor asked, directing the question to Dagnabbit.

The younger dwarf considered the question carefully for a long while, then answered, "I'll take me a group o' warriors, including the Gutbuster Brigade, and backtrack the route to the Surbrin in the north. If we find the raiders, we'll crush 'em and come home. If not, we'll tack south along the river and meet up with ye in Mithral Hall."

Bruenor nodded throughout the recitation of the plan, expecting every word. Dagnabbit was good, but he was also predictable.

"I'd be likin' another shot at them killers," Tred interjected.

His words made Nikwillig, who obviously didn't share the sentiment, look more than a little uncomfortable.

"Forgettin' yer hurt leg?" Nikwillig remarked.

"Bah, Bruenor's priests done me good with their warm hands," Tred insisted, and to accentuate the point the dwarf stood up and began hopping around, and indeed, despite a wince or two, he seemed ready for the road.

Bruenor studied the pair for a moment.

"Well, we can't let ye both get killed, or yer tale'll not be told proper to Emerus Warcrown. So, ye can come on the hunt, Tred, and yerself, Nikwillig, will go back to Mithral Hall with the others."

"King Bruenor, yer words make ye sound like ye're headin' out on the hunt yerself," Dagnabbit remarked, drawing a hard stare from Bruenor.

Bruenor knew the expectations of those around him, particularly of Dagnabbit, who was sworn to secure his king's safety. He knew that the proper course for him, as King of Mithral Hall, would be to head south straightaway with the bulk of his force, back to the security of his kingdom, back where he could direct further counterstrikes in search of this marauding band of orcs and giants. That was what was expected of him, but the mere thought of it made Bruenor's gut churn.

He looked over at Drizzt with a pleading look, and the dark elf offered a slight, knowing nod in response.

"What're ye thinking, elf?" Bruenor asked.

"I would have an easier time finding the monsters than Pwent and his wild band," Drizzt replied. "An easier time even than good Dagnabbit here, though I doubt not his prowess at hunting orcs."

"Then ye come with me," Dagnabbit offered.

There was a slight crack in his voice, showing that he saw where this might be heading, and showing that he was not too pleased by the prospect.

"I will go," Drizzt agreed, "but with my friends around me. Those whom I have come to trust the most. Those who best recognize how to compliment my every move."

He nodded in turn to Catti-brie, to Wulfgar, and to Regis, then paused for a moment and turned directly to Bruenor—and nodded. A smile widened on the face of the dwarf king.

"No, no, no," Dagnabbit remarked immediately. "Ye cannot be taking me king into the wilds."

"I believe the choice is Bruenor's to make, my friend, not yours, and not mine," Drizzt replied. He returned Bruenor's grateful smile and asked the king, "One last hunt?"

"Who says it's the last?" came Bruenor's gruff reply.

The friends chuckled, then laughed all the harder when Dagnabbit stomped his heavy boot on the ground and exclaimed, "Dagnabbit!"

"Bah, but yerself can come along, ye dumb dwarf," Bruenor said to his young commander. "And yerself," he added, looking over at Tred, who nodded grimly.

"And ye bring some fighters with ye!" Dagnabbit insisted.

"Pwent and his boys," said Bruenor.

"No!" Dagnabbit shouted emphatically.

"But you just said . . ."

"That was afore I thinked yerself was goin'."

Bruenor patted his hands in the air to calm the excited dwarf.

"Not Pwent, then," he said, understanding his young commander's concern. Pwent could start a fight with a rock, so it was said in Mithral Hall, and hurt himself and everyone around him badly before he won the scuffle. "Ye pick the group yerself. Twenty o' yer best—"

"Twenty-five," Dagnabbit argued.

"Well, get 'em ready soon," Bruenor said to Dagnabbit, and to all of them. "I'm wanting to be on the road this same day. We got orcs and giants to squish!"

The dwarf looked around at all his friends and noted that Wulfgar's grin was not as wide as those of Drizzt, Catti-brie, and even Regis. Bruenor nodded his understanding to his adopted son, his implied permission for Wulfgar, now a father and a husband, to opt out of the hunt if he saw fit to do so.

Wulfgar tightened his jaw in response, returned the nod, and strode away.

"Ye can't be thinkin' what I'm thinkin' ye're thinkin'!" said Shingles McRuff.

He was one of the toughest looking critters in all of Mirabar, a short and exceedingly stout dwarf whose nasty attitude was always clearly shown on his ruddy, weathered face. He was missing an eye, and simply never bothered to fill in the empty socket, just covered it with an eye patch. Half of his black beard was torn away, the right side of his face showing as one big scar.

"Well, I'm thinkin' what I'm thinkin'," Torgar Hammerstriker replied, "and I'm not knowin' what ye're thinkin' I'm thinkin'!"

"Well, I'm thinkin' that ye're thinkin' o' leavin'," Shingles stated bluntly, and that got the attention of all the other dwarves in the crowded tavern in the highest subterranean level of the city. "Don't know what the marchion said to ye, bud, but I'm betting it ain't nothing next to what yer grandpa'd be sayin' to ye if yer grandpa was still here to be sayin' things to ye."

Torgar threw up his hands and waved away the words, and the looks of all the others.

At least he tried to, for several other dwarves moved in close, pulling up chairs, and more than one started the same question: "Ye heading out o' Mirabar, Torgar?"

Torgar ran his hands through his thick hair.

"Course I ain't, ye durned fools!" he said, rather unconvincingly. "Me father's father's father's father's father spent his days here."

Despite his bluster, even Torgar could recognize the hint of doubt in his own statements, and that made him ask himself if he really was thinking of leaving Mirabar. He was as mad as a demon at Elastul, to be sure, but was there really a notion, deep in his head and deep in his heart, that it might be time for him to end the Hammerstriker dynasty in Mirabar?

He ran his hands through his thick hair again, and again, and ended up shouting, "*Bah!*" in the faces of those around him.

He stood up so forcefully that his chair skidded out behind him, and he stomped away, grabbing a flagon of ale from the bar as he passed and tossing back a coin to the obviously amused tavern keeper.

Out in the cavern that housed the cluster of buildings in the First Below—the highest section of Mirabar's Undercity—Torgar looked all around him, noting the structures and noting the striations of the stone that housed them, stone so familiar to him that he felt as if it was a part of him, and of his heritage.

"Stupid Elastul," he muttered under his breath. "Stupid all o' ye, not seein' King Bruenor and his boys for the friends they be."

He walked away, unaware that his last statements had been overheard by several others, including Shingles, all huddled near the open window of the tavern.

"He's meanin' it," another dwarf remarked.

"And I'm thinkin' that he's gonna go," said another.

"Bah, whaddya know aside from which drink ye're drinkin'?" Shingles blustered at them. "If ye're even knowin' which drink ye're drinkin'!"

"I'm knowing!" shouted another dwarf, from across the way. "So I'm thinkin' that I'm not drinkin' enough o' what I'm drinkin'!"

That brought a roar, and cries of rounds from several parts of the tavern.

Shingles McRuff just grinned at them all, though, and kept looking out the window, though Torgar, his old buddy and comrade at arms, was long out of sight.

Despite his disclaimer and Torgar's denial, Shingles could not disagree with the consensus that Torgar was indeed serious about leaving Mirabar. The arrival of King Bruenor and the boys from Mithral Hall had put a face on a previously faceless enemy, a face that Torgar and many others had come to see as a friend. A rival, perhaps, but certainly no enemy. The treatment Elastul and the other leaders, mostly human, had shown to Bruenor and to the Mirabarran dwarves who had gone to hear Bruenor's tales or buy the wares from Icewind Dale had not set well with Torgar or with many others.

For the first time since the incident, Shingles McRuff seriously considered the recent events and the wider implications of them.

He didn't much like where his thoughts were suddenly, and already, leading him.

"Guilt's a funny thing, now ain't it?" Delly Curtie playfully asked Wulfgar when he returned to her and Colson at their wagon.

"Guilt?" came the skeptical response. "Or an understanding of my responsibilities?"

"Guilt," Delly answered without the slightest hesitation.

"In taking on a family, I accepted the responsibility of protecting that family."

"And what do ye think will happen to me and Colson surrounded by two hundred friendly dwarves? Ye're not abandoning us out in the wilds, Wulfgar. We're going to safety. 'Tis yerself that's walking to danger!"

"And even in that, I am abandoning my respons—"

"Oh, don't ye start that again!" Delly interrupted, and loudly, drawing the attention of several nearby dwarves. "Ye do as ye must. Ye live the life ye were meant to live."

"You came all the way out here with me . . ."

"Livin' the life I'm choosin' to live," Delly explained. "I'm not wanting to lose ye—not for a moment—but I know that if ye abandon yer heart to stand with me and Colson all the day, then I've already lost ye. Come to Mithral Hall if that's what's truly in yer heart, me love, but if not, then get yerself out on the road with Bruenor and th' others."

"And what if I die out there, away from you?"

It was not a question asked out of fear, for Wulfgar was not afraid of dying out on the road. He was an adventurer, a warrior, and as long as he could hold faith that he was following the true course of his life, then whatever was put before him would be acceptable.

Of course, he wouldn't die on the road without a fight!

"I think about it all the time," Delly admitted, "because I'm knowin' that ye've got to be going. And if ye die on the road, then know that yer Colson will be proud o' her daddy. For a bit, I thought about changing yer heart, about tricking ye into staying by me side, but that's not who ye are. I see it on yer face—a face that's smiling all the wider when the wild wind is blowin' across it. Me and Colson can accept whatever fate ye find at the end o' yer road, Wulfgar son of Beornegar, so long as ye're walking the road of yer heart."

She moved up close as she spoke, kneeling in front of the sitting Wulfgar and draping her arms over his shoulders.

"Just give an orc a good smack for me, will ya?'"

Wulfgar was smiling then as he looked into her sparkling eyes—sparkling more than they ever had back in the days when Delly had worked in Arumn's tavern in the seedy bowels of Luskan. Something about the road, the fresh air, the adventure, the child, had gotten into the woman, and Delly seemed to grow more beautiful, more wholesome, more healthy with every passing day.

Wulfgar pulled her close and hugged her tightly. His thoughts went back to the day when Robillard had dropped him in the center of Luskan, presenting him with two choices: the road south and security beside Delly and Colson, or the road north, to join his friends in adventure. Hearing Delly's words, the sincerity in her voice, the love and admiration accompanying it, Wulfgar was never more glad of his choice, of that northward turn, and never more sure of himself.

And never more in love with this woman who had become his wife.

"I will give him *two* good smacks for you," Wulfgar answered, and he moved in to kiss his wife.

"Nah," Delly said, pulling back teasingly. "Yer first one'll send him flyin' far enough."

She didn't move away again as Wulfgar's lips found hers, in a long and leading kiss, gentle at first but then pressing more urgently. The barbarian started to stand, easily lifting the lithe Delly up with him, guiding her to the privacy of their covered wagon.

Colson woke up then and started to cry.

Wulfgar and Delly could only laugh.

Thibbledorf Pwent hopped around, uttering a series of sounds that amply reflected his frustration and disappointment, and kicking at every stone he passed, even those far too big to be kicked. Still, if the tough dwarf felt any pain, he didn't show it much, just an occasional grunt within the steady stream of curses, and an added hop here or there after a particularly vicious kick at a particularly stubborn rock.

Finally, after circling King Bruenor for many minutes of random cursing, Pwent hopped to a stop, and put his stubby hands on his hips.

"Ye're going for a fight, and a fight's where me and me boys belong!"

"We're going to pay back a small band o' orcs and a couple o' giants," Bruenor corrected. "Won't be much of a fight, and even less o' one if Pwent and his boys are there."

"It's what we do."

"And too well!" Bruenor cried.

Pwent's eyes widened.

"Huh?"

"Ye durned fool!" Bruenor scolded. "Don't ye see that this'll be me last time? When we get back to Mithral Hall, I'll be the king again, and what a boring title that is!"

"What're ye talkin' about? Ye're the best king . . ."

Bruenor silenced him with a wave and an exaggerated look of disgust.

"Talkin' with lying emissaries, making pretty with fancy fool lords and fancier and more foolish ladies . . . Ye think I'll get to use me axe much in the next hunnerd years? Only if another army o' damned drow come a'knocking at our doors! So now I get the chance, one last chance, and ye're thinking to steal all me fun with yer killer band. And I thinked ye was me friend."

That set Pwent back on his heels, putting the whole situation in a light he had never begun to imagine.

"I am yer friend, King Bruenor," Pwent said somberly, as reserved as Bruenor or anyone else had ever seen him. "I'll be takin' me boys back to Mithral Hall to get the place ready for yer arrival."

He paused and offered Bruenor a sly wink—well, it was intended to be sly, at least, but from Pwent it just came out as an exaggerated twitch.

"And I'm hopin' ye won't be back anytime soon," Pwent went on, with more comprehension than Bruenor had expected. "Might be just one small band that hit the boys from Felbarr, but might be that ye'll find a bunch o' other small bands betwixt here and that one, and a bunch more on yer way back home. Good fighting, King Bruenor. May ye notch yer axe a thousand more times afore ye see yer shining halls once more!"

With great cheering and fanfare, promises of death to the orcs and giants, and eternal friendship between Mithral Hall and Citadel Felbarr, the band of Bruenor and his dear friends, along with Dagnabbit, Tred, and twenty-five stout warriors, moved off from the main group, turning north into the mountains. Dwarves were not a bloodthirsty race, but they knew how to celebrate when the occasion was a war against goblinkind and giantkin, their most hated of foes.

As for the friends, as one (even Regis!) they felt energized and refreshed to be on the road to adventure once again, and so the only regrets that fine morning were felt by those who had not been chosen to go.

For the dark elf, it was old times and new times all rolled together, the same camaraderie that had so enriched his life of recent years, his old band marching together into adventure in rugged lands, and yet, with a better understanding of each other and of their respective places in the world. The day was full of promise indeed!

What Drizzt Do'Urden did not understand was that he was walking headlong into the saddest day of his life.

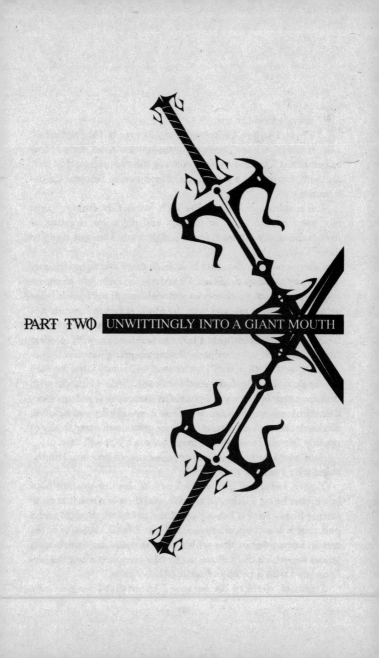

PART TWO UNWITTINGLY INTO A GIANT MOUTH

I am not afraid to die.

There, I said it, I admitted it . . . to myself. I am not afraid to die, nor have I been since the day I walked out of Menzoberranzan. Only now have I come to fully appreciate that fact, and only because of a very special friend named Bruenor Battlehammer.

It is not bravado that makes such words flow from my lips. Not some needed show of courage and not some elevation of myself above any others. It is the simple truth. I am not afraid to die.

I do not wish to die, and I hold faith that I will fight viciously against any attempts to kill me. I'll not run foolishly into an enemy encampment with no chance of victory (though my friends often accuse me of just that, and even the obvious fact that we are not yet dead does not dissuade them from their barbs). Nay, I hope to live for several centuries. I hope to live forever, with my dear friends all about me every step of that unending journey.

So, why the lack of fear? I understand well enough that the road I willingly walk—indeed, the road I choose to walk—is fraught with peril and presents the very real possibility that one day, perhaps soon, I, or my friends, will be slain. And while it would kill me to be killed, obviously, and kill me even more to see great harm come to any of my dear friends, I will not shy from this road. Nor will they.

And now I know why. And now, because of Bruenor, I understand why I am not afraid to die.

Before, I expected that my lack of fear was due to some faith in a higher being, a deity, an afterlife, and there remains that comforting hope. That is but a part of the equation, though, and a part that is based upon prayers and blind faith, rather than the certain knowledge of that which truly sustains me, which truly guides me, which truly allows me to take every step along the perilous road with a profound sense of inner calm.

I am not afraid to die because I know that I am part of a

something, a concept, a belief, that is bigger than all that is me, body and soul.

When I asked Bruenor about this road away from Mithral Hall that he has chosen, I put the question simply: what will the folk of Mithral Hall do if you are killed on the road?

His answer was even more simple and obvious: they'll do better then than if I went home and hid!

That's the way of the dwarves—and it is an expectation they place upon all of their leaders. Even the overprotective ones, such as the consummate bodyguard Pwent, understand deep down that if they truly shelter Bruenor, they have, in effect, already slain the King of Mithral Hall. Bruenor recognizes that the concept of Mithral Hall, a theocracy that is, in fact, a subtle democracy, is bigger than the dwarf, whoever it might be, who is presently occupying the throne. And Bruenor recognizes that kings before him and kings after him will die in battle, tragically, with the dwarves they leave behind caught unprepared for his demise. But countering that seeming inevitability, in the end, is that the concept that is Mithral Hall will rise from the ashes of the funeral pyre. When the drow came to Mithral Hall, as when any enemy in the past ever threatened the place, Bruenor, as king, stood strong and forthright, leading the charge. Indeed, it was Bruenor Battlehammer, and not some warrior acting on his behalf, who slew Matron Baenre herself, the finest notch he ever put into that nasty axe of his.

That is the place of a dwarf king, because a dwarf king must understand that the kingdom is more important than the king, that the clan is bigger than the king, that the principles of the clan's existence are the correct principles and are bigger than the mortal coil of king and commoner alike.

If Bruenor didn't believe that, if he couldn't honestly look his enemies coldly in the eye without fear for his own safety, then Bruenor should not be King of Mithral Hall. A leader who hides when danger reveals itself is no leader at all. A leader who thinks himself irreplaceable and invaluable is a fool.

But I am no leader, so how does this apply to me and my chosen road? Because I know in my heart that I walk a road of truth, a road of the best intentions (if sometimes those intentions are misguided), a road that to me is an honest one. I believe that my way is the correct way (for me, at least), and in my heart, if I ever do not believe this, then I must work hard to alter my course.

Many trials present themselves along this road. Enemies and other physical obstacles abound, of course, but along with them come the pains of the heart. In despair, I traveled back to Menzoberranzan, to surrender to the drow so that they would leave my friends alone, and in that most basic of errors I nearly cost the woman who is most dear to me her very life. I watched a confused and tired Wulfgar walk away from our group and feared he was walking into danger from which he would never emerge. And yet, despite the agony of that parting, I knew that I had to let him go.

At times it is hard to hold confidence that the chosen fork in the road is the right one. The image of Ellifain dying will haunt me forever, I fear, yet I hold in retrospect the understanding that there was nothing I could have truly done differently. Even now knowing the dire consequences of my actions on that fateful day half a century ago, I believe that I would follow the same course, the one that my heart and my conscience forced upon me. For that is all that I can do, all that anyone can do. The inner guidance of conscience is the best marker along this difficult road, even if it is not foolproof.

I will follow it, though I know so well now the deep wounds I might find.

For as long as I believe that I am walking the true road, if I am slain, then I die in the knowledge that for a brief period at least, I was part of something bigger than Drizzt Do'Urden.

I was part of the way it should be.

No drow, no man, no dwarf, could ever ask for more than that.

I am not afraid to die.

—Drizzt Do'Urden

8

AROUND THE EDGES
OF DISASTER

"We're lost!" the yellow-bearded dwarf roared.

He took a threatening step forward, nearly tripping over his long, wagging beard. He was a square-shouldered creature, with hardly a neck to speak of, and a face full of exaggerated features: a huge nose, long and wide; a great mouth of large teeth showing under the pronounced yellow whiskers; and wild dark eyes set in wide sockets, seeming all the wilder as he wound up into one of his more animated moods. Though his heavy plate mail was lying by the bedrolls, he still wore his great helm, fashioned of metal and the towering antlers of a ten-point deer.

"How can we be lost, ye danged fool?" he said. "Ye got all them birds leadin' ye, don't ye?"

The other dwarf, his older brother, shrugged and gave a plaintive, "*Oooo*" sound.

He looked down at his feet, clad in sandals and not the typical heavy dwarven boots, and kicked a nearby rock, sending it bouncing into the brush.

"Ye said ye could get me there!" Ivan Bouldershoulder roared on. "A shortcut? Yeah, a danged shortcut that's got us somewhere. Near to Mithral Hall? No! But somewhere, and ye're right, ye stupid doo-dad, ye got us here fast!"

The blustering dwarf stood up straight and adjusted his battered chain mail jerkin, fixing the bandoleer of tiny crossbow bolts that crossed from his left shoulder to his right hip.

"Tick, tick, tick, boom," his brother warned for the hundredth time, waggling a finger at those special crossbow bolts, each fitted with a small vial of oil of impact.

In response, the angry Ivan drew out a handheld crossbow, an exact replica of the kind favored by the dark elves of the Underdark, and waggled it back at Pikel.

"Boom, yerself, ye stupid doo-dad!"

Pikel's eyes rolled up into his head and he whispered a quick chant. Before Ivan could tell him to knock it off, a small branch snapped down at the yellow-bearded dwarf's extended arm, enwrapping the wrist and tugging back up to put Ivan on the tips of his toes.

"Ye don't want to play like this," Ivan warned. "Not now."

"No boom," Pikel said firmly, waggling his finger like a scolding mother.

He seemed perfectly ridiculous, of course, as he usually did, with his long, green-dyed beard parted in the middle and pulled up over his large ears, then braided together with his long hair to run halfway down his back. He wore light green robes, layered and tied with a thick rope at his waist, and with voluminous sleeves that hung down over his hands if he held his arms at his side.

Ivan gave a little laugh, one that promised his older brother that he'd be meeting a fist very soon.

Pikel just ignored him and walked to the side of their small encampment, where a bowl of vegetable stew was boiling over the fire. The pair had been out of the Spirit Soaring cathedral in the mountains above the small town of Carradoon for more than a tenday, accepting Cadderly's invitation to them to represent him and his wife Danica and all the cathedral in the formal coronation of King Bruenor Battlehammer of Mithral Hall. Ivan and Pikel had been muttering about going to see Mithral Hall for years, ever since Drizzt Do'Urden and Catti-brie had come through the Spirit Soaring on the road to find a lost friend. With things settled comfortably along the Snowflake Mountains, and with the great event of Bruenor's forthcoming coronation, the time seemed perfect.

Just out of the Snowflake Mountains, their road barely begun, Pikel, who was a druid in his heart and in practice, had informed his brother that he could guide them more swiftly on their long journey. He could talk to animals after all, though he hardly seemed able to talk to anyone else except for Ivan, who understood his every grunt. He could predict the weather with a high degree of accuracy, and there was one more little trick up Pikel's wide sleeve, a mode of teleportation that druids understood, using the connectedness of trees to step into one and emerge through another, many miles away.

Ivan and Pikel had done just that, once thus far, and with more than a little complaining from Ivan, who thought the whole trip perfectly unnatural. They had come out into a deep, dark forest. At first, Ivan had figured that they had entered Shilmista, the elf woodland across the Snowflakes from Carradoon, but after a day of wandering in the dark place, both he and Pikel had come to realize that the tone of this particular forest was very different from the magical land ruled by Elbereth and his dancing kin. This forest, wherever it was and whatever it was, was darker and more foreboding than that airy forest of Shilmista. The wind held a deeper bite, as if they had gone further north.

"Ye gonna let me down?" Ivan called from his perch beneath the entrapping tree.

"Uh-uh."

Ivan gave a little chuckle, held his free hand out under the trapped arm and dropped the handheld crossbow to his own waiting grasp. He moved fast, bringing the weapon up to his face, hooking the bowstring under his top teeth and pushing it straight up until it clicked in the readied position, then he bit the weapon's handgrip, holding it in his mouth, while he reached down to pull a small dart from his bandoleer.

"*Oooo!*" Pikel howled when he noticed. He lifted a small log from beside the fire and uttered a quick chant, proclaiming it a "Sha-la-la," and charged for his brother.

Ivan calmly and deliberately set the quarrel in place on the crossbow, then took up the weapon, pointing it at the entangling branch.

Realizing that the howling Pikel was too close, though, the yellow-bearded dwarf matter-of-factly lowered the weapon the charging Pikel's way and fired.

The quarrel hit Pikel's raised enchanted club squarely, the quarrel sticking home, then collapsing on itself. A blinding, concussive flash halted Pikel's charge, and left the stunned dwarf standing there, his beard and hair smoking on the right side, his right arm still upraised, but holding only a blackened stump instead of an enchanted cudgel.

"Oooo," the druid dwarf moaned.

"Yeah, and yer tree is next!" Ivan promised, and he put the crossbow back in his mouth, his hand going for another dart.

Pikel hit him with a flying tackle that became more of a *flying* tackle when the hugging dwarves flew backward, only to be pulled forward by the strong branch, and of course, to rebound backward again.

And so they went, bouncing back and forth, Pikel grabbing at the crossbow and at Ivan's pumping arm, and Ivan punching Pikel, though they were too tightly embraced for him to do any real damage. All the while, the stubborn branch held strong, and the two struggling dwarves only seemed to gain momentum on their back and forth and all-around ride.

They were nearing the highest point of one such bounce when Pikel's enchantment let go, sending a ball of Bouldershoulder soaring into the air, to land with a communal "*Oof,*" and go rolling away.

They rolled past the fire, very close, and Ivan yelped when he burned the tip of his nose. They crashed through the lean-to Pikel had constructed, sending twigs flying. At one point, Pikel managed to wriggle away enough to begin casting another enchantment, so Ivan slapped his strong hand over his brother's mouth. Pikel promptly bit him.

It would have gone on for many minutes—it usually did when the Bouldershoulder brothers were involved, but a low growl from the fire pit stopped both dwarves dead in their roll, each with a fist heading in strong for the other's face. As one, the prone brothers turned their heads, to see a large black bear pawing at the hot vegetable stew.

Ivan shoved Pikel away and leaped to his feet.

"Praise Moradin!" he yelled as he looked around for his mighty axe. "Got me a new cloak!"

Pikel's shriek rent the night air and silenced every night bird for a hundred yards around.

"Shut yer trap!" Ivan ordered.

He rushed out to the side, spying his weapon, and heard his brother chanting again as he started past. Ivan expected to get his with another relatively harmless but ultimately annoying trick of nature.

When the excited Ivan had his axe in hand, he turned back to the fire . . . to see Pikel sitting in front of the contented bear, resting comfortably against its thick fur.

"Ye didn't," Ivan moaned.

"Hee hee hee."

With a growl, Ivan lifted his arm and sent his axe twirling down to stick into the sod.

"Damned Cadderly," he bitched, for in Ivan's eyes, Cadderly had created a monster in Pikel.

It was Cadderly who had first made a pet of a wild animal, a white squirrel he had named Percival, of all things. Taking that cue, Pikel had become rather famous for the friends he had made (*infamous* to Ivan, who thought the whole thing quite embarrassing) at the Spirit Soaring cathedral, particularly among Cadderly and Danica's children. To date, those friends included a great eagle, a pair of bald-headed vultures, a weasel family, three chickens, and a stubborn donkey named Bobo.

And now a bear.

Ivan sighed.

The bear gave a soft moan and seemed to fall over, settling comfortably on the ground, where it started snoring almost immediately. So did Pikel.

Ivan sighed more deeply.

"I do not demand applause, no," the gnome Nanfoodle explained, his little arms crossed over his thin chest, one large foot tapping anxiously on the floor, "but it would be appreciated, yes!"

Standing at no more than three and a half feet, with a long, pointy, crooked nose, his head bald but for a semicircular mane of wild white hair that stuck straight out above his ears and all the way back around, Nanfoodle was not an imposing figure. He was, however, one of the most celebrated alchemists in the North, a fact that Elastul and Shoudra Stargleam knew well.

The Marchion of Mirabar began clapping, his smile wide and sincere, for Nanfoodle has just brought him a piece of specially treated metal, smelted and fashioned of ore taken from the mines just a tenday before. Coated with the new formula the ingenious gnome had concocted, this plate was stronger than the others made of the same batch.

To the side, the Sceptrana was too busy continuing her inspection of the various pieces to join in the applause, but she did offer an appreciative nod to the gnome, which Nanfoodle gladly accepted. The two were great friends and had been since before Elastul had hired Nanfoodle and brought him to Mirabar, mostly on the recommendation of Shoudra.

"And with your new treatment for the metals, our pieces will prove the best in the North," Elastul said.

"Well . . ." The gnome hesitated. "They will be better than they were, but . . ."

"But? There can be no 'buts,' my dear Nanfoodle. Sceptrana Shoudra has contracts to secure, and it will take the finest—not merely better, but the finest!—to reclaim much of the commerce lost in recent years."

"The ore from our rivals is richer, and their techniques impeccable," Nanfoodle explained. "My treatment will increase the strength and durability of our products by a fair amount, but I doubt that we'll outshine the ore of Mithral Hall."

Elastul seemed to collapse in his seat, his hands clenched at his side.

"But we have improved!" Nanfoodle said with great enthusiasm, hoping the emotion would prove infectious.

It didn't.

"I do believe that this is the first time any measurable improvement through alchemical treatments has ever been honestly noted," Shoudra Stargleam added, and she quietly tossed a wink Nanfoodle's way.

"Despite the outlandish claims of many alchemists, there have been few—nay, not few, but *no*, improvements that are not magical in nature.

"And any improvement will help," Shoudra went on. "There are many previous clients who are on the borderline of decisions between Mirabar and Mithral Hall, and if we can improve our quality without raising our prices, then I believe I may sway more than a few our way."

Elastul did begin to brighten at that, even started to nod, but Nanfoodle chimed in, "Well . . ."

"Well?" the marchion asked suspiciously.

"The adamantine flakes needed in the treating solution do not come cheap," the gnome admitted.

Elastul dropped his head into his hands. Behind him, the four Hammers muttered a few select curses.

"You are using adamantine?" Shoudra asked. "I thought you were experimenting with lead."

"I was," the gnome answered. "And all of the blending formula was developed with lead as the additive base." He gave a shrug. "But that only weakened the end product, unfortunately."

"Wait," Elastul bade him with biting and obvious sarcasm. The marchion came up straight in his chair, his finger pointing as if he had suddenly caught on to the big picture. "You have found a way to blend the metals? And in doing so, if you use a stronger metal, you get a better product, but if you use a cheaper one, well, then you get a weaker product?"

"Yes, Marchion," Nanfoodle admitted, lowering his huge head against the biting sarcasm.

"Ever heard of *alloys*, dear Nanfoodle?"

"Yes, Marchion."

"Because I think you just re-invented them all over again."

"Yes, Marchion."

"How much am I paying you?"

"Enough," Shoudra Stargleam cut in, moving near to the marchion and dropping her hand on his forearm to calm him. "This may be the first step to a great benefit. If Nanfoodle's technique eases the expensive process, then it is not without benefit. In any case, this seems the first step on a potentially profitable road. A good start, I would say!"

Her exuberance did make the gnome stand a bit straighter, but Marchion Elastul merely offered a sarcastic smirk in response.

"Well, by all means, good Nanfoodle," he said. "Do not waste my time and coin in easing me along the whole of the process. Back to work, for you, and not to return until we are *much* farther along."

The gnome gave a curt bow and scampered out of the room. When he was gone, Marchion Elastul gave a great, frustrated roar.

"Alchemy is the science of boast," Shoudra said.

It was advice she had offered many times in the past. Elastul was spending huge sums on his team of alchemists and in truth, this was the greatest advance they had heard of thus far.

"This will not do," he said somberly, as if his anger had been thrown out in that previous roar. "King Bruenor walks into our city and sets it all into confusion. They are beating us with their ore and with their demeanor. This will not do."

"Our markets remain strong for all the items that do not need the fine and expensive Mithral Hall ore," Shoudra reminded. "Those items, the hoes and plows, the hinges and wheel strips, outnumber the swords and breastplates by far. Mithral Hall has cut down one portion of our business alone."

"The one portion that defines a mining city."

"True enough," Shoudra had to agree, but she merely shrugged.

She had never been overly excited about the return of the neighboring dwarven stronghold and had always figured that Clan Battlehammer were better neighbors than the previous inhabitants of the place, the evil grey dwarves.

"Their momentum mounts," Elastul said, and he seemed to be talking more to himself than to Shoudra. "King Bruenor, the legend, returns to them now."

"King Gandalug Battlehammer was fairly well known himself," Shoudra sarcastically replied. "Returning from the ages lost, and all."

Elastul shook his head with every word. "Not like Bruenor, who wrested back control of the hall in our time. With his strange friends and hearty clan, Bruenor reshaped the northland, and his return is significant,

I fear. With Bruenor back on the throne, you will find an even harder time in securing the contracts we need to prosper."

"Not so."

"It is not a chance I wish to take," Elastul snapped. "Witness what his reputation alone did to shake our own city. A simple pass through, and half the dwarves are muttering his praises. No, this cannot stand."

He sat back and put a finger to his pursed lips. Behind them, a smile gradually widened, as if some devious plan was formulating.

Shoudra looked at him curiously and said, "You cannot be thinking . . ."

"There are ways to see that Mithral Hall's reputation drops a few notches."

"Ways?" an incredulous Shoudra asked.

"We have dwarves here who have befriended King Bruenor, yes? We have dwarves among us who now call the King of Mithral Hall their friend, and he returns the compliment."

"Torgar will commit no sabotage against Mithral Hall," Shoudra reasoned, seeing easily enough where this was leading.

"He will if he doesn't know he's doing it," Elastul said mysteriously, and for the first time since Nanfoodle had arrived with the initial, misguided news, the marchion's smile was wide and genuine.

Shoudra Stargleam just looked at the man doubtfully. She had often heard his devious plotting, for he spent a great portion of his time on his throne doing just that. Almost always, though, it was just his wishful thinking at work. Despite his bluster, and even more than that, the bluster of the four Hammers who always stood behind him, Elastul wasn't really a man of action. He wanted to protect what he had and even try to improve it in a safe and secure manner, such as hiring alchemists, but to go an extra step, to actually attempt sabotage against Mithral Hall, for example, and thus risk starting a war, simply was not the man's style.

It was entertaining to watch, though, Shoudra had to admit.

9

BECAUSE THAT'S HOW WE DO IT

For Tred McKnuckles, the sight was as painful as anything he had ever witnessed. By his estimation, the people of Clicking Heels had treated him and Nikwillig with generosity and tender care, had jeopardized their own safety by getting into a conflict that had not even involved them. Nikwillig and he had done that to them by approaching their town, and they had reacted with more kindness and openness than a pair of lost dwarves from a distant citadel could have expected.

And now they had paid the price.

Tred walked about the ruins of the small village, the blasted and burned houses, and the bodies. He chased away the carrion birds from one corpse, then closed his eyes against the pain, recognizing the woman as one of the caring faces he had seen when he had first opened his eyes after resting against the weariness of the difficult road that had brought him there.

Bruenor Battlehammer watched the dwarf's somber movements, noting always the look on Tred's face. Before there had been a desire for vengeance—the dwarves' caravan had been hit and destroyed, and Tred had lost friends and a brother. Dwarves could accept such tragedies as an inevitability of their existence. They usually lived on the borderlands of the wilderness, and almost always faced danger of one sort or another, but the look on Tred's tough old face was somewhat different, more subdued, and in a way, more pained. A good measure of guilt had been thrown into the tumultuous mix. Tred and Nikwillig had stumbled into Clicking Heels on their desperate road, and as a result, the town was gone.

Simply, brutally, gone.

That frustration and guilt showed clearly as Tred made his way about the smoldering ruins, especially whenever he came upon one of the many orc corpses, always giving it a good kick in the face.

"How many're ye thinking?" Bruenor asked Drizzt when the drow returned from the outlying countryside, checking tracks and trying to get a clearer picture of what had occurred at the ruins of Clicking Heels.

"A handful of giants," the drow explained. He pointed up to a ridge in the distance. "Three to five, I would make it, based on the tracks and the remaining cairns of stones."

"Cairns?"

"They had prepared well for the attack," Drizzt reasoned. "I would guess that the giants rained boulders on the village in the dark of night, softening up the defenses. It went on for a long time, hours at least."

"How're ye knowing that?

"There are places where the walls were hastily repaired—before being knocked down once more," the drow explained. He pointed to a remote corner of the village. "Over there, a woman was crushed under a boulder, yet the townsfolk had the time to remove the stone and drag her away. In desperation, as the bombardment continued, a group even left the village and tried to sneak up on the giants' position." He pointed up toward the ridgeline, to a boulder tumble off to the side of where he had found the giant tracks and the cairns. "They never got close, with a host of orcs laying in wait."

"How many?" Bruenor asked him. "Ye say a handful o' giants, but how many orcs came against the village?"

Drizzt looked around at the wreckage, at the bodies, human and orc.

"A hundred," he guessed. "Maybe less, maybe more, but somewhere around that number. They left only a dozen dead on the field, and that tells me that the villagers were completely overwhelmed. Giant-thrown boulders killed many and methodically tore away the defensive positions. A third of the village's fighting force were slaughtered out by the ridge, and that left but a score of strong, hearty frontiersmen here to defend. I don't think the giants even came into the town to join in the fight." His lips grew very tight, his voice very grave. "I don't think they had to."

"We gotta pay 'em back, ye know?"

Drizzt nodded.

"A hunnerd, ye say?" Bruenor went on, looking around. "We're outnumbered four to one."

When the dwarf looked back at the drow, he saw Drizzt standing easily, hands on his belted scimitars, a look both grim and eager stamped upon his face—that same look that inspired both a bit of fear and the thrill of adventure in Bruenor and all the others who knew the drow.

"Four to one?" Drizzt asked. "You should send half our force back to Pwent and Mithral Hall . . . just to make it interesting."

A crooked smile creased Bruenor's weathered old face. "Just what I was thinking."

"Ye're the king, damn ye! Ain't ye knowin' what that means?"

Dagnabbit's less than enthusiastic reaction to Bruenor's announcement that they would hunt down the orcs and giants to avenge the destruction of the town and the attack on Tred's caravan came as no surprise to the dwarf king. Dagnabbit was seeing things through the lens offered by his position as Bruenor's appointed protector—and Bruenor did have to admit that at times he needed protecting from his own judgment.

But this was not one of those times, as far as he was concerned. His kingdom was but a few days of easy marching from Clicking Heels, and it was his responsibility, and his pleasure, to aid in cleansing the region of foul creatures like orcs and renegade giants.

"One thing it means is that I can't be lettin' the damned orcs come down and kill the folks about me kingdom!"

"Orcs *and* giants," Dagnabbit reminded. "A small army. We didn't come out here to—"

"We come out here to kill them that killed Tred's companions," Bruenor interrupted. "Seems likely it's the same band to me."

To the side, Tred nodded his agreement.

"And a bigger band than we thought," the stubborn Dagnabbit argued. "Tred was saying that there were a score and a couple o' giants, but 'twas more 'n that that leveled this town! Ye let me go back and get Pwent and his boys, and a hunnerd more o' me best fighters, and we'll go and get the durned orcs and giants."

Bruenor looked over at Drizzt. "Trail'll be cold by then?" he pleaded more than asked.

Drizzt nodded and said, "And we'll find little advantage in the way of surprise with an army of dwarves marching across the hills."

"An army that'll kill yer orcs and giants just fine," said Dagnabbit.

"But on a battlefield of their choosing," Drizzt countered. He looked to Bruenor, though it was obvious that Bruenor needed little convincing. "You get an army and we can, perhaps, find a new trail to lead to our enemies. Yes, we will defeat them, but they will see us coming. Our charge will be through a rain of giant boulders and against fortified positions—behind rock walls, or worse, up on the cliff ledges, barely accessible and easily defended. If we go after them now and hunt them down quickly and with surprise, then we will choose and prepare the battlefield. There will be no flying boulders and no defended ledges, unless we are the ones defending them."

"Sounds like ye're looking to have a bit o' fun," Catti-brie snidely remarked, and Drizzt's smile showed that he couldn't honestly deny that.

Dagnabbit started to argue, as was, in truth, his place in all of this, but Bruenor had heard enough. The king held up his hand, silencing his commander.

"Go find the trail, elf," he ordered Drizzt. "Our friend Tred's looking to spill a bit o' orc blood. Dwarf to dwarf, I'm owing him that."

Tred's expression showed his appreciation at the favorable end to the debate. Even Dagnabbit seemed to accept the verdict, and he said no more.

Drizzt turned to Catti-brie. "Shall we?"

"I was thinkin' ye'd never ask. Ye bringing yer cat?"

"Soon enough," Drizzt promised.

"Regis and I will run liaison between you and Bruenor," Wulfgar added.

Drizzt nodded, and the harmony of the group, with everyone understanding so well their place in the hunt, heightened Bruenor's confidence in his decision.

In truth, Bruenor needed that boost. Deep within him came the nagging worry that he was doing this out of his own selfish needs, that he might be leading his friends and followers into a desperate situation all because he feared, even loathed, the statesmanlike life that awaited him at the end of his road.

But, looking at his skilled and seasoned friends beginning their eager preparations, Bruenor shrugged many of those doubts aside. When they were done with this bit of business, when all the orcs and giants were dead or chased back into their deep holes, he'd go and take his place at Mithral Hall, and he'd use this impending victory as a reminder of who he was and who he wanted to be. There would be the trappings of bureaucratic process, the seemingly endless line of dignitary visitors who had to be entertained, to be sure, but there would also be adventure. Bruenor promised himself that much, thinking again of the secrets of Gauntlgrym. There would be time for the open road and the wind on his wild red beard.

He smiled as he silently made that promise.

He had no idea that getting what you wished for might be the worst thing of all.

"It's all rocks and will be a difficult track, even with so many of them," Drizzt noted when he and Catti-brie entered the rocky slopes north of the destroyed village.

"Or perhaps not," the woman replied, motioning for Drizzt to join her.

As he came beside her, she pointed down at a dark gray stone, at a patch of red marking its smooth surface. Drizzt went down to one knee, removed a leather glove and dipped his finger, then brought it up before his smiling face.

"They have wounded."

"And they're letting them live," Catti-brie remarked. "Civilized group of orcs, it seems."

"To our advantage," Drizzt remarked. He ended short and turned to see a large form coming around the bend.

"The dwarves are readied for the road," Wulfgar announced.

"And we've found them a road to walk," Catti-brie explained, pointing down to the stone.

"Orc blood or a prisoner's?" Wulfgar asked.

The question took the smiles from Drizzt and Catti-brie, for neither of them had even thought of that unpleasant possibility.

"Orc, I would guess," said Drizzt. "I saw no signs of mercy at the village, but let us move, and quickly, in case it is the other."

Wulfgar nodded and headed away, signaling to Regis, who relayed the sign to Bruenor, Dagnabbit, and the others.

"He seems at ease," Catti-brie remarked to Drizzt when Wulfgar had left them, the barbarian fading back to his position ahead of the dwarf contingent.

"His new family pleases him," Drizzt replied. "Enough so that he has forgiven himself his foolishness."

He started ahead, but Catti-brie caught him by the arm, and when he turned to face her, he saw her wearing a serious look.

"His new family pleases him enough that it does not pain him to see us together out here, hunting side by side."

"Then we can only hope to one day share Wulfgar's fate," Drizzt replied with a wry grin. "One day soon."

He started off, then, bounding across the uneven rock surfaces with such ease and grace that Catti-brie didn't even try to pace him. She knew the routine of their hunting. Drizzt would move from vantage point to vantage point all around her while she meticulously followed the trail, the drow serving as her wider eyes while her own were fixed upon the stone before her feet.

"Don't ye be too long in calling up yer cat!" she called to him as he moved away, and he responded with a wave of his hand.

They moved swiftly for several hours, the blood trail easy enough to follow, and by the time they found the source—an orc lying dead along the side of the path, which brought a fair bit of relief—the continuing trail lay obvious before them. There weren't many paths through the mountains, and the ground outside the lone trail stretching before them was nearly impossible to cross, even by long-legged frost giants.

They signaled back through their liaisons and waited for the dwarves then set camp there.

"If the trail does not split soon, we will catch up to them within two days," Drizzt promised Bruenor as they ate their evening meal. "The orc has been dead as long as three days, but our enemies are not moving swiftly or with purpose. They may even be closer than we believe, may even have doubled back in the hopes of finding more prey along the lower elevations."

"That's why I doubled the guard, elf," Bruenor replied through a mouth full of food. "I'm not looking to have a hunnerd orcs and a handful o' giants find me in me sleep!"

Which was precisely how Drizzt hoped to find the hundred orcs and the handful of giants.

They hustled along the next day, Drizzt and Catti-brie spying many signs of the recent passing, like the multitude of footprints along one low, muddy dell. In addition to showing the way, the continuing indications lent credence to Drizzt's estimate of the size of the enemy force.

The drow and Catti-brie knew that they were gaining, and fast, and that the orcs and giants were making no effort to conceal themselves or watch their backs for any apparent pursuit.

And why should they? Clicking Heels, like all the other villages in the Savage Frontier, was a secluded place, a place where, under normal circumstances, the complete disaster and destruction of the village might not be known by the other inhabitants of the region for tendays or months, even in the summertime when travel was easier. This was not a region of high commerce, except in the markets of places like Mithral Hall, and not a region where many journeyed along the rugged trails. Clicking Heels was not on the main road of commerce. It existed on the fringes, like a dozen or more similar communities, comprised mostly of huntsmen, that rarely if ever even showed up on any map.

These were the wilds, lands untamed. The orcs and giants knew all of this, of course, as Drizzt and Catti-brie understood, and so the couple didn't think it likely that their enemies would have sentries protecting their retreat from a village crushed with no survivors.

When the couple joined the dwarves for dinner that second evening, it was with complete confidence that Drizzt reasserted his prediction to Bruenor.

"Tell your fellows to sleep well," he explained. "Before the setting of tomorrow's sun, we will have first sight of our enemies."

"Then afore the rising o' the sun the next day after that, our enemies'll be dead," Bruenor promised.

As he spoke, he looked over at the dwarf he had invited to dine with him that night.

Tred replied with a grim and appreciative nod then dug into his lamb shank with relish.

The terrain was rocky and broken, with collections of trees, evergreens mostly, set in small protected dells against the backdrop of the increasingly towering mountains. The wind swept down and circled about, rebounding off the many mountainous faces. The winding paths of swift-running streams cascaded down the slopes, silver lines against a background of gray and blue. For the inexperienced, the mountain trails would be quietly deceiving, leading a traveler around, in, up, and down circles that ultimately got him nowhere near where he intended to be or taking him on a wide-ranging path that ended abruptly at a five-hundred-foot drop.

Even for Drizzt and his friends, so attuned with the ways of the wild, the mountains presented a huge challenge. They could pursue the orc force readily enough, for the correct trail was clearly marked to the trained eyes of the drow, but finding a way to flank that fleeing force as the trail grew fresher would not be so easy.

On one plateau of a particularly wide mountain, fed by many trails and serving as a sort of hub for them all, Drizzt found a tell-tale marker. He bent over a patch of mud, its edge depressed by the step of a recent boot.

"The print is fresh," he explained to Catti-brie, Regis, and Wulfgar. He rose up from his crouch, rubbing his muddied fingers together. "Less than an hour."

The friends glanced around, focusing mostly on the higher ridgeline that loomed to the north.

Catti-brie was first to catch sight of the movement up there, a hulking giant form gliding around a line of broken boulders.

"Time for Guenhwyvar," Wulfgar remarked.

Drizzt nodded and pulled the statue from his belt pouch, then placed it on the ground and summoned the magical panther to his side.

"We should pass word to Bruenor as well," the barbarian added.

"Ye do it," Catti-brie replied, speaking to Wulfgar. "Ye can get there quicker than the little one with yer longer legs."

Wulfgar nodded; it made sense.

"We'll better locate and assess the enemy while you fetch the dwarves," Drizzt explained. He glanced off at Regis, who was already moving—to the west and not the north. "Flanking?"

"I go this way, you go north, and she goes east," Regis explained.

His three friends smiled, glad to see a bit of the old Regis returned, for the giant they had spotted had been moving west to east and by going west, Regis was almost assuring that his two hunting friends would find the orc and giant band before he did.

"Guenhwyvar comes with me to the north, in a direct line toward the enemy," Drizzt explained. "She alone can run without inviting suspicion. We four will meet back here right before the sunset."

With final nods and determined looks, they split apart, each moving swiftly along the appointed trail.

It was a strange feeling for Regis, being out alone in the wilderness without Drizzt or any of the others protectively at his side. Back in Ten-Towns, the halfling had often ventured out of Lonelywood by himself, but almost always along familiar trails, particularly the one that would take him to the banks of the great lake Maer Dualdon and his favorite fishing hole.

Being alone in the wilds, with known, dangerous enemies not too far away, felt strangely refreshing. Despite his very real fears, Regis could not deny the surge of energy coursing through his diminutive body. The rush of excitement, the thrill of knowing that a goblin might be hiding behind any rock, or that a giant might even then be taking deadly aim at him with one of its huge boulder missiles. . . .

In truth, this wasn't an experience that Regis planned to make the norm of his existence, but he understood that it was a necessary risk, one leading to the greater good, and one that he had to accept.

Still, he wished he hadn't been the first to encounter the orcs, a group of a dozen stragglers lagging behind their main lines. Caught up in his own thoughts, the distracted halfling almost walked right into their midst before ever realizing that they were there.

Drizzt didn't like what he was seeing. High up on a rocky ledge, the drow lay flat on his belly peering over an encampment of several scores of orcs—what he had expected. Just beyond the camp, though, loomed a quartet of behemoths: huge frost giants, and not the dirty rogues one might expect to find consorting with orcs. These were handsome creatures, clean and richly dressed, adorned with ornamental bracelets and rings, and fine furs that were neither particularly new nor particularly weather-beaten.

The giants were part of a larger, more organized clan—obviously a part of the network the Jarl Grayhand, a name not unknown to Drizzt and the dwarves of Mithral Hall, had formed in this part of the Spine of the World.

If the old Grayhand was loaning some of his mighty warriors out to

an orc clan, the implications might prove darker than one flattened village and an ambush on a band of dwarves.

Drizzt looked all around, wondering if there was a way for him to
get closer to the giants, to try to overhear their conversation. He could
only hope they'd be speaking in a language that he could comprehend.

The cover between him and the orc camp was not promising,
though, nor was the climb down the almost sheer cliff facing. Beyond
that, the sun was already hanging low in the sky, and he didn't have
much time if he hoped to rejoin his friends in the appointed place at the
appointed hour.

He lingered for many more minutes, watching from afar the limited
interaction between the giants and orcs. His attention piqued when one
large and powerful orc, wearing the finest garments of all the filthy
band, and with a huge, decorated axe strapped across its back,
approached the giant quartet. The orc didn't go in the hesitating manner
of some of the others, who had been either bringing food to the behemoths or simply trying to navigate past them in as unobtrusive a manner
as possible. This orc—and Drizzt understood that it had to the leader,
or at least one of the leaders—strode up to the giants purposefully and
without any apparent trepidation and began conversing in what seemed
to be a jovial manner.

Engaged, straining to hear whatever tidbit he might, even if only a
burst of laughter, Drizzt was hardly aware of the approach of an orc
sentry until it was too late.

From one high vantage point, Catti-brie noted where the orcs and
giants had stopped to set their camp, far to the west of where she had
entered the higher, northern ridgeline. She realized that Drizzt was likely
already surveying their encampment, and she could get there, but her
estimate told her that she'd probably arrive on the spot just in time to
accompany Drizzt, if they found each other, back to their assigned meeting spot. Thus, the woman spent her time running past the east end of
the enemy encampment, checking the ground over which the orcs and

giants would likely traverse in the morning—unless, of course, they decided to break camp early and march on through the night, which would favor the orcs, no doubt, though probably not be to the liking of the giants.

With the eye of a trained tactician, which she, as the adopted daughter of Bruenor Battlehammer, most certainly was, she looked for advantageous assault points. Bottlenecks in the trail, high ground where dwarves could send rocks and hammers spinning down at their enemies. . . .

Despite her many duties, the woman was the first of the four to return to the rendezvous point. Wulfgar returned soon after her with Bruenor, Dagnabbit, and Tred McKnuckles at his side.

"They have encamped almost directly north of this point," the woman explained.

"How many?" Bruenor asked.

Catti-brie gave a shrug. "Drizzt will know. I was searching the ground ahead to see where and how we might strike tomorrow."

"Ye find any good killin' spots?"

Catti-brie answered with a wicked smile, and Bruenor eagerly rubbed his hands together, then looked over at Tred and offered a nudge and a wink.

"Ye'll get yer payback, friend," the dwarf king promised.

As so often in the past, luck alone saved Regis. He skittered behind a convenient rock without notice from the group of orcs, who were engaged in an argument over some loot they had pilfered, probably from the sacked village.

They argued, pushed and shouted at each other, and deciding to divide the loot up privately amongst themselves, they suddenly quieted. Instead of continuing along the trail to join up with the larger band, they plopped themselves down right there, sending a couple ahead to fetch some food.

That afforded Regis a lovely eavesdropping position while they rambled on about all sorts of things, answering many questions for the halfling and leading him to ask many, many more.

———❦———

Drizzt could not have been in a more disadvantageous situation, lying face down between a rise of stone and a boulder, peering over a ledge and with someone, something—likely an orc—moving up behind him. He ducked his head and shrugged the cowl of his cloak up a bit higher, hoping the creature would miss him in the dim light, but when the footsteps closed, the drow knew that he had to take a different course.

He shoved up to his knees and gracefully leaped to his feet from there, spinning around and drawing his scimitars, moving them as quickly as possible into a defensive position, trying to anticipate the attacker's thrust. If the creature had come straight on, Drizzt would have been caught back on his heels from the outset.

But the orc, and it was an orc, hadn't charged, and didn't charge. It stood back, hands upraised and waving frantically, having dropped its weapon to the ground at its feet.

It said something that Drizzt didn't completely comprehend, though the language was close enough to the goblin tongue, which the drow did know, for him to understand that there was some recognition there, spoken in an almost apologetic tone. It seemed as if the orc, recognizing a drow elf, feared that it was intruding.

The obvious fear didn't surprise Drizzt, for the goblinkin were usually terrified of the drow—as were most reasoning races—but this went beyond that, he sensed. The orc wasn't surprised, as if the appearance of a drow elf near to this force was not unexpected.

He wanted to question the creature further but saw a black flash to the side of the orc and knew his opportunity had passed.

Guenhwyvar came across hard and fast, in a great leap that put the panther about chest level with the orc.

"Guen, no!" Drizzt cried as the cat flew past.

The orc's throat erupted in blood and the creature went flying down to the stone. Drizzt rushed to it, turning it over, thinking to stem the flow of blood from its throat.

Then he realized that the orc had no throat left at all.

Frustrated that an opportunity had flitted away, but grateful that Guenhwyvar had seen the danger from afar and come rushing in to rescue him, Drizzt could only shake his head.

He hid the dead orc as well as possible in a crevice, and with Guenhwyvar at his side, he started back to the rendezvous, having discovered more questions than answers.

"Plenty of ground to shape to our liking," Catti-brie assured them all when they had reassembled on the plateau below the enemy's position. "We'll get the fight we want."

None disagreed, but Bruenor wore a concerned expression.

"Too many giants," he explained when all the others had focused on him. "Four'd make a good enough fight by themselves. I'm thinking we got to hit them afore the morning. Trim the numbers."

"Not an easy thing to do, if we're still wanting surprise tomorrow," Catti-brie added.

They bounced a few ideas back and forth, possible plans to lure out the giants, and potential areas where they could hit at the brutes away from the main force. There seemed no shortage of these, but getting them out wouldn't be an easy task.

"There may be a way . . ." Drizzt offered, the first words he had contributed to the planning.

Replaying the scene with the orc, the reactions of the creature toward him, Drizzt wondered if his heritage might serve him well.

They agreed on a place, and the six and Guenhwyvar, minus Drizzt, started away, while the drow moved back toward his last position overlooking the encampment. He stayed there for just a few moments, his keen eyes cutting the night and discerning an approach route toward the separate giant camp, and he was gone, slipping away as silently as a shadow.

"He'll bring 'em down from the right," Bruenor said when they reached the appointed ambush area.

The dwarf was facing a high cliff, with a rocky, broken trail running left and right in front of it before him.

"Can ye get up there, Rumblebelly?"

Regis, standing at the base of the cliff, was already picking his course. He had discerned a few routes already to the ledge he was hoping to reach, but he wanted an easier one for a companion who was not quite as nimble as he.

"You want to get in on the kill?" he asked Tred McKnuckles, who was standing beside him and looking more than a little overwhelmed by the frantic planning and implementation of the seasoned companions.

"What d'ya think?" the dwarf shot back.

"I think you should put that weapon on your back and follow me up," Regis replied with a wry grin, and without further ado, the halfling began his climb.

"I ain't no damn spider!" Tred yelled back.

"Do you want the kill or not?"

It was the last thing Regis meant to say, and the last thing he had to say, for Tred, grumbling and growling to make a robbed dwarf proud, began his ascent, following the exact course of footholds and handholds Regis had taken. It took him a long time to get to the ledge, and by the time he arrived, Regis was already sitting comfortably with his back against the wall, twenty-five feet above the ground.

"See if you can break off a large chunk of that rock," the halfling remarked, nodding to the side, where a fair-sized boulder had lodged itself on the ledge.

Tred looked at the solid stone, a thousand pounds of granite, doubtfully.

"Ye think ye can drop it off?" came a call from below from Cattibrie.

Regis moved forward to regard her, and Tred looked on even more doubtfully.

Catti-brie didn't wait for an answer but moved to the side to confer with Wulfgar. The barbarian rushed away, returning a few moments later with a long and thick broken branch. He positioned himself below the ledge, then reached up as far as he could, and when it was apparent that he still couldn't reach his companions with the branch, he tossed it up.

Regis caught it and pulled it up beside him. Smiling, he handed it to the bewildered Tred.

"You'll see," the halfling promised.

To the side, on another ledge at about the same height as Regis and Tred's, Guenhwyvar gave a low growl, and poor Tred seemed more unsettled than ever.

Regis just grinned and moved back into position to watch the trail behind.

When he heard them talking in a language that was close enough to Common to be understood, Drizzt's hopes for his plans climbed a bit. He was on the fringes of the encampment, out in the shadows behind a large rock. Neither the orcs nor the giants had set any guards, obviously secure in their victory.

The giants' conversation was small talk mostly, giving the drow no real information. That didn't concern him too much. He was more interested in finding a chance to approach one of them alone, to play his hunch that this group was somewhat familiar with dark elves.

He got his chance almost an hour later. One of the giants was snoring, a sound not unlike an avalanche. Another, the only female of the quartet, lay beside him, near sleep if not already so. The remaining two continued their conversation, though with the long lags of silence attributable to drowsiness. Finally, one of the pair stood up and wandered off.

Drizzt took a deep breath—dealing with creatures as formidable as frost giants was no easy task. In addition to their great size, strength, and fighting prowess, frost giants were not blathering idiots like their hill giant and ogre cousins. By all accounts, they were often quite sharp of mind, and not easily fooled. Drizzt had to count on his heritage, and the reputation that he hoped would precede him.

He crept in under cover of the shadows to within a few feet of the sitting behemoth.

"You missed some treasure," he whispered.

The giant, obviously sleepy, started a bit and fell back to one elbow, turning his head to regard the speaker as it asked, "What?"

Seeing the dark elf, the giant did move more ambitiously, snapping back up to a straight-backed position.

"Donnia?" it asked, a name that Drizzt did not recognize, except to recognize that it was indeed a name, a drow name.

"An associate," he replied quietly. "You missed a great treasure."

"Where? What?"

"At the village. A huge chest of gems and jewels, buried beneath one of the fallen buildings."

The giant looked around, then leaned in more closely.

"You offer this?" he asked suspiciously, so obviously not convinced that the drow, that *any* drow, would walk in and give such information away.

"I cannot carry so much," Drizzt explained. "I cannot carry one tenth of that which lies within. While I could ferry the treasure away one arm-load at a time, I suspect there is more still, buried beneath a slab I can't budge."

The giant looked around again, its movements showing that it was more than a little interested. Not far to the side, one of its companions snored, coughed, and rolled over.

"I will share with you, fifty-fifty, and with your kin, if you believe we need them," Drizzt said, "but not with the orcs."

A wicked smile that crossed the giant's face told Drizzt that his understanding of the race relationships within the enemy band was not far from the mark.

"Let us continue this discussion, but not here," Drizzt said, and he began fading back into the shadows.

The giant looked around yet again, then moved into a crouch and crept after him, following eagerly into the night, moving quietly along a rocky trail to a small clearing protected behind by a sheer cliff wall.

On a ledge on that wall, some ten feet above the head of the towering giant, two sets of curious eyes looked on.

"What will Donnia Soldou think of this?" the giant asked.

"Donnia need not know," Drizzt replied.

The giant's shrug told him much, told him that Donnia, whoever she might be, was not an overriding controlling force but more likely just an associate. That brought a bit of relief to the dark elf. He would hate to think that the orcs and giants were acting at the behest of a drow army.

"I will take Geletha with me," the giant announced.

"Your friend with whom you were speaking?"

The giant nodded. "And we take two shares, you take one."

"That hardly seems fair."

"You cannot move the slab."

"You cannot find the slab." Drizzt continued the banter, trying hard to keep the giant unsuspicious while his friends moved into their final positions.

He figured he wouldn't have to keep it up for long.

When a blue-streaking arrow shot out from behind him, zipped past, and thudded hard into the giant's chest, the drow was not surprised.

The behemoth groaned but was not badly hurt. Drizzt drew his scimitars and leaped around, turning to face Catti-brie's position, still playing the part of the giant's ally.

"Where did it come from?" he shouted. "Lift me that I might see."

"Straight ahead!" roared the great creature.

It started to bend to accommodate the drow, and Drizzt turned fast and ran up its treelike arm. His scimitars slashed hard across the behemoth's face, drawing bright lines of red.

The giant roared and grabbed at him, but the drow had already leaped away, with another blue-streaking arrow sizzling in behind him, slamming the giant yet again.

Shrugging it off, the behemoth continued to move toward Drizzt, until there came a sound like a log splitting. Bruenor Battlehammer's many-notched axe smashed the brute in the back of the knee.

The giant howled and lurched, grabbing the wound, and Catti-brie hit it again with an arrow, this time in the face.

Ignoring the hit as much as possible, the brute lifted a foot, obviously intending to smash Bruenor.

And it was hopping, as Dagnabbit rushed out and planted his warhammer right on top of the giant's set foot.

And a cry of "Tempus!" followed by a second warhammer, this one spinning through the air, changed that course.

Aegis-fang hit the behemoth in the chest, just below its neck, with a force that knocked the giant back against the wall. Wulfgar came in behind the hammer, recalling it magically to his grasp, then charged before the giant had recovered and launched a tremendous smash right into the giant's kneecap.

How the brute howled!

Catti-brie's next arrow hit it right in the face.

Up on the ledge, Tred, with the branch lever tucked tight over one shoulder, looked from the giant to Regis, his expression dumbfounded. He had battled giants before, on many occasions, but never had he seen one so battered so quickly.

He looked past Regis then to Guenhwyvar. The great panther crouched on a ledge to the side, watching the fight, but more than that, watching back toward the east, her ears perked up.

Regis held his hand out toward the ledge, indicating that the target behemoth was in position.

Tred gave a satisfied grunt and bore down on the displaced boulder, setting the lever more solidly and driving on. The rock tilted and tumbled, and the poor giant below, which was just then beginning to regain its senses and set some type of defense against the rushing onslaught of the drow, the barbarian, the woman, and the two fiery dwarves, got a thousand pounds of granite right on top of the head. The crunching sound from its neck echoed off the stone, as did the resounding crash as the boulder bounced away.

Regis gave Tred a salute for the fine shot, but the relief was short-lived, for only then did the halfling and the dwarf come to understand what had so piqued Guenhwyvar's interest and had kept the cat out of the fight. Another giant was charging down the path, and yet another one, a female, behind that.

Regis looked at Tred. "We could find another rock," he offered, just a hint of fear creeping into his voice.

Behind them, Guenhwyvar leaped onto the shoulder of the charging giant, and as it pounded on down the trail, Tred shrugged and did likewise, using the cat's distraction to get a clear shot at the giant's head with his mighty axe. No crack of stone against stone had ever sounded louder than the report of Tred's axe cracking into the giant's skull.

Regis winced and looked over.

"Or we could do that," the halfling remarked, though the dwarf couldn't hear him.

With great effort, Tred stubbornly hung on to the axe handle, hanging off the back of the giant's head. He rode the behemoth down as it stumbled to its knees, then down to the ground.

Tred rose from the dead behemoth's back and swung around to join the fray against the remaining beast—or tried to, then got jerked back around by his axe, which remained firmly embedded.

He heard a groan, from the side and down, and only then realized—and he was the only one of the band to notice—that Dagnabbit had been in an unfortunate position as the giant had slumped down and was buried beneath the behemoth's great weight.

Drizzt started the counterattack, charging up the path at the furious female frost giant. He saw the giant raise her arm to throw, a large stone in hand, and responded by calling upon his innate drow abilities, summoning a globe of darkness before the creature's face. The drow dived aside, frantically, and the hurled rock clipped the stone where he had been standing. Its rebound sent it skipping fast, brushing Wulfgar in the shoulder and sending him flying, then just missing Catti-brie, taking Taulmaril from her hands and bloodying her fingers. She fell to her knees, clutching her hands, her face locked in a grimace of pain.

Drizzt came in hard at the giant. The behemoth kicked across at him, and the drow went into a leaping, rolling somersault right over the flying foot, landing gracefully and spinning about, his deadly scimitars cutting two deep lines in the back of the huge calf.

Bruenor came in next and hard, driving in against the giant's other shin with his axe. The giant swatted him aside with a brutal slap, but the dwarf just accepted the bouncing ride along the rocks, regained his footing, adjusted his one-horned helmet, and wagged a finger back at the behemoth.

"Now ye're makin' me mad, ye overfed orc!"

The giant kicked at Drizzt again, but he was too quick for that, skipping aside time and time again, and spinning about to cut a wicked slash whenever presented an opening.

Apparently realizing that it was overmatched, the behemoth kicked one last time, shortening the blow in an effort not to thump the drow, but to just keep him at bay. The giantess turned to the south and started to run along the broken ground instead of the path, where her long legs would give her an advantage.

Or she tried to.

Aegis-fang whipped in, smashing the ankle of the giantess's trailing foot, driving that foot behind the other ankle and tripping the behemoth up.

She fell hard to the stone, her breath blasted out by the impact.

She tried to rise but had no chance. Drizzt was there, running up her back. And Guenhwyvar was there, leaping onto her shoulders and biting hard at the back of her neck. And Catti-brie was there, holding Khazid'hea, her devilishly sharp sword, gingerly in her injured grasp. And Bruenor was there with his axe, with Wulfgar behind him with the mighty warhammer back in his grasp.

And Tred came in, escorting a shaken, but not too badly hurt Dagnabbit.

Up on the ledge behind them, Regis watched and cheered. He called out when he noticed that the first felled giant was moving again, albeit groggily, the behemoth struggling to rise. Wulfgar rushed back and put Aegis-fang to swift and deadly work on the creature's huge head.

"I never seen nothing like it," Tred admitted as the band made their way back toward the main force of waiting dwarves.

"It's all about shaping the battlefield," Bruenor explained.

"And none do it better 'n King Bruenor!" Dagnabbit added.

"None, unless it's him," Bruenor replied, nodding his chin toward Drizzt, who was tending Catti-brie's hands as they walked.

She had at least one broken finger but seemed more than ready to continue.

There would be no rest for the band that night. There was another battlefield to properly shape, in preparation for an even larger fight.

10

NOT WELCOME

"Uh uh," Pikel said stubbornly, stamping his foot hard and standing before the wide oak, barring Ivan's way into the enchanted tree.

"What are ye saying?" Ivan shot back. "Ye openin' the door just to keep it blocked, ye dopey fool?"

Pikel pointed past his brother to the bear, which was sitting and watching, its expression forlorn.

"Ye ain't takin' the bear!" Ivan bellowed, and he came forward.

"Uh uh," Pikel said again, waggling his finger and shifting to fully block the way.

Nose to nose, Ivan glowered at his brother, but he heard the bear growling behind him soon enough and realized this next fight wouldn't be even.

"Ye can't be taking him," the yellow-bearded dwarf reasoned. "Ye might be breakin' up his bear family, and ye wouldn't want to be doing that!"

"Oooo," said Pikel, seeming caught off guard for just a second before his face brightened.

He came forward and whispered into Ivan's ear.

"How do ye know he ain't got no family?" Ivan roared in protest, and Pikel whispered some more.

"He told ye?" Ivan bellowed in disbelief. "The stupid bear told ye? And ye're believing him? Ye ever think that he might be fibbing? That he might be telling ye that just to get away from his . . . cow or his doe or his . . . bearess, or whatever they're calling a she-bear?"

"Bearess, hee hee hee," said Pikel, and giggling, he whispered some more.

"He's a *she*-bear?" Ivan asked, and he glanced back. "How're ye knowin' it's a . . . never mind, don't ye be telling me. It ain't no matter, anyway. He-bear or she-bear, he . . . she . . . it, ain't goin'."

Pikel's face seemed to sink, his bottom lip getting pressed forward in a most pitiful pout, but Ivan held his ground. He wasn't about to do this strange tree-walking, unsettling under the best of conditions, with a wild bear beside him.

"Nope, it ain't," he said calmly. "And when we're missin' Bruenor's coronation, ye can tell Cadderly why. And when the winter's finding us out here, and yer friend's gone to sleep, ye watch me skin her for some warm blankets! And when . . ."

Pikel's low moan stopped his fiery brother's tirade, for Ivan surely recognized the defeat in Pikel's tone.

The green-bearded Bouldershoulder walked past Ivan and over to his bear. He spent a long while grooming the back of the gentle animal's ears, scratching and pulling ticks, and gently placing the insects down on the ground.

Of course, whenever he put down a bloated one, Ivan made a point of picking it up, holding it high, and popping it between stubby fingers.

A few moments later, Pikel's bear ambled away, and though Pikel remarked that he thought the creature was quite sad, Ivan frankly saw no difference. The bear was going on its way, and any way would have likely been good enough for the bear.

Pikel walked past Ivan again. He took up his newest walking stick and knocked three times on the trunk, then bowed low and reverently as he asked the tree's permission to enter.

Ivan didn't hear anything, of course, but apparently his brother did, for Pikel half-turned and held his arm out Ivan's way, inviting the yellow-bearded brother to lead the way.

Ivan deferred and responded by motioning for Pikel to go ahead.

Pikel bowed again and motioned for Ivan to lead.

Ivan deferred again and motioned more emphatically.

Pikel bowed yet again, still with complete calm, and motioned for Ivan to lead.

Ivan started to motion back yet again but changed his mind in mid-swing, and shoved his brother through instead, then turned and charged the tree.

To smack face-first into the solid trunk.

─────────✦─────────

With his pale, almost translucent skin, and blue eyes so rich in hue they seemed to reflect the colors around him, the elf Tarathiel seemed a tiny thing. Though not very tall, he was lean and seemed all the more so with his angular features and long pointed ears. That was all an errant vision, though, for the elf warrior was a formidable force indeed and certainly would be seen as no tiny thing to any enemy tasting the bite of his fiercely-sharp, slender sword.

Crouching in the high, windblown pass, a day's flight from his home in the Moonwood, Tarathiel recognized the sign clearly enough. Orcs had been through. Many orcs, and not too long ago. Normally that wouldn't have concerned Tarathiel too much—orcs were a common nuisance in the wilds of the valley between the Spine of the World and the Rauvin Mountains—but Tarathiel had tracked the band, and he knew from whence they'd come. They'd come out of the Moonwood, out of his beloved forest home, bearing many, many felled trees.

Tarathiel gnashed his teeth together. He and his clan had failed, and miserably, in the defense of their forest home, for they had not even located the orcs quickly enough to chase them off. Tarathiel feared what that might mean for the near future. Would the lack of defense prompt the ugly brutes to return?

"If they do, then we will slaughter them," the moon elf remarked, turning to speak to his mount, who stood grazing off to the side.

The pegasus snorted in reply, almost as if he'd understood. He threw his head about and tucked his white-feathered wings in tighter over his back.

Tarathiel smiled at the beautiful creature, one of a pair he had rescued a few years earlier from these same mountains, after their sire and dam had been killed by giants. Tarathiel had found the felled pair, smashed down by thrown boulders into a rocky dell. He could tell from the dead mare's teats that she had recently given birth, and so he had spent the better part of a tenday searching the area before finding the pair of foals. That pair had done well in the Moonwood, growing strong and straight under the guidance—not the ownership—of Tarathiel's small clan. This one, which he had named Sunset because of the reddish tinges in his white hair all along his long, glistening mane, welcomed him as a rider. Tarathiel had named Sunset's twin Sunrise, because her shining white mane was highlighted by a brighter color red, a yellowish pink hue. Both pegasi were about the same height, sixteen hands, and both were well-muscled, with strong, thick legs and wide, solid hooves.

"Let us go and find these orcs and show them a little rain," the elf said slyly, tossing a wink at his mount.

Sunset, as if he had understood again, pawed the ground.

They were up in the air soon after, Sunset's huge, powerful wings driving hard or spreading wide to catch the updrafts off the mountain cliffs. They soon spotted the orc band, a score of the creatures, trudging along a trail higher up in the mountains.

So attuned were mount and rider that Tarathiel was easily able to guide Sunset with just his legs, swooping the pegasus down from on high, flashing through the air some fifty yards above the orcs. The elf's bow worked furiously, firing arrow after arrow down at the orcs.

They scrambled and shouted curses, and Tarathiel guessed that more got hurt by diving frantically behind rocks or over ridges than felt the sting of his arrows. He went up and around the bend and flew on for some distance before turning Sunset around. He wanted to give the orcs time to regroup, time to think that the danger had passed. And he wanted to come in faster this time. Much faster.

The pegasus climbed higher into the sky, then banked a sharp turnabout and went into a powerful dive, wings working hard. They came around the corner much lower, just above the reach of the orcs had any been carrying a pole arm or long spear. From that height, despite the swift flight, Tarathiel's bow rang true, plugging one unfortunate orc right in the chest, throwing it back and to the ground.

Sunset soared past, a host of thrown missiles climbing harmlessly into the air behind them.

Tarathiel didn't push his luck for a third run. He banked to the southeast and set off from the mountains, soaring fast for home.

"How was I to know yer stupid spell had run out?" Ivan bellowed against his brother's continuing laughter. The yellow-bearded dwarf rubbed some blood off his scraped nose. "I didn't see no stupid door when ye said there was a door, so how'm I to be knowing when the door that ain't there anyway ain't there no more?"

Pikel howled with laughter.

Ivan stepped forward and launched a punch, but Pikel knew it was coming, of course, and he snapped his head forward, dropping his cooking pot helmet into his waiting, and blocking, hand.

Bong! And Ivan was hopping about in pain once more.

"Hee hee hee."

Ivan recovered in a few moments and went hard for his brother, but Pikel stepped into the tree, disappearing from sight.

Ivan stopped short and settled his senses then jumped in behind his brother. The world turned upside down for the poor dwarf.

Literally.

Pikel's tree-transport was not an easy ride, nor was it a level or even upright one. The brothers were rushed along the root network, magically melded into the trees, flowing through the roots of one to the adjoining roots of another. They went up fast and dropped suddenly—Pikel howling "Weeee!" and Ivan trying hard to keep his stomach out of his mouth.

They spun corkscrew motions along one winding route, then went through a series of sharp turns so violent that Ivan bit the inside of one cheek then the other.

It went on for many minutes, and finally, mercifully, the brothers came out. Ivan, who had somehow caught up to and surpassed Pikel, stumbled face-down in the dirt. Pikel came out hard and fast behind him, landing right atop his brother.

It always seemed to happen exactly like that.

With a great heave, Ivan had his brother bouncing away, but even that shove did little to stop Pikel's continuing laughter.

Ivan leaped up to throttle him, or tried to, for he was too disoriented, too dizzy, and his stomach was churning a bit too much. He ambled a step forward, two to the side, then after a pause, a third and a fourth to the side, to bang against a tree. He almost caught himself but tripped over a root and went down to his knees.

Ivan looked up and started to rise, but a rush of dizziness held him there, clutching at his churning stomach.

Pikel, too, was dizzy, but he wasn't fighting it. Like one of Cadderly's little children, he was up and laughing, trying to walk a straight line and inevitably falling to the ground, enjoying every second of it.

"Stupid doo-dad," Ivan muttered before he threw up.

* * *

Tarathiel watched the play of Sunset and Sunrise, the pegasi obviously glad to be reunited. They trotted across the small lea, whinnying and playfully nipping at each other.

"You never grow tired of watching them," came a higher-pitched, beautifully melodic voice behind him.

He turned to see Innovindil, his dearest friend and lover, walking onto the lea. She was smaller than he, with hair as yellow as his was black, and eyes as strikingly blue. She had that look on her face that so enchanted Tarathiel, a smile just a little bit crooked on the left, rising up sharply there to give her a mysterious, I-know-more-than-you-know look.

She moved beside him, to take his waiting hand.

"You've been gone too long," she scolded.

She brought her free hand up and tousled Tarathiel's hair, then dropped it lower and gently caressed his slender, strong chest.

His expression, which had been soft and bright as he had observed the pegasi at play, and brighter still at Innovindil's approach, darkened.

She asked, "Did you find them?"

Tarathiel nodded and said, "A band of orcs, as we suspected. Sunset and I came upon them in the mountains to the north, dragging trees they felled from the Moonwood."

"How many?"

"A score."

Innovindil gave that wry smile. "And how many are now alive?"

"I killed at least one," Tarathiel replied, "and sent the others scrambling."

"Enough to make them reconsider any return?"

Again the elf nodded.

"We two could go out and find them again," Tarathiel offered, returning the smile. "It will take a day at least to catch up to them, but if we kill them all, we can be sure they will not return."

"I have a better way to spend the next few days," Innovindil replied. She moved closer and gently kissed her husband on the lips. "I'm glad you have returned," she said, her voice growing more husky, more serious.

"As am I," he agreed, with all his heart.

The pair walked off from the lea, leaving the two pegasi to their play. They headed in the direction of the small village of Moonvines, their home, the home of their clan.

They had barely left the lea, though, when they spotted a campfire in the distance.

A campfire in the Moonwood!

Tarathiel handed his bow over to Innovindil and drew out his slender sword. The two set out at once, moving with absolute silence through the dark trees. Before they had gotten halfway to the distant fire, they were met by others of their clan, also armed and ready for battle.

"Ye made a stew again!" Ivan bellowed. "Ain't no wonder me belly's always growling at me of late! Ye won't let me eat any meat!"

"Uh-uh," said Pikel, waggling that finger, a gesture that was growing more and more annoying to Ivan, spawning fantasies of biting that stubby and crooked finger off at the top knuckle. At least then, he'd have some meat, he mused.

"Well, I'm getting me some real food!" Ivan roared, hopping to his feet and hoisting his heavy axe. "And it'd be a lot easier on the deer, or whatever I'm findin', if ye'd use yer spells to hold the thing still so I can kill it clean."

Pikel crinkled his nose in disgust and stood tapping one foot, his arms crossed over his chest.

"Bah!" Ivan snorted at him, and he started away.

He stopped, seeing an elf perched on a branch before and above him, bow drawn back.

"Pikel," the dwarf said quietly, hardly moving, and hardly moving his lips. "Ye think ye might talk to this tree afore me?"

"Uh oh," came Pikel's response.

Ivan glanced back, to see his brother standing perfectly still, hands in the air in a sign of surrender, with several grim-faced elves all around him, their bows ready for the kill.

All the forest came alive around the brothers, elf forms slipping from every shadow, from behind every tree.

With a shrug, Ivan dropped his heavy axe over his shoulder and to the ground.

11

ON A FIELD
OF THEIR CHOOSING

They seemed nervous as they moved along the trail, a single giant among the horde, with the other three inexplicably missing.

Watching them from the boughs of an evergreen, concealed at a height just above the giant, Drizzt Do'Urden recognized that level of alertness clearly and knew that he and his friends would have to be even more precise. The giant was the key to it all, the drow recognized, and had explained as much to Dagnabbit and Bruenor when they were setting out the forces. With that belief firmly in hand, Drizzt had taken a bit of his own initiative, moving up ahead of the concealed dwarves. He was ready, with his formidable panther ally, to make what he hoped would be the decisive first strike.

The trail was clearly defined as it moved through the copse of trees in the small, sheltered dell. Drizzt held his breath and tightened against the trunk of the pine when the orcs wisely sent lead runners in to inspect the area. He was glad that he had convinced Bruenor and Dagnabbit to set the ambush just past that place.

The orc scouts milled about down below, slipping in and out of the shadows, kicking through leafy piles. A pair took up defensive positions, while another pair headed back out the way they had entered, signaling for the approach.

On came the caravan, marching easily and without too much

apparent concern.

The lead orcs passed below Drizzt's position. He looked across the trail, to Guenhwyvar, motioning for the cat to be calm, but be ready.

More and more orcs filtered below, then came the giant, walking alone and with a great scowl upon his face.

Drizzt set himself upon the branch he had specifically selected, drawing out his scimitars slowly and keeping them low, under the sides of his cloak so that their gleaming metal and magical glow would not give him away.

The giant marched through, one long stride after another, eyes straight ahead.

Drizzt leaped out, landing on the giant's huge shoulder, his scimitars slashing fast as he scrambled away, leaping off the other side and into the second pine as the giant reached up to grab at him. The drow ranger hadn't done much damage—he hadn't intended to—but he did turn the behemoth, just enough, and got its arms, eyes, and chin moving upward.

When Guenhwyvar leaped out the other way, she had an open path to the giant's throat, and there she lodged and dug in, tearing and biting.

The giant howled, or tried to, and snapped his huge hands onto the cat. Guenhwyvar didn't relent, digging deeper, biting harder, tearing and crushing the behemoth's windpipe, opening arteries.

Below, the orcs scrambled to get out of the way of stomping boots and breaking branches.

"What's it?" one orc yelled.

"A damned mountain cat!" another howled. "A great black one!"

The giant finally tugged stubborn Guenhwyvar free, not even realizing that he was taking a good portion of his own neck along with the cat. With another great effort, the giant brought the cat in close, under his huge arms, and began to crush her. Guenhwyvar gave a loud, pitiful wail.

Drizzt, wincing at the sound, dismissed her to her astral home. The giant folded a bit more tightly, the panther it had been squeezing turning to insubstantial mist.

The behemoth reached up to his neck, patting the spurting blood wildly, frantically. He stumbled to and fro, scattering terrified orcs, before finally staggering to his knees, then falling down, gasping, into the dirt.

"It kilt the cat!" one orc yelled. "Buried the damned thing right under it!"

A couple of orcs rushed to aid the giant, but the floundering, terrified behemoth slapped them aside. Scores of orcs had their attention squarely on the prone behemoth, wondering if it would rise again.

Which is why they didn't notice the stealthy dark elf, slipping down the tree and into position.

Which is why they didn't notice the dwarves moving in a bit closer, hammers ready to throw, melee weapons in easy reach.

There was much yelling, screaming, suggestions and pleas from the confused orcs, when finally one turned enough to see the force creeping in against them. Its eyes went wide, it lifted its finger to point, and it opened its mouth to cry out.

That yell became a communal thing, as a score or more dwarves joined in the chorus, running forward suddenly, launching their first missile barrage, then wading in, axes, hammers, swords, and picks going to fast and deadly work.

In the back, one orc tried to direct the response—until a scimitar slashed into its back and through a lung. Off to the side, another orc took up the lead—until an arrow split the air, knocking into a tree beside its head. More concerned with its own safety than with organizing against the dwarves, the would-be leader ducked, scrambled, and simply ran away.

Just when those orcs closest to the dwarves seemed to begin some semblance of a defense, in came Wulfgar, his warhammer swatting furiously, slapping aside orcs two at a time. He took a few stinging hits but didn't begin to slow, and he didn't begin to lessen his hearty song to Tempus, his god of battle.

Off to the side of the battle, Catti-brie was both pained and overjoyed. She kept taking up her bow and lowering it in frustration. Her battered fingers simply would not allow for enough accuracy for her to dare shooting anywhere near to her friends. That, plus the fact that she had no idea where Drizzt might be in that morass of scrambling, screaming orcs.

It pained her greatly to be out of the fight, but she saw that it was going as well as they could have hoped. They had taken the orcs completely off their guard, and the fierce dwarves would not begin to relent such an advantage.

Even more brilliant and inspiring to Catti-brie were the movements of Wulfgar. He strode with confidence, such ferocity, with a surety of his every deadly strike. This was not the man she had been engaged to, who became unsure, fearful, and protective. This was not the man who had walked away from them when they had set out to destroy the Crystal Shard.

This was the Wulfgar she had known in Icewind Dale, the man who had charged gladly beside Drizzt into the lair of Biggrin. This was the Wulfgar who had led the barbarian countercharge against the minions of Akar Kessell back in that frozen place. This was the son of Beornegar, returned to them, and fully so, from the clutches of Errtu.

Catti-brie could not hide her smile as she watched him wade among the enemies, for she somehow instinctively knew that no sword or club would harm him this day, that somehow he was above the rest of them. Aegis-fang tossed orcs aside as if they were mere children, mere inconveniences. One orc rushed behind a sapling, and so Wulfgar growled more loudly, shouted more loudly, and swung more powerfully, taking out the tree and the huddling creature behind it.

By the time Catti-brie managed to tear her stare away from the man, the fight was over, with the remaining orcs, still outnumbering the dwarves at least three to one, fleeing in every direction, many throwing down their weapons as they ran.

Bruenor and Dagnabbit moved their troops fast and sure, to cut off as many as possible, and Wulfgar paced all fleeing near him, chopping them down.

Off to the other side, Catti-brie saw one group of three rush into the trees, and she lifted her bow but was too late to catch them with an arrow.

The shadows within the group of trees deepened, engulfed in magical darkness, and the ensuing screams told her that Drizzt was in there and that he had that situation well in hand.

One orc did come rushing out, running right toward her, and she lifted Taulmaril to take it down.

But then it fell, suddenly and hard, tripped up by a lump that appeared on the ground before it, and Catti-brie merely shook her head and grinned when she saw the diminutive form of Regis unfold and rise up. The halfling darted forward and swung his mace once and again, then winced back from the crimson spray, a sour look upon his face. He looked up, noted Catti-brie, and just shrugged and melted back into the grass.

Catti-brie looked all around, her bow ready if needed, but she put it up and replaced the arrow in her magical, always-full quiver.

The short and brutal fight was done.

In all Faerûn there was no tougher race than the dwarves, and among the dwarves there were few to rival the toughness of Clan Battle-hammer—especially those who had survived the harshness of Icewind Dale—and so the battle was long over, and the dwarves had regrouped before several of them even realized that they had been injured in the battle.

Some of those wounds were deep and serious; at least two would have proven fatal if there had not been a pair of clerics along with the party to administer their healing spells, salves, and bandages.

Numbered among the wounded was Wulfgar, the proud and strong barbarian gashed in many places by orc weapons. He didn't complain any more than a reflexive grunt when one of the dwarves poured a stinging solution over the wounds to clean them.

"Are ye all right then?" Catti-brie asked the barbarian when she found him sitting stoically on a rock, waiting his turn with the overworked clerics.

"I took a few hits," he replied, matter-of-factly. "Nothing as hurtful as the chop Bruenor put on me when first we met, but. . . ."

He ended with a wide smile, and Catti-brie thought she'd never seen anything more beautiful than that in all her life.

Drizzt joined them then, nursing one hand.

"Clipped it on an orc's hilt," he explained, shaking it away.

"Where's Rumblebelly?" Catti-brie asked.

The drow nodded toward the place where Catti-brie had seen Regis trip up one orc.

"He won't end a fight without searching the bodies of the dead," Drizzt explained. "He says it's the principle of the thing."

They sat and talked for just a bit longer, before a louder argument off to the side drew their attention.

"Bruenor and Dagnabbit," Catti-brie remarked. "How am I guessin' what that's about?"

She and Drizzt rose to leave. Wulfgar didn't follow, and when they turned to question him, he waved them away.

"He's hurtin' a bit more than he's sayin'," Catti-brie remarked to Drizzt.

"But he could take a hundred times those wounds and still be standing," the drow assured her.

By the time they arrived, they had already discerned the cause of the argument, and it was exactly as Catti-brie had guessed.

"I'm heading for Mithral Hall when I'm telling ye I'm heading for Mithral Hall!" Bruenor roared, poking his finger hard into Dagnabbit's chest.

"We got wounded," Dagnabbit replied, staying strong to his unfortunate task of trying to protect the stubborn king.

Bruenor turned to Drizzt. "What're ye thinking?" he asked. "I'm sayin' we should move along from one town t' the next, all the way to Shallows. Wouldn't do to let 'em get run over without a warning."

"The orcs're dead and scattered," Dagnabbit put in, "and all their giant friends're lying dead too."

Drizzt wasn't sure he agreed with that assessment at all. The dress and cleanliness of the giants had told him that these were not rogues but were part of a larger clan. Still, he decided to keep that potentially devastating news to himself until he could gather more information.

"*These* orcs and *these* giants!" Bruenor bellowed before the drow could respond. "Might that there are more of 'em, running in packs all about!"

"Then all the more reason to go back, regroup, and get Pwent and his boys to join us," Dagnabbit replied.

"We take Pwent and his boys to Shallows and the last thing they'll be worryin' about're stupid orcs," Bruenor said.

Several around him, Drizzt included, caught on to the joke and appreciated the tension-breaking levity. Dagnabbit, his scowl as deep as ever, didn't seem to catch it.

"Well, ye're making more than a bit o' sense," Bruenor admitted a moment later. "The way I'm seein' it, we got a couple o' responsibilities here, and none I'm willing to ignore. We got to get our wounded back. We got to tell the folk o' the region about the danger and help 'em get prepared, and we got to get ourselves ready for fighting nearer to Mithral Hall."

Dagnabbit started to respond, but Bruenor stopped him with an upraised hand and continued on, "So let's send back a group with the wounded, and with orders to tell Pwent and his boys to lead a hunnerd to set up a base north o' Keeper's Dale. They can send another two hunnerd to block the low ground along the Surbrin north o' Mithral Hall. We'll make the rounds and work off that."

"A good plan, and I'm agreein'," said Dagnabbit.

"A good plan, and ye got no choice," Bruenor corrected.

"But . . ." Dagnabbit interjected, even as Bruenor turned to Drizzt and Catti-brie.

The dwarf king swung back to his commander.

"But ye're among them that's taking the wounded back to Mithral Hall," Dagnabbit demanded.

Drizzt was certain that he saw smoke coming out of Bruenor's ears at that remark and was almost as certain that he'd be spending the next few minutes pulling Bruenor off Dagnabbit's beard.

"Ye telling me to go and hide?" Bruenor asked, walking right up to the other dwarf, so that his nose was pressing against Dagnabbit's.

"I'm telling ye that it's me job to keep ye safe!"

"Who gived ye the job?"

"Gandalug."

"And where's Gandalug now?"

"Under a cairn o' rocks."

"And who's taking his place?"

"Yeah, that'd be yerself."

Bruenor assumed a bemused expression and posture, dropping his hands on his hips and smirking at Dagnabbit as if the ensuing logic should be perfectly obvious.

"Yeah, and Gandalug told me ye'd be saying this," Dagnabbit remarked, seeming defeated.

"And what'd he tell ye to tell me when I did?"

The other dwarf shrugged and said, "He just laughed at me."

Bruenor punched him on the shoulder. "Ye go and get things set up as I told ye," he ordered. "Leave us with fifteen, not countin' me boy and girl, the halfling, and the drow."

"We gotta send at least one priest back with the hurt ones."

Bruenor nodded. "But we'll keep th' other."

With that settled, Bruenor joined Catti-brie and Drizzt.

"Wulfgar's among them wounded," Catti-brie informed him.

She led him back to where Wulfgar was still sitting on the rock, tying a bandage tight about one thigh.

"Ye wantin' to go back with the group I'm sending?" Bruenor asked him, moving over to better inspect the many wounds.

"No more than you are," Wulfgar replied.

Bruenor smiled and let the issue drop.

Later on, eleven dwarves, seven of them wounded and one being carried on a makeshift stretcher, started off for the low ground to the south, and the trails that would take them home. Fifteen others, led by Bruenor, Tred, and Dagnabbit, and with Drizzt, Catti-brie, Regis, and Wulfgar running flank, moved off to the northeast.

12

SPIN

"If they did not run away, the day was ours," Urlgen insisted to his fuming father. "Gerti's giants fled like kobolds!"

King Obould furrowed his brow and kicked the face-down body of a dead orc, turning it half up then letting it drop back to the dirt, utter contempt on his ugly face.

"How many dwarfs?" he asked.

"An army!" Urlgen cried, waving his arms emphatically. "Hundreds and hundreds!"

To the side of the young commander, an orc screwed up his face in confusion and started to say something, but Urlgen fixed the stupefied creature with a wicked glare and the warrior snapped his mouth shut.

Obould watched it all knowingly, understanding his son's gross exaggeration.

"Hundreds and hundreds?" he echoed. "Then Gerti's missing three would have done you's no good, eh?"

Urlgen stammered over a reply, finally settling on the ridiculous proclamation that his forces were far superior, whatever the dwarves' numbers, and that an added trio of giants would have indeed turned his tactical evasion into a great and sweeping victory.

Obould took note that never once had his son, there or when Urlgen had first arrived in the cavern complex, mentioned the words "defeat" or "retreat."

"I am curious of your escape," the orc king remarked. "The battle was pitched?"

"It went on for long and long," Urlgen proclaimed.

"And still the dwarfs did not encircle? You's got away."

"We fought our way through!"

Obould nodded knowingly, understanding full well that Urlgen and his warriors had turned tail and fled, and likely against a much smaller force than his son was indicating—likely against a force that was not even numerically equal to their own. The orc king didn't dwell on that, though. He was more concerned with how he might lessen the disaster in terms of his tentative and all-important alliance with Gerti.

Despite his bravado and respect for his own forces—orc tribes that had thrown their allegiance to him—the cunning orc leader understood well that without Gerti, his gains in the region would always be restricted to the most desolate patches of the Savage Frontier. He would be doomed to repeat the fiasco of the Citadel of Many Arrows.

Obould also knew that Gerti wasn't going to be pleased to learn that one of her giants was dead, lying amid a field of slaughtered orcs. With that unsettling thought in mind, Obould made his way to the fallen giant, the behemoth showing few wounds other than the fact that his throat was almost completely torn away.

He looked over at Urlgen, his expression puzzled, and offered a prompting shrug.

"My scouts said it was a big cat," his son explained. "A big black cat. Jumped from that tree to the throat. Killed the giant. Giant killed it."

"Where is it?"

Urlgen's mouth twisted, his formidable fangs pinching into his lower lip. He looked around at the other orcs, all of whom immediately began turning questioning looks at their comrades.

"Dwarfs musta taken it. Probably wanting its skin."

Obould's expression showed little to indicate that he was convinced. He gave a sudden growl, kicked the dead giant hard, and stormed away, furrowing that prominent brow of his and trying hard to figure out how he might parlay this disaster into some sort of advantage over Gerti. Perhaps he could shift the blame to the three deserters, explaining that in the future her giants would have to be more forthcoming of their intentions to the orcs they accompanied on raids like this.

Yes, that might work, he mused, but then a cry came in from one of the many scouts they had sent out into the surrounding areas. That call soon led to a dramatic redirection of thinking for the frustrated and angry orc king.

Soon after, Obould furrowed his brow even more deeply as he looked over the second scene of battle, where three giants—the missing three giants, including one of Gerti's dear friends—lay slaughtered. They weren't far from where Urlgen had set his camp the night before the catastrophic battle, and it was obvious to Obould that the trio were missing from the march because they had been killed before that last march began. He knew it would be obvious to Gerti, who surely would investigate if he pushed the issue that the disaster was more the fault of her giants than his orcs.

"How did this happen?" he asked Urlgen.

When his son didn't immediately respond, the frustrated Obould spun around and punched him hard in the face, laying him low.

"Obould is frightened," Ad'non Kareese announced to his three co-conspirators.

Ad'non had followed Obould's forces to both battlegrounds and had met with the orc king soon after, counseling, as always, patience.

"He should be," said Kaer'lic Suun Wett, and the priestess gave a little cackle. "Gerti will roll him into a ball and kick him over the mountains."

Tos'un joined in the priestess's laughter, but neither Ad'non nor Donnia Soldou seemed overly amused.

"This could break the alliance," Donnia remarked.

Kaer'lic shrugged, as if that hardly mattered, and Donnia shot her an angry look.

"Would you be content to sit in our hole in boring luxury?" Donnia asked.

"There are worse fates."

"And there are better," Ad'non Kareese was quick to put in. "We have an opportunity here for great gain and great fun, and all at a minimal risk. I prefer to hold this course and this alliance."

"As do I," Donnia seconded.

Kaer'lic merely shrugged and seemed bored with it all, as if it did not matter.

"What about you?" Donnia asked Tos'un, who was sitting off to the side, obviously listening and obviously amused, but giving little indication beyond that.

"I think we would all do well to not underestimate the dwarves," the warrior from Menzoberranzan remarked. "My city made that mistake once."

"True enough," agreed Ad'non, "and I must tell you that Urlgen's report of the size of the dwarven force seemed greatly exaggerated, given the battleground. More likely, the dwarves were greatly outnumbered and still routed the orcs—and killed four giants besides. Their magic may have been no less formidable."

"Magic?" Kaer'lic asked. "Dwarves possess little magic, by all accounts."

"They had some here, as far as I can discern," Ad'non insisted. "The orcs spoke of a great cat that felled the giant, one that apparently disappeared after doing its murderous business."

Off to the side, Tos'un perked up. "A *black* cat?"

The other three looked at the Menzoberranyr refugee.

"Yes," Ad'non confirmed, and Tos'un nodded knowingly.

"Drizzt Do'Urden's cat," he explained.

"The renegade?" Kaer'lic asked, suddenly seeming quite interested.

"Yes, with a magical panther that he stole from Menzoberranzan. Very formidable."

"The panther?"

"Yes, and Drizzt Do'Urden," Tos'un explained. "He is no enemy to be taken lightly, and one who threatens not only the orcs and giants on the battleground, but those quietly behind the orcs and giants as well."

"Lovely," Kaer'lic said sarcastically.

"He was among the greatest of Melee-Magthere's graduates," Tos'un explained, "and further trained by Zaknafein, who was regarded as the greatest weapons master in all the city. If he was at that battle, it explains much about why the orcs were so readily defeated."

"This one drow can sway the tide of battle against a host of orcs and a foursome of giants?" Ad'non asked doubtfully.

"No," Tos'un admitted, "but if Drizzt was there, then so was—"

"King Bruenor," Donnia reasoned. "The renegade is Bruenor's closest friend and advisor, yes?"

"Yes," Tos'un confirmed. "Likely the pair had some other powerful friends with them."

"So Bruenor is out of Mithral Hall and roaming the frontier with a small force?" Donnia asked, a wry smile widening on her beautiful face. "How fine an opportunity is this?"

"To strike a wicked blow against Mithral Hall?" Ad'non asked, following the reasoning.

"And to keep Gerti interested in pursuing our present course," said Donnia.

"Or to show our hand too clearly and bring the wrath of powerful enemies upon us," said the ever-cynical Kaer'lic.

"Why priestess, I fear that you have grown too fond of luxury, and too forgetting of the pleasures of chaos," Ad'non said, his growing smile matching Donnia's. "Can you really so easily allow this opportunity for fun and profit pass you by?"

Kaer'lic started to respond several times but retreated from every reply before she ever voiced it.

"I find little pleasure in dealing with the smelly orcs," the priestess said, "or with Gerti and her band, who think they are so positively superior, even to us. More pleasure would I find if we turned Obould against Gerti and let the giants and the orcs slaughter each other. Then we four could quietly kill all those left alive."

"And we would be alone up here, in abject boredom," said Ad'non.

"True enough," Kaer'lic admitted. "So be it. Let us fester this war between the dwarves and our allies. With King Bruenor out of his hole, we may indeed find an interesting course before us, but with all caution! I did not leave the Underdark to fall victim to a dwarven axe, or to the blade of a drow traitor."

The others nodded, sharing the sentiment, particularly Tos'un, who had seen so many of his fellows fall before the armies of Mithral Hall.

"I will go to Gerti and soften the blow of this present disaster," Donnia said.

"And I back to Obould," said Ad'non. "I will wait for your signal before sending the orc king to speak with the giantess."

They departed at once, eagerly, leaving Kaer'lic alone with Tos'un.

"We are winding our way into a deep chasm," the priestess observed. "If our allies betray us at the end of a dwarven spear, then our flight will by necessity be long and swift."

Tos'un nodded. He had been there once before.

Obould's every step was forced as he made his way through the caverns of Gerti's complex, very conscious of the many scowls the frost giant sentries were throwing his way. Despite Ad'non's assurances, Obould knew that the giants had been told of their losses. These creatures weren't like his own race, the orc king understood. They valued every one of their clan, every one of their kind. The frost giants would not easily dismiss the deaths of four of their kin.

When the orc king walked into Gerti's chamber, he found the giantess sitting on her stone throne, one elbow on her knee, her delicate chin in her hand, her blue eyes staring straight ahead, unblinking.

The orc walked up, stopping out of the giant's reach, fearing that Gerti would snap her hand out and throttle him. He resisted the urge to speak out about the disaster and decided that he would be better off waiting for Gerti to start the conversation.

He waited for a long, long while.

"Where are their bodies?" Gerti finally asked.

"Where they fell."

Gerti looked up at him, her eyes going even wider, as if her rage was boiling over behind them.

"My warriors can not begin to carry them," Obould quickly explained. "I will have them buried in cairns where they fell, if you desire. I thought you would wish to bring them back here."

That explanation seemed to calm Gerti considerably. She even rested back in her seat and nodded her chin at him as he finished his explanation.

"You will have your warriors lead my chosen to them."

"Course I will," said Obould.

"I was told that it is possible your son's rash actions may have brought powerful enemies upon the band," Gerti remarked.

Obould shrugged. "It is possible. I was not there."

"Your son survived?"

Obould nodded.

"He fled the fight, along with many of your kin."

There was no mistaking the accusatory edge that had come into Gerti's voice.

"They had only one of your kin with them when the battle was joined, and that giant went down fast," Obould was quick to reply, knowing that he could not let Gerti go down this road with him if he wanted to get out of that place with his head still on his shoulders. "The other three wandered off the night before without telling anyone."

From Gerti's expression, the orc recognized that he had parsed those words correctly, rightly redistributing the blame for the disaster without openly accusing the giants of any failings.

"Do we know where the dwarves went after the fight?"

"We know they did not head straight out for Mithral Hall," Obould explained. "My scouts have found no sign of their march to the south or east."

"They are still in our mountains?"

"I'm thinking that, yeah," said the orc.

"Then find them!" Gerti demanded. "I have a score to settle, and I always make it a point to pay my enemies back in full."

Obould fought the desire to let a grin widen on his face, understanding that Gerti needed this to remain solemn and serious. Still, containing the excitement building within him was no easy task. He could see from Gerti's eyes and could tell from the tone of her voice that this defeat would not hold for long, that she and her giants would become even more committed to the fight.

King Obould wondered if his dwarf counterpart had any idea of the catastrophe that was about to drop on him.

13

THERE, I SAID IT . . .

A slight shift of Torgar's head sent the heavy fist sailing past, and the dwarf wasted no time in turning around and biting the attacker hard on the forearm. His opponent, another dwarf, waved that bitten arm frantically while punching hard with the other, but tough Torgar accepted the beating and bit down harder, driving in close to lessen the impact of the blows.

Pushing, twisting, and driving on with his powerful legs, Torgar took his opponent right over a table and chair. The two of them crashed down hard, wood splintering around them.

They weren't the only dwarves in the tavern who were fighting. Fists and bottles flew wildly, foreheads pounded against foreheads, and more than one table or chair went up in the air, to come crashing down on an opponent's head.

The brawl went on and on, and the poor barkeep, Toivo Foamblower, gave up in frustration, falling back against the wall and crossing his thick forearms over his chest. His expression ranged from bemused to resigned, and he didn't get overly concerned for the damage to his establishment because he knew that the dwarves involved would be quick with reparations.

They always were when it came to taverns.

One by one the combatants left the bar, usually at the end of a foot or headfirst through the long-since shattered windows.

Toivo's grin grew as the crowd thinned to see that the one who had started it all, Torgar Hammerstriker, was still in the thick of it. That had been Toivo's prediction from the beginning. Tough Torgar almost never lost a bar brawl when the odds weren't overwhelming, and he never ever lost when Shingles was fighting beside him.

Though not as quick as some others with his fists, the surly old Shingles knew how to wage a battle, knew how to keep his enemies off their guard. Toivo laughed aloud when one raging dwarf charged up to Shingles, raised bottle in hand.

Shingles held up one finger and put on an incredulous look that gave the attacker pause. Shingles then pointed at the upraised bottle and wagged his finger when the attacker saw that there were still some traces of beer inside.

Shingles motioned for the dwarf to pause and finish the drink. When he did, Shingles brought out his own full bottle, moved as if to take a deep swallow, then smashed it into his attacker's face, following it with a fist that laid the dwarf low.

"Well, throw 'em all out, then!" Toivo yelled at Torgar, Shingles, and a pair of others when the fight at last ended.

The four moved about, lifting semi-conscious dwarves, ally and enemy alike, and unceremoniously tossing them out the broken door.

The four remaining combatants started to make their way out then, but Toivo called to Torgar and Shingles and motioned them back to the bar where he was already setting up drinks.

"A reward for the show?" Torgar asked through fat lips.

"Ye're paying for the drinks and for a lot more than that," Toivo assured him. "Ye durned fool. Ye thinkin' to start trouble all across the city?"

"I ain't starting no trouble. I'm just sharing the trouble I'm seein'!"

"Bah!" the barkeep snorted, wiping a pile of broken glass from the bar. "What kind o' greetings did ye think Bruenor'd be getting from Mirabar? His hall's killin' our business."

"Because they're better'n us!" Torgar cried. He stopped short and brought a hand up to his stinging lips. "They're making the better armor and the better weapons," he said, more in control, and with a bit of a lisp.

"The way to beat 'em is to make our own works better or to find new places to sell. The way to beat 'em is—"

"I'm not arguing yer point and not agreeing with ye, neither," Toivo interrupted, "but ye been running about shouting yer grief all over town. Ye durned fool, can ye be expectin' any less than ye're getting? Are ye thinking to raise all the dwarfs against the marchion and the council? Ye looking to start a war in Mirabar?"

"Course not."

"Then shut yer stupid mouth!" Toivo scolded. "Ye come in here tonight and start spoutin' yer anger. Ye durned fool! Ye know that half the dwarfs in here are watching their gold chests withering, and knowing well that the biggest reason for that's the reopening o' Mithral Hall. Are ye not to know that yer words aren't finding open ears?"

Torgar gave a dismissive wave and bent low to his drink, physically closing up as a reflection of his impotence against Toivo's astute observation.

"He's got a point," said Shingles beside him, and Torgar shot him a glare.

"I ain't tired o' the fighting," Shingles was quick to add. "It's just that we wasted a lot o' good brew tonight, and that can't be a good thing."

"They got me riled, is all," Torgar said, his tone suddenly contrite and a bit defeated. "Bruenor ain't no enemy, and making him one instead o' honestly trying to beat him and his Mithral Hall boys is a fool's road."

"And yerself ain't never been fond o' the folks up top. Not the marchion or the four fools that follow him about, scowling like they was some great warriors," Toivo said with more than a bit of sympathy. "Ain't that the truth?"

"If Mithral Hall was a human town, ye think the marchion and his boys would be so damned determined to beat 'em?"

"I do," Toivo answered without hesitation. "I just think Torgar Hammerstriker wouldn't care so much."

Torgar dropped his head to his arms, folded on the bar. There was truth in that, he had to admit. Somewhere deep inside him was the understanding that Bruenor and the boys from Mithral Hall were kin of the blood. They had all come from the Delzoun Clan, way back beyond the memories of the oldest dwarves. Mithral Hall, Mirabar, Felbarr . . . they were all connected by history and by blood, dwarf to dwarf. On a very basic level, it galled Torgar to think that petty arguments and commerce would come between that all-important bond.

Besides, given the evening he had spent with the visitors from Mithral Hall, Torgar had found that he honestly liked them.

"Well, I'm hopin' ye'll stop shouting so we can stop the fighting," Shingles said at length. He nudged Torgar, and gave the ringleader a wink when he looked up. "Or at least slow it down a bit. I'm not a young one anymore. This is gonna hurt in the mornin'!"

Toivo patted Torgar on the shoulder and walked off to begin his clean-up.

Torgar just lay there, head down on the bar all the night long. Thinking.

And wondering, to his own surprise, if the time was coming for him to leave Mirabar.

"Hope th' elf don't catch 'em and kill 'em tonight," Bruenor grumbled. "He'll take all the fun."

Dagnabbit fixed his king with a curious stare, trying hard to read the unreadable. There had only been a pair of tracks, after all, a couple of unfortunate orcs running scared from the rout. The last few days had been the same, chasing small groups, often just one or two, along this mountain trail or that. As Bruenor was complaining, more often than not, Drizzt, Catti-brie, Wulfgar, and Regis had come upon the fleeing creatures first and had them long dead before the main band ever caught up.

"Not many left for catching," Dagnabbit offered.

"Bah!" the dwarf king snorted, placing his empty bowl of stew on the ground beside him. "More'n half the hunnerd runned off and we ain't catched a dozen!"

"But every day's sending them that's left into deep holes. We ain't to chase 'em in there."

"Why ain't we?"

The simple question was quite revealing, of course, for Bruenor said it with a raging fire behind his fierce eyes, an eagerness that could not be denied.

"Why're ye out here, me king?" Dagnabbit quietly asked. "Yer dark elf friend and his little band can be doin' all that's left to be done, and ye're knowing it, too!"

"We got Shallows to get to and warn, along with th' other towns."

"Another task that Drizzt'd be better at, and quicker at, without us."

"Nah, the folk'd chase off the damned elf if he tried to warn 'em."

Dagnabbit shook his head. "Most about are knowing Drizzt Do'Urden, and if not, he'd just send Catti-brie, Wulfgar, or the little one in to warn 'em. Ye know the raiding band's no more, though more'n half did run off. Ye know they're scattering, running for deep holes, and won't be threatening anyone anytime soon."

"Ye're figuring that the raiding band's all there was," Bruenor argued.

"If there's more than that, then all the more reason for yerself to be back in Mithral Hall," said Dagnabbit, "and ye're knowin' that, too. So why're ye here, me king? Why're ye really here?"

Bruenor settled himself squarely on the log he had taken as a seat and fixed Dagnabbit with a serious and determined stare.

"Would ye rather be out here, with the wind in yer beard and yer axe in yer hands, with an orc afore ye to chop down, or would ye rather be in Mithral Hall, speakin' to the pretty emissaries from Silverymoon or Sundabar, or arguin' with some Mirabarran merchant about tradin' rights? Which would ye rather be doin', Dagnabbit?"

The other dwarf swallowed hard at the unexpected and direct question. There was a political answer to be made, of course, but one that Bruenor knew, and Dagnabbit knew, would ultimately be a lie.

"I'd be beside me king, because that's what I'm to do . . ." the young dwarf started to dodge, but Bruenor was hearing none of it.

"*Rather*, I asked ye. Which would ye rather? Ain't ye got no preferences?"

"My duty—"

"I ain't askin' for yer duty!" Bruenor dismissed him with a wave of his hand. "When ye're wanting to talk honestly, then ye come talk to me again," he blustered. "Until then, go and fetch me another bowl o' fresher stew, cuz this pot's all crusty. Do yer duty, ye danged golem!"

Bruenor lifted his empty bowl and presented it to Dagnabbit, and the younger dwarf, after a short pause, did take it. He didn't get up immediately, though.

"I'd rather be out here," Dagnabbit admitted. "And I'd take a fight with an orc over a day at the forge."

Bruenor's smile erupted beneath his flaming red beard.

"Then why're ye asking me what ye're asking me?" he asked. "Are ye thinkin' that I'm not akin to yerself? Just because I'm the king don't make me wanting any different from any other Battlehammer."

"Ye're fearing to go home," Dagnabbit dared to say. "Ye're looking at it as the end o' yer road."

Bruenor sat back and shrugged, then noticed a pair of purple eyes staring at him from the brush to the side.

"And I'm still thinking that I'm wanting more stew," he said.

Dagnabbit stared at him hard for a few moments, chewing his lip and nodding.

"I'm hoping that the durned elf don't kill 'em all tonight meself," he said with a grin, and he rose to leave.

As soon as Dagnabbit had walked off, Drizzt Do'Urden moved out of the brush and took a seat at Bruenor's side.

"Already dead, ain't they?" Bruenor asked.

"Catti-brie is a fine shot," the drow answered.

"Well, go and find some more."

"There will always be more," the drow replied. "We could spend all our lives hunting orcs in these mountains." He held a sly look over Bruenor until the dwarf looked back at him. "But you know that, of course."

"First Dagnabbit and now yerself?" Bruenor asked. "What're ye wantin' me to say, elf?"

"What's in your heart. Nothing more. When first we started on the road, you went with great anticipation, and a skip in your determined stride. You were seeing Gauntlgrym then, or at least the promise of a grand adventure, the grandest of them all."

"Still am."

"No," Drizzt observed. "Our encounter in Fell Pass showed you the trouble your plans would soon enough encounter. You know that once you get back to Mithral Hall, you'll have a hard time leaving again. You know they will try to keep you there."

"Few guesses, elf?" Bruenor said with a wave of his hand. "Or are ye just thinkin' ye know more than ye know?"

"Not a guess, but an observation," Drizzt replied. "Every step of the way out of Icewind Dale has been heavier than the previous one for Bruenor Battlehammer—every step except those that temporarily turn us aside from our destination, like the journey to Mirabar and this chase through the mountains."

Bruenor leaned forward and grabbed Dagnabbit's empty bowl. He gave it a shake, dunked it in the nearly-empty stew pot, then brought it in and licked the thick broth from his stubby fingers.

"Course, in Mithral Hall I might be getting me stew served to me in fine bowls, on fine platters, and with fine napkins."

"And you never liked napkins."

Bruenor shrugged, his expression showing Drizzt that he was certainly catching on.

"Appoint a steward, then, and at once upon your return," the drow offered. "Be a king on the road, expanding the influence of his people, and searching for an even more ancient and greater lost kingdom. Mithral Hall can run itself. If you did not believe that, you never would have gone to Icewind Dale in the first place."

"It's not so easy."

"You are the king. You define what a king is. This duty will trap you, and that is your fear, but it will only do so if you allow yourself to be trapped by it. In the end, Bruenor Battlehammer alone decides the fate of Bruenor Battlehammer."

"I'm thinkin' ye're making it a bit too easy there, elf," the dwarf replied, "but I'm not saying ye're wrong."

He ended with a sigh, and drowned it in a huge gulp of hot stew.

"Do you know what you want?" Drizzt asked. "Or are you a bit confused, my friend?"

"Do ye remember when we first went huntin' for Mithral Hall?" Bruenor asked. "Remember me trickin' ye by makin' ye think I was on me dyin' bed?"

Drizzt gave a little laugh—it was a scene he would never forget. They, leading the folk of Ten-Towns, had just won victory over the minions of Akar Kessell, who possessed the Crystal Shard. Drizzt had been taken in to Bruenor, who seemed on his deathbed—but only so that he could trick the drow into agreeing to help him find Mithral Hall.

"I did not need much convincing," Drizzt admitted.

"I thinked two things when we found the place, ye know," said Bruenor. "Oh, me heart was pumping, I tell ye! To see me home again . . . to avenge me ancestors. I'm tellin' ye, elf, riding that dragon down to the darkness was the greatest single moment o' me life, though I was thinkin' it was the last moment o' me life when it was happening!"

Drizzt nodded and knew what was coming.

"And what else were you thinking when we found Mithral Hall?" he prompted, because he knew that Bruenor had to say this out loud, had to admit it openly.

"Thrilled, I was, I tell ye truly! But there was something else . . ." He shook his head and sighed again. "When we got back from the southland and me clan retook our home, a bit o' sadness found me heart."

"Because you came to realize that it was the adventure and the road more than the goal."

"Ye're knowin' it, too!" Bruenor blurted.

"Why do you think that I, and Catti-brie, were quick to leave Mithral Hall after the drow war? We are all alike, I fear, and it will likely be the end of us all."

"But what a way to go, eh elf?"

Drizzt gave a laugh, and Bruenor was fast to join in, and it seemed to Drizzt as if a great weight had been lifted off the dwarf's shoulders. But the chuckling from Bruenor stopped abruptly, a serious expression clouding his face.

"What o' me girl?" he asked. "What're ye to do if she gets herself killed on the road? How're ye not to be blaming yerself forever more?"

"It is something that I have thought of often," Drizzt admitted.

"Ye seen what it done to Wulfgar," said Bruenor. "Made him forget his place and spend all his time looking out for her."

"And that was his mistake."

"So, ye're saying ye don't care?"

Drizzt laughed aloud.

"Do not lead me to places I did not intend to go," he retorted. "I care—of course I do—but you tell me this, Bruenor Battlehammer, is there anyone in all the world who loves Catti-brie, or Wulfgar, more than yourself? Will you then put them in Mithral Hall and hold them safely there?

"Of course you would not," Drizzt continued. "You trust in her and let her run. You let her fight and have watched her get hurt—only recently. Not much of a father, if you ask me."

"Who asked ye?"

"Well, if you did . . ."

"If I did and ye told me that, I'd kick ye in yer skinny elf arse!"

"If you did and I told you that, you'd kick empty air and wonder why a hundred blows were raining upon your thick head."

Bruenor scoffed and tossed his bowl to the ground, then pulled off his one-horned helm and began rapping hard on his head.

"Bah! Ye'd need more'n a hunnerd to get through this skull, elf!"

Drizzt smiled and didn't disagree.

Dagnabbit returned then to find his king in a fine mood. The younger dwarf looked at Drizzt, but the drow merely nodded and grinned all the wider.

"If we're wantin' to make Shallows in two days, we gotta set straight out," Dagnabbit remarked. "No more chasin' orcs after this group's dead."

"Then no more chasing orcs," said Drizzt.

Dagnabbit nodded, seeming neither surprised nor upset.

"Rushing me home, still," Bruenor said with a shake of his head, broth flying from his wild beard. He brought a hand up and wiped the beard down.

"Or we might be using Shallows as the front base," Dagnabbit offered. "Put a link line to Pwent an' his boys at both camps outside o' Mithral Hall, and spend the summer runnin' the mountains near to Shallows. The folks'll appreciate that, I'm thinking."

A look of astonishment melted into a smile on Bruenor's face.

"And I'm liking the way ye're thinking!" he said as he took the bowl for his third helping. "Making sure there's not too much for Rumblebelly when he gets in," Bruenor offered between gulps. "Can't let him get too fat again if we're walkin' mountain roads, now can we?"

Drizzt settled back comfortably and was quite pleased for his dwarf friend. It was one thing to know your heart, another thing to admit it.

And something altogether different to allow yourself to follow it.

Torgar walked his post on Mirabar's northern wall, a slight limp in his stride from a swollen knee he had suffered in the previous night's escapade. The wind was up strong this day, blowing sand all about the dwarf, but it was warm enough so that Torgar had loosened his heavy breastplate.

He was well aware of the many looks, scowls mostly, coming at him from the other sentries. His actions with Bruenor had resulted in downward spiral, with arguments growing across the city and with many fists being raised. Torgar was tired of it all. All he wanted was to be left alone to his duties, to walk the wall without conversation, without trouble.

When he noted the approach of a well-groomed dwarf wearing bright robes, he knew he wouldn't get his wish.

"Torgar Hammerstriker!" Councilor Agrathan Hardhammer called.

He moved to the base of the ladder leading to the parapet, hiked up his robes and began to climb.

Torgar kept walking the other way, looking out over the wall and feigning ignorance, but when Agrathan called again, more loudly, he realized that to delay would only bring him more frustration.

He paused and leaned his strong, bruised hands on the wall, staring out to the empty, open land.

Agrathan moved up beside him, and similarly leaned on the wall.

"Another battle last night," the councilor stated.

"When they're askin' for a fist, they're getting a fist," Torgar replied.

"And how many are ye to fight?"

"How many're needin' a good kick?"

He looked at Agrathan, and saw that the councilor was not amused.

"Yer actions're tearing Mirabar apart. Is that what ye're looking to do?"

"I'm not looking to do anything," Torgar insisted, and honestly. He turned to Agrathan, his eyes narrowing. "If me speaking me mind's doing what ye say, then the problem's been there afore I speaked it."

Agrathan settled more comfortably against the wall and seemed to relax, as if he was not disagreeing.

"Many of us have been shaking our heads at the Mithral Hall problem. Ye know that. We're all wishin' that our biggest rivals weren't Battlehammer dwarves! But they are. That's the way of it, and ye know it, and if ye keep pressing that point into everyone's nose, ye're to bend those noses out of shape."

"The rivalry and the arguin' are as much our own fault as the Battlehammers'," Torgar reminded. "Might that a deal benefiting us both could be fashioned, but how're we to know unless someone tries?"

"Yer words aren't without merit," the councilor agreed. "It's been suggested and talked about at the Sparkling Stones."

"Where most o' the councilors ain't dwarfs," Torgar remarked, and Agrathan fixed him with a cold stare.

"The dwarves are spoken for, and their thoughts are heard at council."

Torgar knew from the dwarf's look and icy tone that he had hit a nerve with Agrathan, a proud and long-serving councilor. He thought for a moment to take back his bold and callous statement, or at least to exclude his present company, but he didn't. He felt as if he was being carried away by an inner voice that was growing independent of his common sense.

"When ye joined the Axe of Mirabar, you took an oath," Agrathan said. "Are ye remembering that oath, Torgar Hammerstriker?"

Now it was Torgar's turn to issue a cold stare.

"The oath was to serve the Marchion of Mirabar, not the King of Mithral Hall. Ye might be wise to think on that a bit."

The councilor patted Torgar on the shoulder—many seemed to be doing that lately—and took his leave.

Torgar remembered his oath and weighed that oath against the realities of present day Mirabar.

14

THEY THOUGHT THEY HAD SEEN IT ALL

"Well, ain't this a keg o' beer in a commode," Ivan grumbled.

He was moving around the small lea that the elves were using as a temporary prison for the two intruders. Using some magic that Ivan did not understand, the moon elves had coaxed the trees around the lea in close together, blocking all exits with a nearly solid wall of trunks.

Ivan, of course, was none too happy with that. Pikel reclined in the middle of the field, hands tucked comfortably behind his head as he lay on his back, staring up at the stars. His sandals were off and the contented dwarf waggled his stubby toes happily.

"If they hadn't taked me axe, I'd be making a trail or ten!" Ivan blustered.

Pikel giggled and waggled his toes.

"Shut yer mouth," Ivan fumed, standing with hands on hips and staring defiantly at the tree wall.

He blinked a moment later and rubbed his eyes in disbelief as one of the trees drifted aside, leaving a clear path beyond. Ivan paused, expecting the elves to enter through the breach, but the moments slipped past with no sign the their captors. The dwarf hopped about, started for the break, then skidded to a stop and swung around when he heard his brother giggling.

"Ye did that," Ivan accused.

"Hee hee hee."

"Well if ye could do that, then why've we been sitting here for two days?"

Pikel propped himself on his elbows and shrugged.

"Let's go!"

"Uh uh," said Pikel.

Ivan stared at him incredulously. "Why not?"

Pikel hopped to his feet and jumped all around, putting a finger to pursed lips and saying "*Shhhhh!*"

"Who ye shushing?" Ivan asked, his expression going from angry to confused. "Ye're talking to the damned trees," he realized.

Pikel looked at him and shrugged.

"Ye're meaning that the damned trees'll tell the damned elfs if we walk outta here?"

Pikel nodded enthusiastically.

"Well, shut 'em up!"

Pikel shrugged helplessly.

"Ye can move 'em, and ye can walk through 'em, but ye can't shut 'em up?"

Pikel shrugged again.

Ivan stomped a boot hard on the ground. "Well, let 'em tell the elfs! And let them elfs try to catch me!"

Pikel put his hands on his hips and cocked his head to the side, his expression doubtful.

"Yeah, yeah," Ivan called to him, waving his hand and not wanting to hear any of it.

Of course he had no weapon. Of course he had no armor. Of course he had no idea of where he was or of how to get out of there. Of course he wouldn't likely get fifty feet into the forest before being recaptured, probably painfully.

But none of that really mattered to the outraged dwarf. He just wanted to do something, do *anything*, to stick his finger in the eyes of his captors. That was the way of dwarves, after all, and of Ivan beyond the norm for his taciturn race. It was better to head-butt your enemy, even if he was wearing a full-faced plated helmet, even if it was spiked, than to stand helplessly before him.

Determined, Ivan strode through the Pikel-made gap and down the forest trail.

Pikel sighed and moved to retrieve his sandals. Hearing a commotion beyond the lea, he merely shrugged yet again and fell back to the grass and stared up at the stars. Perfectly content.

"Never would I have believed that a dwarf could move a tree without using an axe," Innovindil remarked.

She stood at Tarathiel's side, on a low branch overlooking the lea, observing the brothers.

"He truly is possessed of druidic magic," Tarathiel agreed. "How is that possible?"

Innovindil giggled. "Perhaps the dwarves are moving to a higher state of consciousness, though it is hard to believe when you consider that one as the source."

Looking at Pikel and his waggling toes, Tarathiel found it hard to disagree with the last part of her statement.

The pair watched silently as Ivan stormed out of the meadow then patiently waited the few minutes it took for the struggling dwarf to be reunited forcibly with his brother, a trio of elves dragging him back.

"This could get dangerous," Innovindil remarked.

"We still can't be sure of their intentions," Tarathiel replied.

She had been pushing him all day to resolve the issue with the dwarves, leaning heavily in favor of escorting them to the edges of the Moonwood and letting them go.

"Then test him," Innovindil said, her tone showing that she had just found a revelation. "If he is a druid, as he seems, then there is one way to prove it. Let Pikel Bouldershoulder find his judge at Montolio's grove."

Tarathiel stroked his thin chin, a smile growing as he considered the words. Perhaps Innovindil was on to something, which really didn't surprise Tarathiel when he thought about it. Ever had Innovindil been the farsighted one, finding roads out of the darkest dilemmas.

He looked to her appreciatively, but she was eyeing the field, concern growing on her fair face. She nodded his way and bade him to follow, then hopped down from the branch and moved onto the field, where it looked like the confrontation between the yellow-bearded Bouldershoulder and the three elves might be about to explode.

"Hold fast, Ivan Bouldershoulder," she called, and the attention of all five turned to her. "Your ire is not justified."

"Bah!" the dwarf snorted, so predictably. "Ye're locking me in, elf? How'd ya think I'd take it?"

"And I am certain that if one of us went into your homeland, he would find himself welcomed with open arms," came the sarcastic reply.

"Probably would," Ivan retorted, offering a snort at Pikel, who merely giggled. "Cadderly's always been a soft one, even for a human!"

"Your *dwarven* homeland," the quick-on-her-feet Innovindil clarified.

"Nah," Ivan had to agree, "but why would an elf want to go there?"

"Why would a pair of dwarves walk out of a tree?" came the reply.

Ivan started to argue, but realized the futility of that.

"Point for yourself," he agreed.

"And how does a dwarf coax a tree to move aside?" the elf asked, looking at Pikel.

"Doo-dad," came the giggling response, with Pikel poking his thumb into his chest.

"Well, that is a common sight," Tarathiel said sarcastically.

"Nothing common about that one," Ivan agreed.

"So please excuse our confusion," said Innovindil. "We do not wish to hold you captive, Ivan Bouldershoulder, but neither can we readily dismiss you and your curious brother. You must appreciate that you have intruded into our home, and the security of that home remains above all else."

"I'll give ye that point, too," the dwarf replied, "but ye gotta be appreciatin' that I got better things to do than sit here and watch the stars. Damned things don't even move!"

"Oh, but they do," Innovindil enthusiastically replied, thinking she may have found a commonality, a way to thin the ice, if not break it all together.

Her hopes only grew when Pikel hopped up and gave an assenting squeal.

"Some do, at least," the elf explained.

She moved closer to Ivan and pointed to one particularly bright star, low on the horizon, just above the tree line. She continued for just a moment, until she took the time to look at Ivan and see him staring at her incredulously, hands on his hips.

"I think ye're missin' me point," he said dryly.

"True enough," the elf admitted.

"It ain't like we ain't been with elfs afore," Ivan explained. "Fought aside a whole flock o' them in Shilmista Forest, chasing off the orcs and goblins. They was glad for me and me brother!"

"Me brudder!" Pikel agreed.

"And perhaps we will come to be, as well," said Innovindil. "In truth, I predict exactly that, but I beg your patience. This is too important for us to make any hasty choices."

"Well, ain't that like an elf," Ivan replied with a resigned, but clearly accepting, sigh. "Seen one in Carradoon, gone to market to buy some wine. Took her time, she did, moving front to back and back to front across the winery, then course she bought the first bottle she'd seen."

"And that elf enjoyed the experience of the purchase, as we wish to enjoy the experience of learning about Ivan and Pikel Bouldershoulder," Innovindil explained.

"Ye'd be learning more if ye'd let us off this stupid field."

"Perhaps, and perhaps soon."

As she finished Innovindil glanced at Tarathiel, who obviously wasn't sharing her generous thoughts. She gave him a hard nudge in the ribs.

"We shall see," was all that he would admit, and that grimly.

Thibbledorf Pwent kicked a stone, launching it many feet through the air.

"Bruenor's expecting better of ye," scolded Cordio Muffinhead, the cleric who had accompanied the wounded back to Mithral Hall.

They had found Pwent and the Gutbuster Brigade camped along the high ground north of Keeper's Dale, the battlerager having gone back out after escorting the main force into Mithral Hall.

What a sight that meeting had been, with Cordio and the others waving frantically to slow down the insane charge of Pwent and his boys. The relief had been palpable when Cordio had at last been able to explain that Bruenor and the others were fine and were moving along a different and roundabout course on their way back to Mithral Hall, checking in with the various settlements, as a good king must now and again.

"If he's knowin' me at all, then he should be knowin' that I'm about to set off to find the fool!" Pwent argued.

"He's knowing that ye're a loyal warrior, who's to do what ye're told to do!" Cordio yelled back at him.

Pwent hopped aside and did a three-step to another stone, kicking it with all his strength. This one was much larger, though, and not quite detached from the ground, and so it hardly moved. Pwent did well to hide his newly-acquired limp.

"Ye got two camps to organize," Cordio said sternly. "Quit breakin' yer toes and get yer runners to Mithral Hall. Ye build a camp here and get one set up on the Surbrin, north o' the mines."

Pwent spat and grumbled, but he nodded and went to work, barking orders that sent the Gutbusters scrambling. That same day, what had been a casual camp awaiting Bruenor's return was transformed into a small fortress with walls of piled stones, perched on the north side of a mountain north of Keeper's Dale.

The next morning, two hundred warriors left Mithral Hall, heading north to join up with the Gutbusters, while at the same time a hundred and fifty warriors moved out of Mithral Hall's eastern gate and marched north along the banks of the Surbrin, laden with supplies for constructing the second forward outpost.

Thibbledorf Pwent immediately set his Gutbusters into a liaison mode, working the direct trails between the two camps.

It tormented Pwent to stay so far south and wait, but he did his job, though he continually sent scouting parties to the north and northeast, searching for some sign of his beloved, and absent, king. It remained foremost in his thoughts that Bruenor wouldn't have ordered the establishment of advanced camps unless he believed they might be needed.

That only made the waiting all the more unsettling.

───────── ✦ ─────────

"He truly is a druid?" Tarathiel asked, hardly believing his ears as a pair of his clan reported the news to him that Pikel's spells were not some trick, that the dwarf did indeed seem to have druidic magic about him.

Beside him, Innovindil could hardly contain her grin. She was truly enjoying these unexpected guests, and indeed, she had been spending quite a bit of time with Ivan, the surly one, who was about as perfectly dwarflike as any dwarf she had ever seen. She and Ivan had swapped many fine tales over the past few days, and though he remained a prisoner it was fairly obvious that Innovindil's contact with Ivan had brightened his mood and lessened the trouble he was causing.

Still, Tarathiel thought her a fool for bothering.

"He prays, sincerely so, to Mielikki," said one of the observers, "and there can be no doubt of his magical abilities, many of which could not be replicated by any cleric of a dwarf god."

"It makes little sense," Tarathiel remarked.

"Pikel Bouldershoulder makes little sense," said the other, "but he is what he appears to be, by all that we can discern. He is a woodland priest, a 'Doo-dad,' as he himself puts it."

"How powerful is his magic?" asked Tarathiel, who had always held druids in great respect.

The two observers looked at each other, their expressions showing clearly that this was a question they had feared.

"It is difficult to discern," said the first. "Pikel's magic is . . . sporadic."

Tarathiel looked at him curiously.

"He seems to throw it as he needs it," the other tried to explain. "Minor dweomers, mostly, though every now and again he seems possessed of a quite potent spell, one that would only be expected of a high-ranking druid, their equivalent of a high priest."

"It seems almost as if he has caught the goddess's fancy," said the first. "As if Mielikki, or one of her minions, has taken a direct interest in him and is watching over him."

Tarathiel paused a moment to digest the information, then said, "You still have not answered my question."

"He is no more dangerous than his brother, certainly," the first replied. "Surely no threat to us or to the Moonwood."

"You are certain?"

"We are," answered the second.

"Perhaps it is time for you to speak with the dwarves," Innovindil offered.

Tarathiel paused again, thinking. "Do you think Sunrise will bear him?" he asked.

"To Montolio's grove?"

Tarathiel nodded. "Let us see if the image of Mielikki's symbol will look kindly upon this 'Doo-dad' dwarf."

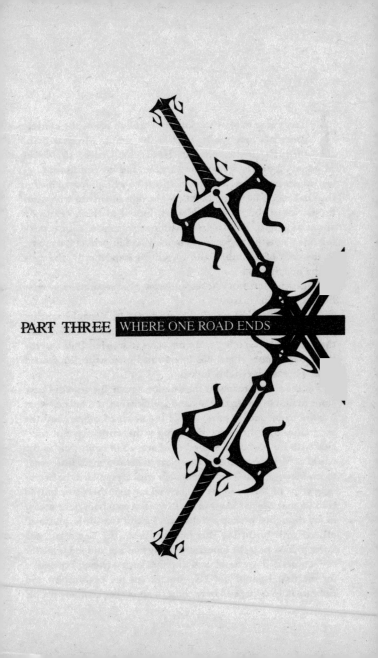

PART THREE WHERE ONE ROAD ENDS

I have come to view my journey through life as the convergence of three roads. First is the simple physical path, through my training in House Do'Urden, to Melee-Magthere, the drow school for warriors, and my continued tutelage under my father, Zaknafein. It was he who prepared me for the challenges, he who taught me the movements to transcend the basics of the drow martial art, indeed to think creatively about any fight. Zaknafein's technique was more about training one's muscles to respond, quickly and in perfect harmony, to the calls of the mind, and even more importantly, the calls of the imagination.

Improvisation, not rote responses, is what separates a warrior from a weapons master.

The road of that physical journey out of Menzoberranzan, through the wilds of the Underdark, along the mountainous trails that led me to Montolio, and from there to Icewind Dale and the loved ones I now share, has intertwined often with the second road. They are inevitably linked.

For the second road was the emotional path, the growth I have come to find in understanding and appreciation, not only of what I desire to be and to have, but of the needs of others, and the acceptance that their way of looking at the world may not coincide with my own. My second road started in confusion as the world of Menzoberranzan came clear to me and made little sense to my views. Again it was Zaknafein who crystallized the beginning steps of this road, as he showed me that there was indeed truth in that which I knew in my heart—but could not quite accept in my thoughts, perhaps—to be true. I credit Catti-brie, above all others, with furthering this journey. From the beginning, she knew to look past the reputation of my heritage and judge me for my actions and my heart, and that was such a freeing experience for me that I could not help but accept the philosophy and embrace it. In doing so I have come to appreciate so many people of various races and various cultures and various viewpoints. From each I learn, and in learning, with such an open mind, I grow.

Now, after all these adventurous years, I have come to understand that there is indeed a third road. For a long time, I thought it an extension of the second, but now I view this path as independent. It is a subtle distinction, perhaps, but not so in importance.

This third journey began the day I was born, as it does for all reasoning beings. It lay somewhat dormant for me for many years, buried beneath the demands of Menzoberranzan and my own innate understanding that the other two paths had to be sorted before the door to this third could truly open.

I opened that door in the home of Montolio deBrouchee, in Mooshie's Grove, when I found Mielikki, when I discovered that which was in my heart and soul. That was the first step on the spiritual road, the path more of mystery than of experience, more of questions than of answers, more of faith and hope than of realization. It is the road that opens only when the needed steps have been taken along the other two. It is the path that requires the shortest steps, perhaps, but is surely the most difficult, at least at first. If the three paths are each divergent and many-forked at their beginning, and indeed, along the way—the physical is usually determined by need, the emotional by want, the spiritual—?

It is not so clear a way, and I fear that for many it never becomes so.

For myself, I know that I am on the right path, but not because I have yet found the answers. I know my way is true because I have found the questions, specifically how, why, and where.

How did I, did anyone, get here? Was it by a course of natural occurrences, or the designs of a creator or creators, or are they indeed one and the same?

In either case, why am I here? Is there indeed even a reason, or is it all pure chance and randomness?

And perhaps the most important question to any reasoning

being, where will my journey take me when I have shrugged off this mortal coil?

I view this last and most important road as ultimately private. These are questions that cannot be answered to me by anyone other than me. I see many people, most people, finding their "answers" in the sermons of others. Words sanctified by age or the perceived wisdom of authors who provide a comfortable ending to their spiritual journey, provide answers to truly troubling questions. No, not an ending, but a pause, awaiting the resumption once this present experience of life as we know it ends.

Perhaps I am being unfair to the various flocks. Perhaps many within have asked themselves the questions and have found their personal answers, then found those of similar ilk with whom to share their revelations and comfort. If that is the case, if it is not a matter of simple indoctrination, then I envy and admire those who have advanced along their spiritual road farther than I.

For myself, I have found Mielikki, though I still have no definitive manifestation of that name in mind. And far from a pause or the ending of my journey, my discovery of Mielikki has only given me the direction I needed to ask those questions of myself in the first place. Mielikki provides me comfort, but the answers, ultimately, come from within, from that part of myself that I feel akin to the tenets of Mielikki as Montolio described them to me.

The greatest epiphany of my life came along this last and most important road: the understanding that all the rest of it, emotional and physical—and material—is naught but a platform. All of our accomplishments in the external are diminished many times over if they do not serve to turn us inward. There and only there lies our meaning, and in truth, part of the answer to the three questions is the understanding to ask them in the first place, and more than that, to recognize their penultimate importance in the course of reason.

The guiding signs of the spiritual journey will rarely be obvious, I believe, for the specific questions found along the road are often changing, and sometimes seemingly unanswerable. Even now, when all seems aright, I am faced with the puzzle of Ellifain and the sadness of that loss. And though I feel as if I am on the greatest adventure of my life with Catti-brie, there are many questions that remain with me concerning our relationship. I try to live in the here and now with her, yet at some point she and I will have to look longer down our shared path. And both of us, I think, fear what we see.

I have to hold faith that things will clarify, that I will find the answers I need.

I have always loved the dawn. I still sit and watch every one, if my situation permits. The sun stings my eyes less now, and less with each rising, and perhaps that is some signal that it, as a representation of the spiritual, has begun to flow more deeply into my heart, my soul, and my understanding of it all.

That, of course, is my hope.

—Drizzt Do'Urden

15

INTOLERANCE

"Ye're really meaning to do this?" Shingles asked Torgar when he found his friend, fresh off his watch, at his modest home in the Mirabar Undercity, stuffing his most important belongings into a large sack.

"Ye knowed I was."

"I knowed ye was talking about it," Shingles corrected. "Didn't think yer brain was rattled enough for ye to actually be doin' it."

"Bah!" Torgar snorted, coming up from his packing to look his friend in the eye. "What choice are they leavin' to me? Agrathan comin' to me on the wall just to tell me to shut me mouth . . . Shut me mouth! I been fightin' for the marchion, for Mirabar, for three hunnerd years. I got more scars than Agrathan, Elastul, and all four o' his private guards put together. Earned every one o' them scars, I did, and now I'm to stand quiet and hear the scolding of Agrathan, and that on me watch, with th' other sentries all lookin' and listenin'?"

"And where're ye to go?" Shingles asked. "Mithral Hall?"

"Yep."

"Where ye'll be welcomed with a big hug and a bottle o' ale?" came the sarcastic reply.

"King Bruenor's not me enemy."

"And not near the friend ye're thinkin'," Shingles argued. "He's to be wonderin' what bringed ye there, and he'll think ye a spy."

It was a logical argument, but Torgar was shaking his head with every word. Even if Shingles proved right on this point, the potential consequences still seemed preferable to Torgar than his present intolerable situation. He was getting up in years and remained the last of the Hammerstriker line, a situation he was hoping to soon enough correct. Given all that he had learned over the last few tendays of King Bruenor, and more importantly, of his own beloved Mirabar, he was thinking that any children he might sire would be better served growing up among Clan Battlehammer.

Perhaps it would take Torgar months, even years, to win the confidence of Bruenor's people, but so be it.

He stuffed the last of his items into the sack and hoisted the bulging bag over his shoulder, turning for the door. To his surprise, Shingles presented him a mug of ale, then held up his own in toast.

"To a road full o' monsters ye can kill!" the older dwarf said.

Torgar banged his mug against the other.

"I'll be clearing it for yerself," he remarked.

Shingles gave a little laugh and took a deep drink.

Torgar knew that his response to the toast was purely polite. Shingles's situation in Mirabar was very different than his own. The old dwarf was the patriarch of a large clan. Uprooting them for a journey to Mithral Hall would be no easy task.

"Ye're to be missed, Torgar Hammerstriker," the old dwarf replied. "And the potters and glass-blowers're sure to be losin' business, not having to replace all the jugs and mugs ye're breakin' in every tavern in town."

Torgar laughed, took another sip, handed the mug back to Shingles, and continued for the door. He paused just once, to turn and offer his friend a look of sincere gratitude, and to drop his free hand on Shingles's shoulder in a sincere pat.

He went out, drawing more than a few stares as he moved along the main thoroughfare of the Undercity, past dozens and dozens of dwarves. Hammers stopped ringing at the forges he passed. All the dwarves of Mirabar knew about Torgar's recent run-ins with the authorities, about the many fights, about his stubborn insistence that the visiting King Bruenor had been badly mistreated.

To see him determinedly striding toward the ladders leading to the overcity with a huge sack on his back. . . .

Torgar didn't turn to regard any of them. This was his choice and his journey. He hadn't asked anyone to join him, beyond his remark to Shingles a moment before, nor did he expect any overt support. He understood the magnitude of it all and quite clearly. Here he was, of a fine and reputable family who had served in Mirabar for centuries, walking away. No dwarf would undertake such an act lightly. To the bearded folk, the hearth and home were the cornerstone of their existence.

By the time he reached the lifts, Torgar had several dwarves following him, Shingles included. He heard their whispers—some of support, some calling him crazy—but he did not respond in any way.

When he reached the overcity, the late afternoon sun shining pale and thin, he found that word of his trek had apparently preceded him, for a substantial group had assembled, human and dwarf alike. They followed him toward the eastern gate with their eyes, if not their feet. Most of the remarks on the surface were less complimentary toward the wayward dwarf. Torgar heard the words "traitor" and "fool" more than a few times.

He didn't react. He had expected and already gone through all of this in his thoughts before he had stuffed the first of his clothes into the sack.

It didn't matter, he reminded himself, because once he crossed out the eastern gate, he'd likely never see or speak with any of these folks ever again.

That thought nearly halted him in his walk.

Nearly.

The dwarf replayed his conversation with Agrathan over and over in his mind, using it to bolster his resolve, to remind himself that he was indeed doing the right thing, that he wasn't forsaking Mirabar so much as Mirabar, in mistreating King Bruenor, and in scolding any who dared befriend the visiting leader, had forsaken him. This was not the robust and proud city of his ancestors, Torgar had decided. This was not a city determined to lead through example. This was a city on the decline. One more determined to bring down their rivals through deceit and sabotage than to elevate themselves above those who would vie with them for markets

Just before he reached the gate, where a pair of dwarf guards stood looking at him incredulously and a pair of human guards stood scowling at him, Torgar was hailed by a familiar voice.

"Do not be doing this," Agrathan advised, running up beside the stern-faced dwarf.

"Don't ye be tryin' to stop me."

"There is more at stake here than one dwarf deciding to move," the councilor tried to explain. "Ye understand this, don't ye? Ye're knowing that all your kinfolk are watching ye and that your actions are starting dangerous whispering among our people?"

Torgar stopped abruptly and turned his head toward the frantic Agrathan. He wanted to comment on the dwarf's accent, which was leaning more toward the human way of speaking than the dwarven. He found it curiously fitting that Agrathan, the liaison, the mediator, seemed to speak with two distinct voices.

"Might be past time the dwarfs o' Mirabar started asking them questions ye're so fearin'."

Agrathan shook his head doubtfully, gave a shrug and a resigned sigh.

Torgar held the stare for a moment longer, then turned and stomped toward the door, not even pausing to consider the expressions of the four guards standing there, or the multitude of folks, human and dwarf alike, who were following him, the horde moving right up to the gate before stopping as one.

One brave soul yelled out, "Moradin's blessings to ye, Torgar Hammerstriker!"

A few others yelled out less complimentary remarks.

Torgar just kept walking, putting the setting sun at his back.

"Predictable fool," Djaffar of the Hammers remarked to the soldiers beside him, all of them astride heavily armored war-horses.

They sat behind the concealment of many strewn rocks on a high bluff to the northeast of Mirabar's eastern gate, from which a lone figure had emerged, walking proudly and determinedly down the road.

Djaffar and his contingent weren't surprised. They had heard of the exodus only a few moments before Torgar had climbed the ladder out of the Undercity, but they had long-ago prepared for just such an eventuality. Thus, they had ridden out quietly through the north gate, while all eyes had been on the dwarf marching toward the eastern one. A roundabout route had brought them to this position to sit and wait.

"If it were up to me, I'd kill him here on the road and let the vultures have his rotting flesh," Djaffar told the others. "And good enough for the traitor! But Marchion Elastul's softer in the heart—his one true weakness—and so you understand your role here?"

In response, three of the riders looked to the fourth, who held up a strong net.

"You give him one chance to surrender. Only one," Djaffar explained.

The four nodded their understanding.

"When, Hammer Djaffar?" one of them asked.

"Patience," the seasoned leader counseled. "Let him get far from the gate, out of sight and out of their hearing. We have not come out here to start a riot, but only to prevent a traitor from bringing all of our secrets to our enemies."

The grim faces looking back at Djaffar assured him that these hand-picked warriors understood their role, and the importance of it.

They caught up to Torgar a short while later, with dusk settling thick about the land. The dwarf was sitting on a rock, rubbing his sore feet and shaking the stones out of his boots, when the four riders swiftly approached. He started to jump up, even reached for his great axe, but then, apparently recognizing the riders for who they were, he just sat back down and assumed a defiant pose.

The four warriors charged up and encircled him, their trained mounts bristling with eagerness.

A moment later, up rode Djaffar. Torgar gave a snort, seeming hardly surprised.

"Torgar Hammerstriker," Djaffar announced. "By the edict of Marchion Elastul Raurym, I declare you expatriated from Mirabar."

"Already done that meself," the dwarf replied.

"It is your intention to continue along the eastern road to Mithral Hall and the court of King Bruenor Battlehammer?"

"Well, I'm not for thinking that King Bruenor's got the time for seein' me, but if he asked, I'd be goin' to see him, yes."

It was all said so casually, so matter-of-factly, that the faces of the five men tightened with anger, which seemed to please Torgar all the more.

"In that event, you are guilty of treason to the crown."

"Treason?" Torgar huffed. "Ye're declarin' a war on Mithral Hall, are ye?"

"They are our known rivals."

"That don't make me goin' there treason."

"Espionage, then!" Djaffar yelled. "Surrender now!"

Torgar studied him carefully for a moment, showing no emotion and no indication of what might happen next. He did glance over at his heavy axe, lying to the side.

That was all the excuse the Mirabarran guards needed. The two to Torgar's left dropped their net between them and spurred their horses forward, running past on either side of the dwarf, plucking him from his seat and bouncing him down to the ground in the strong mesh.

Torgar went into a frenzy, tearing at the cords, trying to pull himself free, but the other two guards were right there, drawing forth solid clubs and dropping from their mounts. Torgar thrashed and kicked, even managed to bite one, but he was at an impossible disadvantage.

The soldiers had the dwarf beaten to semi-consciousness quickly, and managed to extricate him from the net soon after, unstrapping and removing his fine plate armor.

"Let the city find slumber before we return," Djaffar explained to them. "I have arranged with the Axe to ensure that no dwarves are on the wall this night."

Shoudra Stargleam was not truly surprised, when she thought about it, but she was surely dismayed that night. The sceptrana stood on her balcony, enjoying the night and brushing her long black hair when she noted a commotion by the city's eastern gate, of which her balcony provided a fine view.

The gates opened wide and some riders entered. Shoudra recognized Djaffar of the Hammers from his boastfully plumed helmet. Though she could make out few details, it wasn't hard for the Sceptrana to guess the identity of the diminutive figure walking behind the riders, stripped down to breeches and a torn shirt and with his hands chained before him, on a lead to the rear horse.

She held quiet but did nothing to conceal herself as the prisoner caravan wound its way right beneath her balcony.

There, shuffling along behind the four, and being prodded by the fifth, came Torgar Hammerstriker, bound and obviously beaten.

They hadn't even let the poor fellow put his boots on.

"Oh, Elastul, what have you done?" Shoudra quietly asked, and there was great trepidation in her voice, for she knew that the marchion might have erred and badly.

The knock on her door sounded like a wizard's thunderbolt, jarring Shoudra from her restless sleep. She leaped out of bed and scrambled reflexively to answer it, only half aware of where she was.

She pulled the door open, then stopped cold, seeing Djaffar standing there leaning on the wall outside her apartment. She noted his eyes, roaming her body head to toe, and became suddenly conscious of the fact that she was wearing very little that warm summer's night, just a silken shift that barely covered her.

Shoudra edged the door closed a bit and moved modestly behind it, peering out through the crack at the leering, grinning Hammer.

"Milady," Djaffar said with a tip of his open-faced helm, glinting in the torchlight.

"What is the hour?" she asked.

"Several before the dawn."

"Then what do you want?" Shoudra asked.

"I am surprised that you retired, milady," Djaffar said innocently. "It was not so long ago that I saw you, quite awake and standing on your balcony."

It all began to make sense to Shoudra then, as she came fully awake and remembered all that she had seen that far from ordinary night.

"I retired soon after."

"With many questions on your pretty mind, no doubt."

"That is my business, Djaffar." Shoudra made sure that she injected a bit of anger into her tone, wanting to put the too confident man on the defensive. "Is there a reason you disturb my slumber? Is there some emergency concerning the marchion? Because, if there is not . . ."

"We must discuss that which you witnessed from your balcony, milady," Djaffar said coolly, and if he was the slightest bit intimidated by Shoudra's powerful tone he did not show it.

"Who is to say that I witnessed anything at all?"

"Exactly, and you would do well to remember that."

Shoudra's blue eyes opened wide. "My dear Djaffar, are you threatening the Sceptrana of Mirabar?"

"I am asking you to do what is right," the Hammer replied without backing down. "It was under the orders of the marchion himself that the traitor Torgar was arrested."

"Brutally . . ."

"Not so. He surrendered to the lawful authority without a fight," Djaffar argued.

Shoudra didn't believe a word of it. She knew Djaffar and the rest of the four Hammers well enough to know that they loved a fight when the odds were stacked in their favor.

"He was brought back to Mirabar under the cover of darkness for a reason, milady. Surely you can understand and appreciate that this is a sensitive matter."

"Because the dwarves of Mirabar, even those who disagree with Torgar, would not be pleased to learn that he was dragged into the city in chains," Shoudra replied.

Though there was a substantial amount of sarcasm in her voice, Djaffar ignored it completely and merely replied, "Exactly."

The Hammer gave a wry smile.

"We could have left him dead in the wilderness, buried in a place where none would ever find him. You do understand that, of course, as you understand that your silence in this matter is of prime importance?"

"Could you have done all of that? In good conscience?"

"I am a warrior, milady, and sworn to the protection of the marchion," Djaffar answered with that same grin. "I trust in your silence here."

Shoudra just stared at him hard. Finally recognizing that he wasn't going to get any more of an answer than that, Djaffar tipped his helm again and walked away down the corridor.

Shoudra Stargleam shut her door, then turned her back and leaned against it. She rubbed her eyes and considered the very unusual night.

"What are you doing, Elastul?" she asked herself quietly.

In the room next to Shoudra's, another was asking himself that very same question. Nanfoodle the alchemist had been in Mirabar for several years but had tried very hard to keep away from the politics of the place. He was an alchemist, a scholar, and a gnome with a bit of talent in illusion magic, but that was all. This latest debacle, concerning the arrival of the legendary King of Mithral Hall, whom Nanfoodle had dearly wanted to go and meet, had him more than a bit concerned, however.

He had heard the loud knock, and thinking it was on his own door, had scrambled from his bed and rushed to answer. When he had arrived there, though, he already heard the voices, Shoudra and Djaffar, and recognized that the man had come to speak with her and not him.

Nanfoodle had heard every word. Torgar Hammerstriker, one of the most respected dwarves in Mirabar, whose family had been in service to the various marchions for centuries, had been beaten on the road and dragged back, secretly, in chains.

A shiver ran up Nanfoodle's spine. The whole episode, from the time they had learned that Bruenor Battlehammer was knocking on their gate, had him quite unhinged.

He knew that it would all come to no good.

And though the gnome had long before decided to remain neutral on anything politic, to do his experiments and take his rewards, he found himself at the house of a friend the next day.

Councilor Agrathan Hardhammer was not pleased by the gnome's revelations. Not at all.

"I know," Agrathan said to Shoudra as soon as she opened her door that next morning, the dwarf having gone straight from his meeting with Nanfoodle to the sceptrana's apartment.

"You know what?"

"What you know, about the treatment and return of a certain disgruntled dwarf. Torgar was dragged in by the Hammers last night, in chains."

"By one Hammer, at least."

"Djaffar, curse his name!" said Agrathan.

The dwarf's ire toward Djaffar surprised Shoudra, for she had never heard Agrathan speak of any of the individual Hammers at all before.

"Elastul Raurym is the source of the decision, not Djaffar or any of the other Hammers," she reminded.

Agrathan banged his head on the door jamb.

"He is blowing the embers hot in a room full of smokepowder," the dwarf said.

Shoudra did not disagree—to a point. She understood Agrathan's frustration and fears, but she also had to admit that she understood Elastul's reluctance in letting the dwarf walk away. Agrathan knew Mirabar's defenses as well as any and knew their production capacities and the state of their various ore veins as well. The sceptrana didn't honestly believe that it would ever come to war between Mithral Hall and Mirabar, but if it did. . . .

"I believe that Elastul felt he had no choice," Shoudra replied. "At least they did not murder the wayward dwarf on the road."

That statement didn't have the effect Shoudra had hoped for. Instead of calming Agrathan, the mere mention of that diabolical possibility had the dwarf's eyes going wide, and his jaw clenching tightly. He calmed quickly, though, and took a deep, steadying breath.

"It might have been the smarter thing for him to do," he said quietly, and it was Shoudra's turn to open her eyes wide. "When the dwarfs of Mirabar learn that Torgar's a prisoner in his own town, they're not to be a happy bunch—and they will learn of it, do not doubt."

"Do you know where they're keeping him?"

"I was hoping that you'd be telling me that very thing."

Shoudra shrugged.

"Might be time for us two to go and talk to Elastul."

Shoudra Stargleam did not disagree, though she understood better than Agrathan, apparently, that the meeting would do little to resolve the present problem. In Elastul's eyes, obviously, Torgar Hammerstriker had committed an act of betrayal, of treason even, and Shoudra doubted that the unfortunate dwarf would be seeing the world outside his prison cell anytime soon.

She did go with Agrathan to the marchion's palace, though, and the two were ushered in to Elastul's audience chamber forthwith. Shoudra noted that all of the normal guards and attendants in the room were absent, other than the four Hammers, who stood in their typical position behind the marchion. She also noted the look that Djaffar shot her way, one suggestive and uncomfortable, one that made her want to pull her robe tighter about her.

"What is the urgency?" the marchion asked at once, before any formal greetings. "I have much to attend this day."

"The urgency is that you've put Torgar Hammerstriker in prison, Marchion," Agrathan bluntly replied, and he added with great emphasis, "Torgar *Delzoun* Hammerstriker."

"He is not being mistreated," Elastul replied, and he added, "As long as he does not resist," when he took note of Shoudra's doubtful look.

"I have asked for, and expect, discretion on this matter," the marchion went on, obviously aiming this remark at Shoudra.

"She wasn't the one who told me," Agrathan answered.

"Then who?"

"Not important," the dwarf replied. "If you intend to hunt any who'd speak of this, then ye'd do better trying to hold water from dripping through your fingers."

Elastul didn't seem pleased at all by that remark, and he turned a frown upon Djaffar, who merely shrugged.

"This is important, Marchion," Agrathan said. "Torgar is not just any citizen."

"Torgar is not a citizen," Elastul corrected. "Not anymore, and by his own volition. I am charged with the defense of Mirabar, and so I have taken steps to just that effect. He is jailed, and he shall remain jailed until such time as he recants his position on this matter, publicly, and forsakes this ludicrous idea of traveling to Mithral Hall."

Agrathan started to respond, but Elastul cut him off.

"There is no debate over this, Councilor."

Agrathan looked to Shoudra for support, but she shrugged and shook her head.

And so it was. Marchion Elastul considered Mithral Hall an enemy, obviously, and every step he took seemed to ensure that his perception would become reality.

Both Agrathan and Shoudra hoped that Elastul understood fully the implications of this latest action, for both feared the reaction should the truth of Torgar's imprisonment become general knowledge around the city.

The dwarf's remark about hot embers in a smokepowder filled room seemed quite insightful to Shoudra Stargleam at that moment.

16

THE HERO

Catti-brie crept silently to the edge of the rocky lip, peering over. As she had expected, the orc's camp lay below her on a flat rock with strewn boulders all around it. There wasn't much of a fire, just a pit of glowing embers. The orc huddled close to it, blocking most of the glow.

Catti-brie scanned the area, allowing her eyes to shift into the spectrum of heat instead of light, and she was glad that she had her magical circlet with her when she spotted the soft glow of a second orc, not so far away, whittling away at a broken branch. She did a quick scan of the area then let her vision shift back to the normal spectrum. Her circlet was a marvelous item indeed, one that helped her to see in the dark, but it was not without its limitations. It operated far better underground, allowing her vision where she would have had none at all than under the night sky. When the stars were out or near the glow of a fire, the magical circlet often only added to the woman's confusion, distorting distances, particularly on heat-neutral surfaces such as broken stones.

Catti-brie paused and stood perfectly still, her eyes unblinking as they adjusted to the dim light. She had already picked a route that would take her down to the orc and had confirmed that route with the magical circlet, intending to go down and capture or slay the creature.

But now there were two.

Catti-brie reached instinctively for Taulmaril as she considered the new odds, but her hand stopped short of grabbing the bow that was strapped across her back. Her fingers remained swollen and bruised, with at least one broken. After practicing earlier that day, she knew she could hardly hope to hit the orcs from that distance.

She went to Khazid'hea instead. Her fabulous sword, nicknamed Cutter because of its fine and deadly blade, could shear through armor as easily as it could cut through cloth. She felt the energy, the eagerness, of the sentient, hungry sword as soon as her hand closed around the hilt. Khazid'hea wanted this fight, as it wanted any fight.

That pull only strengthened as she slowly and silently slid the sword out of its scabbard, holding it low behind the rocky barricade. Its fine edge could catch the slightest glimmer of light and reflect it clearly.

The sword's hunger called out to her, bade her to start moving down the trail and toward the first victim.

Catti-brie almost started away, but she paused and glanced back over her shoulder. She should go and get some of the others, she realized. Drizzt had gone off earlier, but her other friends could not be far away.

It is only a pair of orcs after all, and if you strike first and fast, it will be one against one, she thought—or perhaps it was her sword suggesting that thought to her.

Either way, it seemed a logical argument to Cattie-brie. She had never met an orc that could match her in swordplay.

Before she could further second-guess herself, Catti-brie slipped out from behind the rocky lip and started slowly and quietly down the nearest trail that would get her to the plateau and the encampment.

Soon she was at the orc's level and barely ten feet away. The oblivious creature remained huddled over the embers, stirring them occasionally, while its equally-oblivious companion continued its whittling far to the side.

She moved a half step closer, then another. Barely five feet separated her from the orc then. Apparently sensing her, the creature looked up, gave a cry—

—and fell over backward, rolling and scrambling as Catti-brie stuck it, once and again, before having to turn back to face its charging companion.

The second orc skidded to a stop when Khazid'hea flashed up before it in perfect balance. The orc stabbed viciously with its crude spear, but Catti-brie easily turned her hips aside. It struck again, to similar non-effect, then came forward, retracted suddenly, and thrust again, this time to the anticipated side.

The wrong side.

Catti-brie dodged the second thrust, then started to dodge the third, but stopped as the orc retracted, and dodged out the other way as the spear charged ahead.

She had her chance, and it was one she didn't miss. Across went Khazid'hea, the fabulous blade cleanly shearing the last foot off the orc's spear. The creature howled and jumped back, throwing the remaining shaft at the woman as it did, but a flick of Catti-brie's wrist had that spear shaft spinning off into the darkness.

She rushed ahead, sword leading, ready to thrust the blade into the orc's chest.

And she stopped, abruptly, as a stone whistled across, right before her.

And as she turned to face this newest attacker, she got hit in the back by a second stone, thrown hard.

And a third skipped by, and a fourth hit her square in the shoulder, and her arm, suddenly gone numb, slipped down.

Orcs crawled over the strewn rocks all around the encampment, waving their weapons and throwing more rocks to keep her dancing and off-balance.

Catti-brie's mind raced. She could hardly believe that she had so foolishly walked into a trap. She felt Khazid'hea's continuing urging to her to jump into battle, to slay them all, and wondered for a moment how much control she actually held over the ever-hungry sword.

But no, she realized, this was her mistake and not the weapon's. Normally in this position, she'd play defensively, letting her enemy come to her, but the orcs showed little sign of wanting to advance. Instead they bent to retrieve more stones and came up hurling them at her. She dodged and danced and got hit a few times, some stinging. She picked what she perceived to be the most vulnerable spot in the ring and charged at it, her sword flashing wildly.

It was pure instinct then for Catti-brie, her muscles working faster than her conscious thoughts could follow. Nothing short of brilliant, the woman parried a sword, an axe, and another spear—one, two, three—and still managed to step out to the side suddenly, stabbing an orc who had expected her to move forward. Clutching its belly, that one fell away.

And a second orc joined it, dropping to the stone and writhing wildly while trying to stem the blood flow from its slashed neck.

A twist of Catti-brie's wrist had the weapon of a third orc turned tip down to the stone, leaving her an easy opening for a deadly strike, but as Khazid'hea started its forward rush, a stone clipped the woman's already wounded hand, sending a burst of fiery pain up her arm. To her horror, before she even realized the extent of what had happened, she heard Khazid'hea go bouncing away across the stones.

A spear came out hard at her, but the agile woman turned fast aside, then grabbed it as it thrust past. A step forward, a flying elbow had the orc staggered, and she moved to pull free the weapon and make it her own.

But then a club cracked her between the shoulder blades and her arms went weak, and the spear-holding orc yanked back its weapon and stabbed ahead, gashing the woman across the hip and buttocks. She staggered forward and away, and somehow managed to slap her hand out and turn aside a slashing sword then do it again, though the second block had the tender skin of her palm opened wide.

Every movement was in desperation then, more desperate than Catti-brie had ever been. It occurred to her, somewhere deep in her swirling thoughts, how close to the edge of disaster she and her friends had been and for so long. She noted then, in a flash of clarity before the club hit her again, sending her stumbling to her knees as she tried to run across the camp and leap away into the dark night, how a single mistake could prove so quickly disastrous.

She went down hard to the stone and noted Khazid'hea, not so far away. It was out of her reach, might as well have been across the world, the woman realized as the orcs closed in. She rolled desperately to her back and began kicking out and up at them, anything to keep their weapons away.

"What is it, Guen?" Drizzt asked quietly

He came up beside the panther, whose ears were flattened as she stood perfectly still, staring out into the dark night. The drow crouched beside her and similarly scanned, not expecting to find any enemies about, for he had seen no orc sign at all that day or night.

But something was wrong. The panther knew it, and so did Drizzt. Something was out of place. He looked back down the mountainside, to the distant glow of Bruenor's camp, where all seemed quiet.

"What do you sense?" the drow asked the panther.

Guen gave a low, almost plaintive growl. Drizzt felt his heart racing, and he began looking desperately all around, scolding himself for going off on his own that afternoon, pushing farther into the mountains in an effort to try to spot the lone tower that marked the town of Shallows, and leaving his friends so far behind.

She did a fair job of keeping the orcs off of her for a long, long time, but the angle was too awkward, and the effort too great, and gradually Catti-brie's kicks slowed to inconsequential. She got kicked hard in the ribs, and she had no choice but to curl up and clutch at the pain. Tears flowed freely as the woman realized her error and the consequences of it.

She would never see her friends again. She would never laugh with Drizzt again, tease Regis again, or watch her father take his place as King of Mithral Hall.

She would never have children of her own. She would not watch her daughter grow to womanhood or her son to manhood. She would never hold Colson again or take heart at the smile that had so recently returned to Wulfgar's face.

Everything seemed to pause around her, just for a moment, and she looked up to see the biggest of the orc group towering over her at her feet, lifting a heavy axe in both its strong hands, while the others cheered it on.

She had no defense. She prayed it would not hurt too much.

Up went the axe, and down went the orc's head.

Down, driven down, right into its shoulders at the end of a warhammer's gleaming mithral head. The orc went into a short bounce, but didn't fall right back to the stone as Wulfgar slammed his powerful shoulder into it, launching it right over the prone woman.

With a roar, the son of Beornegar stepped forward, straddling Catti-brie with his strong legs, his powerful arms working mightily to send Aegis-fang sweeping back and forth and all about, driving back the surprised orcs. He clipped one, shattering its side, then stepped forward enough to nail a second with a sweep across its legs that upended it and dropped it howling to the stone. In a rage beyond anything that Catti-brie had ever before seen, a battle fury beyond anything the orcs had ever encountered, the barbarian crouched and turned around, launching Aegis-fang into the chest of the nearest orc, blasting it away. Unlike Catti-brie a few moments before, however, not an orc thought this monstrous human unarmed. Wulfgar charged right into them, ignoring the puny hits of their half-hearted swings and countering with punches that sent orcs flying away.

Catti-brie regained her wits enough to roll to the side toward her lost sword. She retrieved it and started to rise but could hardly find the strength. She stumbled again and thought her attempt would cost her her life and mock Wulfgar's desperate rescue, when an orc rushed beside her. A split second later, though, the woman realized that the creature wasn't trying to attack her but was simply trying to run away.

And why not, she realized when she looked back at Wulfgar. Another orc went flying off into the night, and another was up in the air at the end of one hand clutched tightly around its throat. The orc was large, nearly as wide as Wulfgar, but the barbarian held it aloft easily. The flailing creature couldn't begin to break his iron grasp.

Wulfgar warded off yet another pesky orc with his free hand. Aegis-fang returned to his grasp, and he gave a warding swing, then turned his attention back to the orc he held aloft. With a primal growl, his corded muscles flexed powerfully.

The orc's neck snapped and the creature went limp, and Wulfgar tossed it aside.

On he came, his rage far from abated, Aegis-fang chopping down orcs and scattering them to the night. Bones shattered under his mighty blows as he waded through their fleeing ranks like a thresher through a field of wheat.

And it was over so suddenly, and Wulfgar's arm went down to his side. Trembling visibly, his face appearing ashen even in the meager light, he strode to Catti-brie and reached down to her.

She took his hand with her own and a quick tug had her standing before him on legs that would hardly support her.

That didn't matter, though, for the woman simply fell forward into Wulfgar's waiting grasp. He lifted her in his arms and hugged her close.

Catti-brie buried her face against the man's strong shoulder, sobbing, and Wulfgar crushed against her, whispering calming words in her ear, his own face lost in the her thick auburn hair.

All around them, the night creatures, stirred by the sharp ruckus of battle, gradually quieted and the orcs fled into the darkness, and the night slipped past.

17

MIELIKKI'S APPROVAL

While at first Tarathiel found the constant "*wheeee!*" of Pikel Bouldershoulder annoying, he found that by the time he set Sunset down in the mountain forest and helped the dwarf off the pegasus's back, he had grown quite fond of the green-bearded fellow.

"Hee hee hee," Pikel said, glancing back many times at the pegasus as he followed Tarathiel along.

They had been up and flying for most of the day, and the afternoon light was beginning to wane.

"You are pleased by Sunset?" Tarathiel asked.

"Hee hee hee," Pikel answered.

"Well, I have something else, I hope, that I expect might please you equally," the elf explained.

Pikel looked at him curiously.

"We are nearing the home of a great ranger, now deceased," Tarathiel explained. "An enchanted and hallowed place that has come to be known as Mooshie's Grove."

Pikel's eyes widened so greatly that they seemed as if they would fall out of his head.

"You have heard of it?"

"Uh huh."

Tarathiel smiled and led on through the winding mountain trail, with tall pines all about, the wind swirling around them. They came to the diamond-shaped grove of trees and piled stone walls soon after, the place still looking as if the ranger Montolio was still alive and tending it. There was strong magic about the grove.

Tarathiel only hoped that the last inhabitant of the area he had known was still around. He had taken Drizzt Do'Urden there a few years before, as a measure of the unusual dark elf, and he and Innovindil had decided that a similar test might suit Pikel Bouldershoulder well.

The two went into the grove and walked around, admiring the elevated walkways and the simple, beautiful design of the huts.

"So, you and your brother were heading to the coronation of King Bruenor Battlehammer?" the elf asked to pass the time, knowing that Innovindil was similarly questioning the other brother back in the Moonwood.

"Yup yup," Pikel said, but he was obviously distracted, hopping about, scratching his head and nodding happily.

"You know King Bruenor well, then?"

"Yup yup," Pikel answered.

He stopped suddenly, looked at the elf, and blinked a few times.

"Uh uh," he corrected, and gave a shrug.

"You do not know Bruenor well?"

"Nope."

"But well enough to represent . . . what was his name? Cadderly?"

"Yup yup."

"I see. And tell me, Pikel," Tarathiel asked, "how is it that you have come by such druidic . . . ?"

His voice trailed off, for he noticed that Pikel was suddenly distracted, looking away, his eyes widening. Following the dwarf's gaze, Tarathiel soon enough understood that his question had fallen on deaf ears, for there, just outside the grove, stood the most magnificent of equine creatures in all the world. Large and strong, with legs that could shatter a giant's skull, and a single, straight horn that could skewer two men standing back to back, the unicorn pawed the ground anxiously, watching Pikel every bit as intently as the dwarf was regarding it.

Pikel put his arm above his head, finger pointing up, like his own unicorn horn, and began hopping all about.

"Be easy, dwarf," Tarathiel warned, unsure of how the magnificent, and ultimately dangerous, creature would respond.

Pikel, though, hardly seemed nervous, and with a shriek of delight, the dwarf went hopping across the way, tumbling over the stone wall that lined that edge of the grove, and rushed out toward the beast.

The unicorn pawed the ground and gave a great whinny, but Pikel hardly seemed to notice and charged on.

Tarathiel grimaced, thinking himself foolish for bringing the dwarf to the grove. He took up the chase, calling for Pikel to stop.

But it was Tarathiel who stopped, just as he was going over the stone wall. Across the small field, Pikel stood beside the unicorn, stroking its muscled neck, his face a mask of awe. The unicorn seemed a bit unsure and continued pawing the ground, but it did not ward Pikel away, nor did it make any move to rush off.

Tarathiel sat down on the wall, smiling and nodding, and very glad of that.

Pikel stayed with the magnificent unicorn for some time before the creature finally turned and galloped away. The enchanted dwarf floated back across the field, skipping so lightly that his feet didn't even seem to touch the ground.

"Are you pleased?"

"Yup yup!"

"I think it liked you."

"Yup yup!"

"You know of Mielikki?"

Pikel's smile nearly took in his big ears. He reached under the front of his tunic and pulled forth a pendant of a carved unicorn head, the symbol of the nature goddess.

Tarathiel had seen another wearing a similar pendant, though Pikel's was carved of wood while the other had been made of scrimshaw using the bones of the knucklehead trout of Icewind Dale.

"Will King Bruenor be pleased that one who worships the goddess is in his court?" Tarathiel asked, leading the conversation to a place he thought might prove revealing.

Pikel looked at him curiously.

"He is a dwarf, after all, and most dwarves are not favorably disposed toward the goddess Mielikki."

"*Pffft,*" Pikel scoffed, waving a hand at the elf.

"You believe I am wrong?"

"Yup yup."

"I have heard that there is another in his court so favorably disposed to Mielikki," Tarathiel remarked. "One who trained right here with Montolio the Ranger. A very unusual creature, not so much unlike Pikel Bouldershoulder."

"Drizzit Dudden!" Pikel cried, and though it took Tarathiel a moment to recognize the badly-pronounced name, when he did, he nodded his approval.

If the unicorn hadn't been proof enough, then Pikel's knowledge of Drizzt certainly was.

"Drizzt, yes," the elf said. "It was he I took out here, when first I found the unicorn. The unicorn liked him, too."

"Hee hee hee."

"Let us spend the night here," the elf explained. "We will set out as soon as the sun rises to return to your brother."

That thought seemed quite acceptable, even pleasing to Pikel Bouldershoulder. The dwarf ran off, searching all the grove, soon enough finding a pair of hammocks he could string up.

They spent a comfortable night indeed within the magical aura that permeated Mooshie's Grove.

"He knew Drizzt Do'Urden," Tarathiel said to Innovindil when the two met that following evening, to discuss their respective meetings with the unusual dwarf brothers.

"As did Ivan," Innovindil confirmed. "In fact, Drizzt Do'Urden and Catti-brie, Bruenor's adopted human daughter, are the ties between the priest Cadderly and Mithral Hall. All that Ivan and Pikel, and Cadderly, know of Bruenor they learned from that pair."

"Pikel believes that Drizzt will be with Bruenor," Tarathiel said somberly.

"If he returns to the region, we will learn the truth of Ellifain's current state, of being and of mind."

Tarathiel's eyes clouded over and he looked down. The life and fate of Ellifain Tuuserail was among the saddest and darkest tales in the Moonwood. Ellifain had been but a young child that fateful night, half a century before, when the dark elves had crept out of their tunnels and descended upon a gathering of moon elves out in celebration of the night. All were slaughtered, except for Ellifain, and the baby girl would have found a similar fate had it not been for the uncharacteristically generous action of a particular drow, Drizzt Do'Urden. He had buried the child beneath her dead mother, smearing her with her mother's blood to make it look like Ellifain, too, had been mortally wounded.

While Tarathiel and Innovindil and all the rest of the Moonwood clan had come to understand the generosity of Drizzt's actions and to trust in the remarkable dark elf's account of that horrible night, Ellifain had never gotten past that one terrible moment. The massacre had scarred the elf beyond reason, despite the best efforts of hired clerics and wizards, and had put her on a singular course throughout her adult life: to kill drow elves and to kill Drizzt Do'Urden.

The two had met face to face when Drizzt had once ventured through the Moonwood, and it had taken all that Tarathiel and the others could muster to hold Ellifain in check, to keep her from Drizzt's throat, or more likely, from death at the end of his scimitars.

"Do you think she will reveal herself in an effort to get at him?" Innovindil asked. "Is it our responsibility, in that case, to warn Drizzt Do'Urden and King Bruenor to take care of what elves they allow entry to Mithral Hall?"

Tarathiel shrugged in answer to the first question. A few years before, without explanation, Ellifain had disappeared from the Moonwood. They had tracked her to Silverymoon, where she was trying to hire a swordsman to serve as a sparring partner, with the requirement that he was skilled in the two long weapon style common among drow.

The pair had almost caught Ellifain on numerous occasions, but she had always seemed one step ahead of them. And she had disappeared, simply vanished, it seemed, and the trail soon grew cold. The elves suspected wizardly interference, likely a teleport spell, but they had found none who would admit to any such thing, and indeed, had found none who would even admit to ever meeting Ellifain, despite all their efforts and a great deal of offered gold.

The trail was dead, and the elves had hoped—they still did hope—that Ellifain had given up her life-quest of finding and killing Drizzt, but Tarathiel and Innovindil doubted that to be the case. There was no reason guiding Ellifain's weapon hand, only unrelenting anger and a thirst for vengeance beyond anything the elves had ever known before.

"It is our responsibility as a neighbor to warn King Bruenor," Tarathiel answered.

"We hold responsibilities to dwarves?"

"Only because Ellifain's course, if she still follows it, is not one guided by any moral trail."

Innovindil considered his words for a few moments then nodded her agreement. "She believes that if she can kill Drizzt, she will destroy those images that haunt her every step. In killing Drizzt, she is striking back against all the drow, avenging her family."

"But if warned, and she reveals herself and her intent, he will likely slaughter her," Tarathiel said, and Innovindil winced at the thought.

"Perhaps that would be the most merciful course of all," the female said quietly, and she looked up at Tarathiel, whose face grew very tight, whose eyes narrowed dangerously.

But that expression softened in the face of Innovindil's simple logic, in the undeniable understanding that Ellifain, the true Ellifain, had died that night long ago on the moonlit field, and that this creature she had become was ultimately and inexorably flawed.

"I do not think that Ivan and Pikel Bouldershoulder are the ones to deliver such a message to King Bruenor," Innovindil remarked, and Tarathiel's dark expression brightened a bit, a smirk even crossing his face.

"Likely they would jumble the message and bring about a war between Mithral Hall and the Moonwood," he said with a forced chuckle.

"Boom!" Innovindil added in her best Pikel impression, and both elves laughed aloud.

Tarathiel's eyes went to the western sky, though, where the setting sun was lighting pink fires against a line of clouds, and his mirth dissipated. Ellifain was out there, or she was dead, and either way, there was nothing he could do to save her.

18

A CITIZEN IN
GOOD STANDING

It never took much to fluster the gnome, but this was more than his sensibilities could handle. He walked swiftly along the streets of Mirabar, heading for the connections to the Undercity, but not traveling in a direct line. Nanfoodle was trying hard—too hard—to avoid being detected.

He was cognizant of that fact, and so he tried to straighten out his course and settle his stride to a more normal pace. Why shouldn't he go into the Undercity, after all? He was the Marchion's Prime Alchemist, often working with fresh ore and often visiting the dwarves, so why was he trying to conceal his destination?

Nanfoodle shook his head and scolded himself repeatedly, then stopped, took a deep breath, and started again with a more normal stride and an expression of forced calm.

Well, a calm expression that lasted until he considered again his course. He had told Councilor Agrathan of Torgar's imprisonment and had thought to let his incidental knowledge of the situation go at that, figuring that he had done his duty as a friend—and he truly felt that he was a friend—of the dwarves. However, with so much time behind them and no apparent action coming on Torgar's behalf, Nanfoodle had come to realize that Agrathan had taken the issue no further than the marchion. Even worse, to the gnome's sensibilities, Mirabar's dwarves were still under the impression that Torgar was on the road to, or perhaps had even arrived at, Mithral Hall. For several days, the gnome had wrestled with his conscience over the issue. Had he done enough? Was it his duty as a friend to tell the dwarves, to tell Shingles McRuff at least, who was known to be the best friend of Torgar Hammerstriker? Or was it his duty to the marchion, his employer and the one who had brought him to Mirabar, to keep his mouth shut and mind his own business?

As these questions played yet again in poor Nanfoodle's thoughts, the gnome's strides became less purposeful and more meandering, and he brought his hands together before him, twiddling his thumbs. His eyes were only half-open, the gnome exploring his heart and soul as much as paying attention to his surroundings, and so he was quite surprised when a tall and imposing figure stepped out before him as he turned down one narrow alleyway.

Nanfoodle skidded to an abrupt stop, his gaze gradually climbing the robed, shapely figure before him, settling on the intense eyes of Shoudra Stargleam.

"Um, hello Sceptrana," the gnome nervously greeted. "A fine day for a walk it is, yes?"

"A fine day *above* ground, yes," Shoudra replied. "Can you be so certain that the Undercity is similarly pleasant?"

"The Undercity? Well, I would know nothing about the Undercity . . . have not been down there with the dwarves in days, in tendays!"

"A situation you plan to remedy this very day, no doubt."

"W-why, no," the gnome stammered. "Was just out for a walk. Yes, yes . . . trying to sort a formula in my head, you see. Must toughen the metal . . ."

"Spare me the dodges," Shoudra bade him. "So now I know who it was who whispered in Agrathan's ear."

"Agrathan? The Councilor Hardhammer, you mean?"

Nanfoodle realized how unconvincing he sounded, and that only made him seem more nervous to the clever Shoudra.

"Djaffar was a bit loud in the hallway on the night when Torgar Hammerstriker was dragged back to Mirabar," Shoudra remarked.

"Djaffar? Loud? Well, he usually is, I suppose," Nanfoodle bluffed, thinking himself quite clever. "In any hallway, I would guess, though I've not seen nor heard him in any hallway that I can recall."

"Truly?" Shoudra said, a wry grin widening on her beautiful face. "And yet you were not surprised to hear that Torgar Hammerstriker was dragged back to Mirabar? How, then, is this not news to you?"

"Well, I . . . well . . ."

The little gnome threw up his hands in defeat.

"You heard him, that night, outside my door."

"I did."

"And you told Agrathan."

Nanfoodle gave a great sigh and said, "Should he not know? Should the dwarves be oblivious to the actions of their marchion?"

"And it is your place to tell them?"

"Well . . ." Nanfoodle gave a snort, and another, and stamped his foot. "I do not know!"

He gnashed his teeth for a few moments, then looked up at Shoudra, and was surprised to see an expression on her face that was quite sympathetic.

"You feel as betrayed as I," he remarked.

"The marchion owes me, and you, nothing," the woman was quick to respond. "Not even an explanation."

"Yet you seem to think that we owe him something in return."

Shoudra's eyes widened and she seemed to grow very tall and terrible before the little gnome.

"You owe to him because he *is* Mirabar!" she scolded. "It is the position, not the man, deserving and demanding of your respect, Nanfoodle the Foolish."

"I am not of Mirabar!" the gnome shot back, with unexpected fury. "I was brought in for my expertise, and I am paid well because I am the greatest in my field."

"Your field? You are a master of illusion and a master of the obvious all at once," Shoudra countered. "You are a carnival barker, a trickster and a—"

"How dare you?" Nanfoodle yelled back. "Alchemy is the greatest of the Arts, the one whose truths we have not yet uncovered. The one that holds the promise of power for all, and not just a select few, like those powers of Shoudra and her ilk, who guard mighty secrets for personal gain."

"Alchemy is a means to make a few potions of minor magic, and a bit of powder that blows up more often on its creator than on its intended target. Beyond that, it is a sham, a lie perpetrated by the cunning on the greedy. You can no more strengthen the metal of Mirabar's mines than transmute lead into gold."

"Why, from the solid earth I can create hungry mud at your feet to swallow you up!" Nanfoodle roared.

"With water?" Shoudra calmly asked, the simple reply taking most of the bluster from the excited gnome, visibly shrinking him back to size.

He started to reply, stammering indecipherably, and just gave a snort, and remarked, "Not all agree with your estimation of the value of alchemy."

"Indeed, and some pay well for the unfounded promises it offers."

Nanfoodle snorted again. "The point remains that I owe nothing to your marchion beyond my position to him as my employer," he reasoned, "and only as my *current* employer, as I am a free-lance alchemist who has served many well-paying folks throughout the wide lands of the North. I could walk into Waterdeep tomorrow and find employ at near equal pay."

"True enough," Shoudra replied, "but I have not asked you for any loyalty to Elastul, only to Mirabar, this city that you have come to name as your home. I have been watching you closely, Nanfoodle, ever since Councilor Agrathan came to me with his knowledge of the imprisonment of Torgar. I have replayed many times my encounter with Djaffar, and I know whose door it is that abuts my own. You are out this day, walking nervously, meandering your course, which is obviously to the mines and the dwarves. I share your frustration and understand well that which gnaws at your heart, and so, since Councilor Agrathan has taken little action, you have decided to tell others. Friends of Torgar, likely, in an effort to start some petition against the marchion's actions and get Torgar freed from his cell, wherever that may be."

"I have decided to tell the friends of Torgar only so that they might know the truth," Nanfoodle admitted, and corrected. "What actions they might take are their own to decide."

"How democratic," came the sarcastic reply.

"You just said you share my frustrations," Nanfoodle retorted.

"But not your foolishness, it would seem," Shoudra was quick to respond. "Do you truly understand the implications? Do you truly understand the brotherhood of dwarf to dwarf? You risk tearing the city asunder, of setting human against dwarf. What do you owe to Mirabar, Nanfoodle the Illusionist? And what do you owe to Marchion Elastul, your employer?"

"And what do I owe to the dwarves I have named as my friends?" the little gnome asked innocently, and his words seemed to knock Shoudra back a step.

"I know not," she admitted with a sigh, one that clearly showed that frustration she had spoken of.

"Nor do I," Nanfoodle agreed.

Shoudra straightened herself, but she seemed not so tall and terrible to Nanfoodle, seemed rather a kindred soul, befuddled and unhappy about the course of events swirling around her and outside of her control.

She dropped a hand on his shoulder, a gesture of sympathy and friendship, and said quietly, "Walk lightly, friend. Understand the implications of your actions here. The dwarves of Mirabar are on the fine edge of a dagger, stepping left and right. They among all the citizens bear the least love and the most loyalty to the present marchion. Where will your revelations leave them?"

Nanfoodle nodded, not disagreeing with her reasoning, but he added, "And yet, if this city is all you claim it to be, if this wondrous joy of coexistence that is Mirabar is worthy of inspiring such loyalty, can it suffer the injustice of the jailing of Torgar Hammerstriker?"

Again, his words seemed to set Shoudra back on her heels, striking her as profoundly as any slap might. She paused, closed her eyes, and gradually began to nod.

"Do what you will, Nanfoodle, with no judgment from Shoudra Stargleam. I will leave your choice to your heart. None will know of this conversation, or even that you know of Torgar—not from me, at least."

She smiled warmly at the little gnome, patted him again on the shoulder, and turned and walked away.

Nanfoodle stood there, watching her depart and wondering which course would be better. Should he return to his apartment and his workshop and forget all about Torgar and the mounting troubles between the dwarves and the marchion? Or should he continue as he had intended, knowing full well the explosive potential of his information, and tell the dwarves the truth about the prisoner in the marchion's jail?

No question of alchemy, that most elusive of sciences, had ever perplexed the gnome more than this matter. Was it his place to start an uproar, perhaps even a riot? Was it his place, as a friend, to sit idly by and allow such injustice?

And what of Agrathan? If the marchion had convinced the dwarf councilor to remain silent, as seemed obvious, was Nanfoodle playing the part of the righteous fool? Agrathan must know more than he, after all. Agrathan's loyalty to his kin could not be questioned, and Agrathan had apparently said nothing about Torgar's fate.

Where did that leave Nanfoodle?

With a sigh, the little gnome turned back and started walking for home, thinking himself very foolish and very uppity for even beginning such a course. He had barely gone ten strides, though, when a familiar figure crossed before him, and paused to say hello.

"Greetings to you, Shingles McRuff," Nanfoodle responded, and he felt his stomach turn and his knees go weak.

His short legs churning, Councilor Agrathan burst into Marchion Elastul's audience chamber completely unannounced and with several door guards hot on his heels.

"They *know!*" the dwarf cried, before the surprised marchion could even inquire about the intrusion, and before any of the four Hammers who were standing behind Elastul could scold him for entering without invitation.

"They?" Elastul replied, though it was obvious to all that he knew exactly of whom Agrathan was speaking.

"Word's out about Torgar," Agrathan explained. "The dwarves know what you did, and they're none too happy!"

"Indeed," Elastul replied, settling back in his throne. "And how is it that your people know, Councilor?"

There was no mistaking the accusation in his tone.

"Not from me!" the dwarf protested. "You think I'm pleased by this development? You think it does my old heart good to see the dwarves of Mirabar yelling at each other, throwing words and throwing fists? But you had to know they would learn of this and soon enough. You cannot keep such a secret, Marchion, not about one as important as Torgar *Delzoun* Hammerstriker."

His emphasis on that telling middle name, a distinguished title indeed among the dwarves of Mirabar, had Elastul's eyes narrowing dangerously. Elastul's middle name, after all, was not Delzoun, nor could it be, and to all the marchions of Mirabar, humans all, the Delzoun heritage could be both a blessing and a curse. That Delzoun heritage bound the dwarves to this land, and this land bound them to the marchion. But that Delzoun heritage also bound them to a commonality of their own race, one *apart* from the marchion. Why was it, after all, that every time Agrathan spoke of the weight of Elastul's decision to imprison the traitor Torgar, he used, and emphasized, that middle name?

"So they know," Elastul remarked. "Perhaps that is the proper thing, in the end. Surely most of the dwarves of Mirabar recognize Torgar Hammerstriker as the traitor that he is, and surely many of those same dwarves, merchants among them, craftsmen among them, understand and appreciate the damage the traitor might have caused to us all if he had been allowed to travel to our hated enemies."

"Enemies?"

"Rivals, then," the marchion conceded. "Do you believe that Mithral Hall would not welcome the information that the traitor dwarf might have offered?"

"I am not certain that I believe that Torgar would have offered anything other than his friendship to King Bruenor," Agrathan replied.

"And that alone would be worthy of hanging him," Elastul retorted.

The Hammers laughed and agreed, and Agrathan paled, his eyes going wide.

"You can't be thinking. . . ."

"No, no, Councilor," Elastul assured him. "I have not constructed any gallows for the traitor dwarf. Not yet, at least. Nor do I intend to. It is as I told you before. Torgar Hammerstriker will remain in prison, not abused, but surely contained, until such time as he sees the truth of things and returns to his own good senses. I'll not risk the wealth of Mirabar on his judgment."

Agrathan seemed to calm a bit at that, but the cloud did not leave his soft (for a dwarf, at least) features. He stroked his long white beard and paused for a bit, deep in thought.

"All that you say is true," he admitted, his vernacular becoming more sophisticated as he calmed. "I do not deny that, Marchion, but your reason, for all of its worth, does little to alleviate the fires burning brightly beneath this very room. The fires in the hearts of your dwarf subjects—in a good number of them, at least, who named Torgar Delzoun Hammerstriker as a friend."

"They will come to their senses," Elastul replied. "I trust that Agrathan, beloved councilor, will convince them of the necessity of my actions."

Agrathan stared at Elastul for a long time, his expression shifting to one of simple resignation. He understood the reasoning, all along. He understood why Torgar had been taken from his intended road, and why he had been jailed. He understood why Elastul considered it up to him to calm the dwarves.

That didn't mean that Agrathan believed he had any chance of succeeding, though.

"Well good enough for him, I'm saying," one dwarf cried, and banged his fist on the wall. "The fool would o' telled them all our tricks. If he's to be a friend o' Mithral Hall, then throw him in a hole and leave him there!"

"The words of a fool, if ever I heared 'em," yelled another.

"Who ya callin' a fool?"

"Yerself, ye fool!"

The first dwarf charged forward, fists flying. Those around him, rather than try to stop him, came forward right beside him. They met the name-caller and his friends of similar mind.

Toivo Foamblower leaned back against the wall as the fight exploded around him, the fifth fight of that day in his tavern, and this one looking as if it would be the largest and bloodiest of them all.

Out in the street, just beyond his windows, a score of dwarves were fighting with a score of dwarves, rolling and punching, biting and kicking.

"Ye fool, Torgar," Toivo muttered under his breath.

"And ye bigger fool, Elastul!" he added as he dodged a living missile that soared over him, smashing the wall and a sizeable amount of good stock before falling to the floor, groaning and bitching.

It was going to be a long night in the Undercity. A long night indeed.

The scene was repeated in every bar along the Undercity and in the mines, where miner squared off against miner, sometimes with picks raised, as the news of the imprisonment of Torgar Hammerstriker spread like wildfire among the dwarves of Mirabar.

"Good for Elastul!" was shouted all along the dwarven enclaves, only to be inevitably refuted by a shout of "Damn the marchion!"

Raised voices, predictably, led to raised fists.

Outside Toivo's tavern, Shingles McRuff and a group of friends confronted a host of other-minded dwarves, the group spouting the praises of the man who had "stopped the traitor afore he could betray Mirabar to Mithral Hall."

"Ye're seeming a bit happy that Elastul's quick to jail one o' yer own," Shingles argued. "Ye're thinking it a good thing to have a dwarf rotting in a human jail?"

"Might be that I'm thinking it a good thing to have a traitor to Mirabar rotting in a Mirabar jail!" retorted the other dwarf, a tough-looking character with a black beard and eyebrows so bushy that they nearly hid his eyes. "At least until we've built the dog a proper gallows!"

That brought applause from the dwarves behind him, roars of anger from those beside Shingles, and an even more direct opposition response from old Shingles himself in the form of a well-aimed fist.

The black-bearded dwarf hopped backward beneath the weight of the blow, but thanks to the grabbing arms of his companions, not only didn't he fall, but he came rushing right back at Shingles.

The old dwarf was more than ready, lifting his fists as if to block the attack up high, then dropping to his knees at the very last second and jamming his shoulder into the black-bearded dwarf's waist. Up scrambled Shingles, lifting the outraged dwarf high and launching him into his fellows, then leaping in right behind, fists and feet flying.

Battling dwarves rolled all about the street, and the commotion brought many doors swinging open. Those dwarves who came to view the scene wasted little time in jumping right in, flailing away, though in truth they often had little idea which side they were joining. The riot went from street to street and snaked its way into many houses, and more than one had a fire pit overturned, flames leaping to furniture and tapestries.

Amidst it all, there came the blaring of a hundred horns as the Axe of Mirabar charged down from above, some on the lifts, others just setting ropes and swinging over, trying to get down fast before the rioting swept the whole of the Undercity into disaster.

Dwarf against dwarf and dwarf against man, they battled. In the face of the battle joined by humans, some with weapons drawn, many of the dwarves who had initially opposed Shingles and his like-minded companions changed sides. To many of those in the middle ground concerning the arrest of Torgar, it then became a question of loyalty, to blood or to country.

Though nearly half of the dwarves were fighting beside the Axe, and though many, many humans continued to filter down to quell the riot, it took hours to get the supporters of Torgar under control. Even then, the soldiers of the marchion were faced with the unenviable task of containing more than a hundred prisoners.

Hundreds more were watching them, they knew, and the first sign of mistreatment would likely ignite an even larger riot.

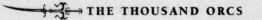

To Agrathan, who came late upon the scene, the destruction along the streets, the bloodied faces of so many of his kin, and even more than that the expressions of sheer outrage on so many, showed him the very danger of which he had warned the marchion laid bare. He went to the Axe commanders one by one, pressing for lenience and wise choices concerning the disposition of the prisoners, always with a grim warning that though the top was on the boiling kettle, the fire was still hot beneath it.

"Keep the peace as best ye can, but not a swing too far," Agrathan warned every commander.

After reciting that speech over and over, after pulling one angry guard after another off a prisoner, the exhausted councilor moved to the side of one avenue and plopped down on a stone bench.

"They got Torgar!" came a voice he could not ignore.

He looked up to see a bruised and battered Shingles, who seemed more than ready to break free of the two men who held him and start the row all over again.

"They dragged him from the road and beat him down!"

Agrathan looked hard at the old dwarf, gently patting his hands in the air to try to calm Shingles.

"Ye knew it!" Shingles roared. "Ye knew it all along, and ye're not for caring!"

"I care," Agrathan countered, leaping up from the bench.

"Bah! Ye're a short human, and not a thing more!"

As he shouted the insult, the guards holding Shingles gave a rough jerk, one letting go with one hand to slap the old dwarf across the face.

That was all the opening he needed. He accepted the slap with a growing grin then leaped around, breaking completely free of that one's grasp. Then, without hesitation, he launched his free fist hard into the gut of the soldier still holding him, doubling the man over and loosening his grasp. Shingles tore free completely, twisting and punching to avoid the grasp of the first man.

The soldier backed, calling for help, but Shingles came in too fast, kicking the man in the shin, and snapping his forehead forward and down, connecting solidly—too solidly—on the man's codpiece. He doubled over and dropped to his knees, his eyes crossing. Shingles came back around wildly, charging for the second soldier.

But when that soldier dodged aside, the dwarf didn't pursue. Instead he continued ahead toward his true intended target: poor Councilor Agrathan.

Agrathan had never been a fighter of Shingles's caliber, nor were his fists near as hard from any recent battles as those of the surly miner. Even worse for Agrathan, his heart wasn't in his defense nearly as much as Shingles's was in his rage.

The councilor felt the first few blows keenly, a left hook, a right cross, a few quick jabs, and a roundhouse that dropped him to the ground. He felt the bottom of Shingles's boot as the dwarf, lifted right off the ground by a pair of pursuing guards, got one last kick in. Agrathan felt the hands of a human grabbing him under the arm and helping him to his feet, an assist the dwarf roughly pushed away.

Gnashing his teeth, wounded inside far more than he could ever be outside, Councilor Agrathan stormed back for the lifts.

He knew that he had to get to the marchion. He had no idea what he was going to say, had no idea even what he expected or wanted the marchion to do, but he knew that the time had come to confront the man more forcefully.

19

MORTAL WINDS
BLOWING

"In all the days of all my life, I have never felt so mortal," Catti-brie said to the whispering wind.

Behind and below her, the dwarves, Regis, and Wulfgar went about their business preparing supper and setting up the latest camp, but the woman had been excused from her duties so that she could be alone to sort through her emotions.

And it was a tumult of emotions beyond anything Catti-brie had ever known. Her last fight had not been the first time the woman had been in mortal peril, surely, and not even the first time she had been helpless before a hated enemy. Once before, she had been captured by the assassin, Artemis Entreri, and dragged along in his pursuit of Regis, but in that instance, as helpless as she had felt, Catti-brie had never really expected to die.

Never like she had felt when caught helpless on the ground at the feet of the encircling, vicious orcs. In that horrible moment Catti-brie had seen her own death, vividly, unavoidably. In that one horrible moment, all of her life's dreams and hopes had been washed away on a wave of . . .

Of what?

Regret?

Truly, she had lived as fully as anyone, running across the land on wild adventures, helping to defeat dragons and demons, fighting to reclaim Mithral Hall for her adoptive father and his clan, chasing pirates on the open seas. She had known love.

She looked back over her shoulder at Wulfgar as she considered this.

She had known sorrow, and perhaps she had found love again. Or was she just kidding herself? She was surrounded by the best friends that anyone could ever hope to know, by an unlikely crew that loved her as she loved them. Companions, friends. It had been more than that with Wulfgar, so she had believed, and with Drizzt . . .

What?

She didn't know. She loved him dearly and always felt better when he was beside her, but were they meant to live as husband and wife? Was he to be the father of her children? Was that even possible?

The woman winced at the notion. One part of her rejoiced at the thought, and believed it would be something wonderful and beautiful. Another part of her, more pragmatic, recoiled at the thought, knowing that any such children would, by the mere nature of their heritage, remain as outcasts to any and all save those few who knew the truth of Drizzt Do'Urden.

Catti-brie closed her eyes and put her head down on her bent knees, curling up as she sat there, high on an exposed rock. She imagined herself as an older woman, far less mobile, and surely unable to run the mountainsides beside Drizzt Do'Urden, blessed as he was with the eternal youth of his people. She saw him on the trails every day, his smile wide as he basked in the adventure. That was his nature, after all, as it was hers. But it would only be hers for a few more years, she knew in her heart, and less than that if ever she was to become with child.

It was all too confusing, and all too painful. Those orcs circling her had shown her something about herself that she had never even realized, had shown her that her present life, as enjoyable as it was, as wild and full of adventure as it was, had to be (unless she was killed in the wilds) a prelude to something quite a bit different. Was she to be a mother? Or an emissary, perhaps, serving the court of her father, King Bruenor? Was this to be her last run through the wilds, her last great adventure?

"Doubt is expected after such a defeat," came a voice behind her, soft and familiar.

She opened her eyes and turned to see Wulfgar standing there, just a bit below her, his arms folded over the bent knee of his higher, lead leg.

Catti-brie gave him a curious look.

"I know what you are feeling," the barbarian said quietly, full of sincerity and compassion. "You faced death, and the looming specter warned you."

"Warned me?"

"Of your own mortality," Wulfgar explained.

Catti-brie's expression turned to incredulity. Wasn't Wulfgar stating the obvious?

"When I fell with the yochlol . . ." the barbarian began, and his eyes closed a bit in obvious pain at the memory. He paused and settled, then opened his eyes wide and pressed on. "In the lair of Errtu, I came to know despair. I came to know defeat beyond anything I had ever imagined, and I came to know both doubt and regret. For all that I had accomplished in my years, in bringing my people together, and into harmony with the folk of Ten-Towns, in fighting beside you, my friends, to rescue Regis, to reclaim Mithral Hall, to . . ."

"Save me from the yochlol," Catti-brie added, and Wulfgar smiled and accepted the gracious compliment with a slight nod.

"For all of that, in the lair of Errtu, I came to know an emptiness that I had not known to exist until that very moment," the barbarian explained. "As I looked upon what I believed to be the last moments of my existence, I felt strangely cold and dissatisfied with my lack of accomplishments."

"After all that you did accomplish?" the woman asked skeptically.

Wulfgar nodded. "Because in so many other ways, I had failed," Wulfgar answered, looking up at her. "In my love for you, I failed. And in my own understanding of who I was, and who I wanted to be, and what I wanted and needed for a life that I might know when the windy trails were no longer my home . . . I had failed."

Catti-brie could hardly believe what she was hearing. It was as if

Wulfgar was looking right through her, and pulling her own words out.

"And you found Colson and Delly," she said.

"A fine start, perhaps," Wulfgar replied.

His smile seemed sincere, and Catti-brie returned that smile, and they went quiet for a bit.

"Do you love him?" Wulfgar asked suddenly, unexpectedly.

Catti-brie started to answer with a question of her own, but the answer was self-evident as soon as she truly considered his words.

"Do you?" she asked instead.

"He is my brother, as true to me as any could ever be," Wulfgar answered without the slightest hesitation. "If a spear were aimed for Drizzt's chest, I would gladly leap in front of it, even should it cost me my own life, and I would die contented. Yes, I love him, as I love Bruenor, as I love Regis, as I love . . ."

He stopped there, and simply shrugged.

"As I, too, love them," Catti-brie answered.

"That is not what I mean," Wulfgar replied, not letting the dodge go past. "Do you love him? Do you see him as your partner, on the trails and in the home?"

Catti-brie looked at Wulfgar hard, trying to discern his intent. She saw no jealousy, no anger, and no signal of hopes, one way or the other. What she saw was Wulfgar, the true Wulfgar, son of Beornegar, a caring and loving companion.

"I do not know," she heard herself saying before she ever really considered the question.

The words caught her by surprise, hung in the air and in her thoughts, and she knew them to be true.

"I have felt your pain and your doubts," Wulfgar said, his voice going even softer, and he moved to her and braced her shoulders with his hands and lowered his forehead against hers. "We are all here for you, in any manner that you need. We, all of us, Drizzt included, are first your friends."

Catti-brie closed her eyes and let herself sink into that comforting moment, losing herself in the solidity of Wulfgar, in the understanding that he knew her pain, profoundly, that he had climbed from depths that she could hardly imagine. She found comfort in the knowledge that Wulfgar had returned from hell, that he had found his way, or at least, that he was walking a truer road.

She, too, would find that path, wherever it led.

"Bruenor told me," Drizzt said to Wulfgar when the drow returned from his extended scouting of the mountains to the northeast.

The drow dropped a hand onto his friend's shoulder and nodded.

"It was a rescue not unlike one of those Drizzt Do'Urden has perfected," Wulfgar replied, and he looked away.

"You have my thanks."

"I did not do it for you."

The simple statement, spoken simply, without obvious malice or anger, widened Drizzt's purple eyes.

"Of course not," he agreed.

The dark elf backed away, staring hard at Wulfgar, trying to find some clue as to where the barbarian's thoughts might be.

He saw only an impassive face, turned toward him.

"If we are to go thanking each other every time one of us stays the weapon hand an enemy has aimed at another, then we will spend our days doing little else," Wulfgar said. "Catti-brie was in trouble, and I was fortunate enough—we were all fortunate enough—to have come upon her in time. Did I do any more or less than Drizzt Do'Urden might have done?"

The perplexed Drizzt said, "No."

"Did I do more, then, than Bruenor Battlehammer might have done, had he seen his daughter in such mortal peril?"

"No."

"Did I do more, then, than Regis would have done, or at least, would have tried to do?"

"I have taken your point," Drizzt said.

"Then hold it well," said Wulfgar, and he looked away once more.

It took Drizzt a few moments to finally catch on to what was happening. Wulfgar had seen his thanks as condescending, as if, some-how, he had done something beyond what the companions would expect of each other. That notion hadn't sat well on the big man's shoulders.

"I take back my offer of thanks," Drizzt said.

Wulfgar merely chuckled.

"Perhaps, instead, I offer you a warm welcome back," Drizzt added.

That turned Wulfgar to him, the barbarian throwing a puzzled expression his way.

Drizzt nodded and walked away, leaving Wulfgar with those words to consider. The drow turned his gaze to a rocky outcropping to the south of the encampment, where a solitary figure sat quietly.

"She's been up there all the day," Bruenor remarked, moving beside the drow. "Ever since he brought her back."

"Lying at the feet of outraged orcs can be an unsettling experience."

"Ye think?"

Drizzt looked over at his bearded friend.

"Ye gonna go to her, elf?" Bruenor asked.

Drizzt wasn't sure, and his confusion showed clearly on his face.

"Yeah, she might be needin' some time to herself," Bruenor remarked. He looked back at Wulfgar, drawing the drow's gaze with his own. "Not exactly the hero she'd expected, I'd be guessin'."

The words hit Drizzt hard, mostly because the implications were forc-ing him to emotional places to which he did not wish to venture. What was this about, after all? Was it about Wulfgar rescuing his former and Drizzt's present love? Or was it about one of the companions rescuing another, as had happened so many times on their long and trying road?

The latter, Drizzt decided. It had to be the latter, and all the rest of it was emotional baggage that had no place among them. Not out where an orc or giant seemed crouched behind every boulder, ready to kill them. Not out where such distractions could lead to incredible disaster. Drizzt nearly laughed aloud as he considered the swirl of thoughts churning within him, including those same protective feelings toward Catti-brie for which he had once scolded a younger Wulfgar.

He focused on the positive, then, on the fact that Catti-brie had sur-vived without serious wounds, and on the fact that this stride Wulfgar had taken, this act of courage and strength and heroism, would likely move him further along his road back from the pits of Errtu's hell. Indeed, in looking at the barbarian then, moving with confidence and grace among the dwarves, a calm expression upon his face, it seemed to Drizzt as if the last edges of the smoke of the Abyss has washed clean of his features.

Yes, Drizzt decided, it was a good day.

"I saw the tower of Shallows at midday," the drow told Bruenor, "but though I was close enough to see it clearly, even to make out the forms of the soldiers walking atop it, I believe we have a couple of days' march ahead of us. I was on the edge of a long ravine when I glimpsed it, one that will take days to move around."

"But the town was still standing?" the dwarf asked.

"Seemed a peaceful place, with pennants flying in the summer breeze."

"As it should be, elf. As it should be," Bruenor remarked. "We'll go in and tell 'em what's been what, and might that I'll leave a few dwarves with 'em if they're needing the help, and—"

"And we go home," said Drizzt, studying Bruenor as he spoke, noting clearly that the dwarf wasn't hearing those words as any blessing.

"Might be other towns needin' us to check in on them," Bruenor huffed.

"I am sure that we can find a few if we look hard enough."

Bruenor either missed the sarcastic grin on Drizzt's face or simply chose to ignore it.

"Yup," the dwarf king said, and he walked away.

Drizzt watched him go, but his gaze was inevitably drawn back up to the high outcropping, to the lone figure of Catti-brie.

He wanted to go to her—desperately wanted to go and put his arms around her and tell her that everything was all right.

For some reason, though, Drizzt thought that would be ultimately unfair. He sensed that she needed some space from him and from everyone else, that she needed to sort through all the emotions that her close encounter with her own mortality had brought bubbling within her.

What kind of a friend might he be if he did not allow her that space?

Wulfgar was with the main body of dwarves that next day on the road, helping to haul the supplies, but Regis remained outside the group, moving along the higher trails with Drizzt and Catti-brie. He spent little time scouting for enemies, though, for he was too busy watching his two friends, and noting, very definitely, the change that had come over them.

Drizzt was all business, as usual, signaling back directions and weaving around with a sureness of foot and a speed that the others, save Guenhwyvar who was not even there this day, could not hope to match. The drow was pretending as if nothing had happened, Regis saw clearly, but it was just that, a pretense.

His zigzagging routes were keeping him closer to Catti-brie, the halfling noted, constantly coming to vantage points that put him in sight of the woman. Truly, the drow's movements surprised Regis, for never before had he seen Drizzt so protective.

Was it protectiveness, the halfling had to wonder, or was it something else?

The change in Catti-brie was even more obvious. There was a coolness about her, particularly toward Drizzt. It wasn't anything overtly rude, it was just that she was speaking much less that day than normally, answering his directions with a simple nod or shrug. The incident with the orcs was weighing heavily on her mind, Regis supposed.

He glanced back at the dwarven caravan then looked all around, ensuring that they were secure for the time being—no sign of any orc or giant had shown that day—then he scrambled forward along the trail, catching up to Catti-brie.

"A chill in the wind this morning," he said to her.

She nodded and kept looking straight ahead. Her thoughts were inward and not on the trail before her.

"Seems that the cold has affected your shoulder," Regis dared to remark.

Catti-brie nodded again, but then she stopped and turned deliberately to regard him. Her stern expression did not hold against the cherubic halfling face, one full of innocence, even though it was obvious that Regis had just made a remark at her expense.

"I'm sorry," the woman said. "A lot on me mind is all."

"When we were on the river, on our way to Cadderly, and the goblin spear found my shoulder, I felt the same way," Regis replied, "helpless, and as if the end of my road was upon me."

"And more than a few have noted the change that has come over Regis since that day."

It was Regis's turn to shrug.

"Often in those moments when we think all is lost," he said, "many things . . . priorities . . . become clear to us. Sometimes, it just takes a while after the incident to sort things out."

Catti-brie's smile told him that he had hit the mark.

"It's a strange thing, this life we've chosen," Regis mused. "We know that the odds tell us without doubt that we'll one day be killed in the wilds, but we keep telling ourselves that it won't be this day at least, and so we walk farther along that same road.

"Why does Regis, no friend of any road, take that walk, then?" Catti-brie asked.

"Because I've chosen to walk with my friends," the halfling explained. "Because we are as one, and I would rather die out here beside you than learn of your death while sitting in a comfortable chair—especially when such news would come with my feelings that perhaps if I had been with you, you would not have been killed."

"It is guilt, then?"

"That, and a desire not to miss the excitement," Regis answered with a laugh. "How much grander the tales are than the experiences. I know that from listening to Bruenor and his kin exaggerating every thrown punch into a battering ram of a fist that could level a castle's walls, yet even knowing it, hearing those tales about incidents that did not include me, fill me with wonder and regret."

"So ye've come to admit yer adventurous side?"

"Perhaps."

"And ye're not thinking that ye might be needing more?"

Regis looked at her with an expression that conveyed that he was not sure what "more" might mean.

"Ye're not thinking that ye might want a life with others of yer own ilk? That ye might want a wife and some . . ."

"Children?" the halfling finished when Catti-brie paused, as if she could not force the word from her lips.

"Aye."

"It has been so many years since I've even lived among other halflings," Regis said, "and . . . well, it did not end amicably."

"It's a tale ye've not told."

"And too long a tale for this road," Regis replied. "I don't know how to answer you. Honestly. For now, I've got my friends, and that has just seemed to be enough."

"For now?"

Regis shrugged and asked, "Is that what's troubling you? Did you find more regrets than you expected when the orcs had encircled you and you thought your life to be at its end?"

Catti-brie looked away, giving the halfling all the answer he needed. The perceptive Regis saw much more than the direct answer to his question. He understood the source of many of those regrets. He had been watching Catti-brie's relationship with Drizzt grow over the last months, and while the sight of them surely did his romantic heart good, he knew that such a union, if it ever came to pass, would not be without its troubles. He knew what Catti-brie had been thinking when the orcs hovered over her. She had been wondering about children, her children, and it was obvious to Regis that children were nothing Drizzt Do'Urden could ever give to her. Could a drow and human even bear offspring?

Perhaps, since elves and humans could, and had, but what fate might such a child find? Was it one that Catti-brie could accept?

"What will you do?" the halfling asked her, drawing a curious look.

Regis nodded ahead on the trail, to the figure of Drizzt walking toward them. Catti-brie looked at him and took a deep breath.

"I will walk the trails as scout for our group," the woman answered coolly. "I will draw Taumaril often and fire true, and when battle is joined I'll leap in with Cutter's gleaming edge slashing down our foes."

"You know what I mean."

"No, I do not," Catti-brie answered.

Regis started to argue, but Drizzt was upon them then, and so he bit back his retort.

"The trails are clear of orc-sign," the drow remarked, speaking haltingly and looking from Regis to Catti-brie, as if suspicious of the conversation he was so obviously interrupting.

"Then we will make the ravine before nightfall," Catti-brie replied.

"Long before, and make our turn to the north."

The woman nodded, and Regis gave a frustrated, "*Hrmmph!*" and walked away.

"What troubles our little friend?" Drizzt asked.

"The road ahead," the woman answered.

"Ah, perhaps there is a bit of the old Regis within him yet," Drizzt said with a smile, missing the true meaning of her words.

Catti-brie just smiled and kept walking.

They made the ravine soon after and saw the gleaming white tower that marked the town of Shallows—the tower of Withegroo Seian'Doo, a wizard of minor repute. Hardly pausing, the group moved along its western edge until long after the sun had set. They heard the howls of wolves that night, but they were far off, and if they were connected in any way to any orcs, the companions could not tell.

They rounded the ravine the next day, turning to the east and back toward the south and took heart, for still there was no sign of the orcs. It seemed as if the group that had hit Clicking Heels might be an isolated one, and those who had not fallen to the vengeful dwarves had likely retreated to dark mountain holes.

Again they marched long after sunset, and when they camped, they did so with the watch fires of Shallows's wall in sight, knowing full well that their own fires could be seen clearly from the town.

Drizzt was not surprised to find a pair of scouts moving their way under the cover of darkness. The drow was out for a final survey of the area when he heard the footfalls, soon coming in sight of the creeping men. They were trying to be quiet, obviously, and having little fortune, almost constantly tripping over roots and stones.

The drow moved to a position to the side of the pair behind a tree and called out, "Halt and be counted!"

It was a customary demand in these wild parts. The two humans stumbled again and fell to low crouches, glancing about nervously.

"Who is it who approaches the camp of King Bruenor Battlehammer without proper announcement?" Drizzt called.

"King Bruenor!" the pair yelled together, and at each other.

"Aye, the lord of Mithral Hall, returned home upon news of the death of Gandalug, who was king."

"He's a bit far to the north, I'm thinking," one man dared reply.

The pair kept hopping about, trying to discern the speaker.

"We're on the trail of orcs and giants who sacked a town to the south and west," Drizzt explained. "Journeying to Shallows, fair Shallows, to ensure that the folk are well, and well protected, should any monsters move against them."

One man snorted, and the other yelled back, "Bah! No orc'll e'er climb the wall of Shallows, and no giant'll ever knock it down!"

"Well spoken," Drizzt said, and the man assumed a defiant posture, standing straight and tall and crossing his arms over his chest. "I take it that you are scouts of Shallows, then?"

"We're wanting to know who it is setting camp in sight of our walls," the man called back

"Well, it is as I told you, but please, continue on your way. You will be announced to King Bruenor. I am certain that he will gladly share his table this night."

The man eased from his defiant posture and looked to his friend, the two seeming unsure.

"Run along!" Drizzt called.

And he was gone, melting into the night, running easily along the rough ground and quickly outdistancing the men so that by the time they at last reached the encampment, Bruenor and the others were waiting for them, with two extra heaping plates set out.

"Me friend here told me ye'd be in," Bruenor said to the pair.

He looked to the side, and so did the scouts, to where Drizzt was dropping the cowl of his cloak, revealing his dark heritage.

Both men widened their eyes at the sight, but then one unexpectedly cried out, "Drizzt Do'Urden! By the gods, but I wondered if I'd ever meet the likes of yerself!"

Drizzt smiled—he couldn't help it, so unused was he to hearing such warm greetings from surface dwellers. He glanced at Bruenor, and noted Catti-brie standing beside the dwarf and looking his way, her expression curious, a bit confused, and a bit charmed.

Drizzt could only guess at the swirl of emotions behind that look.

20

SHARP TURN
IN THE ROAD

They moved along the paths of the Moonwood easily, with Tarathiel, astride Sunset, leading the way. The bells of his saddle jingled merrily, and Innovindil walked with the dwarf brothers right behind. The sky was gray, and the air stifling and a bit too warm, but the elves seemed in a fine mood, as did Pikel, who was marveling at their winding trail. They kept coming upon seeming dead ends and Tarathiel, who knew the western stretch of the Moonwood better than anyone alive, would make a slight adjustment and a new path would open before him, clear and inviting. It almost seemed as if Tarathiel had just asked the trees for passage, and that they had complied.

Pikel so loved that kind of thing.

Among the four, only Ivan was in a surly mood. The dwarf hadn't slept well the previous night, awakened often by Elvish singing, and while Ivan would join in any good drinking song, any hymn to the dwarf gods (which was pretty much the same thing), or songs of heroes of old and treasures lost and treasures found, he found the Elvish styling little more than whining, pining at the moon and the stars.

In fact, over the past few days, Ivan had had about enough of the elves altogether and only wanted to be back on the road to Mithral Hall. The yellow-bearded dwarf, never known for his subtlety, had related those emotions to Tarathiel and Innovindil often and repeatedly.

The four were moving out to the west from the region where the elves of the Moonwood made their main enclave and just a bit to the north, where the ground was higher and they would likely spot the snaking River Surbrin. The dwarves could then use the river as a guide on their southerly turn to Mithral Hall. Tarathiel had explained that they had about a tenday of traveling ahead of them—less, if they managed to float some kind of raft on the river and glide through the night.

Pikel and Innovindil chatted almost constantly along the trail, sharing information and insights on the various plants and animals they passed. Once or twice, Pikel called a bird down from a tree and whispered something to it. The bird, apparently understanding, flew off and returned with many others, lining the branches around the foursome and filling the air with their chirping song. Innovindil clapped her hands and beamed an enchanted smile at Pikel. Even Tarathiel, the far more serious of the two elves, seemed quite pleased. Ivan missed it all, though, stomping along, grumbling to himself about "stupid fairies."

That, of course, only pleased the elves even more—especially when Pikel convinced the birds to make an amazingly accurate bombing run above his brother.

"Think ye might be lending me yer fine bow?" the disgruntled Ivan asked Tarathiel. The dwarf glared up at the branches as he spoke. "I can get us a bit o' supper."

Tarathiel's answer was a bemused smile, which only widened when Pikel added, "Hee hee hee."

"We shan't be accompanying you two to Mithral Hall," Tarathiel explained.

"Who was askin' ye?" Ivan grumbled in reply, but when the two elves fixed him with surprised and a bit wounded looks, the dwarf seemed to retract a bit. "Bah, but why'd ye want to go and stay with a bunch of dwarfs anyway? Course ye could, if ye're wanting to, and me and me brother'd make sure that ye was treated as well as ye treated us two in yer stinkin . . . in yer pretty forest."

"Your compliments roll as freely as a frozen river, Ivan Boulder-shoulder," Innovindil said in a deceivingly complimentary tone.

She tossed a wink to Tarathiel and Pikel, who giggled.

"Aye," said Ivan, apparently not catching on.

He smirked and looked hard at the elf.

"We have much to discuss with King Bruenor, though," Tarathiel remarked then, bringing the conversation back to the issue at hand. "Perhaps you will bid him to send an emissary to the Moonwood. Drizzt Do'Urden would be welcomed."

"The dark elf?" Ivan balked. "Couple o' moon elves like yerselves asking me to ask a drow to walk into yer home? Ye best be careful, Tarathiel. Yer reputation for hospitality to dwarfs and dark elfs might not be sittin' well with yer kin!"

"Not to dark elves, I assure you," the elf corrected, "but to that one dark elf, yes. We would welcome Drizzt Do'Urden, though we have not named him as a friend. We have information regarding him—information that will be important to him and is important to us."

"Such as?"

"That is all that I am at liberty to say at this time," Tarathiel replied. "I'd not burden you with such a long and detailed story to bring to King Bruenor. Without knowledge of that which came before, you would not understand enough to properly convey the information."

"It is out of no mistrust of you two that we choose to wait for King Bruenor's official emissary," Innovindil was quick to add, for a scowl was growing over Ivan's face. "There is protocol that must be followed. This message we ask you to deliver is of great importance, and we let you go with complete confidence that you will not only deliver our words to King Bruenor, but deliver them with our sense of urgency in mind."

"Oo oi!" Pikel agreed, punching a fist into the air.

Tarathiel started to second that, but he stopped suddenly, his expression growing very serious. He glanced around, then at Innovindil, then slid down from his winged mount.

"What's he seein'?" Ivan demanded.

Innovindil locked stares with Tarathiel, her expression growing equally stern.

Tarathiel motioned for Ivan to be quiet then moved silently to the side of the trail, bending low to the ground, head tilted as if he was listening. Ivan started to say something again, but Tarathiel held up a hand, silencing him.

"Oooo," said Pikel, looking around with alarm.

Ivan hopped about, seeing nothing but his three concerned companions.

"What'd ye know?" he asked Tarathiel, but the elf was deep in thought and did not reply.

Ivan rushed across to Pikel and asked, "What'd ye know?"

Pikel crinkled his face and pinched his nose.

"Orcs?" Ivan cried.

"Yup yup."

In a single movement, Ivan pulled the axe from his back and turned, feet set wide apart in solid balance, axe at the ready before him, eyes narrowed and scouring every shadow.

"Well, bring 'em on, then. I'm up for a bit o' chopping afore another long and boring road!"

"I sense them, too," Innovindil said a moment later.

"Dere," Pikel added, pointing to the north.

The two elves followed his finger, then looked back at him, nodding.

"Our borders have seen orc incursions of late," Innovindil explained. "This one, as the others, will be repelled. Trouble yourselves not with these creatures. Your road is to the west and the south, and there you should go and quickly. We will see to the beasts that dare stain the Moonwood."

"Uh-uh," Pikel disagreed, crossing his burly, hairy arms over his chest.

"Bah!" Ivan snorted. "Ye're not for throwin' us out afore the fun begins! Ye call yerselves proper hosts and ye're thinking o' chasin' us off with orcs needin' killing?"

The two elves looked to each other, honestly surprised.

"Yeah, I know, and no, I'm not liking ye," Ivan explained, "but I'm hatin' yer enemies, so that's a good thing. Now, are ye to make a friend of a dwarf and let him chop an orc or fifty? Or are ye to chase us off and hope we're remembering the words ye asked us to deliver to King Bruenor?"

Still the elves exchanged questioning glances, and Innovindil gave a slight shrug, leaving the decision to Tarathiel alone.

"Come along, then," the elf said to the brothers. "Let us see what we can learn before rousing my people against the threat. And do try to be quiet."

"Bah, if we're too quiet, might be that the orcs'll just wander away, and what good's that?"

They moved a short distance before Tarathiel motioned for them to stop and bade them to wait. He climbed onto the pegasus, found a run for Sunset, and lifted into the air, rising carefully in the close quarters, up and out to the north.

He returned almost immediately, setting down before the three, motioning for them to hold silent and to follow him. Up to the north a short distance, the elf led them to the top of a ridge. From that vantage point, Ivan saw that the mystical tree-attuned senses of his companions had not led them astray.

There, in a clearing of their own making, was a band of orcs. It was a dozen at least, perhaps as many as a score, weaving in and out of the shadows of the trees. They carried large axes, perfect for chopping the tall trees, and more importantly (and explaining why Tarathiel had been so quick to return with Sunset) and more atypically, they also each had a long, strong bow.

"I saw them from afar," Tarathiel explained quietly to the other three as they crouched at the ridge top. "I do not believe that they spotted me."

"We must get word to the clan," Innovindil said.

Tarathiel looked around doubtfully. They had been traveling for a couple of days. While he realized that his people would move much more quickly with such dire news as orc intruders, and without having a pair of dwarves slowing them down, he didn't think that they would get there in time to catch the orcs in the Moonwood.

"They must not escape," the elf said grimly, thoughts of the last band retreating into the mountains still fresh in his mind.

"Then let's kill 'em," Ivan replied.

"Three to one," Innovindil remarked. "Perhaps five to one."

"It'll be quick, then," Ivan replied.

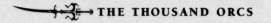

He took up his heavy axe. Beside him, Pikel fished his cooking pot out of his sack, plopped it on his head, and agreed, "Oo oi!"

The elves looked to each other with obvious confusion and surprise.

"Oo oi!" Pikel repeated.

Tarathiel looked at Innovindil for his answer.

"It has been a long time since I have had a good fight," she said with a wry grin.

"Only a dozen—ye'll have longer to wait for any real fight," Ivan said dryly, but the elves didn't seem to pay his remark much heed.

Tarathiel looked over at Ivan and asked, "Where will you fit in?"

"In the middle o' them, I'm hoping," the dwarf answered, pointing toward the distant orcs. "And I'm thinking me axe'll be fitting in real well between them orcs' eyeballs."

That seemed simple enough, and so Tarathiel and Innovindil looked to Pikel, who merely chuckled, "Hee hee hee."

"Don't ye be frettin' about me brother," Ivan explained. "He'll find a way to do his part. I'm not knowin' how—I'm usually not knowin' how even after the fightin's over—but he does, and he will."

"Good enough, then," said Tarathiel. "Let us find the best vantage point for launching our strike."

He moved to Sunset and whispered something into the pegasus's ear, then started away while Sunset walked off in another direction. Innovindil went next, moving as silently as her elf partner. Then came Ivan and Pikel, crunching away on every dry leaf and dead stick.

"Vantage point," Ivan huffed to his brother. "Just walk in, say yer howdies, and start killing!"

"Hee hee hee," said Pikel.

Innovindil also wore a smile at that remark, but it was one edged with a bit of trepidation. Confidence was one thing, carelessness quite another.

With the elves guiding them, and despite the noisiness of the dwarves, the foursome came to the edge of a rocky clearing. Across the way, the orcs were at their work, some chopping hard at one tree, others holding guiding ropes tied off along the higher branches.

"We will hit at them after they have retired," Tarathiel quietly explained. "The sun is high. It should not be long."

Pikel's face grew very tight, though, and he shook his head.

"He's not for watching them cut down a tree," Ivan explained, and the elves looked to each other doubtfully.

Pikel opened a pouch, revealing a cache of bright red berries. His expression grew very serious and very stern. With a grim nod to the others, he walked up to a nearby oak, the widest tree around, and put his forehead against its thick trunk. He closed his eyes and began muttering under his breath.

Still muttering, he stepped *into* the tree, disappearing completely.

"Yeah, I know yer feelings," Ivan whispered to the two elves, who were standing dumbfounded, their mouths hanging open. "He does it all the time."

Ivan's gaze went up to the branches, and he pointed and said, "There."

Pikel exited the trunk some twenty feet above the ground, moving out on a branch that overhung the rocky field.

"Your brother is a curious one," Innovindil whispered. "Many tricks."

"We may need them," Tarathiel added.

He was looking doubtfully at the dozen or more orcs, all with bows on their backs or lying within easy reach. Looking up at Pikel, though, he knew that the dwarves weren't likely to wait, whatever he suggested, so he went into a crouch and began surveying the battlefield, then motioned to Innovindil to fan out to the side.

Ivan walked right between them, crunching through the trees, axe in hand, stepping onto the edge of the clearing.

"Can't be hitting anything that moves, now can ye?" he taunted loudly.

The chopping stopped immediately. All sound from the other side of the clearing halted, and the orcs turned as one, their yellowish, blood-shot eyes wide.

"Well?" Ivan called to them. "Ain't ye never looked death in the eye before?"

The orcs didn't charge across the way. They began to move slowly, deliberately, with a couple barking orders.

"Them're the leaders," Ivan whispered back to the concealed elves. "Pick yer shots."

The orcs never blinked, never took their eyes off the spectacle of the lone dwarf standing barely twenty feet from them, as they slowly began to collect their bows, to string the weapons and bring them up to the ready.

The leaders continued to talk to the others, and it was obvious that they were calling for a coordinated barrage, bidding those already prepared to fire to hold their shots.

The elves fired first, a pair of arrows soaring out from the brush to strike true across the way, Tarathiel's taking one leader in the throat, Innovindil's catching another in the belly, sending it squirming to the ground.

At that same moment, the air before Ivan seemed to warp like a ripple on a pond, and that wave rushed across the clearing as the orcs let fly.

Arrows warped even as they cleared the bows, bending like the strands of a willow tree and flying every which way but straight. Except for one, from the trees to the side, that soared in at Ivan.

The dwarf saw it in time, though, and he jerked down, bringing his axe up to the side and, fortunately, in line with the missile. It clipped the blade, then Ivan's armored shoulder, staggering the dwarf to the side but doing no real damage against the armor he wore.

"Get 'em all, ye durned fool!" Ivan scolded his brother, who giggled from the boughs above him.

Across the way, the orcs looked at their bows as if deceived and saw that most of those, too, had warped under the druidic magic wave, and so they threw them down, drew out swords and spears, and charged wildly.

Two more barely began their run before elven arrows dropped them. Ivan Bouldershoulder resisted the urge to counter with his own charge, and the urge to look up and make sure that his scatterbrained brother was still paying attention.

Another pair of elven arrows soared off, and Tarathiel and Innovindil leaped out beside Ivan, each drawing a slender sword and a long dirk.

The orcs closed, leaping stones and scrambling over boulders, and howling their guttural battle cries.

Handfuls of bright red berries flew out over Ivan and the elves, enchanted missiles that popped loudly and sparked painfully as they hit. Dozens of little bursts settled in and around the charging orcs. The enchanted bombs did little damage, but brought about massive confusion, an opening that neither Ivan nor the elves missed.

Ivan pulled a hand axe from his belt and flung it into the face of the nearest orc, then drew a second and cut down an orc to the side. Out he charged with a roar, his large axe going to work immediately on one stumbling monster, halting its charge with a whack in the chest, then flying wide as Ivan spun past, coming in hard and chopping the creature on the back of the neck.

But it was the movement of the elves, and not ferocious Ivan, that elicited the sincerely impressed "Oooo" from Pikel up above.

Standing side by side, Tarathiel and Innovindil brought their weapons up in a flowing cross before their chests, rising past their faces and going out at the ready to either side, so that Tarathiel's right arm crossed against Innovindil's left, forearm to forearm. They held that touch as they went out against the charge, moving as if they were one, flowing back and forth and turning as they went, Tarathiel crossing behind Innovindil, coming around to the female's right and shifting past, so that they were touching right forearm to right forearm, right foot to right foot, heel against toe.

Not understanding the level of the joining, an orc rushed in at Tarathiel's seemingly exposed back, only to find Innovindil's blade waiting for it, turning its spear aside with ease. Innovindil didn't finish the move, though, but rather went back to an orc that was still off-balance from Pikel's bomb barrage. The elf slid the blade easily through the orc's exposed ribs as it stumbled past. She didn't have to finish that move either, for Tarathiel had understood everything she had accomplished in the parry as surely as if he had done the movement himself. He just reversed his grip on the dirk in his left hand, and while still parrying the blade of the orc he was fighting before him with his sword, he thrust out hard behind, stabbing the attacking spear wielder in the chest.

In a single, fluid movement, Tarathiel extracted the dagger and flipped it into the air, catching it by the tip, then brought his arm toward the orc before him as if he meant to throw the dirk.

The orc flinched, and Tarathiel rotated away.

Innovindil came across, her long sword slashing the confused orc's throat.

Tarathiel stopped the rotation first and dropped his sword arm down and around, hooking his still-moving partner around the waist. He pulled hard, lifting Innovindil off the ground, pulling her over his hip, and whipping her across before him, her feet extended and kicking at the orc that had come in at Tarathiel.

She didn't score any hits on that orc—she wasn't really trying to—but her weaving feet had the creature reacting with its short, hooked blade, striking at her repeatedly and futilely.

As Innovindil rolled across his torso, Tarathiel reached across with his left hand, and she hooked her right elbow over it, and he stopped his rotation completely, except with that arm, playing with Innovindil's momentum to send her spinning out to his left.

At the same time, as soon as she had cleared the way, the male struck out with his right arm, his sword arm. The poor orc, still trying to catch up to Innovindil, never even saw the blade coming.

Innovindil landed lightly, her momentum and spin bringing her right across the path of another orc, her blades slashing high, stabbing low.

In that one short charge and spin, the elves had five orcs dead or dying.

"Oooo," said Pikel, and he looked down at the berries in his hand doubtfully.

Then he caught a movement to the side, moving through the brush, and saw a pair of orcs lifting bows.

He threw before they could fire, the two dozen little explosions making the orcs jump and jerk, stinging and blinding them.

Pikel's arms went out that way, his fingers waggling, calling to the brush around the pair of orcs. Vines and shrubs grabbed at the creatures, and at a third, Pikel realized with a giggle, for he heard the unseen orc roaring in protest below its trapped companions.

Ivan didn't have the grace or coordination of the warrior elves, and in truth, their deadly dance was impressive to the dwarf. Amusing, but impressive nonetheless.

What he lacked in grace, the yellow-bearded dwarf more than made up for in sheer ferocity, though. Rushing past the orc he had chopped down, he met the charge—and hard—of another, accepting a shield rush and setting his legs powerfully. He didn't move. The orc bounced back.

Ivan chopped that leading shield arm hard, his axe creasing the shield, even digging into the arm strapped under it. He jerked the weapon free immediately, lifting the orc into a short turn and forcing it to regain its balance. The dwarf struck again, this time getting the axe head past the blocking shield, chopping hard on the orc's shoulder.

The wounded creature stumbled back, but another rushed past it, and a third behind that.

Ivan was already moving, taking one step back and dropping low. He grabbed up a rock and threw it hard as he came up, thumping the closest orc in the chest, staggering it. As its companion came past it on its left, Ivan went past it on the right. His axe took the stunned orc in the gut, lifting it into the air and dropping it hard on its back.

The second orc skidded to a stop and started to turn—and caught Ivan's axe, spinning end over end, right in the chest.

Ivan, orcs in hot pursuit, charged right in, bowling over the creased orc as it fell and collecting his axe on the way. He kept running to a nearby boulder and leaped up and rolled over it, landing on his feet and falling back against it.

Orcs split around the boulder, charging on, and expecting that Ivan had run out the other side.

His axe caught the first coming by on the left, then went back hard to the right, smashing the lead orc from there as well.

Ivan hopped out behind the backhand, ready to fight straight up, but he found the work ending fast, as elven blades, already dripping orc blood, caught up to his pursuers.

There, facing the dwarf from either side of the boulder, stood Tarathiel and Innovindil. Much passed between the three at that moment, a level of respect that none of them had expected.

Ivan broke the stare first, glancing around, noting that no orcs were in the area except for dead and dying ones. He heard the clatter of the remaining creatures fleeing in the distant trees.

"Got me eight," Ivan announced.

He looked to the orc he had hit with the backhand, blunt side of his axe. It was hurt and dazed, and trying to rise, but before the dwarf could make a move toward it, Tarathiel's sword sliced its throat.

The dwarf shrugged. "All right, seven and a half," he said.

"And yet, I would reason that the one among us who scored the fewest kills was the most instrumental in our easy victory," said Innovindil.

She looked up to the tree to where Pikel had been sitting. A movement to the side turned her gaze, and those of Ivan and Tarathiel, to a tangle of brush from which Pikel was emerging, bloody club in hand and a wide grin on his face.

"Sha-la-la," the dwarf explained, holding forth the enchanted club. He held up three stubby fingers. "Tree!" he announced.

There came a movement behind him. Pikel's smile disappeared, and the dwarf spun around, his club smashing down.

The three across the way winced at the sound of shattering bone, but then Pikel came back up, his smile returned.

"Not quite done?" Ivan asked dryly.

"Tree!" came Pikel's enthusiastic reply, three fingers pointed up into the air.

The day was warm and sunny when the four companions came to the northwestern corner of the Moonwood. From a vantage point up high on a ridge, Tarathiel pointed out the shining line of the River Surbrin, snaking its way along the foothills of the Spine of the World to the west, flowing north to south.

"That will bring you to the eastern gates of Mithral Hall," Tarathiel explained. "Near to it, at least. I suspect you will find your way to the dwarven halls easily enough."

"And we trust that you will deliver our message to King Bruenor and the dark elf, Drizzt Do'Urden," Innovindil added.

"Yup," said Pikel.

"We'll tell 'em," said Ivan.

The elves looked at each other, neither expression holding any doubt at all. The four parted as friends, with more respect between them, particularly from Ivan and Tarathiel, than they had ever expected to find.

PART FOUR THE TURN IN THE ROAD

W e have to live our lives and view our relationship in the present. That is the truth of my life with Catti-brie, and it is also my fear for that life. To live in the here and now, to walk the wind-swept trails and do battle against whatever foe opposes us. To define our cause and our purpose, even if that purpose is no more than the pursuit of adventure, and to chase that goal with all our hearts and souls. When we do that, Catti-brie and I are free of the damning realities of our respective heritage. As long as we do that, we can live our lives together in true friendship and love, as close as two reasoning beings could ever be.

It is only when we look further down the road of the future that we encounter troubles.

On the mountainous trails north of Mithral Hall, Catti-brie recently had a brush with death and more poignantly, a brush with mortality. She looked at the end of her life, so suddenly and brutally. She thought she was dead, and believed in that horrible instant that she would never be a mother, that she would bear no children and instill in them the values that guide her life and her road. She saw mortality, true mortality, with no one to carry on her legacy.

She did not like what she saw.

She escaped death, as she has so often done, as I, and all of us, have so often done. Wulfgar was there for her, as he would have been for any of us, as any of us would have been for him, to scatter the orcs. And so her mortality was not realized in full.

But still the thought lingers.

And there, in that clearer understanding of the prospects of her future, in the clearer understanding of the prospect of our future, lies the rub, the sharp turn in our adventurous road that threatens to spill all that we have come to achieve into a ravine of deadly rocks.

What future is there between us? When we consider our

relationship day by day, there is only joy and adventure and excitement; when we look down the road, we see limitations that we, particularly Catti-brie, cannot ignore. Will she ever bear children? Could she even bear mine? There are many half-elves in the world, the product of mixed heritage, human and elf, but half-drow? I have never heard of such a thing—it was rumored that House Barrison Del'Armgo fostered such couplings, to add strength and size to their warrior males, but I know not if that was anything more than rumor. Certainly the results were not promising, even if that were true!

So I do not know that I could father any of Catti-brie's children, and in truth, even if it is possible, it is not necessarily a pleasant prospect, and certainly not one without severe repercussions. Certainly I would want children of mine to hold so many of Catti-brie's wonderful qualities: her perceptive nature, her bravery, her compassion, her constant holding to the course she knows to be right, and of course, her beauty. No parent could be anything but proud of a child who carried the qualities of Catti-brie.

But that child would be half-drow in a world that will not accept drow elves. I find a measure of tolerance now, in towns where my reputation precedes me, but what chance might any child beginning in this place have? By the time such a child was old enough to begin to make any such reputation, he or she would be undoubtedly scarred by the uniqueness of heritage. Perhaps we could have a child and keep it in Mithral Hall all the years.

But that, too, is a limitation, and one that Catti-brie knows all too well.

It is all too confusing and all too troubling. I love Catti-brie—I know that now—and know, too, that she loves me. We are friends above all else, and that is the beauty of our relationship. In the here and in the now, walking the road, feeling the wind, fighting our enemies, I could not ask for a better companion, a better compliment to who I am.

But as I look farther down that road, a decade, two decades,

I see sharper curves and deeper ravines. I would love Catti-brie until the day of her death, if that day found her infirm and aged while I was still in the flower of my youth. To me, there would be no burden, no longing to go out and adventure more, no need to go out and find a more physically compatible companion, an elf or perhaps even another drow.

Catti-brie once asked me if my greatest limitation was internal or external. Was I more limited by the way people viewed me as a dark elf, or by the way I viewed people viewing me? I think that same thing applies now, only for her. For while I understand the turns our road together will inevitably take, and I fully accept them, she fears them, I believe, and more for my sensibilities than for her own. In three decades, when she nears sixty years of age, she will be old by human standards. I'll be around a hundred, my first century, and would still be considered a very young adult, barely more than a child, by the reckoning of the drow. I think that her brush with mortality is making her look to that point and that she is not much enjoying the prospects—for me more than for her.

And there remains that other issue, of children. If we two were to start a family, our children would face terrific pressures and prejudices and would be young, so very young, when their mother passed away.

It is all too confusing.

I choose, for now, to walk in the present.

Yes, I do so out of fear.

—Drizzt Do'Urden

21

THE AURA
OF BEING KING

Even after the greeting by the guards sent out from Shallows, the response from the town the following morning, when the King of Mithral Hall and his entourage walked through the front gate of the walled town, stunned the group.

Trumpeters sounded from the parapets and from the top of the lone tower that stood along the northern wall of the small town. Though none of the trumpeters was very good, and none dressed in the shining armor one might expect from the court of a larger city like Silverymoon, Bruenor was certain that he had never heard anyone play with more heart.

All the people of the village, more than a hundred, encircled the area beyond the gate, clapping and waving and throwing petals. There were more women than Bruenor had expected from a frontier town and even a few children, including a couple of babies. Perhaps he should be spending quite a bit of time out of Mithral Hall and watching over these developing towns, Bruenor mused. It was not an unpleasant thought. In just looking at the place, it seemed to him as if Shallows was trying hard to become a regular town, a settled place, instead of the pocket of rogues and outlaws he had always thought it and all the other towns of the Savage Frontier to be. He considered his former home then, Ten-Towns, and recalled the evolution of those ten cities into something far more settled than they had been when he had first arrived in Icewind Dale those centuries before.

The dwarf, leading the procession, paused and looked around, past the many cheering people to their sturdy houses. Most were made of stone with supporting wooden frames, and all were built solid, as if the inhabitants meant to be there for a while. Bruenor nodded his silent approval, his gaze gradually moving to the single tower that so clearly marked the town. It was a thirty-foot gray cylinder, flying a pennant of a pair of hands surrounded by golden stars on a red background. A wizard's emblem, obviously, and when the crowd before him parted and a white-bearded old man walked through, dressed in a tall and pointy hat and bright red robes emblazoned in golden stars, it wasn't hard for the dwarf to make the connection.

"Welcome to my humble town, King Bruenor of Mithral Hall," the man said, walking up to stand right before Bruenor. He swept off his hat and fell into a grand bow. "I am Withegroo Seian'Doo, the founder of Shallows and present liege. This honor is unexpected but surely not unwelcome."

"Me greetings to yerself, Withe . . ."

"Withe*groo*."

"Withegroo," Bruenor finished. "And I'm not yet King Bruenor—well, not yet again, if ye get me meaning."

"It was with great sadness that I and my fellow townsfolk here heard of the passing of your ancestor, Gandalug."

"Yep, but the old one had himself a few good centuries, and I'm not thinking we can be askin' for more than that," Bruenor replied.

He looked around, to see the cheery and sincere smiles of the townsfolk, and he knew that he could be at ease there, that he and his friends, even Drizzt who was standing right behind him, were indeed welcomed guests in Shallows.

"Got the word in the west," the dwarf explained. "In Icewind Dale, where me and a few o' me friends were making our homes."

"Did you get lost on your journey home to Mithral Hall?"

Bruenor shook his head.

"Found me a couple o' friends from Felbarr," he explained, and he turned and indicated Tred, who gave an uncomfortable though still gracious bow. "They'd found themselves a bit o' trouble with some orcs."

He noted a shadow cross over Withegroo's wrinkled old face and long, hawkish nose. The man's enormous ears twitched beneath the bristles of his wild white hair, which was sticking out in every direction under the bent brim of his red hat.

Bruenor matched that look with a grave one of his own.

"Ye know the town o' Clicking Heels?" he asked somberly.

Withegroo looked around, to see several of his townsfolk nodding.

"Well, it ain't no more," Bruenor said bluntly. "Orcs 'n giants laid it to waste. Killed them all."

Groans, gasps, and whispers sprang up all around the courtyard.

"We been chasin' the dogs and killed more than a few," Bruenor went on quickly, wanting to put a better light on the tragedy. "Left a handful o' giants and near to a hunnerd orcs layin' dead in the mountains, but we thought it smart to come in here and make sure that Shallows was standing strong."

"Stronger than you can imagine," Withegroo replied.

He stood up straight and tall—and he was tall, well over six feet, tall enough to look Wulfgar in the eye without bending back his head. Unlike Wulfgar, though, the man was stick lean and couldn't have weighed more than half the barbarian's three hundred pounds.

"We have suffered the likes of orcs and giants many times," the wizard continued, "but not once have any crossed the line of our strong walls."

"Old Withegroo lays 'em dead with his lightning!" one man shouted from the side, and others immediately took up the chorus of cheers for the wizard.

Withegroo smiled, somewhat sheepishly, somewhat pridefully, and turned to them, patting his hands humbly to silence the growing chorus.

"I do what I can," the wizard said to Bruenor, turning back to face the dwarf. "I am no novice to battle, and I made my name and my fortune adventuring in dark caves filled with all sorts of beasts."

"And ye bought yerself a town," Bruenor remarked, with no sarcasm in his tone.

"I built myself a tower," the wizard corrected. "I thought this a fine place to live out my days, in study and recollections of adventures past. These good folk"—he turned and swept his hand across the crowd—"found me, one by one and family by family. I believe they recognized the value of having so striking a landmark as my tower in their intended settlement—brings in the dwarf traders, you see."

He ended with an exaggerated wink, which brought a smile to Bruenor's face.

"Bet they weren't minding having a wizard lookin' over them, throwing a few bolts o' lightning at any monsters venturing too close, either," the dwarf said to Withegroo, who took the compliment in stride.

"I do what I can."

"I'm bettin' ye do."

"Well," the wizard said with a deep breath, setting an abrupt change in the conversation. "You have come to check in on us, and an honor it is, King—or soon to be King—Bruenor Battlehammer. You can see that we are secure and strong, but I beg you, do not take quick leave of us. The walls of Shallows and the houses alike are of stone, and may seem cold—though not to a dwarf!—but they mask hearths of warmth and the voices of those with many adventures to share." He stepped back and looked up, addressing the whole company. "You are welcome, one and all. Welcome to Shallows!"

And with that, a great cheer went up form all the townsfolk, and Bruenor motioned for his road-weary group to disperse and relax.

"A bit better welcome than we received from Mirabar," Drizzt remarked to Bruenor, Catti-brie, Regis, and Wulfgar when the dwarf king moved away from Withegroo to rejoin his closest friends.

"Yeah, Mirabar," Bruenor grumbled. "Remind me to knock that place down."

"Not a sign o' orc about," Catti-brie said, "and a town with strong walls and stronger folk, and a wizard backing them. . . ."

She nodded her approval.

"And a southern road awaiting us," Wulfgar put in.

"But not right yet," said Catti-brie. "I'm thinking we should stay on a bit, just to be sure they're safe."

"Ye got a feeling, do ye?" Bruenor asked.

Catti-brie looked around, and despite the festivities, the laughter, and the seemingly normal scene, a cloud crossed her face.

"Yeah, I got it, too," said Bruenor. "But not to worry. We'll be checkin' all the land, and we'll take our march to the Surbrin in the east. Tred's telling me there's a couple more towns down that way. Let's see how many o' the folk in the region are as welcoming to King Bruenor and his friends."

He looked at Drizzt and pointedly added, "All his friends."

The drow shrugged as if it did not matter, and in truth, it did not.

"There are ten thousand more in dark holes who will be led if they believe that they will find greater glory," Ad'non Kareese said to his three companions.

He had just returned from a scouting circuit of the region between the dark elves hideaway and Gerti's complex, including a pair of visits with other minor monster kings: an orc who knew of Obould and a particularly wretched goblin.

"Twenty thousand," Donnia corrected, "at least. The mountain caverns crawl with the little beasts, and the only thing that keeps them in there is their own stupidity and fear. If Obould and Gerti claim this prize, the head of the king of the dwarven stronghold, then we will coax more than a few, I am certain."

"To what end?" Kaer'lic interjected doubtfully. "Then we will only have to look at the beasts scurrying about the surface."

"In chaos we find comfort," Tos'un put in with a wry grin.

"Spoken like a dolt from Menzoberranzan," said Kaer'lic, which only made Tos'un smile even wider.

"To your own tests of worthiness, then," Tos'un replied. "In chaos we find wealth. In chaos we find enjoyment."

Kaer'lic shrugged and didn't argue.

"I have already made some connections with the leaders of the various goblin and orc tribes and have heard hints of one that holds great ties to the more formidable beasts of the Trollmoors to the south," Ad'non remarked.

"Beware the boasts of goblins," said Donnia. "They would tell you that the mountain giants bow to them if they thought you would be impressed."

"Their tunnels stretch long," Ad'non replied.

"I am willing to believe that we can do this," said Tos'un, "and willing to believe that we will enjoy it greatly. I was the biggest doubter when we first tried to tie Obould to Gerti, and I was certain that the giantess would throttle the wretched orc when she learned of the loss of four of her kin, yet look where we are. Obould's scouts are everywhere, running the mountains, tracking this band that we believe contains King Bruenor himself. Once he is found, and Gerti takes her revenge. . . ."

"We can rally thousands to Obould's side," said Ad'non. "We can create a dark swarm that will cover the land for miles around!"

"And?" Kaer'lic asked dryly.

"And let them kill the dwarves, the humans, and each other," Ad'non replied. "And we will be there, always one step behind, yet always one step ahead, to collect our due at every turn."

"And to thoroughly enjoy the spectacle of it all," Donnia added with a wicked grin.

Kaer'lic accepted that reasoning and nodded her approval.

"Be certain that our allies are warned of the presence of a drow who is not a friend," the priestess advised.

She sat back as the others began formulating plans for their next moves. Kaer'lic did like the excitement, but there were other matters that concerned her more. She thought back to some experiences she had faced before finding her two, then three companions, when she had been out of her Underdark city on a mission for the ruling priestesses.

In those thoughts, Drizzt Do'Urden surely came to mind more than once, for he was not the first traitor to Lolth and drow ways that Kaer'lic the Terrible had faced.

It wasn't that she had any particular hatred or vendetta against Drizzt, of course—Tos'un would more likely harbor such resentments, she supposed—but the ever-plotting priestess had to wonder how it would all play out. Would she find unexpected opportunities to pay back old debts? Might the reputation of one renegade drow be put in good service to the Spider Queen, and even more importantly, to a priestess who had fallen out of favor with the goddess?

She smiled and looked around at the other three, all seeming so much more eager to play this out than was she.

Kaer'lic the Terrible, ever the patient one.

They heard the trumpets, and though they were somewhat dim-witted, one of the orc band made the connection between that heralding sound and the troupe they had been tracking.

From across the ravine, the orcs had the same view of Withegroo's tower as Drizzt and his friends had enjoyed only the day before.

Wicked grins splayed on their misshapen, tusked mouths, the orc patrol rushed away, back up into the foothills to where Urlgen, son of Obould, waited.

"Bruenor in the town," the patrol leader informed the tall, cruel orc leader.

Urlgen curled his torn lip, welcoming the information. The orc needed to redeem himself, and nothing short of the death of Bruenor Battlehammer would suffice. Obould blamed him, and so did Gerti, and for any creature living in the cold mountains at the end of the Spine of the World, having those two angry with him was not a good thing.

But they had King Bruenor within their grasp, at rest in a remote town and with little understanding of the catastrophe that was about to befall him.

Urlgen dispatched his messengers with all speed and with orders to press Obould to move quickly. They had the rat in the trap and Urlgen did not want him to slip out.

The orc was exhausted, having spent day after day in rallying others to his cause. Still, King Obould knew that he had to make this journey personally and not deliver the news that Bruenor had been found through any messenger.

He found Gerti sitting on the very edge of her throne, her blue eyes narrow and dangerous, her posture that of a predator anxious to spring.

"You have located King Bruenor and those others who murdered my kin?" she asked before the orc king could even offer a formal greeting.

"A small town," Obould replied. "The one with the lone tower."

Gerti nodded her recognition. With its singular tower, Shallows was quite distinct in this region of abandoned, simple villages and underground dwarven or goblinkin strongholds.

"And you have prepared your forces?"

"An army is out and running already," Obould answered.

Gerti's eyes widened and she seemed about to explode.

"Only to circle south," the orc quickly explained. "The ground is flat and easy to cross there, and King Bruenor must be held in the town."

"They are out to seal the road and nothing more?"

"Yes."

Gerti nodded to one of her attendants, a massive, muscular frost giant clad in shining metal armor and holding the largest, nastiest spear Obould had ever seen. The warrior immediately returned the nod with a bow and started out of the room.

"Yerki will lead my forces," Gerti explained. "They are ready to march at once."

"How many?" the orc had to ask.

"Ten," Gerti replied.

"And a thousand orcs," Obould added.

"Then our contributions to the downfall of King Bruenor Battle-hammer are about the same," remarked the superior-minded giantess.

Obould almost blurted a sarcastic response, but he remembered where he was and how easy it would be for any of Gerti's associates to smash him, and he just chuckled instead.

With her eyes still focused, narrow again and deadly serious, Gerti didn't join in his mirth.

"We must be away at once," Obould explained, shifting the subject a bit. "Three days running to the town."

"Make it in two," Gerti said.

Obould nodded, bowed, and turned around, hustling away from the giantess, but she stopped him as he was about to exit the cave, calling out his name.

The orc turned to face the power that was Gerti.

"Do not fail me . . . again," the giantess warned, putting emphasis on that last, damning word.

But Obould stood tall and straight and didn't back away from Gerti's imposing stare at all. He had ten giants at his disposal. Ten giants!

And a thousand orcs!

TOO CLEAR
A WARNING

Ivan had at first scoffed at Pikel's suggestion that they ride the currents of the River Surbrin to Mithral Hall's eastern gates, but after they set their camp the third night out of the Moonwood, with the river right below them, Pikel surprised his brother by sneaking away in the dark to collect fallen logs. By the time Ivan's snores had turned to the roaring yawns of morning, his green-bearded brother had fashioned a fair-sized raft of notched, interlocking logs, tied together by vines and rope.

Ivan's first reaction, of course, had been one of doubt.

"Ye fool, ye'll get us both drowned to death!" he said, hands on hips, feet wide-spaced, as if expecting Pikel to take the insult with typical grace and leap upon him.

Pikel only laughed and launched the raft. It bobbed in a shallow ebb pool at the river's edge in perfect balance and hardly dipped at all when Pikel hopped aboard.

With a lot of coaxing and many reminders of sore feet, Ivan finally joined his brother on the craft, "just to give it a test!" Before Ivan announced his final intent, Pikel paddled the raft out into the main currents, where it drifted easily.

Ivan's protests were lost in the sheer comfort of the journey, an easy glide. Pikel had fashioned the raft beautifully, creating a couple of amazingly comfortable seats, and even stringing a small hammock at one end of the craft.

Ivan didn't have to ask where his brother had learned to make such things. He knew that Pikel's weird druidic magic had been involved—obviously so! Some of the wood, like the chair he had taken as his own, seemed shaped, not carved, and the oar Pikel was using was covered in designs of leaves and trees so intricate that it would have taken a skilled woodcarver a tenday to fashion it. Pikel had done it in a single night.

They made great time that first day on the Surbrin, and on Pikel's suggestion, they continued right through the night. What a pleasant experience it was, particularly for Pikel, to be gliding on the easy currents under the canopy of twinkling stars. Even Ivan, so much the true dwarf, gained a bit more respect for elves under that amazing summer sky, or at least, he admitted some understanding (to himself!) of the elves' love of stars.

The second day, the river edged closer to the towering mountains, running the line along the eastern edge of the Spine of the World. Shining walls of gray stone, spattered with green foliage and streaks of white, marked the right bank, and sometimes both sides, as the river wove in and out of the rocky terrain. It didn't seem to bother Pikel in the least, but it made Ivan fall more on his guard. They had recently battled orcs, after all, and wouldn't this landscape make for a wonderful ambush?

At Ivan's insistence, they put up on the riverbank that second night, and in truth, the river was becoming a bit too unpredictable and rushed for travel in the dark anyway. Besides, the dwarves needed to re-supply.

Rain found them the next day, but it was a gentle one mostly, though it soaked them and made them miserable. At least the mountains retreated somewhat, the riverbank to the east falling away, and the mountain slopes on the west becoming more rounded and gently up-sloping.

"Think we'll find 'em today?" Ivan asked early on.

"Yup yup," Pikel replied.

Both dwarves retreated into thoughts of the real reason for their journey out of the Spirit Soaring cathedral. They had come to see Mithral Hall, to see King Bruenor's coronation. The prospect of viewing great dwarven halls, something neither of the brothers had done since their youngest years, far more than a century before, incited great joy in Ivan. His mind thought back to the most distant of his memories, to the sound of hammers ringing on metal, the smell of coal and sulfur and most of all mead. He could see again the strong, tall columns that supported the greatest chambers of his own home and believed that those of legendary Mithral Hall would probably exceed even those magnificent works by far.

Yes, to Ivan's thinking, as much as he loved Cadderly, Danica, and the kids, it would be grand to be among his own kind again, and in a place fashioned to the tastes of dwarves.

He looked over at Pikel as he considered his anticipation and wondered, hoped, that perhaps being in a place like Mithral Hall might go a long way into guiding the "doo-dad" back to his true heritage. If Pikel could fashion such work as this raft out of wood, Ivan had to wonder how magnificent his art might be when working with the true dwarven materials of stone and metal.

Of course, Ivan's budding fantasy would have been more convincing to him if, in the middle of his contemplations, Pikel hadn't summoned down a large and incredibly ugly bird to his upheld forearm, then engaged in a long and seemingly detailed conversation with the creature.

"Talkin' to yer own level?" Ivan asked dryly when the vulture flew away.

Pikel turned to his brother with a surprisingly serious expression, then pointed to the western bank and began steering the raft that way.

Ivan knew better than to argue. His often silly brother had proven too many times that the information he could garner from animals could prove vital. Besides, the river was getting a bit more vigorous and Ivan longed to put his feet on solid ground once more.

As soon as they had the boat beached, Pikel grabbed his large sack of supplies, plopped his cooking pot over his head, and leaped away, rushing for the higher ground away from the riverbank. Ivan caught up to him a short time later, on a rocky mound.

Pikel pointed to the southwest, to a cluster of activity against the backdrop of the gray mountains.

"Dwarfs," Ivan remarked.

He narrowed his eyes and shielded them from the glare with his hand. He nodded, affirming his own observation. They were indeed dwarves, and had to be from Mithral Hall, all rushing around, apparently working on defensive fortifications.

He looked back to his brother but found Pikel already moving, cutting a straight line for the construction. Side-by-side they ran along the gently sloping ground, first down then up a steep trail.

A short time later came a roaring command, "Halt and be known! Be liked or be skewered!"

The brothers, understanding the seriousness of that tone, skidded to a stop before the closed iron gates set at the front of a stone wall.

A burly red-bearded dwarf in full battle-mail rushed out through those gates.

"Well, ye don't look like orcs and ye don't smell like orcs," he said.

"Though I'm not for certain what yerself looks and smells like," he added, scrutinizing Pikel.

"Doo-dad," Pikel remarked.

"Ivan Bouldershoulder at yer service, and I'm thinking ye must be in service to King Bruenor. This is me brother Pikel. We're coming outta Carradoon and the Snowflake Mountains, sent by High Priest Cadderly Bonaduce to serve as witnesses to the new king's coronation."

The soldier nodded, his expression showing that while he might not have understood all that Ivan had just said, he seemed to get the gist of it and seemed to think it a perfectly reasonable explanation.

"Cadderly's a friend o' that drow elf that runs about with yer soon-to-be king," Ivan explained, drawing a knowing nod from the soldier. "He's still soon-to-be, ain't he?"

The soldier's expression turned sour for just a moment, his crusty features tightening, then widened in understanding.

"We ain't crowned him yet, as he ain't been in from Icewind Dale."

"We feared we'd miss him," Ivan said.

"Ye would've if he'd've come right in," the soldier explained, "but him and his found orcs on the road and're chasin' them down and putting them back in their filthy holes."

Ivan nodded with sincere admiration.

"Good king," he said, and the soldier beamed.

"Small band and nothin' more, so it won't be long," the soldier explained. He turned to the side and motioned for the brothers to come along. "We're a bit short o' the ale out here," he explained. "Come out fast from the halls to set the camp, while our brothers are up there on the west, setting another."

"Just a small band?" Ivan asked skeptically.

"We're not for taking any chances, Ivan Bouldershoulder," the soldier explained. "We been fighting much o' late, and not too far from our memories are them damned drow coming up from their deep holes. I'm not knowing this Carradoon or them Snowflake Mountains ye're mentioning, but up here's a wild land."

"We just got done fighting a few orcs ourselfs," Ivan replied. He turned to the river and nodded .... in the Moonwood. Me brother put us ....

"Oo," said Pikel, hardly tak ....

"Yeah yeah, ye got us up .... s in a nest o' elves!" Ivan admitted, ... "Orcs crawling everywhere, are the .... to the right place!"

It was spoken like a true dw .... e sentiment enough to slap Ivan on ......

"Let me see what ye're buil .... a trick or two from the south that ye ain't heared of here."

"Ye heading out?" came a soft voice, one that Drizzt Do'Urden surely welcomed.

He looked up from the small pouch he was preparing for the road to see Catti-brie's approach. The two had said little over the past few days. Catti-brie had retreated within herself, for private contemplations that Drizzt wasn't sure he understood.

"Just ensuring that the orcs were indeed chased away," the drow answered.

"Withegroo's got patrols out."

Drizzt offered a doubting smirk.

"Yeah, I was thinking the same thing. They're knowing the ground, at least."

"As I soon will."

"Let me get me bow, and I'll take yer flank," the woman offered.

Drizzt looked up. "It is a dark night," he said.

Looking as if she had just been slapped, Catti-brie also let her gaze move about before settling it enough to stare back at Drizzt.

"I got me a little headpiece here for just such an occasion," she remarked.

From her belt pouch she brought forth the cat's-eye circlet that she often wore, one that magically conveyed heightened vision in very low light.

"Not as keen as a drow's eyes," Drizzt remarked. "The ground is rocky and likely treacherous."

Catti-brie started to argue, to remind him that the circlet had served her even in the Underdark, and that this had never been an issue between them before, but Drizzt interrupted her before she could even get started.

"Remember the rocky climb outside of Deudermont's house?" he asked. "You hardly managed it. After the rain, the rocks here are no doubt equally slick."

Again, Catti-brie looked as if he had just slapped her. His words were true enough. She could not pace him in the daylight, let alone in the dark of night, but was he saying that she would slow him down? Was he, for the first time since his foolish decision to go to Menzoberranzan alone, forsaking the help of his friends?

He nodded, offered the thin veil of a smile, slung his pack over his shoulder, and rose, turning away.

Catti-brie caught him by the arm, forcing him to turn and face her.

"Ye know I can do this," she said.

Drizzt looked at her hard and long. His stern expression melted away into a nod.

"There is no better partner in all the world," he admitted.

"But ye want to go out alone this night," Catti-brie stated more than asked.

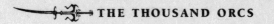

Again the drow nodded.

Catti-brie pulled him close into a hug, and it was one of warmth and love, with just a bit of sadness.

Drizzt went out from Shallows soon after. Guenhwyvar was not with him, but he had the figurine close and knew that the cat would be available to his call should he need her. Barely fifty feet from the torchlit gate, the drow melted into the shadows, becoming one with the dark of night.

He saw the patrols from Shallows several times in the night and heard them long before they came into view. Drizzt avoided them easily every time. He did not want company, but his inner turmoil did little to dull his focus. Out there, in the dark, he was hunting as only a skilled drow might do, roaming the trails and the woods as silently as a shadow. He expected to find nothing, but he was seasoned enough to understand that those honest expectations would lean him toward the precipice of disaster if he embraced them too deeply.

Thus he was not surprised when he found orc-sign. Prints showed themselves to Drizzt's keen drow eyes amidst a circle of sitting stones. They were fresh, very recent, yet there was no sign of any campfire or of any residue from a torch. Night had been on for some time, and all of the patrols from Shallows were human in make-up, and all of them were carrying torches.

But someone had been there, someone human-sized or close to it, and someone traveling in the dark of night without any apparent light source. Given all the recent events, the fact that these were orcs—from the tracks, the drow figured there were two of them—was not hard to determine.

Neither was the trail. The creatures were moving quickly and without much regard to their tracks. Within half an hour's time, Drizzt knew that he had closed considerably.

He did not for a moment wish that Catti-brie or any of the others were at his side. He did not for a moment turn his thoughts away from the task at hand, from the dangers and needs of that very second.

Under the cover of a low tree branch, the drow spotted them. A pair of orcs, crouched on a nearby ridgeline, peered around some lilac bushes toward the distant and well-lit town of Shallows.

Step-by-step, each foot meticulously placed before the other, the drow closed.

Out came his scimitars, and the orcs nearly jumped out of their boots, turning to see curving blade tips in close to their throats. One threw up its hands, but the other, stupidly, went for its weapon, a short, thick sword.

It got the blade out, even managed a quick thrust, but Drizzt's left hand worked a circle around the weapon, turning it down and out wide, while his right hand held his other scimitar poised for a kill on the other orc.

He could easily have killed the attacking orc at that moment—after the turning parry, he had an open strike to the creature's chest—but he was more interested in prisoners than corpses, so he brought his scimitar in against the creature's ribs, hoping the threat alone would end the fight.

But the orc, stubborn to the end, leaped back—right over the north side of the ridge, which was, in fact, a thirty foot cliff.

Holding his scimitar in tight against the second creature, Drizzt skittered up to the cliff edge. He saw the orc bounce once off a rocky protrusion, go into a short somersault, and smash hard onto the stone below.

The other orc bolted away.

Again, Drizzt could have killed it, but he stayed his hand and took up a swift pursuit.

The orc went for the trees, rushing around strewn rocks, falling down one descent and scrambling up the backside. It glanced back many times during its wild flight, thinking and hoping that it had left the dark elf far behind.

But Drizzt was merely off to the side, easily pacing the creature. As it veered around one tree—the same tree from which Drizzt had been watching the pair a few moments earlier—the drow took a more direct route. Leaping onto a low branch, Drizzt ran with perfect balance and the lightest of steps along the limb. He hopped around the trunk to a branch heading out the other way, similarly traversed it, and fell into a roll at its end that landed him on the ground. The dark elf crouched down on one knee, with both blades pointed back at the rushing orc that was now heading straight for him.

The orc shrieked and swerved, and Drizzt feigned a double thrust that sent the creature turning off balance.

Drizzt retracted the blades immediately and spun around, kicking out his trailing foot into the orc's trailing foot as it skittered, forcing its legs crossed and sending it sprawling face down to the rocky ground.

Not really hurt, the orc flattened its hands on the ground and started to push back up, but a pair of scimitar blades touching against the base of its skull convinced it that it might be better to lie still.

Torchlight and noises in the distance told Drizzt that the commotion had roused one of the patrols. He called out to them, bringing them to his side, then bade them to take the prisoner to King Bruenor and Withegroo while he scouted out the rest of the area.

The look on Bruenor's face when Drizzt returned to Shallows some hours later puzzled the drow. Drizzt had expected either frustration from the dwarf because the orc wouldn't talk, or more likely, simple anger, the continuation of the feelings about the tragedy at Clicking Heels.

What he saw on his red-bearded friend's face, though, was neither. Bruenor's look was more tentative in quality, his skin ashen.

"What do you know?" the drow asked his friend, sliding into a seat beside Bruenor, in front of a blazing hearth in the house the folk of Shallows had given them to use.

"He says there's a thousand out there," Bruenor explained somberly. "Says that the orcs 'n giants are all about and ready to squish us flat."

"A ruse to force a lenient hand from his captors," Drizzt reasoned.

Bruenor didn't seem convinced.

"How far'd ye go out, elf?"

"Not very," Drizzt admitted. "I merely ran the town's perimeter, looking for any small bands that might bring havoc."

"Orc says the lands south o' here're crawling with its dirty kinfolk."

"Again, it is a cunning lie, if it is a lie."

"Nah," said Bruenor. "The orc would o' said the north then. That'd be more believable and harder to make sure of. Putting them in the flat-lands to the south makes the truth a patrol away. Besides, the squeal-ing pig wasn't in any flavor to be thinking beyond them words that were coming outta its mouth, if ye get me meaning."

A shudder coursed Drizzt's spine as he did, indeed, get the dwarf's meaning.

"Spoke pretty quick, he did," said Bruenor. The dwarf reached over the low arm of his chair and brought up a flagon of ale, moving it to his waiting lips. "Looks like we might be gettin' a bit more fighting afore we find our way back to Mithral Hall."

"That displeases you?"

"Course not!" Bruenor was quick to retort. "But a thousand's a lot o' orcs!"

Drizzt gave a comforting laugh, reached over and patted Bruenor's arm.

"My dear dwarf," he said, "you and I both know that orcs can't count!"

The drow sat back in his chair, pondering the potentially devastat-ing news.

"Perhaps I should be out again at once," he said.

"Rumblebelly, Wulfgar, and Catti-brie are already on their way," Bruenor explained. "The town's sent scouts o' their own, and old With-egroo's promising to use some magic eyes. We'll know afore the turn o' dark if the orc was squealin' the truth or telling lies."

It was true enough, Drizzt realized, and so he rested back again. He let his lavender eyes close, glad to be among such capable friends, par-ticularly if there was any truth at all to the orc's dire tale.

"And I got Dagnabbit working hard on plans for getting us all outta here if there's too many or for holding off whatever might come if there's not," Bruenor rambled on, oblivious to his friend's descent into deep, deep rest. "Might be that we'll find ourselves a bit o' fun! Ye can't be guessin' how glad I am that I didn't let them talk me into going straight to me home, elf! Aye, this is what any good dwarf's livin' for—a chance to smash an orc face! Aye, and don't ye doubt that I'll be getting me share o' kills. Don't ye doubt it for a minute! I'll be gettin' more than yerself or me girl or me boy all put together."

He lifted his mug in a toast to himself.

"Got room for a hunnerd more notches on me axe, elf! And that's just on the sharpened side!"

23

SWORD AGAINST
SWORD

They were frontiersmen, hunters and by brutal experience, warriors. Not a man or woman of Shallows was unfamiliar with the use of a blade, nor were any inexperienced in killing. Orcs and goblins were all too common in the wilds.

The folk of Shallows knew well the habits of the creatures from the dark mountain holes, knew well the tendencies and the tricks of the wretched orc-kin.

Too well.

The scouting party out of Shallows was not too wary that night, despite the warnings from King Bruenor and his friends, and the tale of the disaster at Clicking Heels. Even as Drizzt was returning with the captured orc, a force of a dozen strong warriors was departing Shallows's southern gate, moving fast along ground comfortably familiar.

They spotted orc-sign soon after and agreed that it was two or three of the creatures at the most. Eager for some sport, the band deserted their information gathering mission and went on the hunt instead, coming down one fairly steep trail into a shallow, boulder-strewn dell. They knew they were close. Every sword, axe, and spear came out at the ready.

The point woman motioned back for the main group to hold fast, then she fell to her belly and started to crawl about a pair of boulders.

A wide grin was on her face, for she expected the duo or trio of orcs to be waiting on the other side of that very rock, oblivious to the fact that they were about to die.

Her grin disappeared as she came around the far side to see not two, not three, but a score of the humanoid creatures, standing ready, weapons drawn.

Confident that she had not been seen but knowing well that her band had been spotted long before—likely as they were descending into the dell—the woman edged back around the boulders and turned into a sitting position. She was thinking to ward her friends away, or at least to assemble them in some kind of defensive position. She started to motion for them to do just that, swinging her arm up from pointing at them to showing the ridge behind.

She froze. Her face, gone stern from its previous smile, slipped into an expression of sheer dread. There, up on the ridge behind her fellows, the woman saw the unmistakable forms of many, many enemies.

A cry from back there, from the trailing human scout, confirmed the horror, and the other members of the party swung around.

A horde of orcs came down fast, howling with every step.

The woman started to scramble up to go and join her companions, but she fell back at the sound of footsteps rushing around and coming over the boulders. The score of orcs went right past her, bearing down on their prey, and the woman knew that her friends were doomed to a man.

Too many enemies, she knew. Too many.

She fell back, recoiling instinctively from the horrible screams of agony that began to erupt all over the bloody battlefield. She saw one man go up several feet into the air at the end of a trio of orc spears. Howling and kicking, he somehow managed to fall back to his feet and somehow hold his balance, though he was surely mortally wounded.

He stood determinedly—until a group of orcs leaped atop him, smashing him down.

The woman melted back, crawling between the paired boulders, squeezing into the dark place underneath their abutting overhangs. She tried to control her breathing, tried to stifle the shrieks welling up within her. From under the stones she could not see the battlefield, but she could hear it well enough. Too well.

She lay there in the dark, terrified, for a long, long while after the cries had abated. She knew that at least one man had been dragged off as a prisoner.

But there was nothing she could do.

She lay there, praying every minute that some orc wouldn't happen by and notice her, and she held back her tears as the long night passed.

Overwhelmed and trembling, sheer exhaustion overcame her.

The sound of birds awakened her the next morning. Still terrified, it took every ounce of willpower she could muster to crawl out of that small cubby-hole. Coming out the way she had gone in, but feet first, was no easy task, physically or emotionally. Every inch that she moved out made her feel more vulnerable, and she almost expected a spear to be thrust into her belly at any time.

When she had to blink away the bright sunlight, she gradually managed to sit up.

There she saw the bodies of her companions, hacked apart—an arm here, a head lying over there. The orcs had slaughtered them, had mutilated them.

Gasping for breath, the woman tried to turn to her side and stand, but stopped halfway and fell to her knees, falling forward to all fours and vomiting.

It took her a long time to manage to stand, and a long time to wander past the carnage of those who had been her companions, her hunting partners, her friends. She didn't pause to reassemble any corpses, to look for lost limbs or lost heads, to count the bodies to try to determine how many, if any, had been taken off as prisoners.

It didn't seem to matter then, for she knew beyond doubt that any who had been dragged away were already dead.

Or wished they were.

She came up out of the dell slowly, cautiously, but no sign of the orc ambush group was to be found. The first step over that lip came hard to her, as did the second, but each subsequent stride moved more quickly, more determinedly, until she was running flat out across the mile of ground she needed to cover to get back to her home.

"It ain't right, I tell ye!" yelled one dwarf, who was a bit too full of the mead. The feisty fellow stood up on his chair and pounded his fist on the table in frustration. "Ye just can't be forgetting all the years! All the damned years! More'n any o' yerselfs'll e'er know!"

He ended by wagging an accusing finger at a group of humans seated at a nearby table in the crowded tavern.

Over at the bar, Shingles watched the spectacle with resignation, and he even gave a knowing nod of what was soon to come, when one the humans wagged a finger back at the drunk dwarf and told him to "sit down and shut his hairy mouth."

Was there anyone in Mirabar whose knuckles were not bruised from recent fights?

"Not another one, I pray," came a quiet voice to the side.

Shingles turned to regard the dwarf who had taken the stool beside him. The old dwarf nodded and lifted his mug to second the sentiment, but he stopped before the mug even lifted from the bar.

"Agrathan?" Shingles asked in surprise.

Councilor Agrathan, dirty and disguised, put a finger to pursed lips, motioning for old Shingles to calm down.

"Aye," he said quietly, looking around to make certain that none were watching. "I heard that trouble was brewing on the streets."

"Trouble's been brewing since yer fool marchion hauled Torgar Hammerstriker back from the road," Shingles pointed out. "Been a dozen fights every day and every night, and now the fool humans are coming down here, and doin' nothing but causing more trouble."

"Those in the city above have come to view this as a test of loyalty," the councilor explained.

"To blood or to town?"

"To town, which to them is of utmost importance."

"Ye're speakin' like a human again," Shingles warned.

"I'm just telling ye the truth of it," Agrathan protested. "If ye don't want to be hearing that truth, then don't be asking!"

"Bah!" Shingles snorted. He buried his face with the mug, swallowing half its contents in one big gulp. "What about the loyalty of the marchion to the folk o' Mirabar? Ain't that countin' for nothing?"

"Elastul's thinking that he did right by the folk of Mirabar by preventing Torgar from going to Mithral Hall, taking our secrets along with him," Agrathan replied, an argument that Shingles and all the others had heard countless times since Torgar's imprisonment.

"More years than ye'll know from the time yer mother dropped ye to the time they plant ye in the ground!" the drunk dwarf at the table shouted even more loudly and more vehemently.

He was wagging a fist at the men, not just a finger. He threw back his chair and staggered toward the men, who rose as one, along with many other humans in the establishment—and along with many, many dwarves, including the drunk's companions, who rushed to hold the drunk back.

"And more years than the marchion's to rule and to live, and more than the ten marchions before him and a good number yet to come," Shingles added privately to Agrathan. "Torgar and his kin been serving since Mirabar's been Mirabar. Ye just can't be throwing a fellow like that in yer jail and not expecting to stir the folk."

"Elastul remains firm that he did the right thing," Agrathan answered.

For just a moment, Shingles thought he caught a look of regret cross the councilor's face.

"I hope ye're telling him that he's a fool, then," Shingles bluntly replied.

Agrathan's expression went to a stern look.

"Ye should be watching your words concerning our leader," the councilor warned. "I took an oath of loyalty to Mirabar and one to Elastul when I took my place at the table of the Sparkling Stones."

"Are ye threatening me, Agrathan?" Shingles quietly and calmly asked.

"I'm advising you," Agrathan corrected. "Many ears are out and about, don't doubt. Marchion Elastul's well aware that there might be trouble."

"More trouble than Mirabar would e'er've knowed if he just let Torgar alone," Shingles grumbled.

Agrathan gave a great sigh. "I come to you to ask ye to help me calm things down a bit. The place is on the edge of a fall. I can smell it."

Even as he finished, the drunken dwarf broke free of his comrades and launched himself at the humans, beginning a brawl that quickly escalated.

"Well?" Agrathan yelled at Shingles as the place began to erupt. "Are you with me or against me?"

Shingles sat calmly, despite the tornado exploding into fury all around him. So there it was, presented calmly, a choice that he had been mulling over for a month. He looked around at the growing fight, man against dwarf and dwarf against dwarf. Of late, Shingles had been playing the part of the calming voice in these nightly brawls, had been taking a diplomatic route in the hopes that Elastul's imprisonment of Torgar would prove a temporary thing, maybe even that Elastul would come to see that he had erred in capturing Torgar in the first place.

"I'm with ye if ye can tell me truly that Elastul'll be lettin' Torgar out soon," he answered.

"The condition hasn't changed," Agrathan replied. "When Torgar denounces his road, Torgar walks free."

"Won't happen."

"Then he won't walk free. Elastul's not moving on this one."

A body came crashing past, flopping over the bar between the pair so quickly that neither was really sure if it had been a human or a dwarf.

"Are you with me or against me?" Agrathan asked again, for the fight was at the critical moment, obviously, just about to get out of control.

"Thought I gived ye me answer three tendays ago," Shingles replied.

As a reminder, he balled up his fist and laid Agrathan low with a single heavy punch.

For all the like-minded dwarves in the tavern that night, those on the line of divided loyalties, Shingles's action came as a signal to fight. For all those, human and dwarf, of the opposite mind, the punch thrown by this leader of Torgar's supporters was a call to arms.

Within seconds, everyone in the tavern was into it, and it began to spill onto the streets. Out there, of course, more were drawn in, mostly dwarves, and more on Shingles's side than opposing.

As the fight tilted Shingles's way, the Axe of Mirabar arrived in force, brandishing weapons and telling the dwarves to disperse. This time, unlike all the previous, the dwarf supporters of Torgar Hammerstriker were ready to take their case to a higher authority.

Many ran off at the first sign of the Axe, only to return in full battle gear, wearing mail and with weapons drawn, in numbers far greater than the ranks of the policing Axe. In the ensuing standoff, more and more of Shingles's allies ran to get their gear, as well, and many of those dwarves opposing Shingles threw insults freely, or warned against the action.

But surprisingly few would go to that next level and take up arms against their kin.

The standoff held for a long time, but as the dwarves' numbers increased—one hundred, two hundred, four hundred—the predominantly human soldiers of the Axe began to shrink back toward the lifts that would take them back to the overcity.

"Ye're not wanting this fight," Shingles called to them. He had taken his position at the front center of the mob of dwarves. "Not over that one dwarf ye got jailed."

"The marchion's word . . ." the leader of the Axe contingent yelled back.

"Won't be much good if ye're all dead, now will it?" Shingles interrupted.

He could hardly believe he was speaking those words aloud, could hardly believe that he, and those following him, were taking this road. It was a path that would lead to the overcity, certainly, and likely right out of the city. This wasn't like the initial riot, which was based solely on shock and sheer emotion. The tone was different. This was a revolt more than a riot.

"Seems ye got yer choice, boys," Shingles bellowed. "Ye want to fight us, then fight us, but one way or th' other, we're gettin' Torgar back among them where he's belongin'!"

As Shingles finished, he noticed the bloodied Agrathan standing off to the side, looking at him plaintively, a desperate expression begging him to reconsider this most dangerous course.

As he finished, the dwarves behind him, hundreds strong, gave out a round of wild cheers and began to move inexorably forward, like a great, unstoppable wave.

The doubt was easily recognizable on the faces of the Mirabarran soldiers, as clear as was the resolve stamped upon the grim face of every dwarf marching behind Shingles.

It wasn't much of a battle, there in the Undercity, in the great corridor just off the lift area. A few hits were traded, a couple of them serious, but the Axe gave way, running back to the room with all the lifting platforms and barring the doors. Shingles's dwarves pounded on them for a bit, but in an orderly fashion, they followed their leader down another side corridor, one that would get them to the surface along a winding, sloping tunnel.

Agrathan, his face bloody and bruised, stood before them, alone.

"Do not do this," the councilor pleaded.

"Get outta our way, Agrathan," Shingles told him, firmly but with a measure of respect. "Ye tried yer way in getting Torgar out—I know ye did—but Elastul's not for listening to ye. Well, he'll be listening to us!"

The cheers behind Shingles drowned out Agrathan's responses and told the councilor beyond all doubt that the dwarves would not be deterred. He turned and ran along the tunnel ahead of the marching mob, who took up an ancient war song, one that had rung out from Mirabar's walls many times over the millennia.

That sound, as much as anything else, nearly broke Agrathan's heart.

The councilor rushed through the positions of the Axe warriors at the tunnel's exit in the overcity, bidding the commanders to wield their force judiciously.

Agrathan ran on, down the streets toward Elastul's palace.

"What is it?" came a cry behind him and to the side.

He didn't slow, but turned his head enough to see Sceptrana Shoudra Stargleam coming out of one avenue, waving for him to wait for her. He kept running and motioned for her to catch up instead.

"They are in revolt," Agrathan told her.

Shoudra's expression after the initial shock showed that she was not so surprised by the news.

"How serious are they?" she asked as she ran along beside Agrathan.

"If Elastul will not release Torgar Hammerstriker, then Mirabar will know war!" the dwarf assured her.

Djaffar was waiting for the pair when they arrived at Elastul's palace. He leaned on the door jamb, seeming almost bored.

"The news beat you here," he explained.

"We must act, and quickly!" Agrathan cried. "Assemble the council. There is no time to spare."

"The council need not get involved," Djaffar began.

"The marchion has agreed to the release?" Shoudra cut in.

"This is a job for the Axe, not the council," Djaffar went on, seeming supremely confident. "The dwarves will be put down."

Agrathan trembled as if he would explode—and he did just that, leaping at the Hammer and putting a lock on the man's throat, pulling Djaffar down to the ground.

A bright flash of light ended that, blinding both combatants, and in the moment of surprise, the Hammer managed to pull away. Both looked to Shoudra Stargleam, the source of the magic.

"The whole of the city will act thusly," the woman said sourly.

Even as she finished the sound of battle, of metal on metal, rang out in the night air.

"This is the purest folly!" Agrathan cried. "The city will tear apart because of—"

"The actions of one dwarf!" Djaffar interrupted.

"The stubbornness of Elastul!" Agrathan corrected. "Show us to him. Will he sit there quiet in his house while Mirabar burns down around him?"

Djaffar started to respond, his expression holding its steady, sour edge, but then Shoudra intervened, stepping up to the man and fixing him with an uncompromising glower. She walked right by him into the house.

"Elastul!" Shoudra called loudly. "Marchion!"

A door to the side banged open and the marchion, flanked by the other three Hammers, swept into the foyer.

"I told you to control them!" Elastul yelled at Agrathan.

"Nothing will control them now," the dwarf shot back.

"Nothing short of the Axe," Djaffar corrected.

"Not even yer Axe!" Agrathan cried, his voice taking on an unmistakable reversion to his Dwarvish accent. "Torgar's part o' that Axe, or have ye forgotten? And five hundred of me . . . of *my* people count among the two thousand of your ranks. You'll have a quarter that won't fight with you, if you're lucky, and a quarter that will join the enemy if you're not."

"Get out there," Elastul told Agrathan, "and speak to them. Your people are sorely outnumbered here, good dwarf. Would you have them slaughtered?"

Agrathan trembled visibly, his lips chewing on words that would not come. He turned and ran out of the house, following the volume of the battle, which predictably led him toward the town's jail.

"The dwarves are more formidable than you believe," Shoudra Stargleam told Elastul.

"We will defeat them."

"To what end?" the Sceptrana asked. It was hard to deter Elastul on such a matter by reasoning concerning losses to his soldiers, since his own safety didn't really seem to be at stake, but by changing the subject to the not-so-little matter of profits, she quickly gained the marchion's attention. "The dwarves are our miners, the only miners we have capable of bringing up proper ore."

"We'll get more," the marchion retorted.

Shoudra shot him a doubtful look.

"What would you have me do?"

"Release Torgar Hammerstriker," the Sceptrana replied.

Elastul winced.

"You have no choice. Release him and set him on the road. He'll not go alone, I know, and the loss to Mirabar will be heavy, but not all the dwarves will depart. Your reputation will not deter other dwarves, perhaps, from coming into the city. The alternate course is one of a bloody battle where there will be no winners, with naught but a shattered Mirabar in its wake."

"You overestimate the loyalty of dwarf to dwarf."

"You underestimate it. To a dwarf, any dwarf, the only thing more precious than gold and jewels is kin. And they're all kin, Elastul, family of Delzoun at their core. I say this as your advisor and as your friend. Let Torgar go, and quickly, before the battle mounts into a full riot, where all reason is flown."

Elastul lowered his gaze in thought, mulling it over with a range of expressions, anger to fear, washing over his face. He looked back up at Shoudra then at Djaffar.

"Do it," he commanded.

"Marchion!" Djaffar started to protest, but his retort was cut short by Elastul's uncompromising stance and expression.

"Do it now!" Elastul demanded. "Go and free Torgar Hammerstriker, and bid him to leave this city forever more."

"He may see your lenience as a reason for staying," Shoudra started to reason, wondering honestly if all of this might be used to further a deeper and better relationship between Elastul and the dwarves.

"He cannot stay and cannot return, under penalty of death."

"That may not prove acceptable to many of the dwarves," Shoudra pointed out.

"Then let those who agree with the traitor go with him," Elastul spat. "Let them go and die on the road to Mithral Hall, or let them get to Mithral Hall and infect it with the same disloyalty and feeble convictions that have too long plagued Mirabar!

"Go!" the marchion roared at Djaffar. "Go now and let us be rid of them!"

Djaffar gave a snarl, but he motioned for one of the other Hammers to accompany him and rushed out into the night.

With a look to Elastul, Shoudra Stargleam joined the Hammers.

The fight outside the jail was more a series of brawls than a pitched battle at the point where the three arrived, but the situation seemed to be fast degenerating, despite Agrathan's pleading efforts to calm the dwarves.

Several hundred were there in support of Shingles and Torgar, opposing perhaps twice that many soldiers of the Axe. Notably, no dwarves showed in the ranks of the Mirabarran garrison, though many dwarf Axe soldiers stood off to the side, arms crossed, faces dour and grim.

Shoudra looked over at Djaffar, who was regarding the dwarf noncombatants with open contempt.

"Do not even think of going against the marchion's orders," the sceptrana warned the stubborn Hammer, "and do not even think of delaying the release of Torgar in the hopes that this battle will erupt before us."

Djaffar turned a wry and wicked grin her way.

"I have spells prepared," Shoudra warned.

It was a bluff, but she didn't back away from the man an inch.

When that didn't work, she reminded, "It is a fight none in Mirabar can win. Look at them, Djaffar. Members of your own Axe stand to the side, torn in their loyalties."

Councilor Agrathan came over then, flustered and with his robes all twisted, as if someone had lifted him by the fine fabric and shook him all about (which, indeed, had happened).

"There's no talking to them!" the frustrated dwarf roared.

"Djaffar can talk to them," Shoudra explained, "for he has the news that Torgar is to be released." She looked over the Hammer, whose eyes had narrowed. "Immediately, on word from the marchion. Torgar will be set upon the road out of Mirabar, here and now, and with all of his personal items returned."

"Praise Dumathoin," Agrathan said with a great sigh of relief.

He rushed off to spread the news, using words, finally, to quell many of the mounting brawls.

"Be done with the foul Torgar, then!" Djaffar spat at Shoudra, an admission of defeat. "And let him be done with us. Let all his smelly little kin walk out with him, for all I care!"

Shoudra accepted that tantrum for what it was, never really expecting anything more than that from Djaffar of the Hammers.

Shoudra took center stage, commanding the attention of all by sending a magical burst of light up above her. All eyes upon her, she gave the announcement that so many of Mirabar's dwarves desperately wanted to hear.

When Torgar Hammerstriker walked out of the Mirabar jail a short while later, he did so to thunderous applause from Shingles and his supporters, mixed in with curses and jeers from many of the humans—and a few groans and mixed sounds from the Axe dwarves, still standing to the side.

Shoudra made her way to Torgar and found Agrathan there as well.

"You are not completely free in your choice of road," the sceptrana explained to the dwarf, her body language and tone telling him that she was no enemy, despite her words. "You are bid to depart the city at once."

"Already decided upon that," Torgar said.

"Give him the night, at least," Agrathan asked of Shoudra. "Allow him his farewells to those he will leave behind."

"I'm not thinking that he's leaving many behind worth saying farewell to," came a gruff voice, and the trio turned to see old Shingles, outfitted in traveling clothes and with a huge pack on his back, moving toward them.

When they looked past the old dwarf, they saw others similarly outfitted, and others across the great square, meeting runners bearing their supplies and traveling gear.

"Ye can't be doing this!" Councilor Agrathan protested, but his was the only protest, for when he looked to Shoudra, he saw her nodding with grim resignation.

Soon after, Torgar Hammerstriker left Mirabar for the last time, along with nearly four hundred dwarves, nearly a fifth of all the dwarves of Mirabar, many of whom had lived in the city for more than a century, and many from families who had served Mirabar since its founding. They all walked with their heads held high and with the conviction that they would not be ill-treated and would not be turned away by the King of Mithral Hall.

"I did not think this possible," Agrathan said to Shoudra as the pair, along with Djaffar, watched the departure.

"Rats leave the ship when it's taking water," Djaffar reminded. "They're seeing more riches in Mithral Hall, the greedy dogs."

"What they are seeing is the possibility that they will have a greater place among their own than we afford them in the city of Marchion Elastul," Shoudra corrected. "The greatest of riches is respect, Djaffar, and few in all Faerûn are more deserving of respect than the dwarves of Mirabar."

Agrathan almost cynically added, "The dwarves of Mithral Hall, you mean," but he bit the words back and reminded himself that he still had sixteen hundred dwarf constituents looking to him for leadership, particularly in this confusing time.

Agrathan knew that it would take a long time for Mirabar to shake off the stench of the recent events.

A very long time.

24

WITH SURPRISING SKILL

Drizzt, Catti-brie, Wulfgar, and Regis sat around a rough map Regis had drawn of the town and the surrounding area and upon which Drizzt had added detail. The mood was dour and fearful—not for themselves, but for the townsfolk. First the orc prisoner had mentioned a huge army encircling the town, then a woman who had been out on patrol had come in, battered and terrified, and reporting that all the others were dead, wiped away by a powerful force of humanoids.

Though she was obviously unnerved, her words told of a well-coordinated group, a dangerous foe beyond the usual expectations.

None of the friends mentioned Clicking Heels that morning, but the images of that flattened town surely played upon all their minds. Shallows was larger than Clicking Heels and much better defended, with a wizard to help, but the signs were getting very dark.

Bruenor came in soon after, his face locked in a scowl.

"Stubborn bunch," the dwarf remarked, moving between Regis and Wulfgar and observing the map with an approving grunt.

"Withegroo cannot be dismissing the claims of the lone survivor," Drizzt came back. "They lost nearly one in ten this morning."

"Oh, he's believin' her, he is," Bruenor explained, "but him and the others're thinking that they're to pay back them that killed their kin. The folk of Shallows are up for a fight."

"Even if that fight's against a foe they can't be beating?" Catti-brie asked.

"Don't know that they're thinking such a foe's about," came Bruenor's response.

The words had barely left his lips when Drizzt and Catti-brie rose up, the woman reaching for her bow, Drizzt going for his cloak.

"I'll go, too," Regis offered.

Wulfgar rose and picked up Aegis-fang.

"The two of ye take the short perimeter," Catti-brie said. "I'll take one round out from there, and let Drizzt do the deep scouting."

"Should we wait for the cover of night?" Regis asked.

"Orcs're better at night than in the day," Catti-brie remarked.

"And we might not have that much time to spare," Drizzt added. He looked to Bruenor and said, "The townsfolk have to agree to let the weak and infirm leave, at least."

"Got Dagnabbit putting together plans for a run even now," the dwarf confirmed, "but I'm not thinking that many o' Shallows's folk'll be wantin' to go out. This is their place, elf, their home and the place of security they've known for many years. They're trusting in Withegroo, and he's one to be trustin', I don't doubt."

"I fear that he might be wrong this time," Drizzt replied. "Every sign darkens the possibilities. If the force allied against Shallows is as strong as indications are, then before too long the folk of the town may all wish that they had gone out."

"Go and see," Bruenor bade him. "I'll make 'em listen while ye're out. I'll get the horses ready and the wagons packed. I'll get me dwarfs in proper order and ready to roll out. I'll be talking with Withegroo again, right off, now that I can catch him alone and without them hollering fools wanting revenge here and now."

"Do ye think he'll hear ye?" Catti-brie asked.

Bruenor gave a shrug and an exaggerated wink, and said, "I'm the king, ain't I?"

On that lighter note, the four scouts rushed out of the building and out of the town. Wulfgar and Regis peeled away to high ground near to the town's walls. Catti-brie found a similar but more defensible vantage point a hundred yards farther out, and Drizzt rushed away from there.

Other scouting groups went out from Shallows as well, but none were nearly as organized, nor nearly as stealthy.

One such group, seven strong, passed Wulfgar and Regis just outside the town's southern gate.

"Well met again," the townsfolk greeted, pausing for just a moment.

"You would do well—better for your town—if you remained inside the walls, preparing defenses should the expected attack come," Wulfgar told the apparent leader: a young man, strong of limb and with a grim and angry expression locked upon his dark, strong features.

The man stopped, his six companions paused behind him, and he shot the barbarian a curious, somewhat angry look.

"We will discern the strength of our common enemy," Wulfgar explained, "and report fully to the town leaders. None can scout the trails better than Drizzt Do'Urden."

The man's look did not soften. It was almost as if he was taking Wulfgar's remarks as a personal affront.

"Every person out here is at risk," Wulfgar went on, not backing down an inch. "For Shallows to lose seven more able-bodied fighters now would not bode well."

The man's nostrils flared and his eyes widened, his expression intense indeed.

Regis motioned to him, bidding him to move off to the side.

"There are other considerations," the halfling remarked, and he offered a sidelong glance at Wulfgar as he spoke, even managing a little telling wink to his large friend.

The scout eyed the halfling suspiciously, but Regis only smiled innocently and turned, nodding for the man to follow. They held a short, private conversation off to the side, and the man from Shallows was smiling and nodding as he returned.

"Back to the town," he ordered his companions, sweeping past them and taking them up in his wake. "Our friends here are correct and we're splitting our forces apart before we even know what it is we're soon to fight."

There came some murmuring of dissent and confusion but the speaker was obviously the appointed and accepted leader, and the group started back the way they'd come.

"Do you never feel the slightest twinge of regret when employing your magical ruby?" Wulfgar asked Regis when the others had moved off.

"Not when it's for their own good," Regis replied, grinning from ear to ear. "We both heard that group coming from fifty feet away. I think the orcs would have, as well." He turned and looked out to the south. "And if there are nearly as many as we've been led to believe, I likely just saved those seven from death this day."

"A temporary reprieve?" Wulfgar asked, the jarring question catching Regis off his guard and stealing the smile from his cherubic face.

He and the barbarian looked at each other, but then Wulfgar looked past him, the barbarian's blue eyes widening.

Regis spun around, looking to the south once more, and there he saw Catti-brie running flat out toward them, waving her arms and her bow in the air.

Regis winced. Wulfgar leaped ahead as the woman staggered suddenly, grasping at her shoulder. Only then did Regis and Wulfgar understand that she was being pursued by archers.

Regis spun around and saw the seven scouts from Shallows rushing back his way.

"To the town!" he yelled to them. "To the town and man the walls. Have the gate ready to swing wide for us!"

By the time the halfling turned back, Catti-brie and Wulfgar had joined up and were both running back toward him, with Wulfgar supporting the wounded woman.

Behind them, coming out of the brush and around the rocks, rushed a horde of orcs.

Regis paused and watched, measuring the distance, and only then did he realize that he wouldn't be doing Wulfgar and Catti-brie much good if they had to sweep him up in their wake.

He turned and ran, reaching the gate at about the same time as his two friends. They scrambled in and the gate was closed and secured behind them, and after a cursory look at Catti-brie's wound, which was superficial, the three rushed for the ladders and the wall parapets.

The orcs came on, a great number indeed, and horns blew throughout the town, with folk rushing all around.

The wave didn't approach, though, but rather swung around in a fierce charge, howling all the louder as they ran back to the south.

"That would be Drizzt," Regis remarked.

"Buying us time," Catti-brie concurred.

She looked up at Wulfgar as she spoke, and he at her, both of them grim-faced and concerned.

The first boulder bounced across the stony ground and hit the town wall a few minutes after sunset. Surprisingly, it had come from the north, from across the narrow ravine.

Horns blew and the militiamen of Shallows rushed to their defensive positions, as did Dagnabbit's dwarves, and King Bruenor and his friends.

A second boulder bounced in, this time closer.

"Can't even see 'em!" Bruenor growled at his three friends as they stood along the northern wall, peering into the gloom.

"There!" Regis cried out, pointing to a boulder tumble.

The others squinted and could just make out the forms of giants across the way.

Catti-brie put her bow up immediately, taking aim, then lifting the angle to compensate for the great distance. She let fly, her arrow cutting a lightninglike line across the darkening sky.

She didn't hit a giant, but the flash at impact told her that she was in the general area at least. She lifted her bow, gritting her teeth against the pain in her fingers and shoulder, which had been creased by an orc's arrow. Before she let fly, though, she had to stop and grab onto Wulfgar, for all the wall was shaking then, hit by a thrown rock.

"Take cover!" came the cry from the lead sentry.

Catti-brie got her bow back up and fired off her second shot, but then she and all her friends were scrambling as one boulder smashed into the courtyard behind them and another landed short of the wall but skipped in hard. Another hit the wall squarely, and another hit the northeastern juncture then skipped along the eastern wall, clipping stones and soldiers.

"How many damned giants are there?" Bruenor asked as he and the others scrambled for cover.

"Too many," came Regis's answer.

"We gotta find a way to counter them," the dwarf king started to reason, but before he could gain any momentum for that thought, a cry from the southern wall told him and his friends that they had other more immediate problems.

By the time Bruenor, Wulfgar, Regis, and Catti-brie reached the southern wall to stand beside Dagnabbit and the other dwarves, the orcs' charge was on in full. The field before the city seemed black with the rushing horde, and the air reverberated with their high-pitched keening. Hundreds and hundreds came on, not slowing at all as the first barrage of arrows went out from Shallows's strong wall.

"This is gonna hurt," Bruenor remarked, looking to his friend and to Dagnabbit.

"Gonna hurt them orcs," Dagnabbit corrected with a grim nod. "We take the center!" he cried to his fifteen remaining warriors. "None come through that gate! None come over the wall!"

With cheers of "Mithral Hall!" and "King Bruenor!" Dagnabbit's well-drilled warriors clustered in the appointed area, the most vulnerable spot on Shallows's southern wall. As one, they took up their dwarven arrows and their well-balanced throwing hammers, and they crouched. The orcs were throwing spears and launching arrows of their own. The dwarves held their ground atop the wall until the last possible second, then leaped up and whipped their hammers into the leading edge of the orc throng, interrupting the charge.

Shallows's bowmen sent a volley out from the walls, and Catti-brie put the Heartseeker to devastating work, her streaks of arrow lightning cutting lines through the enemy ranks.

An agonized cry from behind told them all that one of the townsfolk had caught a giant-thrown rock, and the continuing explosions and ground-shaking made it clear that the giants hadn't let up their barrage in the least.

Dagnabbit's dwarves let fly a second volley before leaping from the wall into the courtyard to bolster the gate defenses, King Bruenor joining them. The bowmen and Catti-brie continued to drive into the orcs' ranks as the blackness closed.

Ropes and grapnels came up over the walls, many catching hold. The orcs, seemingly oblivious to the rain of death, leaped onto them and began scrambling up, while others below threw themselves at the gates, the sheer weight of the force bending the heavy locking bars.

"I wish Drizzt was here!" a terrified Regis cried.

"But he is not," Wulfgar countered, and the two shared a look.

With a growl of determination, Wulfgar nodded for the halfling to follow, and away they went, running along the parapet. The mighty barbarian grabbed grapnels and ropes, using his great strength to pull them free even if they were taut from the weight of orcs climbing on the other side.

At one point, an orc crested the wall just as Wulfgar reached for the supporting grapnel. The barbarian howled and spun. The orc roared and started to swing its heavy club.

And a silver-streaking arrow caught it in the armpit and blew it aside.

Wulfgar glanced back at Catti-brie for just a moment then pulled free the grapnel.

Another orc caught the wall-top as the barbarian tossed the rope back over. It started to pull itself up.

Regis's mace smashed it in the face once, then again.

"More to the east!" Wulfgar cried.

He rushed along to secure a breach where several orcs were even then coming over the wall, doing close battle with a group of Shallows's bowmen.

Regis started to follow but skidded to a stop as the reaching hands of another orc showed on the wall-top right before him. He lifted his mace, but he changed his mind and met the orc with a dazzling, spinning ruby instead.

The orc held in place, truly mesmerized by the spinning gem, its magic reaching out with promises and warm feelings. In a split second, the creature harbored no doubts that the halfling holding the amazing gemstone was its best friend.

"How strong are you?" Regis asked, but the orc didn't seem to understand.

"Strong?" the halfling said more forcefully, and he lifted one arm and made a muscle—not much of one, but a muscle nonetheless.

The orc smiled and grunted.

Regis motioned for it to slip back down, just a bit, and grab the rope again. The creature complied.

Then the halfling patted both his hands emphatically, gesturing for the orc to hold its place right there. Again it complied, and that one rope, at least, was blocked for the time being.

Regis glanced to the right to see Catti-brie staring at him in disbelief. He shrugged then turned back to the left, just in time to see Wulfgar lift an orc high overhead and throw it into a pair of others as they tried to get over the wall. All three fell back outside.

In other places the wall defense wasn't so secure, and orcs poured in, leaping down to the courtyard.

There, centering the defense, stood seventeen toughened dwarves—Dagnabbit and Bruenor among them. As the orcs came down, the dwarves swarmed over them, axes and hammers slashing and smashing.

Bruenor led that charge, hitting the first orc before it had even touched down from its leap. He caught it in the legs and sent it spinning right over, to land face down. Not bothering to finish the kill, the dwarf plowed on, shield-rushing a second orc as it hit the ground. The two of them came together with enough impact to rattle Bruenor's teeth.

The dwarf bounced back and shook his head fiercely, his lips wagging. He swung his axe reflexively across in front of him, thinking that the orc might even then be bearing down on him.

He hit only air, though, and when he recovered his wits a bit, he looked ahead to see that the orc hadn't taken the hit as well as he. The creature was sitting, leaning backward on stiffened arms, its head lolling side to side.

It hardly seemed fair to Bruenor, but war wasn't fair. He charged forward, past the orc, slowing only enough so that he could crease its skull with his heavy axe.

The sheer ferocity of the assault had caught Drizzt off his guard. Barely away from the group he had turned, the drow had been skipping down one descent when he had first caught sight of the charging orcs. Avoiding them had been easy enough, but by the time Drizzt had been able to scramble out of the bowl and head back toward Shallows, the leading edge of the assaulting force was far ahead of him. He saw his three friends in the distance, running back for the town. He saw Catti-brie get clipped by an arrow, and he breathed a great sigh of relief when she, escorted by Wulfgar and Regis, got behind the town's strong walls.

From the shadows of a tree, the drow watched the orc horde sweep past him. He knew he couldn't get back to the town to fight, and perhaps die, beside his friends.

A group of orcs passed below him, and he considered leaping in among them and slashing them down.

But he held his position in the tree, tight to the trunk. It occurred to him that these particular orcs he had chosen to avoid might be the ones who would slay one of his friends, but he dismissed that devastating thought at once, having no time for such distractions. The choices lay clear before him—he could either join in the battle, out there among the horde, or use the distraction of the battle to scout out the truth of their enemies.

The drow surveyed the sweeping lines of orcs, charging headlong for Shallows. How much could he really do out there? How many could he kill, and how much of an effect would a few less orcs really have on this fight?

No, Drizzt had to trust that his friends and the townsfolk would hold.
He had to trust that this was likely an exploratory assault, the first rush,
the test of defenses.

Shallows would be better off after that initial battle if they understood the true size and strength of their enemy, the location of the orc
camps and their defenses.

As the last of the horde swept past beneath him, Drizzt dropped
lightly from the tree and sprinted off, not back to the north and the town,
but to the east, moving along behind the main bulk of the enemy force.

He could hardly lift his arms anymore, so many swings had he taken,
so many orcs had he thrown, but Wulfgar pressed on with all the power
he could muster, throwing himself against any and all who crested the
southern wall.

Blood ran from a dozen wounds on Wulfgar, and on Regis, who
fought valiantly, if less effectively, beside him, putting mace and gemstone to work. As one group of four orcs came over the wall simulta-
neously, Wulfgar looked back to his right, a silent plea for Catti-brie,
but she was not there.

Panicked, the barbarian looked out over the wall, and the distraction
as the orcs closed in nearly cost him dearly.

Nearly—but then an arrow sizzled down past him, clipping one orc
and smashing into the stone with a blinding flash. Wulfgar glanced
back over his shoulder, relief flooding through him as he noted Catti-
brie in a new position at the top of the lone tower that so distinguished
Shallows.

The woman let fly another arrow and nodded grimly at Wulfgar.

He turned back to meet the resumed charge, to sweep one orc away
with his hammer, then he turned to Regis to help the halfling as another
of the brutes bore down on him. The orc stopped suddenly, staring hard
at a spinning ruby.

Wulfgar plowed ahead, shouldering the nearest orc back over the
wall, but taking a stinging hit from the other's club. Grunting away the

pain, Wulfgar took another hit—a solid blow to the forearm—but he rolled his arm around the weapon and pulled it in close, tucking it under his arm and moving nose to nose with the wretched orc.

The creature started to bite at him, or tried to, but Wulfgar snapped his forehead into the orc's face, flattening its nose and dazing it enough for him to shove it back from him. Knowing the creature was stunned, he released his hold on the club and grabbed the front of the orc's dirty leather armor instead. A quick turn and a heave had that orc flying out of the town.

Turning for the orc Regis had entranced, Wulfgar glanced back up at the tower, where Catti-brie and a couple of the town's archers were launching arrow after arrow into the throng beyond the wall.

Wulfgar paused, noting another presence up there. It was the old wizard Withegroo. The man was chanting and waving his arms.

"It's breaking in!" came a dwarf's cry from the courtyard below.

Wulfgar snapped his gaze that way to see Bruenor and his kin running roughshod over the orcs in the courtyard, scrambling back to reinforce the gate.

Out of the corner of his eye, though, he saw a small flare come out from above, a tiny ball of fire gracefully arcing out over the wall.

He felt a flash of heat as Withegroo's fireball exploded.

That shock snapped the orc standing before Regis out of its enchantment, and before the halfling could react, the creature stabbed straight out at him.

With a yelp, Regis fell back into the courtyard.

Wulfgar leaped upon the orc, bearing it down to the ground beneath him. Face down, the orc managed to push up to its elbows, but Wulfgar had it by the head then with both hands. With a roar of outrage, the barbarian drove the creature's head down to the stone parapet, again and again, even after the orc stopped fighting, even after the once solid skull became a misshapen, crushed, and bloody thing.

He was still bashing the orc down when a strong hand grabbed him by the shoulder.

Wulfgar spun frantically, angrily, but held back when he saw Bruenor staring down at him.

"They've run off, boy," the dwarf explained, "and I'm thinking that one's not to be causing us no more trouble."

Wulfgar rose, shoving the orc down one final time.

"Regis?" he asked breathlessly.

Bruenor nodded to the courtyard. The halfling was sitting up halfway, though he hardly seemed conscious of the events around him. Blood showed at his side and several dwarves tended him frantically.

"Bet that one hurt," Bruenor said grimly.

25

THE KEPT
HALFLING

He felt as if he was awakening from a dream, a very bad dream. He felt a tightness in the side, but as he considered a sensation there, along his belly, Regis was very surprised that it didn't hurt much more.

The halfling's eyes popped open wide as the last scenes of battle—the orc thrusting its sword into his gut—played clearly in his mind. He had tried to jump back and had lost his footing almost immediately, falling from the wall.

Regis reflexively rubbed the back of his head—that fall had hurt! In retrospect, though, it had also likely saved his life. If he had been standing with his back to a wall, he'd have been thoroughly skewered, no doubt. He propped himself up on his elbows, recognizing the small side room to the cottage in Shallows. The light was dim around him, night had likely fallen in full outside.

He was alive and in a comfortable bed, and his wounds had been tended. They had turned back the orc tide.

Regis's wave of hope shook suddenly—as his body shook—when the thunderous report of a giant-hurled boulder slammed a structure somewhere nearby.

"Live to fight another day," the halfling mumbled under his breath.

He started out of the bed, wincing with each movement, but stopped when he heard familiar voices outside his small room.

"A thousand at the least," Drizzt said quietly, grimly.

Another rock shook the town.

"We can break through them," Bruenor answered.

Regis could imagine Drizzt shaking his head in the silence that ensued. The halfling crept out of his bed and to the door, which was open just a crack. He peered into the other room, to see his four companions sitting around the small table, a single candle burning between them. What struck the halfling most were the number of bandages wrapped around Wulfgar. The man had taken a beating holding the wall.

"We can't go north because of the ravine," Drizzt finally replied.

"And they've giants across it," Catti-brie added.

"A handful, at least," the drow agreed. "More, I would guess, since their bombardment has continued unabated for many hours now. Even giants get tired, and some would have to go and retrieve more rocks."

"Bah, they ain't done much damage," Bruenor grumbled.

"More than ye think," Catti-brie replied. "Now they're taking special aim at Withegroo's tower. Hit it a dozen times in the last hour, from what I'm hearing."

"The wizard showed himself in the last battle with the fireball," Drizzt remarked. "They will focus on him now."

"Well, here's hoping he's got more to throw than a single fireball, then," said Catti-brie.

"Here's hoping we all have more to give," Wulfgar chimed in.

They all sat quietly for a few moments, their expressions grim.

Regis turned around and leaned heavily on the wall. He was truly relieved that Wulfgar was alive and apparently not too badly hurt. He had feared the barbarian slain, likely while trying to defend him.

Of course it had come to this, the halfling realized. Ever since they had been fighting bandits on the road in Icewind Dale, Regis had been trying to fit in, had been trying to find a way where he would not only be out of harm's way but would actually prove an asset to his friends.

He had found more success than any of them had expected, particularly in the fight at the guard tower in the Spine of the World, when they had discovered the place overrun by ogres.

In truth, Regis was quite proud of his recent exploits. Ever since he had taken that spear in the shoulder on the river, when the friends were journeying to bring the Crystal Shard to Cadderly, Regis had come to view his place in the world a bit differently. Always before, the halfling had looked for the easy way, and in truth that was the way he most wanted to take even now, but his guilt wouldn't allow it. He had been saved that day on the river by his friends, by the same friends who had traveled halfway across the world to rescue him from the clutches of Pasha Pook, by the same friends who had carried him along, often literally, for so many years.

And so of late he had tried with all his might to find some way to become a greater asset to them, to pay them back for all they had done for him.

But never once had Regis believed that his luck would hold. He should have died atop that ogre tower in the Spine of the World, far to the west, and he should have died on the wall of Shallows.

His hand slipped down to his wounded belly as he considered that.

He turned around and peered out at the four friends again, the real heroes. Yes, he had been the one carried on the shoulders of the folk of Ten-Towns after the defeat of Akar Kessell. Yes, he had been the one who had ascended to a position of true power after the fall of Pook, though he had so quickly squandered that opportunity. Yes, he was spoken of by the folk of the North as one of the companions, but crouching there, watching the group, he knew the truth of it.

In his heart, he could not deny that truth.

They were the heroes, not he. He was the beneficiary of fine friends.

As he tuned back to the conversation, the halfling realized that his friends were talking of alternative plans to fighting, of sneaking the villagers away or of sending for help from the south.

The halfling took a deep and steadying breath, then stepped out into the room just as Bruenor was saying to Drizzt, "We can't be sparing yer swords, elf. Nor yer cat. Too long a run to Pwent. Even if ye could get there, ye'd not get back in time to do anythin' more then clean up the bodies."

"But I see no way for us to take a hundred villagers out of Shallows and run to the south," the drow replied.

He stopped short to regard Regis, as did the others.

"Ye're up!" Bruenor cried.

Catti-brie stood from her chair and moved to guide Regis to the seat, but the halfling, whose side was still stiff and tight, didn't really want to bend. Standing seemed preferable to sitting.

"Up halfway, at least," he answered Bruenor.

He winced as he spoke but waved Catti-brie away, motioning for her to keep her seat.

"You are made of tougher stuff than you seem, Regis of Lonelywood," Wulfgar proclaimed.

He held up a flagon in toast.

"And quicker feet," Regis replied with a knowing grin. "You don't believe that my descent from the wall was anything but intentional, do you?"

"A cunning flank!" Wulfgar agreed and all the friends shared a laugh.

It was a short-lived one, for the grim reality of the situation remained.

"We'd not get the folks of Shallows to follow us out in any case," Catti-brie put in when the conversation got back to the business at hand. "They're thinking to hold against whatever comes against them. They've great faith in themselves and their town and greater faith in their resident mage."

"Too much so, I fear," said Drizzt. "The force is considerable, and the giant bombardment could go on for days and days—there is no shortage of stones to throw in the mountains north of Shallows."

"Bah, they ain't doing much damage," Bruenor argued. "Nothing that can't be fixed."

"A townsman was struck and killed by a stone today," Drizzt answered. "Another two were hurt. We haven't many to spare."

Regis stepped back a bit and let the four ramble on with their defensive preparations. The idea of "ducking yer head and lifting yer axe," as Bruenor had put it, seemed to be the order of the day, but after the ferocity of the first attack, the halfling wasn't sure he agreed.

The giants hadn't crossed the ravine and yet the orcs had almost breached the wall, and the southern gates had been weakened by the press of enemies. While Shallows would continue to see a thinning of their forces as men and dwarves were injured, the orcs' numbers would likely grow. Regis understood the creatures and knew that others might be fast to the call if they believed victory to be imminent and riches to be split.

He almost announced then that he would take the initiative and leave Shallows for the south, that he would find a way to Pwent and the others and return beside a dwarven army. He owed his friends that much at least.

He almost announced it, but he did not, for in truth, the prospect of sneaking away to the south through an army of bloodthirsty orcs shook Regis to his spine. He would rather die beside his friends than out there, and even worse than dying would be getting captured by the orcs. What tortures might those beasts know?

Regis shuddered visibly, and Catti-brie caught the movement and offered a curious glance.

"I'm a bit chilled," Regis explained.

"Probably because you lost so much blood," said Drizzt.

"Get yerself back in yer bed, Rumblebelly," said Bruenor. "We'll take care o' keeping ye safe!"

Yes, Regis pondered, and the thought made him wince. They'd keep him safe. They were always keeping him safe.

They knew the second assault would come soon after sunset.

"They're being too quiet," Bruenor said to Drizzt. The pair was standing on the northern wall, peering out across the ravine to where the giant had been. "Restin' to come on, no doubt."

"The giants won't approach," Drizzt reasoned. "Not while the defense is still in place. They'll not face a wizard's lightning when they can strike from afar with complete safety."

"Complete?" Bruenor asked slyly, for he and Drizzt had just been discussing that very issue, and they had just come to the conclusion that

Drizzt should go out and bring the fight to the giants or distract them from their devastating bombardment at least.

Now the drow was hesitating, and Bruenor knew why.

"We could use yer swords here, don't ye doubt," the dwarf said.

Drizzt eyed him curiously.

"But we'll hold without ye," Bruenor added. "Don't ye doubt that, either. Ye go and get 'em, elf. Keep their damned rocks off our heads and leave the little orcs to us."

Drizzt looked back to the north and took a deep breath.

"And now ye're asking all them questions in yer head again, ain't ye?" Bruenor remarked. "Ye're thinking that maybe ye were wrong in telling Catti-brie not to go. Ye're thinking that maybe ye were wrong in thinking to go out at all. Ye're thinking that everything ye're doing is wrong. But ye know better'n that, elf. Ye know where we're standing, and that's under the shadow o' flying rocks. As much as ye're thinking ye don't want to be away from yer friends, yer friends're thinking they don't want ye away."

Drizzt offered him a smile.

"Yet you believe that I have to go, as we discussed," he finished for the dwarf.

"We don't stop or at least slow them giants, and there's no Shallows to defend," the dwarf answered. "Seeming pretty simple from where I'm looking at it. Ye're the only one who can get across that ravine fast enough to make a difference, despite the arguing ye got from me girl when we decided ye should go."

At the mention of Catti-brie, Drizzt turned a bit and glanced back over his shoulder, up to the top of Withegroo's battered tower where the woman stood, bow in hand, looking out over the parapets. She glanced down at Drizzt and noticed his stare. She offered a wave.

"I'll not be away for long," the drow promised Bruenor, returning Catti-brie's wave with a salute of his own.

"Ye'll be as long as ye're needing to be," Bruenor corrected. "I'm thinking is ye can keep them giants off us through the next fight, we'll hold, and if we hold strong, then might be that them orcs'll give it up or break apart enough for us to get through and run to the south."

"Or at least to get some runners through with news for Thibbledorf Pwent," Drizzt added.

"Dagnabbit's working on that very thing," Bruenor assured him with a wink and a nod.

The dwarf didn't have to say any more. They both knew the truth of it. Shallows had to hold through the next couple of fights, either to weaken the orcs enough for a full breakout to the south or to make their enemies give up altogether.

As the bottom rim of the sun began to flirt with the western horizon, Drizzt went out over Shallows's wall, avoiding the northern gate, as he expected it was being watched. He slipped down beside the wider guard tower on the town's northwestern corner and moved off as stealthily as possible, rock to rock, brush to brush, belly-crawling across any open expanses. He made the lip of the ravine, and there he waited.

The dusk grew around him. He could hear the sounds of the stirring orcs to the south, and the grating of boulders being piled by the giants just a few hundred yards from his position, across the ravine. The drow pulled his cloak up tight around him and closed his eyes, falling into a meditative state, forcing himself to become the pure warrior. He had no honest idea of how he might divert the giants, though that was the goal his friends so desperately needed him to achieve.

The mere thought of those companions he had left behind shattered that meditative state and had Drizzt looking back over his shoulder at the battered town. The last image he had seen of Catti-brie, grim-faced and accepting, flashed over and over in his mind.

"Go," she had bade him earlier in the day when he had argued, for purely selfish reasons, against the course.

That was all she had said, but Drizzt knew better than to believe that other, darker thoughts weren't crossing her mind, as they surely were his own. They were going to try to hold the town, against the odds, and Drizzt and his friends had been forced to split up.

He had to wonder if he would ever see any of them alive again.

The drow let his forehead slip down to the earth, and he closed his eyes again. He wasn't scared—not for himself, at least—but he had seen the orc force, and he knew that there were several giants across the way.

This band was organized, determined, and had them terribly outnumbered. Was this the end of his beloved band?

Drizzt lifted his head and stubbornly shook it, dismissing the question within a swirl of memories of other enemies overcome. Of the verbeeg lair with Wulfgar and Guenhwyvar. Of the fight to reclaim Mithral Hall. Of the wild chase on Calimport's streets to save Regis. And most of all, of the war with the army of Menzoberranzan, defending Mithral Hall against a terrible foe.

Then the dark elf couldn't even dwell on past victories, couldn't dwell on anything. He moved his consciousness purposefully across his limbs and torso, attuning himself, body and mind, into a singular warrior entity.

The sun dipped below the western horizon.

The Hunter moved over the lip of the ravine, sliding along the rock faces like the shadow of death.

It started almost exactly as the assault of the previous night, with giant boulders raining down across the town and a frenzied horde of orcs charging hard from the south. The defense followed much the same course, with Wulfgar centering the defense of the parapet and Bruenor's dwarves bolstering the gate.

This time, though, Bruenor was with his barbarian friend—and with Regis, who despite the advice of his friends that he should remain at rest, would not be left out.

On the tower behind the wall, Catti-brie sent the first responses out against the orc charge—a line of flashing arrows slashing across the southern fields—as much to put some light out there and mark the enemy advance as in hope of hitting anything.

When the orcs were but fifty feet from the wall, the other archers opened up. It was a devastating barrage made all the more powerful by one of Withegroo's fireballs.

Many orcs died in that moment, but the rest pressed on, rushing to the base of the wall and throwing their grapnels or setting ladders. One group bore a ram between two lines of orcs and pressed straightaway to the gate. Their initial hit almost took it down.

Bruenor, Regis, and Wulfgar met the first breach on that wall top. A pair of orcs scrambled onto the parapet, and Wulfgar caught one even as it spun over the wall, lifting it high, throwing it back outside, and taking one of its following companions down with it. Bruenor took a different tactic, coming in hard for the second orc even as it stood straight. The dwarf feigned high and ducked low, shouldering the orc across the knees and upending it. A twist and shove by the dwarf had the orc falling—not outside to join the one Wulfgar had thrown, but inside, to the courtyard, where Dagnabbit and the other dwarves waited.

As soon as the orc flew away, Bruenor hopped up. Regis rushed by him, or tried to, as another orc crested the wall, but the dwarf caught the halfling by the shoulder, pulled him back defensively, and stepped forward. A swipe of Bruenor's axe took that second orc down, and the dwarf's foam-emblazoned shield got a third, right on the head, as it too tried to come over.

Behind him, Regis tried to help, but in truth the halfling found himself more often ducking the back-swing of Bruenor's constantly chopping axe than any orc's weapon. Regis turned toward Wulfgar instead and found the barbarian in no less of a battle frenzy, whipping Aegis-fang back and forth with abandon, shoulder-blocking orcs back over the wall.

Regis hopped to and fro as more and more orcs tried to gain the wall, but he simply could not fit between or beside his ferocious friends.

One orc came up and over fast. Wulfgar, his hammer caught on another to the right side, just let go with his left hand and slapped the creature past him. The orc stumbled but caught itself and would have turned to attack the barbarian, except that Regis dived down low, cutting across its ankles and tripping it up.

The clever halfling got more than he bargained for, though, as the orc hooked him with its feet and pulled him along for the ride. Not wanting to take that fall again—and particularly not when he heard the gates groan in protest under yet another thunderous hit—Regis let go of his little mace and grasped desperately at the lip of the wall.

"Rumblebelly!" he heard Bruenor cry, his worst fears then realized.

He knew that he would be a distraction—a potentially deadly distraction—to his friends.

"Fight on!" the halfling cried back.

He let go, dropping the ten feet to the ground. He landed in a roll to absorb the blow, but nearly fainted as he came rolling across his wounded side. He was just to the west of the southern gate and saw that the gate was about to crash in. He grabbed his dropped mace and looked to the side to the grim-faced dwarves.

He knew he would be of no real help to them.

He knew what he had to do. He had known since he heard his friends remarking that they simply could not spare Drizzt's blades in the defense of the town.

Regis turned around and ran for the western wall. He heard Dagnabbit yell out to him to "Stand fast!" but he ignored the call, making the wall and turning north along it.

Soon he was on the parapet in the northwestern corner, the same place where Drizzt had gone out before him. Regis took a deep breath and looked back and up, to see Catti-brie staring at him incredulously.

He saluted her, then he willed his legs to move him over the wall.

"I am no evoker," Withegroo lamented after casting his fireball.

A few orcs had been killed, but unfortunately the rusty wizard hadn't put the blast where he had intended to, and he had done little more than momentarily delay the assault.

He leaned on the southern rim of his tower top, beside Catti-brie and a trio of other archers, and watched the battle unfold. He didn't have many effective spells to throw, so he knew he'd have to choose his castings carefully.

He saw a breach at the southeastern corner, orcs rolling up over the wall and leaping down to the courtyard below, and nearly threw one of a pair of lightning bolts he had prepared. He held the shot, though, seeing the dwarves of Mithral Hall rushing to the spot and overwhelming the orcs as they touched down.

Even as the old wizard breathed easier, he saw a second breach open up, a pair of orcs climbing onto the parapet in the southwestern corner. These didn't leap right down, but rather lifted heavy bows.

Withegroo beat one to the punch, waggling his fingers and sending a series of magical bolts out at the creature, burning it, staggering it, and ultimately dropping it to the stone.

Its companion responded by turning the bow up toward the tower top and letting fly a wild shot.

Before Withegroo could respond with a second spell, Catti-brie took aim on the orc and fired, her magical arrow snapping it down to the stone.

The wizard patted her shoulder, but she couldn't even pause long enough to acknowledge the teamwork. Too many other targets were already presenting themselves along the southern wall.

Then came the howls, to the east and to the west as the second wave came on, of scores and scores of orcs riding worgs.

Then came a heavier rain of boulders, ten at a time it seemed, falling heavily across the town.

Shallows shook under the weight of another battering blow to the southern gate. A hinge burst wide and one of the double-doors twisted inward.

He crossed the steep-sided and rocky ravine as quickly as possible, leaping from stone to stone and scrambling on all fours. As he came up the northern facing, he paused to look back at Shallows, and he knew then that his guess about the giants had been correct. They were more than five in number—likely twice that, at least. Since the beginning of the first assault, they had been taking turns throwing the rocks, conserving their strength, in shifts of two or three at a time.

But they were out in full as the assault escalated. The bombardment that echoed behind Drizzt Do'Urden was nothing short of spectacular, and devastating.

It pained Drizzt profoundly to think that his friends were in that town.

He shook the disturbing thought from his mind and pressed onward, scaling the rock face with the same sure-footed agility that had propelled him through the Underdark for all those years.

His mind whirled with all the possibilities, but he did find his center, his necessary meditative state. If there were a dozen giants up there, how might he begin to do battle with them? How might he engage them in any manner to distract them, to buy his friends and the other gallant defenders of Shallows some respite, at least, while they fended the town from the orc hordes?

As soon as Drizzt reached the lip of the ravine, he spotted the cluster of stones and the giants—nine by his count. The drow pulled the magical figurine from his pouch and brought forth his feline companion. He had Guenhwyvar rush off to the north and await his signal.

Drizzt reached for his scimitars then glanced back at Shallows. He wondered if there was some way he could get his friends out of there, but he quickly realized that even if Bruenor, Wulfgar, Catti-brie, and Regis were all beside him, they would find this enemy beyond even their skills. Nine giants, and not the more common and far less formidable hill giants, but nine cunning and mighty frost giants.

Drizzt corrected his count when he saw yet another moving in toward the band, carrying a bulging sack that the drow knew to be filled with rocks.

Could he, perhaps, lead his friends and the rest of Bruenor's dwarves out there? With Dagnabbit and Tred and the others, they might prepare a battlefield on which they could defeat the giants.

But considering the ravine he had just exited, the drow realized that line of reasoning to be one of folly. They could never get that group across the ravine in any short amount of time and without being detected—and how vulnerable they would be among the steep, sharp rocks down below with half a score of giants raining boulders on them.

Drizzt took a deep breath and forced himself to focus on the task at hand. He reached for his scimitars reflexively, but then moved his hands aside, leaving them in their sheaths. He had fooled the frost giants once before. . . .

"Hold!" he cried, walking to the edge of their position. "Another enemy has revealed itself to the north and west, not so far from here!"

The giants stared at him incredulously. Some looked to each other, and Drizzt recognized clearly the doubt stamped upon their faces.

"A second group of dwarves!" Drizzt cried, pointing out to the northwest. "A larger force, but one heading straight to reinforce Shallows, and one I am certain has not yet learned of your position out here."

"How many?" a giantess asked.

Drizzt noticed that some of the others were reaching for stones.

"Two score," the drow improvised, trying hard to put an urgent edge to his tone, to bring the obviously skeptical giants to action.

"Two score," one of the other giants echoed, and Drizzt noted clearly the dry edge in its tone.

He knew then, beyond any doubt, that his ploy would not work. Not this time, not on this group.

Drizzt was moving before the volley of rocks came at him, and that warrior reflex alone saved him from being battered to pulp then and there. He summoned a globe of darkness at his back as he rushed out of the boulder cluster then ran straight off to the rockier and more broken ground.

Half the giants gave chase.

In those first strides out of the cluster, all hope of deception flown, Drizzt fell into himself—into the warrior, into the Hunter. He was pure instinct, feeling the giants' movements around him before he saw them, sensing and anticipating his enemy.

He cut left and a boulder skipped past—one that would have crushed the life from him had he not veered off.

Cutting back to the right, he slipped into a narrow channel between two rock walls, brought up another globe of darkness, then leaped and scrambled over the wall to his right, rolling down behind a jut of stone.

He knew he couldn't sit and wait. It wasn't just about eluding the pursuit for self-preservation. It was about keeping the giants, as many as possible, away from their bombardment, and so, as the last of the chasing five rushed past, Drizzt sprang back the other way, managing to slash the trailing behemoth across the back as he went.

The giant gave a howl and its companions turned to follow.

Drizzt yelled for Guenhwyvar.

The mad rush throughout the stony mountainsides, one that would last all night long, was on.

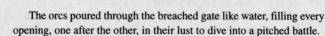

The orcs poured through the breached gate like water, filling every opening, one after the other, in their lust to dive into a pitched battle.

Or at least, they started to.

From on high came the first and most devastating response, a blinding stroke of lightning slashing down past the startled Catti-brie, cutting before the startled Mithral Hall dwarves to explode against the metal gates in a multitude of bluish arcs.

Many orcs fell to Withegroo's stroke. Many were killed, others stunned and others blinded, and when Dagnabbit and Tred led the charge to secure the gate, the off-balanced and confused orcs proved easy prey.

Hammers thumped and axes chopped. Orcs squealed and bones shattered.

But the orcs still had the gate opened, and more poured in, pushing aside their smoking comrades, scrambling madly to get at the dwarves.

From the tower, Catti-brie sent a line of arrows at the blasted gates and the incoming orcs, but only for a moment. The wall top remained primary to her, where Wulfgar, Bruenor, and a handful of Shallows's townsfolk were fighting back a swarm of hungry attackers.

The dwarf and the barbarian quickly worked their way above the broken gate back-to-back. They turned, with Wulfgar facing out over the wall and Bruenor looking down at the mounting battle in the town's courtyard.

Catti-brie watched them curiously, then understood as Bruenor patted Wulfgar's broad back. With a cry to Clan Battlehammer, the soon-to-be Tenth King of Mithral Hall leaped down from on high, right into the midst of the swarming orcs.

"Bruenor," Catti-brie mouthed silently, desperately, for he disappeared almost at once in the swirling mob, almost as if he had leaped right into the mouth of a whirlpool.

The woman shook away the horrible image immediately and turned her attention back to the wall to Wulfgar, who was fast becoming a lone figure of defiance up there.

Catti-brie fired left of him, then right, each arrow taking down an orc as it tried to come over the wall. Her hand was aching badly, she could hardly draw the bowstring, but she had to, just as Wulfgar, with all his wounds and all his weariness, had to stand there and hold that wall.

She fired again, grimacing in pain, but scoring another hit. There was hardly any self-congratulation in that fact, though, for in looking at the wall, at the sheer number of orcs, Catti-brie wondered grimly if she could possibly miss.

He dived behind a rock, praying that the orcs were so concerned with the town that they had not seen him come out over the wall. He hunched lower, trembling with terror as worg-riding orcs swept past him, left and right, and others leaped the stone he was hiding behind—and leaped him as well.

He could only hope that he had gotten far enough from the wall so that when they were forced to stop, he could slip away.

It seemed that he had, for the worg-riders split left and right as they neared the wall, drawing out bows and sending arrows randomly over the wall.

Regis put his legs back under him and started to slowly rise.

He heard growling and froze, turning slowly, to see the bared fangs of a worg not three feet from his face. The orc atop it had its bow drawn, taking a bead on Regis's skull.

"I brought this!" Regis cried breathlessly, desperately, holding up his ruby and giving it a spin.

The halfling threw up his free arm to block as the worg's snapping jaw came for his face.

"I will sweep them from the wall!" Withegroo proclaimed in outrage as another of his townsmen went down under the press, far to Wulfgar's left.

The wizard waggled his fingers and swept his arms about, preparing to launch a second devastating lightning bolt. At that desperate moment, it certainly seemed as if Shallows needed one.

A rock hit the tower top and skipped across it, slamming the back of Withegroo's legs and crushing him against the tower's raised lip.

Catti-brie and the other archers rushed to him as he started to slump down, grimacing in agony, his eyes rolling up into his head.

More rocks hit the tower, the giants having apparently found the range, and it shuddered again and again. Another skipped across the top, to smash against the wall near the fallen wizard.

"We can't hold the tower!" one of the town's archers cried.

He and his companions pulled their beloved Withegroo from the trapping rock and gently lifted him.

"Come on!" the man cried to Catti-brie.

The woman ignored him and held her ground, keeping her focus on the wall and Wulfgar, who desperately needed her then. She could only hope that no rock would skip in behind her and take her down the same way.

Crying out for Mithral Hall and Clan Battlehammer—and with a lone and powerful voice yelling for his lost brother and Citadel Felbarr—the dwarves met the orcs pouring in through the gate and those coming down off the wall with wild abandon. At least it seemed to be that, though in truth the dwarves held their defensive formation strong, even in the midst of the tumult.

They saw Bruenor leap down from on high. Dagnabbit, spearheading the wedgelike formation, swung the group around to get to their fighting king.

Bruenor's many-notched axe swept left and right. He took a dozen hits in the first few moments after leaping from the wall but gave out twice that. While the orcs' blows seemed to bounce off of him without effect, his own swipes took off limbs and heads or swept the feet out from under one attacker after another.

The orcs pressed in on him, and he fought them back time and again, roaring his clan's name, spitting blood, taking hits with a smile and almost every time paying back the orc that had struck him with a lethal retort. Soon, with dead orcs piled around him, few others would venture in, and Bruenor had to charge ahead to find battle. Even then, the orcs gave ground before him, terrified of this bloody, maniacal dwarf.

The other dwarves were beside him, and Bruenor's exploits inspired them to even greater ferocity. No sword or club could slow them, no orc could stand before them.

The tide stopped flowing in through the battered and hanging gates. Amidst a shower of crimson mist and cries of pain and rage, the tide began to retreat.

None of the turn in the courtyard below would have mattered, though, if Wulfgar could not hold strong on the wall. Like a tireless gnomish machine, the barbarian swept Aegis-fang before him. Orcs leaped over the wall and went flying back out.

One orc came in hard with a shoulder block, thinking to knock Wulfgar back and to the ground, but the orc's charge ended as it hit the set barbarian. It might as well have tried to run right through Shallows's stone wall.

It bounced back a step, and Wulfgar hit it with a short right cross, staggering it. The orc went up in the air, grabbed by the throat with one hand. With seemingly little effort, Wulfgar sent it flying.

Behind that missile, though, the barbarian saw another orc, this one with a bow, aimed right for him.

Wulfgar roared and tried to turn, knowing he had no defense.

The orc flew away as a streaking arrow whipped past, burrowing into its chest.

Wulfgar couldn't even take the second to glance back and nod his appreciation to Catti-brie. Bolstered in the knowledge that she was still there, overlooking him, covering his flanks with that deadly bow of hers, the barbarian pressed on, sweeping another orc from the wall, and another.

The sudden blowing of many, many horns out across the battlefield did nothing to break the fanatic fury of the dwarves. They didn't know if the horns signaled the arrival of more enemies, or even of allies, nor did they care.

In truth, the dwarves, fighting for their clan, fighting for the survival of their king who stood tallest among them, needed no incentive and had no time for trepidation.

Only after many minutes, the orc mob thinning considerably, did they come to understand that their enemy was in retreat, that the town had held through the second assault.

Bruenor centered their line just behind the blasted gates, all of them breathing hard, all of them covered in blood, all of them looking around.

They had held, and scores of orcs lay dead or dying in and around the courtyard and the wall, but not a dwarf, not a defender in all the town, would consider the fight a victory. Not only the gates had been compromised, but the walls themselves had been badly damaged. In many places, mixed among the dead orcs, were the bodies of many townsfolk, warriors Shallows simply could not spare.

"They're gonna come back," Tred said grimly.

"And we're gonna punch 'em again!" Dagnabbit assured him, and he looked to his king for confirmation.

Bruenor returned that stare with one that showed a bit of uncharacteristic confusion on the crusty old dwarf king's intense face. He started some movement—it seemed a shrug—and he fell over.

With the battle ended, King Bruenor could no longer deny the wounds he had taken, including one sword stab when he had first leaped down from on high that had found a seam in his fine armor and slipped through to his lung.

Up above the fallen dwarf, Wulfgar slumped on the wall in complete exhaustion, and with more than a few wicked wounds of his own, oblivious to the fall of his friend down below—until, that is, he heard the shriek of Catti-brie. He glanced up to see the woman looking down from the tower, her gaze leading to the courtyard below him, her wide eyes and horrified expression telling him so very much.

26

POINT AND COUNTERPOINT

"Too many dead!" King Obould scolded his son, though not loudly, when he arrived on the scene south of Shallows and observed the body-strewn field.

Despite his obvious anger and disappointment at the course of the battle thus far and the resiliency of Shallows's defenders, Obould had brought several hundred more orcs with him. As he had gone about the caverns of the Spine of the World with news of the entrapment of the dwarf king of Mithral Hall, many tribes had been eager to join in the glory of the slaughter.

"The town is softened, and their dead lay thick about our own," Urlgen argued, his voice rising.

Obould shot Urlgen a threatening glare, then led his son's gaze to the three large orcs standing together off to the side, each a chief of his respective tribe.

"We think the wizard is dead," Urlgen went on. "A rock hit the top of his tower and he did nothing at the end of the battle."

"Then why did you run away?"

"Too many dead," Urlgen echoed sarcastically.

Obould's eyes narrowed into that particular look the orc king had, which told all standing near to him to dive for cover. Urlgen did no such thing, though. The young, strong upstart puffed out his chest.

"The town will not stand against the next attack," Urlgen insisted. "And now, with more warriors, we can finish them easily."

Obould was nodding with every word of the seemingly obvious assessment, but then he replied, "Not now."

"They are ripe!"

"Too many dead," said Obould. "Use the giants to knock down their walls with rocks. Use the giants to topple the tower. We chase them out or leave them nothing to hide behind. Then we kill them, every one."

"Half the giants are gone," Urlgen informed his father.

Obould's bloodshot eyes widened, his jaw going tight with trembling rage.

"Chasing a scout from the town," Urlgen quickly added.

"Half!"

"A dangerous scout," said Urlgen. "One who holds a black panther as a companion."

Urlgen's face eased almost immediately. Ad'non had warned them about Drizzt Do'Urden, as Donnia had warned the giants. Given everything the drow had told the orc king about this unusual dark elf, it seemed that having half the giants chasing him away might not be so bad a trade off.

"Tell the giants who remain to throw their stones," Obould instructed. "Big stones. And send arrows of fire into the town. Burn it and bash it! Stomp it down flat! And tighten the ranks around the enemy. No escape!"

Urlgen's tusky smile showed his complete agreement. The two orcs both looked back at the battered town with supreme confidence that Shallows would fall and that all within would soon enough be dead.

A boulder clipped the stone above him, bouncing wildly past and showering him with chips of broken stone.

Drizzt ducked his head against the stinging shower and doggedly went back to his work, tightening a belt around a twisted ankle. That done, he stood gingerly and shifted his weight to the wounded foot, nodding grimly when it would still support his weight.

Still, where to go?

The pursuit had been dogged, a handful of giants chasing him through the long night. He had used every trick he knew—backtracking and setting strategic globes of darkness, climbing one tree and rushing across its boughs to another and another, coming down far to the side and sprinting off in a completely different direction—but still the giants hounded him.

It occurred to Drizzt that someone was guiding them. Given his reception at the first giant camp, when they had thought him an ally of some unknown drow, he could render a guess as to who—or at least what—that someone might be.

As dawn broke over the eastern horizon, and with the unerring pursuit close behind, Drizzt realized that his greatest advantage was fast diminishing. He understood, too, that his companion needed to be sent away to her rest.

"Guen," he called softly.

A moment later the great panther leaped across the narrow channel above Drizzt, settling on a stone at his shoulder height, a few feet away.

"Rest easy and rest quickly," Drizzt bade the panther, willing her away. "I will need you again, and soon I fear."

The cat gave a low growl that blew away on the wind, as Guenhwyvar seemed to dissipate in the air, becoming less than substantial, becoming the grayish mist, then nothing tangible at all.

Loud voices from not too far behind told Drizzt that he had better get moving. He took some comfort in the fact that he had led so many giants away from the battle at Shallows, and indeed, he had taken them far to the northwest, to the rougher and higher rocky ground. Every once in a while, the drow came out on a high ridge that offered him a view of the distant, battered town, and each time he could only clutch at the hope that his friends were all right, that they had held strong, or perhaps even that they had found a way to slip out and make a run to the south.

A boulder skipped into the narrow channel then, followed by the roar of the giants, and Drizzt had no further time for contemplation. He darted off as quickly as his twisted ankle would allow, moving on all fours at times as he scaled the steep inclines.

He was tiring, though, and he knew it, and he knew, too, that giants did not tire as quickly as the smaller races. He couldn't keep up the run for much longer, if the pursuit remained so dogged, nor could he hope to turn and face his pursuers. If it was one giant, perhaps, or even two, he might try, but not this many. All his warrior skills wouldn't hold him for long against a handful of mighty frost giants.

He needed another solution, a different escape route, and he found it in the form of a dark opening among a tumble of boulders against one rocky cliff facing. At first he thought the cave within to be nothing more than the sheltered and darkened area formed by the formation of the rocks, but then he saw a deeper opening at the back of the alcove, a crack in the ground barely wide enough for him to slip through. He fell to his belly and peered in, breathed in. His Underdark senses told him that this was no little hole in the ground, but something large and deep.

Drizzt crawled back out and surveyed the area. Did he want to end the chase then and there? Could his friends afford for him to release the giants of their pursuit, when the behemoths would surely turn right back to their stone-throwing positions?

But what choice did he really have? This pursuit was going to end soon either way, he knew.

With a reluctant sigh, the drow slipped into the cave and moved a bit deeper into the darkness, then sat and listened, and let his eyes adjust to the dramatic shift of light.

Within minutes, he heard the giants milling around outside, and their grumbling told him that they knew exactly where he had gone. The light in the cave increased slightly as the boulder tumble outside was thrown away. After more angry grumbling, including a suggestion that they go and get some orcs or someone named Donnia—and Drizzt recognized that as a drow name—to pursue the drow into the cave, the hole was blocked by a giant's face. How Drizzt wished he had Catti-brie's bow in hand!

More roars of protest and grumbling ensued, but only briefly, and the cave went perfectly dark. The ground shook beneath Drizzt, as the giants piled stones over the opening, sealing him in.

"Wonderful," Drizzt whispered.

He wasn't really worried for himself, though, for he could tell from the feel of the air that he would find another way out of the cave. How long that might take, though, he could not guess.

He feared that by the time he got out and circled back to Shallows, there would be no town standing.

His left arm was all but useless. He knew that the bone had been shattered under the worg's tremendous bite, and the torn skin was taking on the unhealthy color of a dire infection, but he couldn't worry about that.

Regis pressed the charmed orc to urge the exhausted mount on faster, though feared that he was pushing his luck more than pushing the obviously angry worg. With the limitations of their shared vocabulary, the halfling had somehow managed to convince the orc that he knew where they could find big treasure, and a horde of weapons for the other orcs, and so the dim-witted creature had beaten its worg into submission, and into letting go of Regis's shattered arm, and had forced the snarling and nipping creature to take a second rider on its broad back.

It certainly hadn't been a comfortable or comforting ride for Regis. Sitting before the big, smelly orc placed the halfling's dangling feet to the sides of the worg's neck—within nipping distance, he found out, whenever the great wolf slowed.

As they left the battlefield far behind that night and pressed on through the morning, the halfling had found the orc's resistance growing. He used his enchanted, mesmerizing ruby constantly on the orc, not ordering it but rather tempting it, again and again, with techniques the sneaky halfling had perfected on the streets of Calimport years before.

But even with the gemstone, Regis knew that he was on the edge of disaster. The worg could not be so tempted—certainly not as much as the taste of halfling flesh would tempt such a cruel creature—and the orc was not a patient thing. Even worse, several times, the halfling thought he would simply faint and fall off, for his shattered arm was shooting lines of burning, overwhelming, and disorienting pain through him.

He thought of his friends, and he knew that he could not falter, not for himself and not for them.

All Regis could think to do was to keep them running fast to the south and hope that some opportunity opened before him where he could kill the pair, or at least where he could slip away. And despite his trepidation, the halfling understood well that he could never have covered as much ground on foot as they had on the worg. When the dawn brightened the ground the next morning, they found that the mountains to the south, across the eastern stretches of Fell Pass, were much closer than those they had left behind.

The orc wanted to sleep, something that Regis knew he could not allow. The halfling was sure that as soon as the brute closed its eyes, the worg would make a meal of him.

"Into the mountains," he told it with his halting command of the Orcish language. "We camp here and dwarves will find us."

Grumbling, the orc pressed the overburdened worg on.

As they came into the foothills, Regis watched every turn and every ridge, looking desperately for a place where he could make his escape. A small cliff face, perhaps, where he could quietly slip over and disappear into the brush below, or a river that might wash him far enough away from these two wretched companions.

He saw a couple of promising spots but let them pass by, too afraid to make such a break. He tried to bolster his resolve by reminding himself of the predicament of his friends to the north, but still he saw nothing that offered more than a fleeting hope.

Still, from the tone of the orc's complaints, Regis understood that he would have to do something soon.

"We gonna camp," the orc informed him.

Regis's eyes went wide and he looked around desperately for a way out. His darting eyes looked down to his small mace, belted at his hip.

He thought of taking it out then and there and smashing the worg atop the head. He couldn't get his hand to move to it, though, whatever the logic, for he knew beyond doubt that he would have to be perfect, and that the blow would have to fell the creature, which he sincerely doubted it would. Even without the wound to his arm, Regis was no match for a worg, and he knew it. He couldn't begin to hurt the thing before those snapping jaws found his throat.

The only thing keeping him alive was the orc, the worg's master.

The halfling nearly fell over when the orc stopped the mount suddenly, on a small and level landing along the mountainside. Regis remembered to leap off the worg's back only when the snarling creature turned and nipped at his foot. He ran to the side and the worg turned and darted at him, but the orc intercepted and scolded it, kicking it in the rump as it turned around.

The worg retreated across the way, looking back at Regis with its hateful eyes, a stare that told him that as soon as the orc fell asleep, the great wolf would have him dead.

He found his solution in the fact that this particular clearing was surrounded by trees. Deathly exhausted and afraid, and terribly sore from his ordeal, Regis moved to an appropriate tree and started to climb.

"Where you's going?" the orc demanded.

"I'll keep the first watch," Regis replied.

"The dog will watch." The orc indicated the worg, which looked at Regis and bared its filthy fangs.

"As will I!" the halfling insisted.

He scrambled up the tree as fast as his broken arm would permit, moving well out of the orc's reach as quickly as he could manage.

He found a nook and settled his back against the trunk, his legs stretched out over a branch, and tried to secure himself as much as possible. He thought to go down and prod the orc into moving along, but in truth, he knew that they all needed rest, particularly the worg—though if the thing fell over dead of exhaustion, the halfling wouldn't shed a tear.

Every few seconds, Regis glanced back to the north, toward distant Shallows, and thought of his friends.

He could only hope they were still alive.

"Three buildings burning strong," Dagnabbit informed Catti-brie and Wulfgar as they kept a vigil at Bruenor's bedside.

They had set up the infirmary in the low workmen tunnels beneath

Withegroo's tower, a series of connecting passageways that allowed for inspections at key points of the tower's supporting base structure. This was actually the strongest section of the town, even stronger than the tower above, for the dwarves Withegroo had hired to build his tower had fashioned the tunnels first, reinforcing them against weather and enemies alike, for they alone had provided shelter during the months of the tower's construction.

Still, the cramped tunnels were hardly suited for their present purposes as makeshift bunkers. The friends were in the largest room—the only place that could rightly be called a room—and Wulfgar couldn't even stand up straight. He had to belly crawl through a ten-foot passageway to get in.

"The buildings are stone," Catti-brie argued.

"With a lot of wood support," said the dwarf. He moved beside Bruenor and sat down. "Giants threw a few firepots, and the rocks are coming in fast now."

"It's an organized group," said Wulfgar.

"Aye," Dagnabbit agreed, "and they're blocking all the south. We got no way out." He looked at Bruenor, so pale and weak, his broad chest barely rising with each breath. "Exceptin' that way."

Bruenor surprised them all, then, by opening one eye and even managing to turn his head toward Dagnabbit.

"Then ye take a bunch o' stinkin' orcs along for yer ride," the dwarf said, and he sank back into his bed.

Catti-brie was there in an instant, hovering over him, but after a quick inspection she realized that he had slipped off into that semiconscious state once again.

"Where's Rockbottom?" she asked, referring to the one cleric who had remained with their group of dwarves when the expeditionary force had split.

"Tending Withegroo, though I'm thinking the old mage's about finished," Dagnabbit answered. "Rockbottom says he's done all he can for Bruenor for now, and he's thinking like I'm thinking that we're gonna be needin' that wizard to have any chance o' getting outta here."

Catti-brie bit back her urge to scream at poor Dagnabbit, for she realized that despite his seemingly callous attitude toward Bruenor, he was as torn up as she was about the dwarf king's predicament. Dagnabbit was above all else pragmatic, though. He was the commander of Mithral Hall's forces, and always followed the road that promised the best chance of positive result, whatever the emotional burden. Cattibrie understood that he was as angry and frustrated as she at their helplessness, at having to sit there and watch the life ebb out of Bruenor.

Dagnabbit moved to the side of Bruenor's bed and gently lifted the signature one-horned helm off the dwarf king's head, rolling it about in his hands.

"Even if we find a way outta here, I don't know if we can take him with us," the dwarf said quietly.

Wulfgar was up in an instant, towering over Dagnabbit despite his necessary crouch.

"You would leave him?" he roared incredulously.

Dagnabbit didn't shrink from the barbarian's wild stare. He looked from Bruenor to Wulfgar, then back to his beloved king.

"If bringing him means throwing out all chance of us running by them, yeah," he admitted. "Bruenor'd not want to go if going meant getting them he loves slaughtered, and ye're knowing that."

"Get Rockbottom back in here to tend to him."

"Rockbottom can't do a thing for him, and ye heared it yerself when last he was here," said Dagnabbit. "Damned orc got him good. He'll be needin' a bigger priest than Rockbottom, might be even that he'll be needin' a whole bunch o' priests."

Wulfgar started toward Dagnabbit, but Catti-brie grabbed him by the arms and forced him to stop and look at her. He saw only sympathy there, a complete understanding of, and agreement with, his frustrations.

"We'll make our choices as we see them," the woman said softly.

"If we are to run to the south, then I will carry Bruenor all the way to Mithral Hall," Wulfgar said, casting a stern look at Dagnabbit.

The commander didn't flinch, but he did, after a moment, nod.

"Well if ye do, then ye know that me and me boys'll do all we can to keep ye running and to keep them damned orcs off ye."

That calmed Wulfgar, even though he, Catti-brie, and Dagnabbit all knew that those were words of the heart, not of the mind. In truth, to all three, the point seemed moot anyway. A few scouts had dared to slip out of Shallows in the hours since the end of the second battle and the reports of the tightening ring of orcs showed no chance of any large-scale escape.

They were trapped, Bruenor was dying, Drizzt and Regis were both missing, and there was nothing they could do about it.

Punctuating that disturbing logic, another giant boulder smashed against the tower above them, and cries of "Fire! Fire!" echoed down the low tunnels leading to the small, smoky room.

"Town lost thirty in the fighting," Dagnabbit informed them. "Counting the twelve killed afore the first fight."

"Almost a third," said Catti-brie.

"And most o' them men—some o' their best fighters," said the dwarf. "Two o' me own are dead, another five down too hurt to fight. If they come on again, we'll be hard pressed to hold."

"We'll hold," Wulfgar said grimly.

"After seein' ye on the wall, I'm almost believing ye," the dwarf replied.

"Almost?" Catti-brie asked.

Dagnabbit, who had seen the extent of destruction to the fortifications above, could only offer a shrug in reply.

"We hold or we die," said Catti-brie.

"We gotta get out," Dagnabbit remarked.

"Or get help in," said Catti-brie. "Regis got over the wall, though I'm not for knowing if he's dead on the field outside, or if he's running for help." She looked to Wulfgar as she explained, "Right after he went over the wall, the orcs on worgs came charging in."

After the fight, the friends had searched the ground west of Shallows as much as possible, but had found no sign of Regis. That had brought them some hope, at least, but in truth, both of them feared the halfling captured or dead.

"Even if he got away, I'm not for hoping that'll do anyone but himself any good," said Dagnabbit. "How long will it take him to find

Pwent? It'll take an army to get through to us, I'm thinking, and not just them Gutbusters. And how long will it take them to gather an army to our aid?"

"As long as it takes," said Wulfgar. "Until then, we must hold."

Dagnabbit started to reply, seeming as if to argue the point, but then he just blew a long sigh.

"Stay with King Bruenor," he bade Catti-brie. "If any're to keep his heart beating, it's yerself. Keep him warm, and wish him well from me and all me boys if he walks his journey to the other side."

He looked to Wulfgar.

"Help me and me boys fix what defenses we can?" he asked the man.

With a nod and a determined look to Catti-brie, the barbarian lifted his bloodied frame and crawled out of the small tunnel to begin the work of shoring up the defenses.

Such as they were.

He caught himself just as he was about to fall off of the branch, and when he realized that, when he realized where he was, the halfling had to spend a long moment telling his heart not to leap out of his chest. The fall probably wouldn't have been so bad, a few bruises and scratches, but Regis knew all too well what awaited him on the ground: a snarling, vicious worg.

He settled himself quickly and looked over the impromptu encampment. The orc was snoring contentedly between a pair of shading rocks, while the worg was curled right at the base of Regis's tree.

Wonderful, the halfling thought.

The sun was up and the day bright and warm, and Regis's heart told him that this was his last and only chance, that he had to find some way out of there. Would the orc still consider him a friend when it awoke? Would the gem-enhanced promises he had made of treasures and new weapons still hold strong in the dim-witted creature's thinking? If not, how could he use his ruby once again? How could he even get close enough to a hostile orc with that hungry worg wanting nothing more than to make a meal of him?

Regis put his head down and fought hard to hold back his sobs, for it seemed to him that it had all been for naught. He wished that he was back in Shallows with his friends, that if he was to die, as he surely believed he was, it would be with Bruenor and the others, with the friends who had walked the road beside him.

Not like this. Not torn apart by a cruel worg on a lonely mountain pass.

"Stop it!" Regis scolded himself, more loudly than he had intended.

Below him, the worg looked up, gave a long, low growl, then put its head back atop its paws.

"No time for self pity," the halfling whispered. "Your friends need you, Regis, so what are you going to do for them? Sit here and cry?"

No, he decided, and he sat up straighter and resolutely shook his head. Even that motion made his broken arm throb more. It was time to rouse the orc, to hope that the creature was still under the sway of the enchanted ruby, or to find some other way if it was not. If he had to fight them both, orc and worg, then he'd fight and be done with it. His friendship with those who had risked themselves time and again for his sake demanded no less.

Seeming taller, feeling taller, Regis rolled over the side of the branch and caught a foothold below, moving down the tree to a better vantage point where he could rouse the orc and judge its demeanor.

He stopped, though, and suddenly, his head snapping around, as something came bouncing into the encampment.

An old boot.

The worg leaped at it and tore at it with snapping jaws—and those jaws were snapping indeed, as a series of small explosions erupted from within the boot.

The worg yelped and howled, and leaped up into the air, doing a complete somersault.

The most curious looking creature Regis had ever seen rushed in to join the dance: a green-bearded dwarf wearing light green robes, open sandals on his dirty feet, and a cooking pot on his head. The dwarf ran right up to the worg and began waggling his fingers and his lips. The great wolf stopped its yammering and its hopping and froze in place, ears going back, eyes going wide.

With a sound that could only be described as a shriek, the worg put its tail between its legs and ran away.

"Hee hee hee," said the dwarf.

"What?" roared the awakened orc, its protesting cry cut short—as tended to happen when a battle-axe crushed the speaker's skull.

From behind the tumbling orc came a second dwarf, this one with a brilliant yellow beard, and dressed in more conventional dwarven attire—except for a tremendous helm that sported the huge antlers of a full-grown buck.

"Ye should o' killed the damned dog, too," the yellow bearded dwarf roared. "I'm hungry!"

As the green-bearded creature started wagging his finger in a scolding manner, Regis moved down the tree as quickly as his aching arm would permit.

"Who are you?" he called.

Both dwarves spun on him—and the yellow-bearded one almost launched his deadly axe Regis's way.

"No friend o' orcs . . . like yerself!" the yellow-bearded dwarf roared.

"No, no, no!" Regis insisted coming to the ground and waving his empty hand up in a sign of submission, his other arm tucked in close to his side. "I have come from the town of Shallows."

"Don't know it," said the yellow-bearded dwarf.

He looked to the other, who agreed with a "Nope, nope."

"And King Bruenor Battlehammer," Regis went on.

"Ah, now ye're talking!" said the dwarf with the yellow-beard. "Ivan Bouldershoulder at yer service, little one. And this's me brother—"

"Pikel!" Regis cried.

He had heard quite a bit about these two from Drizzt and Catti-brie, though in truth, no spoken words could do the specter of Pikel Bouldershoulder justice.

"Aye," said Ivan, "and tell me, little one, how're ye knowin' that, and what're ye doing with the likes o' them two?"

"We have to hurry," Regis replied, urgency suddenly flying back into his tone. "Bruenor's in trouble—they all are!—and I have to get to Mithral Hall . . . no, to the camp that Thibbledorf Pwent was supposed to be building north of the hall."

"Yeah, that's where we're goin'," said Ivan. "To Pwent. We took a circular route, but a bird told me brother where they were at. We were just fixing to go there when another bird told me brother about the orc and his puppy."

"He talks to a lot of birds, does he?" Regis asked dryly.

"Aye, and to the trees. Come along and he'll get us there afore ye can ask me how."

"There is no time," Regis said to the Bouldershoulders, to Thibbledorf Pwent and to the other leaders at the second dwarven outpost, some twenty miles across uneven, rocky ground north of Keeper's Dale, the vale heralding the main entrance to Mithral Hall. "Bruenor and the others don't have the four extra days it will take for the runners to gather the army and return here."

"Bah, they'll do it in three!" one of the outpost bosses, a crusty little fellow named Runabout Kickastone, insisted. "Ain't ye never seen a mad dwarf run?"

"Three's three too many!" roared Pwent, who had been leaning toward the north ever since Regis and the Bouldershoulders had arrived with the dire news of Shallows's predicament.

Indeed, Thibbledorf Pwent had been leaning to the north since Bruenor had separated from him and sent him to the south.

"We only got a hunnerd!" said Runabout. "And from what the little one's saying, a hunnerd ain't to do much!"

"Ye got the Gutbusters!" Pwent roared right back. "Them orcs'll think they're outnumbered, don't ye doubt!"

"And you've got clerics," added Regis, who knew they had to be away at once, and who guessed easily enough that some of his friends were likely in desperate need of some healing magic.

Runabout sighed and looked around, planting his hands on his hips.

"We might be doin' some good if we can get to the town," he admitted. "Shorin' up defenses and healing them that's hurt and all that. Don't sound like we'll be getting there with any kind o' ease, though."

Off to the side, Pikel hopped over to Ivan and began whispering excitedly into his brother's ear. All the others turned to watch and listen, though they couldn't really make out any clear words or meanings.

"Me brother's got some berries that'll make ye walk longer and faster," Ivan explained. "Takin' away yer need to stop and eat or drink. That'll get us up there all the faster, with short camps."

"Getting up there's sounding like the easy part," the ever-doubting Runabout replied, and before he had even finished, Pikel hopped up to Ivan and put his lips near his brother's ear again.

Ivan's expression turned sour, his face full of doubt, and he began to shake his head, but as Pikel continued, ever more excitedly, the dwarf slowly settled and began to listen more intently.

Finally, Pikel hopped back and Ivan turned an incredulous stare upon him and asked, "Ye think?"

"Hee hee hee."

"What?" Thibbledorf Pwent, Regis, and Runabout all demanded at once.

"Well, me brother's got a plan," Ivan haltingly explained. "Crazy plan . . ."

"Yes!" said Pwent, punching his fist into the air.

"But a plan's a plan, at least," Ivan went on. He looked to Pikel and asked again, "Ye think?"

"Hee hee hee."

"Well?" prompted Runabout.

"Well, are we to stand here jawing or to get going?" Ivan shot right back. "Ye got a big, strong wagon?"

"Yes," Runabout answered.

"Ye got a lot o' wood? Especially them big logs ye been using to hold the stone walls in place?"

Runabout looked around and slowly nodded.

"Then get all yer wood and get yer biggest and strongest wagons, and get all yer boys into line on the road north," said Ivan.

"What about yer brother's plan?" Runabout asked.

"I'm thinkin' it'd be better if I tell ye on the way," Ivan responded. "Both because we can't be standing here talking while yer king's in trouble, and because . . ." He paused and looked at the giggling Pikel, then admitted, "Because when ye hear it, ye might think we'd've been better waiting for the army."

"Hee hee hee," said Pikel.

Within the hour, the hundred dwarves and Regis set out from the outpost, pulling huge wagons laden with tons of strong wood. Pikel wasn't pulling and wasn't even walking. Rather, the dwarf moved from wagon to wagon, working the wood with his druidic magic, considering each piece and how it might fit into his overall design, and giggling. Despite the gravity of the situation, despite the fact that they were walking into an obviously desperate battle, Pikel was always giggling.

27

WHEN HOPE
FADES

Catti-brie sat in the dim light of a single candle, staring at Bruenor, her beloved father, as he lay on the cot. His face was ashen, and it was no trick of the light, she knew. His chest barely moved, and the bandages she had only recently changed were already blood-stained yet again.

Another rock hit close outside, shaking the ground but not even stirring Catti-brie, for the explosions had been sounding repeatedly. The bombardment had increased in tempo and ferocity. Every twentieth missile or so was no rock but a burning fire pot that spread lines of devastation, often igniting secondary fires within the town. Three blazes had already been put out in the wizard's tower, and Dagnabbit had warned that the integrity of the structure had been compromised.

They hadn't moved Bruenor, though, for there was nowhere else to go.

Catti-brie sat and stared at her father, remembering all the good times, all the things he had done for her, all the adventures they had shared. Her mind told her that that was over, though her heart surely argued against that conclusion.

In truth, they were waiting for Bruenor to die, for when he took his last breath, they—all who remained—would crawl out of their holes and over the battered walls and make their desperate run to the south. That was their only hope, slim though it was.

But Catti-brie could hardly believe she was sitting there waiting for Bruenor to die. She could hardly accept that the toughened old dwarf's chest would sometime soon go still, that he would no longer draw breath. She had always thought he would outlive her.

She had witnessed his fall once before and had thought him dead, when he had ridden the shadow dragon down into the gorge in Mithral Hall. She remembered that heartbreak, the unbelievable hole she had felt in her heart, the sense of helplessness and the surreal nature of it all.

She was feeling that again, all of it, only this time the end would come before her eyes, undeniably and with no room for hope.

The woman felt a strong hand on her shoulder then and turned to see Wulfgar moving in beside her. He draped his arm across her shoulders, and she put her head on his strong chest.

"I wish Drizzt would return," Wulfgar remarked quietly, and Catti-brie looked at him. "And with Regis beside him," the barbarian said. "We should all be together for this."

"For the end of Bruenor's life?"

"For all of it," Wulfgar explained. "For the run to the south, or the last stand here. It would be fitting."

They said no more. They didn't have to. Each was feeling the exact same thing, each was remembering the exact same things.

Up above, the rain of boulders continued.

"How many orcs are there?" Innovindil asked Tarathiel.

The two elves were far from the Moonwood, flying through the night on their winged horses. She had to shout to be heard, and even then her voice carried thinly on the night breezes.

"Enough so that the security of our own home will surely be compromised," Tarathiel answered with all confidence.

They were in the foothills to the north of the town of Shallows, looking back at the hundreds of fires of orc camps and at the flames engulfing sections of the town, most notably the lone tower that so clearly marked the place.

The pair set down on one high ridge to better converse.

"We cannot help them," Tarathiel said to his more compassionate companion as soon as they set down and he could better see the look upon her fair face. "Even if we could get to the Moonwood and rouse all the clan, we'd not return in time to turn the tide of this battle. Nor should we try," he added, seeing her doubting expression. "Our first responsibility is to the forest we name as our home, and if this black tide turns to the east and crosses the Surbrin, we will know war soon enough."

"There is truth in your words," Innovindil admitted. "I wonder if we might go there, though, and perhaps pull some from the disaster before the darkness closes in over them."

Tarathiel shook his head and painted on an expression that showed no room for debate.

"Orc arrows would chase us every inch," he argued, "and if they brought down Sunrise and Sunset, what good would we do for anybody? Who would fly to the east and warn our people?"

He pressed on with the argument, though Innovindil didn't need to hear it. She understood her responsibilities, and just as importantly, her limitations. She knew that the catastrophe to the south was far beyond the ability of her and her friend, and all their clan, to correct.

It pained her, it pained them both, to watch the town of Shallows die, for though the elves of the Moonwood were no friends to any of the humans in the area, neither were they enemies.

They could only watch.

It was a difficult climb, made all the more so because of the swelling and soreness in his twisted ankle. Hand over hand, Drizzt pulled himself up the long and narrow natural chimney, chasing the last flickers of diminishing daylight up above.

Diminishing daylight.

The drow paused, more than halfway up the three hundred foot climb. The worse thing about the fading afternoon light above was that Drizzt knew it was not the day after he had first crawled into the cave, but was the day after that. The size of the caverns had truly surprised him. It was a vast underground network, and he had spent nearly two days wandering through it, looking for a way back to the surface. Following lighter air, the drow had found many dead ends, chutes and openings too small for him to exit through.

He was beginning to suspect that he had found another, but he continued his climb. Still, each foot traversed made it clearer to him that this too was a dead end. The light above had shone brilliantly when first he had seen it, a welcomed contrast to the darkness of the caverns, but that had been due to the angle of the sun, the drow realized, and not the width of the opening.

He continued up another hundred feet before he knew for certain that he would have to double back, that the opening would admit no more than an arm or perhaps his head.

With a quiet reminder to himself that his friends needed him, Drizzt Do'Urden started back down.

An hour later, he was walking as swiftly as his sore ankle and his sheer exhaustion would permit. He considered doubling back, moving all the way to where he had first entered the tunnels in the hope that he might move the barriers the giants had constructed there, but he shook that thought away.

The sun had long risen before the drow found the next opening, and this time the exit was large enough.

Drizzt came out into the daylight, blinking against the stinging brilliance, letting his eyes adjust as much as possible. Then he spent a long while studying the mountains around him, trying to find some recognizable landmark that would guide him back to Shallows. The angle was too different, though. Observing the sun told him east from west, and north from south, though, so he started south. He was hoping to hit the Fell Pass, and hoping that he would find his bearings once the ground had somewhat leveled out.

He tore a sleeve from his shirt and tightened the splint around his ankle, then trotted away, ignoring the pain. He watched the sun pass its zenith above him, then move to the western horizon and drop behind.

Hours later, he found the Fell Pass and recognized the ground.

He ran on to the east across the foothills, urgency growing with each stride. A short while later, he saw a distant glow against the lightening sky of the southeast. He rushed up over one hill, finding a better viewpoint and saw, in the distance, flames climbing into the night sky.

Withegroo's tower.

His heart pumping more out of fear than from exertion, Drizzt ran on. He saw a glowing ball sail across the sky, north to south. When it hit it burst into flame in the battered town.

Drizzt didn't veer to the south, instead charging straight for the giants' position, determined to deter them yet again. His hand went to his onyx figurine, though he didn't bring the panther to him just yet.

"Be ready, Guenhwyvar," he said quietly. "Soon we find battle."

Drizzt knew that fire in the night distorted distances greatly, and so he was not surprised at how long it took him to get back near the town and the attacking giants.

He moved to the northern rim of the ravine in clear sight of Shallows. He could see the defenders rushing around. The tower was burning, though not nearly as brightly as before, and most of the activity was centered around it.

The giants seemed to be concentrating on that particular target as well.

Drizzt took out the figurine and set it on the ground, determined to bring forth Guenhwyvar and charge straight on into the giant encampment. He paused, though, noting a familiar figure atop that burning tower.

Drizzt couldn't make out much, but one thing showed clearly to him: a one-horned helmet that he knew so very well.

"Defy them, Bruenor," the drow whispered, a wry grin on his face.

Almost in response, a series of missiles smashed against that tower, one clipping right near the brightest burning fires and sending a shower of sparks through the night sky.

There the dwarf remained, atop the structure, directing the forces on the ground.

Drizzt's smile widened, or started to, for then there came a loud groaning and scraping sound from the south. Eyes wide with horror, Drizzt watched the tower lean, watched the dwarf atop it scramble to the edge, diving desperately for the rim.

The tower toppled to the south, and half fell over, half crumbled, so that the poor doomed dwarf fell down amidst tons of crushing stone.

Drizzt didn't even realize his own movements, didn't even register that his legs hadn't supported him through that terrible sight, that he was sitting down on the stone.

He knew beyond any doubt that no one in all the world could have survived that catastrophe.

A chill rushed through him. His hands trembled and tears filled his violet eyes.

"Bruenor," he whispered over and over.

His hands reached out to the south, into the empty air, with nothing to hold on to.

28

BOWING BEFORE
THE WRONG GOD

She could see nothing, could feel only the pain of raw scrapes all
around her arms and shoulders, and the discomfort of breathing in
chunks of stony dust. She groped around in the darkness of the partially
collapsed tunnel, searching desperately for her father.

Luck was with her, for the area around which Bruenor lay had survived the catastrophe almost intact. Catti-brie got up beside her father,
gently running her hands over his face, then putting her ear low to his
mouth, to find that he was still breathing, shallow though it was.

The woman turned around, trying to get her bearings, trying to figure
out which way would provide the shortest route to the surface, though
she wondered if she should even go to the surface at all. Had the orcs
come on in full after the fall of Withegroo's tower, which surely had
fallen? If so, she wondered if she would be better off staying there, in
the dark, for as long as she could manage before trying to find a way
out of the town altogether so she could head for the south.

That seemed the safer course, perhaps, but Wulfgar was up there,
and Dagnabbit and the others were up there, and the townsfolk were
up there, and if the orcs had indeed come on, the battle would be desperate.

Catti-brie crawled to the side of the small chamber and began to
claw at the stone, digging free several chunks and a mound of dirt and

stone dust. Her fingers bled but she pushed on. The ground above her groaned ominously, but she pushed on, ignoring the exhaustion that crept through her as the minutes passed.

She hit a rock too big for her to move. Undaunted, the woman started working at the side of the stone, and she jumped back as the rock suddenly shifted.

Morning light streamed in as the boulder went away, hoisted and tossed aside by the strong arms of Wulfgar.

He reached in for her and she gave him her hand and the barbarian gently pulled her from the small tunnel.

"Bruenor?" Wulfgar asked desperately.

"He's the same," Catti-brie replied. "The collapse didn't touch his room. Dwarves built it well."

As she finished, the woman looked around at the devastation. The tower had half fallen over and half collapsed in on itself, and it had taken out several buildings on its toppling descent, leaving a long line of rubble. She wanted to ask so many questions then, about who had survived and who had fallen, but she could find no words, her jaw just drooping open.

"Dagnabbit is gone," Wulfgar informed her. "Three other dwarves were lost with him, and at least five townsmen."

Catti-brie continued her scan, hardly believing the devastation that had befallen the town. Most of the buildings were down or badly damaged, and little remained of the wall. When the orcs came on—and she knew it would be soon since she could hear their horns blowing and drums beating in the south—there would be no organized defense, just fighting from street to street, and before the bitter end, from tunnel to tunnel.

She looked to Wulfgar and gathered strength from his stoic expression and his wide shoulders. He'd kill more than a few before the orcs finished him, Catti-brie knew, and she decided that she would too. A wry smile widened on her face, and Wulfgar looked at her curiously.

"Well, if it's to end, then it's to end in a blaze o' fighting!" she said, nodding and grinning.

It was either that or fall down and weep.

She put her hand on Wulfgar's shoulder, and he on hers.

"They're coming," came a voice behind them.

They turned to see Tred, battered and bloody, but looking more than ready for a fight. The dwarf stood sidelong, one hand hidden behind his back, the other holding his double-bladed axe.

Wulfgar pointed out several positions in a rough circle around the cave entrance leading back to Bruenor.

"We'll hold these four positions," he explained, "and fall back behind one pile after another to join up right here."

"And then?" asked Tred.

"We fall back into the caves, or what's left of them," the barbarian said. "Let the orcs crawl in and be killed until we are too weary to strike at them."

Tred looked around, then nodded his agreement though he understood, as they all did, the ultimate futility of it all. Certainly some orcs, thirsty for blood, would foolishly come into the caves after them, but soon enough the wicked creatures would realize that time was on their side, that they could just wait out the return of the defenders, or even worse, that they could start fires and smoke the defenders out of the caves.

"It'll be me honor to die beside yer King Bruenor and to die beside the fine children of the king. He was a fine and brave one, that Dagnabbit," Tred said somberly, glancing over at the long pile of broken stone. "Citadel Felbarr would've been proud to call him one of our own. I'm wishing we had the time to dig him out."

"It is a fitting grave," Wulfgar replied. "Dagnabbit stood tall and defied them, and at the moment of his fall he called to the dwarf gods. He knew that he had done well. He knew that he had honored his people and his race."

A solemn and silent moment passed, all three bowing their heads in deference to the fallen Dagnabbit.

"I got me some orcs to chop," Tred announced.

He saluted the pair and moved off, organizing the remaining few into battle groups to defend three of the positions.

Soon after, the bombardment increased once again but there was plenty of cover with so many piles of rubble, and there was little left to destroy. The giants' prelude seemed more an annoyance than anything else. The rain of boulders ended as the orcs, many riding worgs, came on, howling their battle cries.

Catti-brie started the fight for the defenders, popping up from behind the rubble pile and letting fly a streaking arrow that hit a worg squarely in the head, stopping it in its tracks and launching its rider through the air. The woman let fly again to the side, for there was no shortage of targets with orcs swarming over the all but destroyed walls. She drove her arrows into their ranks, taking one, sometimes even two, down with every shot.

But still they came on.

"Stay with the bow," Wulfgar instructed her.

He rose up strong and tall and met the orcs' charge, Aegis-fang sweeping the leading orcs away, launching them through the air.

All around the pair, the defenders of Shallows rose to meet the charge, humans and dwarves fighting desperately side by side. For a while, it seemed as if no orc's blow could fell any of them, as if any hit they suffered was a minor thing, shrugged off and retaliated immediately and brutally. Bodies piled all around the four defended positions, and almost all of them at first were orc and worg.

The momentum couldn't hold, though, nor could the defense. The defenders, even in their desperate frenzy, knew it.

Wulfgar swept his warhammer tirelessly, battering through any defenses the orcs trying to stand before him could possibly manage. Occasionally one of the creatures managed to slip under the blow, or duck back from it, but before the orc could them come on, a streaking silver arrow drove it down.

Catti-brie put Taulmaril up again and again, her enchanted quiver never emptying. Whenever she could manage, she aimed for a worg instead of an orc, considering the snarling wolves to be the more dangerous foe. Most of the time, though, the woman didn't even bother to aim, nor did she have to.

Even with that devastating line of fire, and with Wulfgar fighting more brilliantly and brutally than she had ever witnessed, the orcs, like the incoming tide, began to press in, swarming through holes.

Catti-brie let fly an arrow, put another up and spun around, blasting away an orc point-blank. Another was there, though, and she had to take up her bow like a staff and fend the creature off.

A second joined it, and she almost yelled for Wulfgar. Almost, but she held her words, realizing that any distraction to him would surely bring about his swift downfall. The woman whipped Taulmaril out before her viciously, back and forth, forcing the two orcs back. She dropped the bow and in the same fluid movement brought forth Khazid'hea, her fine-edged sword.

The orcs pressed on, a thrusting spear coming in hard at her right. A downward parry sheared the spear's tip cleanly off, and the orc, surprised by the lack of any real impact with the parry, overbalanced just a bit.

Enough for Catti-brie to turn her hand over and stab out quickly, taking the creature in the chest.

Back came Khazid'hea, just in time to ring against the heavy blade of the second orc's sword. One on one, this creature would be no match for Catti-brie.

But two others joined it, on either side, and Catti-brie was working furiously to fend off the trio. Behind her, she heard an impact, followed by Wulfgar's grunt.

But she couldn't help him, and he couldn't help her.

Catti-brie worked her blade all the more ferociously, turning aside thrust after stab after slash. Frustration grew within her, for she was making no headway, and she was working far too hard to maintain the pace.

The orc before her and to the right moved suddenly, and in a way she could not have anticipated. At first, she thought the creature was charging her, but quickly she realized that it was just flying by, launched at the end of a heavy dwarven axe. Tred stepped forward behind it, launching a backhand that doubled over the second of the trio, the one standing right before Catti-brie. The woman reacted quickly, diverting all of her attention to the orc on her left. She came forward suddenly, turned Khazid'hea over the orc's sword and down. The orc, both weapons down low, charged forward, trying to bowl her over, but the woman nimbly side-stepped the charge then stepped right past the orc.

As the blades disengaged, she flipped her grip around and stabbed out behind her, severing the creature's spine.

"Defenses falling!" Tred cried, running to join the battered Wulfgar and nearly getting his head torn off by one of Aegis-fang's wild swings. "We're backing to the hole!"

Wulfgar grunted his accord and swiped away yet another orc, then fell back behind the rubble barricade.

A worg came flying over it, leaping for his throat.

Catti-brie, her bow retrieved, took the wolf in the flank, the powerfully enchanted arrow throwing it out to the side, quite dead.

She looked up to see a horde of others charging in, though, and expected they would be overwhelmed quickly. She heard a noise behind her on the ground and turned to see old Withegroo, his features gaunt and strained. He could hardly stand, his body trembling from the exertion of even being upright, but the look in his eyes was not dull, and he moved his lips with determination wrought of sheer rage.

His fireball stopped the charge of worg and orc, and brought the defenders a little more time, but the exertion cost Withegroo dearly. He managed a smile as he launched his devastating bomb, then he looked at Catti-brie and winked.

He fell over, and before she even went to him the woman knew that he was dead.

Withegroo's blast had defeated the charge of one flank, but the orcs did not scramble from the magical display. The dwindling defenders backed and backed some more, and when they heard horns blowing in the south they knew it was more orcs joining the already overwhelming odds.

Or were those horns some other signal? the defenders had to wonder, as the press suddenly lightened. They were practically backed to the end of the line by then, with several already forced down into the tiny tunnels.

The defenders of Shallows regrouped in a tight ring and battled on. Before long, Catti-brie and Wulfgar were back to their original defensive position, and this time with few orcs standing before them.

Still the horns blew in the south, and as the fighting subsided,

Wulfgar dared to run to the highest mound he could find and peered out that way.

"What in the Nine Hells?" he called.

Tred, Catti-brie, and a few others joined him, and their incredulity was no less intense. There, rolling north and pulled by a strange looking team of more than twenty straggly mules, came a huge wooden totem. It was a gigantic statue of an orc face, but with a singular, grotesque eye.

"Gruumsh," Tred McKnuckles said. He spat upon the ground as if the mere mention of the orc god put a foul taste in his mouth. "They're bringing their clerics up," he reasoned. "A ceremony for their final victory, I'm guessin'."

The orcs that had been battling only moments before, filled the field to the south of the town, all pointing and cheering, many falling to their knees, prostrating themselves before the image of their revered, and feared, god.

Across the ravine, Drizzt heard the horns, though from his low vantage point creeping in on the giants' position, he couldn't see what the fuss was about. Even the giants standing up above him were talking excitedly, confused and pointing out to the south.

Drizzt spotted Guenhwyvar across the way, moving in for an attack. He caught the cat's attention with a wave of his hand, and motioned for her to hold her position. He looked around, wondering how he could find a better vantage point without being seen. He started out but stopped almost immediately. The giants, not so startled anymore, were conversing angrily. He couldn't understand very much of what they were saying, but he recognized that they were somewhat put off by the orcs—he heard something about the orc priests stealing all their glory.

A flicker of hope came to Drizzt that perhaps their enemies were about to split ranks, though he knew it was likely far too late to make any real difference.

The driver, huddled under heavy robes, cracked his whip above the long line of pulling beasts, and the dirty and shaggy creatures tugged harder, propelling the huge wagon and great statue of Gruumsh One-Eye, god of the orcs, along the sloping and rocky ground.

All of the orcs had turned their attention from Shallows, and the tiny pocket of hopelessly outnumbered defenders, to this new arrival. They bowed and fell to their knees in droves beside the wagon's course.

"What is this?" one orc commander asked the leader of the army, Urlgen, son of Obould.

Urlgen considered the strange scene with a perfectly confused expression, his tusks chewing at his lips.

"Obould has brought many allies," was all he could say, and all he could think.

Was his father elevating the glory of this attack? Was he tying the attacks directly to some edict of the orc god's?

Urlgen didn't know, and like the rest of his army his movements crept him closer to the great rolling statue. Unlike most of the others, though, Urlgen didn't focus entirely on that idol. He considered the curious team, perhaps the most unkempt and straggly looking team of . . . of what? Urlgen didn't even really know what the creatures were. Mules? Small oxen? Rothé, perhaps, taken from the corridors of the Underdark?

From there, the unusually smart orc scrutinized the drivers. One was taller and broader than the other, though both were short by orc standards. Perhaps the second—more a passenger than a driver, he seemed—was a child, but Urlgen couldn't really tell, since both wore heavy cloaks that included wide, low cowls.

The wagon rolled to a stop some hundred or so feet from the town, which Urlgen thought rather foolish, since it left them in range of that horrible human woman and her nasty bow. The orc leader glanced back that way, and he did see several of the defenders watching, as were his own minions.

The larger driver stood up and lifted his arms above his head. The sleeves of his cloak slipped down to reveal gnarly hands and a hairy forearm that didn't seem very orclike.

Before anyone could truly take note of that, though, the driver grabbed a lever of some kind located on the front of the statue, right below the tusk-filled mouth.

He said something that sounded like, "Hee hee hee," and yanked the lever down.

"Well, here's one less priest for the damned Gruumsh," Catti-brie said with bitter determination.

She lifted Taulmaril and leveled it the driver's way, but Tred grabbed her arm and stayed the shot.

"One won't be makin' any difference," he said, "and something's not right about all this besides."

Catti-brie started to ask what he meant, but in truth she could sense it too. Something about the team and the drivers struck her as odd, even from a distance.

Her eyes widened when she heard the grinding sound that followed the orc shaman's pull of the lever, and they widened some more as the great statue seemed to grow, then split apart, the four sides breaking in the middle and falling out to form four wide planks.

Out onto those planks, from the hollow inside of the statue, ran dwarves—many dwarves—in the full battle array of the unmistakable Gutbusters!

One in particular led the way, wearing black, ridged armor and a helmet with a spike that was half again the height of the dwarf wearing it.

"It's Pwent!" Catti-brie cried.

Even as she spoke, Thibbledorf Pwent leaped out, roaring and flailing. He ducked his head with perfect timing to skewer one orc as he landed atop another, smashing it to the ground. Catti-brie lost sight of him then but winced anyway, for she knew his technique. She knew that he was jostling about wildly atop the orc, his sharpened armor shredding it.

His boys followed with equal abandon, running to the end of a plank and leaping wildly atop the confused throng of orcs. One after another they went, dwarven catapult balls raining death from on high. Even more dwarves appeared a moment later, throwing off camouflaging blankets that someone must have enchanted to make them look like a team of mules, and charging out from the yokes. How many fine targets they found in those first confusing seconds, with so many orcs kneeling on the ground, bowing forward.

The massacre became a fight soon after, but even then the orcs were outmatched. Many were running, caught by surprise, and as was typical for any goblinkin, ranks broke apart at the first sign of retreat.

The dwarven ranks stayed tight and strong and swept toward the town, with groups breaking away at the slightest sign of pursuit to chase off the orcs.

"Ye Battlehammers was always known for yer timing!" Tred McKnuckles cried, then he yelped and leaped aside as a great rock smashed down and bounced past.

"Damn giants again!" the dwarf cried.

Catti-brie ran to the remnants of the northern wall and lifted her bow.

"Move as you shoot!" Wulfgar warned, and indeed, as soon as the first arrow made its way out across the ravine, a volley of great stones came in at the position where the arrow had been fired.

It did Drizzt Do'Urden's heart good to see those telltale arrows sailing across the ravine, but even that good news—that Catti-brie was apparently still fighting—did not distract him from his course. The giants had started their bombardment in full force again, and that, he knew, he could not allow. He called Guenhwyvar into action, then scrambled up to the side of the giants' position himself, moving high up on a pile of boulders unnoticed by the behemoths.

The drow advanced without a sound, leaping out and crossing behind one giant, his scimitars slashing hard. He hit the ground running, executing a perfect double stab at the back of another's knee, and kept right on going, around the rocks on the other side.

Giants turned to follow, and one lifted its arms to throw a stone at the fleeing drow.

Instead of executing the throw, the giant caught a flying panther in its face—all six hundred pounds of raking claws. Guenhwyvar went for the eyes, not the kill, and scraped them deep, blinding the giant before leaping aside.

All the giants were scrambling, but Drizzt held no illusions that he and Guenhwyvar could keep them occupied for long. Nor did he think that he could possibly kill many, even any, of them, but maybe he and the panther could blind a few or get a few to chase them away.

He came back around the rocks the same way he had gone in and did indeed catch the closest giant off its guard, managing another few nasty stabs before scrambling the other way. The pursuit was better this time, though—was too good—with giants flanking both ways and another pair pursuing directly.

Drizzt moved to put his back to a wall, ready to make a final, desperate stand.

The nearest giant charged in.

Before it got to Drizzt, though, the behemoth winced and grabbed at its neck. As it spun around, the dark elf clearly saw the feathered fletching of a pair of arrows buried in the giant's neck. Drizzt's jaw dropped open when the brute moved just a bit to the side.

There, up above him to the north, sat a pair of elves astride flying horses.

The giants scrambled.

Drizzt rushed out to the side, stabbed yet another, then kept on running, leaping past some boulders. Few giants paid him any heed, though. A couple off to the side were still futilely trying to keep up with Guenhwyvar as the panther leaped all around them. Several of the others were moving fast for more rocks—to throw at the elves, obviously.

Drizzt couldn't let them get organized. He moved to the rock pile on the west. When one giant stooped and reached for a stone, he leaped out, slashing the behemoth hard across its fingers. The giant retracted the hand, and it, and a companion, gave chase on the drow.

This time Drizzt didn't turn and didn't slow, leading the giants off and yelling for Guenhwyvar to do the same across the way. The drow ranger saw a stone go flying into the air and heard the shriek of a pegasus a moment later, though when he looked to the north, both elves were still up there, flying around and firing their bows.

Drizzt sprinted out across some open ground, often glancing back at the destroyed town, hoping to catch some sign of his friends.

He saw nothing definitive, just a swarm of orcs charging for the town. Drizzt had to turn away, running to the north with a pair of giants close behind him.

"We got no time!" Thibbledorf Pwent cried, charging into Shallows. "Gather up yer things and yer wounded and follow me to the wagon!"

"We need a cleric!" Wulfgar yelled at him. "At once! We've wounded too badly hurt to be moved!"

"Then ye might need to leave 'em!" Pwent yelled back..

"One of them is Bruenor Battlehammer!" Wulfgar yelled back.

"*Cleric!*" yelled Pwent. "And get the one on the wagon with the green beard," the battlerager cried to another dwarf. "He's got more tricks than a den o' drunken wizards."

"Get 'em moving!" another dwarf cried. "Get the wounded on the wagon and get all the dead dwarfs ye can up there with 'em. We're not for leaving Battlehammers behind for the buzzards or the orcs!"

"How did ye find us so fast?" Catti-brie started to ask Pwent, but she stopped and smiled when she saw the obvious source of the daring rescue. The second driver, the little one, whom she recognized clearly once his cowl was pulled back. "Regis," the woman said.

With her heart busting, she moved to hug him but backed away quickly when she saw him wince as she put pressure against his arm.

"Someone had to feed the wolf," the halfling said with a sheepish shrug.

Catti-brie bent low and kissed him on the head, and Regis blushed deeply.

And they were moving, a whirlwind of scrambling dwarf warriors buzzing like a swarm of angry bees around the exhausted defenders of Shallows, a ragtag group. Of the hundred humans and twenty-six dwarves who had begun the defense of the town, less than a score were leaving of their own strength, and only another ten, Bruenor among them, were still drawing breath at all.

Hardly a victory.

29

WHERE ROADS MEET
AND ROADS DIVERGE

They ran in flanking lines left and right of the main wagons. Others pulled hard at the largest wagon—the orc god statue discarded—that bore the wounded, including King Bruenor Battlehammer. On the cart with him rode Regis, who was too injured to do much of anything else, and Pikel Bouldershoulder, the doo-dad, who used his enchanted berries and roots on Bruenor's wounds.

"He'll draw out the sickness," Ivan assured Wulfgar and Tred as they ran along behind that wagon. "Me brother's got some tricks, he does."

Wulfgar nodded grimly and took heart in the words, for Catti-brie had told him a short while before that Bruenor did seem to be resting more easily.

"Ain't that that's worrying me," Tred put in. "We're seeing orc sign all about, and if they come on now. . . ."

"They will be without their giant friends, who were left on the other side of the ravine," Wulfgar insisted.

"True enough," Tred admitted, though his dour expression did not brighten, "but I'm thinking we'll be finding a tougher fight with them orcs, even with yer boys from Mithral Hall here, when them orcs ain't so surprised that yer boys from Mithral Hall're here!"

There really wasn't much that Wulfgar could say against such logic. He had seen the orc force, and he knew that those legions, despite being scattered and with many slaughtered outside of Shallows, would still prove overwhelming to this contingent in a level fight. Even as they had begun the run the previous day, they had all known that their only real hope was that the orcs had been too scattered to regroup in time to catch them before they reached the safety of Mithral Hall, or at least before they met up with the dwarven army rolling out of that fortress.

But already the signs were showing their hopes to be in vain. All through the night—in which the dwarves, utilizing more of Pikel's wondrous berries, had kept moving—they had heard the calls of worgs, left and right, shadowing them. Earlier the second day, they had caught sight of a dust cloud rising in the north, not so far behind, and they knew that they were being pursued.

Pwent had proposed a possible scenario to them that morning. The battlerager figured that the orc worg-riders would flank and circle in front of the dwarves, trying to slow their run, thus giving the pursuing main force time to catch up and overwhelm them. The dwarves had decided that if such a blockade had been formed, they would lower their heads and blast straight through it.

Wulfgar could only hope that it didn't come to that. They barely had enough to take turns pulling the wagon of wounded, and Pwent and his boys were reaching the end of their tolerance. Pikel's berries were amazing indeed, but they did not provide magical strength. They merely allowed the body to draw on its deeper resources. After the run to the north, the desperate fight, and the beginning of the run back to the south, Wulfgar could plainly see that those reserves were reaching their end. Even worse, those who had come from the prolonged defense of Shallows, himself included, were all carrying grievous wounds.

Another fight would likely be the end of all of them and at the least would eliminate any hope Wulfgar had of getting his beloved father back to Mithral Hall alive.

And so that afternoon, when scouts reported a growing cloud of dust to the west, the barbarian moved to the wagon to join Catti-brie, Regis, and Bruenor.

"That'll mark the end of it," Catti-brie remarked, staring out at the cloud.

Her demeanor, so removed from the ever-optimistic presence that Wulfgar had always known, caught him off guard and surprised Regis as well.

"We'll fight them and beat them!" Regis replied. "And if more catch us, we'll fight them, too!"

"Indeed," Wulfgar agreed. "I would not see Aegis-fang in the hands of an orc, even if that means I must kill every orc in all the North. And I will see Bruenor back to Mithral Hall, where he will find his strength anew and resume the throne that is so rightfully his."

The words were empowering to both Regis and Catti-brie, and their appreciative looks to Wulfgar became grins and even laughter when Pikel Bouldershoulder chimed in with an enthusiastic "Oo oi!"

The dwarves closed ranks around the wagons, though they maintained their swift pace. Pwent began directing his charges, moving his most seasoned fighters to the delicate areas of defense, and calling out to his boys to be ready. At one point, he moved beside the wagon.

"There'll be a few hunnerd of 'em, judging by what me scouts're seeing," the battlerager explained. He added with an exaggerated wink, "Nothing me and me boys can't handle."

Wulfgar nodded, as did the others, but they all knew the truth of the matter. Being intercepted by several hundred orcs would be bad enough, but even if they could indeed win out against such odds, they would find themselves caught by an equal or larger group from behind because of the inevitable delay.

"Take up your bow," Wulfgar bade Catti-brie as he handed her Taulmaril. "Shoot well."

"Perhaps I could go out under a flag of truce and speak with them," Regis offered, pointedly pulling the enchanted ruby pendant over his shirt collar.

Wulfgar shook his head.

"They'd have ye dead even if ye managed to snare a few o' them with yer lies," Catti-brie remarked.

"Promises, not lies," Regis corrected.

He shrugged helplessly and looked down at the ruby then tucked it away.

The dwarven ranks tightened. It was obvious that they had been spotted by the intercepting force, and their choices were few. A turn to the east would likely put them into another group of orcs, and to stop and try to form some semblance of defense might bring the pursuing orcs upon them as well.

They plowed ahead, gripping weapons in one hand, wagon yokes in the other.

"We gotta make that ridge afore 'em!" Thibbledorf Pwent cried to his fellows, pointing ahead to some higher ground.

The dwarves responded by lowering their aching shoulders even more and charging on. They reached the base of the ridge and started up the slope, hardly slowing.

But they didn't get there first.

"The wing is not broken, but it is bruised badly and will not carry Sunset for any distance," Innovindil told Tarathiel when he and Sunrise returned to her in the mountain cave, some miles north east of the place where they had battled the giants.

Even with the glancing hit by the thrown rock, they had managed to outdistance the pursuing giants and had been fortunate to find a cave where they could put up for the time being.

"The giants have given up the chase, I believe," Tarathiel replied. "They will not find us."

"But neither will we get back to the Moonwood anytime soon," Innovindil reasoned, "or at least, not both of us."

Her expression as she finished was as clear a signal to Tarathiel that she wanted him to climb onto Sunrise and fly off for home as if she had spoken the words directly.

"I am not certain that our report to our people would be complete enough to properly prepare them for what is to come," he replied somberly.

"What have you seen?"

Tarathiel's expression held a grim edge.

"They are crawling out of their holes," he told her, "all to the north and the west. The orcs and goblins are rising as one, and we have seen that the giants, too, are with them. I fear that the force that sacked the town of Shallows is but a small portion of what we will discover."

"Then all the more reason for you to fly to our people."

Tarathiel looked to his mount and seemed, for just a moment, to be leaning that way, but then he looked back at his companion and stood resolute.

"I'll not leave you," he said. "The elves of the Moonwood will not be caught off their guard, whether I fly there or not."

Innovindil started to argue but changed her mind almost immediately. She did not want to be left out there alone, however brave she might sound. She did not know the region as did Tarathiel, and she truly feared for Sunrise. Though the pegasus would survive the wound, it had been so valiant in holding its position above the giants through the pain and shock that the elf had no intention of allowing Sunrise to do anything but heal, even if protecting the pegasus was at the cost of her own life. She knew that Tarathiel felt the same way.

"And we have something else to learn, and now may be our only chance to do so," Tarathiel added after a short pause.

"You believe that the dark elf escaped the fight with the giants," Innovindil reasoned.

"It is possible that Ellifain is out there, as well."

"It is probable that Ellifain is dead," said Innovindil, and Tarathiel could only nod.

Initial shock, the adrenaline of an approaching, desperate battle, fast shifted to confusion among the ranks of the battleragers and the others in the fleeing caravan, for there, on the ridge before them, stood dwarves—a host of dwarves—and arrayed with the colors not of Mithral Hall, but with the axe symbol of Mirabar.

"Who are ye, and what're ye about?" the lead dwarf cried, and he lifted his helm back off his face.

"Torgar!" Regis cried, surely recognizing the dwarf.

A perplexed expression came over the dwarf's face, and he motioned to his fellows to spread wide, left and right. He, along with several others, came down to the ragtag group.

"Well, yer King Bruenor's got our weapons, and so's Mithral Hall, whatever his fate," Torgar proclaimed when Wulfgar and the others filled him in on the desperate battle and the retreat to Mithral Hall. "We come out to ask King Bruenor for his friendship, and now I'm thinking we can prove our own to him and his. Ye just keep on yer run and me and mine'll follow ye close."

"Ye let me and me own run with ye, Torgar o' Mirabar," Thibbledorf Pwent cut in as he stepped forward, showing his ridged, blood-stained armor in all its gory glory. "We give them orcs a reason to run!"

"Luck has shone upon us," Wulfgar whispered to Catti-brie a moment later, as the five hundred reinforcements found positions around the retreating caravan.

They both looked to Bruenor and to Pikel, still tirelessly tending the dwarf king and the other wounded. Apparently sensing their looks, Pikel turned to regard them and offered a wink and a hopeful nod.

Catti-brie couldn't help but smile but then couldn't help but look back to the north.

"You're thinking of Drizzt," Wulfgar observed.

"As soon as we get Bruenor back to Mithral Hall, we'll head out to find him," Regis said, joining in on the conversation.

Catti-brie shook her head with even greater resolve. "He will see to himself and trust that we will see to our safety and the security of Mithral Hall. When his job is done out there, he will come home."

Both Wulfgar and Regis looked at her with surprise, but both inevitably agreed. Without information to the contrary, they knew they had to trust in Drizzt, and in truth, who in all the world was better suited to survive in the hostile environment of the orc-infested North? More practically, none of them were really fit to head back out. Certainly Regis was in no shape to be walking a dangerous road anytime soon.

Catti-brie continued to stare to the north, and without even realizing it, she began chewing nervously on her bottom lip.

Wulfgar grabbed her forearm and gave a gentle, comforting squeeze.

"Elastul told you?" Nanfoodle asked Shoudra when the two met up in the corridor of their building a few nights later.

"He instructed me to go with you," Shoudra replied, her tone making it clear that she was none too pleased with the order.

"He has erred and continues to do so," the little gnome said. "First he chases Bruenor off, then imprisons Torgar, and now . . ."

"This is hardly the same thing," said Shoudra.

"Is it so different? Will the remaining dwarves in Mirabar be pleased when they learn of our antics in Mithral Hall? Do we even have a hope of succeeding there, given that more than four hundred of Mirabar's dwarves will precede our arrival?"

"Elastul is counting on just that fact to gain us the confidence of Bruenor and his kin."

"To what end? Treachery?" asked the glum gnome.

Shoudra started to respond, but just shrugged. "We will see what we find when we arrive in Mithral Hall," she said after a moment's reflection.

Nanfoodle considered her words and her demeanor for a moment, then his face brightened.

"I plan to follow your lead in the cavern of Clan Battlehammer," he said, "even if that lead diverges from the edicts of Marchion Elastul."

Shoudra looked around cautiously, her expression bidding the gnome to speak no more of such foolishness.

In her own heart, though, the Sceptrana did not disagree. Elastul's edict had been direct and simple: Go to Mithral Hall and check on the traitor dwarves, and while they're there, do some serious damage to their rival's operations.

Better, Shoudra thought, that they go to Mithral Hall to reach out to

King Bruenor through Torgar Hammerstriker and the others. After the disaster that had befallen Mirabar, they might find a new and stronger alliance with their fellow mining city, one that would benefit them all.

She could only sigh and wish things were different, though, for she knew Elastul well enough to understand the absurdity of even hoping that she could realize such an outcome.

EPILOGUE

With every stone he turned, Drizzt Do'Urden held his breath, expecting to find one of his friends buried beneath it. The destruction of Shallows had been complete by his estimation. He had no idea what the pile of shaped wood on the field just south of the town might be, but he supposed that the orcs had brought great siege engines with them in the final assault.

Not that they had needed any, given the damage the giants had wrought upon the town.

He took heart at the many dead orcs and worgs littered about the scene, but the fact that many had died right at the entrance to the substructure tunnels, logically the last line of defense, told him that the end had surely been bitter.

He found no bodies in those tunnels, at least, lending him some hope that his friends had been captured and not killed.

And he found a familiar one-horned helmet.

Hardly finding the strength to bend without falling over, the drow touched the crown of Bruenor Battlehammer and gently lifted it, turning it over in his hands. He had hoped that his eyes had deceived him from across the ravine that terrible night, when the flaming tower had fallen. He had hoped that Bruenor had somehow been able to leap away and escape the catastrophe.

The drow forced himself to look around, to poke at the rubble near to the helmet. There, under tons of stone, he found the end of a crushed hand, a gnarled, dwarf's hand.

So, he believed, he had found Bruenor's grave.

And were Wulfgar and Regis buried there too? And what of Catti-brie?

The images that flitted about in his whirling thoughts weighed heavily on Drizzt Do'Urden. He remembered thinking it would be better to adventure on the open road—even if it were to cost him his life, even if it were to cost Catti-brie's life—than to live a life in one secure place.

How hollow those thoughts felt to him in that terrible moment.

Strangely, he thought of Zaknafein then, of his family and his days in Menzoberranzan, of the tragedies that had marked his early life. He thought of Ellifain too, of all that he had tried to do for her that fateful night under the stars, and of her ultimate end.

He thought of his friends, some surely lost, and likely all dead, and was stabbed by the futility of it all. For all his life since his days with Zaknafein, his departure from Menzoberranzan, his days with Montolio and with the friends he had come to love above all others in Icewind Dale, Drizzt Do'Urden had followed a line of precepts based upon discipline and ultimate optimism. He fought for a better world because he believed that a better world could and would be made. He had never held any illusions that he would change the whole world, of course, or even a substantial portion of it, but he had always held strongly that fighting to better just his own little pocket of the world was a worthwhile course.

And there was Ellifain. And there was Bruenor.

He looked down at the helmet and rolled it over in his hands.

In all likelihood he had lost every close friend he had ever known.

Except for one, the drow realized when Guenhwyvar stirred beside him.

Three days later, Drizzt Do'Urden sat on the rocky slopes of a mountain, listening to the cacophony of horns around him and watching the progression of lines of torches moving along nearly every mountain trail. All that had happened had been but a prelude, he understood then. The orcs were massing, bringing a fair number of goblins along with them, and even worse, they had allied with the frost giants in greater numbers than any could have anticipated.

What had gone from a raid on a caravan from Citadel Felbarr had escalated to the sacking of two towns and to a threat to every life in the North. In just watching the progression, Drizzt could see that Mithral Hall itself would soon be threatened.

And, he believed, Mithral Hall was a leaderless place.

In truth, though, none of that realization sank very deeply into the thoughts and heart of Drizzt Do'Urden that dark night on a mountain slope, and when he saw the campfire of a small off-shoot of the massing humanoid force not too far away, all thoughts of anything but the immediate situation flew from him.

The drow produced his onyx figurine and called forth Guenhwyvar, then drew out his scimitars and started his slow walk toward the encampment. He didn't blink; his face showed no emotion at all.

It was time to go to work.

R·A·SALVATORE

THE HUNTER'S BLADES TRILOGY
BOOK II

1

ANGER'S REMINDER

Drizzt didn't like to think of it as a shrine. Propped on a forked stick, the one-horned helmet of Bruenor Battlehammer dominated the small hollow that the dark elf had taken as his home. The propped helm was set right before the cliff face that served as the hollow's rear wall, in the only place within the natural shelter that got any sunlight.

Drizzt wanted it that way. He wanted to see the helmet. He wanted to never forget. And it wasn't just Bruenor he was determined to remember, and not just his other friends.

Most of all, Drizzt wanted to remember who had done this horrible thing to him and to his world.

He had to fall to his belly to crawl between the two fallen boulders and into the hollow, and even then the going was slow and tight. Drizzt didn't care; he actually preferred it that way. The total lack of comforts, the almost animalistic nature of his existence, was good for him, was cathartic, and even more than that, was yet another reminder to him of what he had to become, of who he had to be if he wanted to survive out there. No more was he Drizzt Do'Urden of Icewind Dale, friend to Bruenor and Catti-brie, Wulfgar and Regis. No more was he Drizzt Do'Urden, the ranger trained by Montolio deBrouchee in the ways of nature and the spirit of Mielikki. No, now he was that lone drow who had wandered out of Menzoberranzan. Now he was that refugee from

2

the city of dark elves, who had forsaken the ways of the priestesses who had so wronged him and who had murdered his father.

Now he was the Hunter, the instinctual creature who had defeated the dark ways of the Underdark, and who would repay the orc hordes for the death of his dearest friends.

Now he was the Hunter, who sealed his mind against all but survival, who put aside the emotional agony of the loss of Ellifain.

Drizzt knelt before the sacred totem one afternoon, watching the splay of sunlight on the tilted helmet. Bruenor had lost one of the horns on it years and years before, long before Drizzt had come into his life. The dwarf had never replaced the horn, he had told Drizzt, because it was a reminder to him always to keep his head low.

Delicate fingers moved up and felt the rough edge of that broken horn. Drizzt could still catch the smell of Bruenor on the leather band of the helm, as if the dwarf was squatting in the dark hollow beside him. As if they had just returned from another brutal battle, breathing heavy, laughing hard, and lathered in sweat.

The drow closed his eyes and saw again that last desperate image of Bruenor. He saw Withegroo's white tower, flames leaping up its side, a lone dwarf rushing about on top, calling orders to the bitter end. He saw the tower lean and tumble, and watched the dwarf disappear into the crumbling blocks.

He closed his eyes all the tighter to hold back the tears. He had to defeat them, had to push them far, far away. The warrior he had become had no place for such emotions. Drizzt opened his eyes and looked again at the helmet, drawing strength in his anger. He followed the line of a sunbeam to the recess behind the staked headgear, to see his own discarded boots.

Like the weak and debilitating emotion of grief, he didn't need them anymore.

Drizzt fell to his belly and slithered out through the small opening between the boulders, moving into the late afternoon sunlight. He jumped to his feet almost immediately after sliding clear, and put his nose up to the wind. He glanced around, his keen eyes searching every shadow and every play of the sunlight, his bare feet feeling the cool ground beneath him. With a cursory glance all around, the Hunter sprinted off for higher ground.

He came out on the side of a mountain spur just as the sun disappeared behind the western horizon, and there he waited, scouting all the region as the shadows lengthened and twilight fell.

Finally, the light of a camp fire glittered in the distance.

Drizzt's hand went instinctively to the onyx figurine in his belt pouch. He didn't take it forth and summon Guenhwyvar, though. Not this night.

His vision grew even more acute as the night deepened around him, and Drizzt ran off, silent as the shadows, elusive as a feather on a windy autumn day. He wasn't constricted by the mountain trails, for he was too nimble to be slowed by boulder tumbles and broken ground. He wove through trees easily, and so stealthily that many of the forest animals, even wary deer, never heard or noted his approach, never knew he had passed unless a shift in the wind brought his scent to them.

At one point, he came to a small river, but crossed in four great strides, leaping from wet stone to wet stone in such perfect balance that even their water-splashed sides did little to trip him up.

He had lost sight of the fire almost as soon as he came down from the mountain spur, but he had taken his bearings from up there and he knew where to run, as if anger itself was guiding his long and sure strides.

Across a small dell and around a thick copse of trees, the drow caught sight of the campfire once more, and he was close enough to see the silhouettes of the forms moving around it. They were orcs, he knew at once, from their height, their broad shoulders, and their slightly hunched manner of moving. A couple were arguing—no surprise there—and Drizzt knew enough of their guttural language to understand their dispute to be over which would keep watch. Clearly, neither wanted the duty, nor thought it anything more than an inconvenience.

The drow crouched behind some brush not far away and a wicked grin grew across his face. Their watch was indeed inconsequential, he thought, for alert or not, they would not take note of him.

They would not see the Hunter.

* * * * *

The brutish sentry dropped his spear across a big stone, interlocked his fingers and inverted his hands, his knuckles cracking more loudly than snapping branches.

"Always Bellig," he bitched, glancing back at the campfire and the many forms gathered around it, some lying, others tearing at scraps of putrid food. "Bellig keep watch. You sleep, you eat. Always Bellig keep watch."

He continued to grumble and complain, and continued to look back at the encampment for a long while. Bellig turned back, to see facial features chiseled from ebony, to see a shock of white hair, and to see eyes—those eyes! Purple eyes! Flaming eyes!

Bellig instinctively reached for his spear—or started to, until he saw the flash of a gleaming blade to his left and another to the right. He tried to bring his arms in close to block, but he was far too slow to catch up to the dark elf's blades.

The orc tried to scream, but by that point, the scimitars had cut two deep lines, severing his throat.

Bellig clutched at the mortal wounds and the blades came back, then back again, and again.

The dying orc turned as if to run to his comrades, but the scimitars struck again, this time at his legs, their fine edges easily parting muscle and tendon.

Bellig felt a hand grab him as he fell, guiding him down quietly to the ground. He was still alive, though he had no way to draw breath. He was still alive, though his lifeblood deepened in a dark red pool around him.

His killer moved off . . . so quietly.

* * * * *

"Arsh, get yourself quiet over there, stupid Bellig," Oonta called from under the boughs of a wide-spreading elm not far to the side. "Me and Figgle is talking!"

"Him's a big mouth," Figgle the Ugly agreed.

With his nose missing, one lip torn away, and green-gray teeth all twisted and tusky, Figgle was a garish one even by orc standards. He had bent too close to a particularly nasty worg in his youth, and had paid the price.

"Me gonna kill him soon," Oonta remarked, drawing a crooked smile from his sentry companion.

A spear soared in, striking the tree between them and sticking fast.

"Bellig!" Oonta cried as he and Figgle stumbled aside. "Me gonna kills you sooner!"

With a growl, Oonta reached for the quivering spear, as Figgle wagged his head in agreement.

"Leave it," came a voice, speaking basic Orcish but too melodic in tone to belong to an orc.

Both sentries froze and turned around to look in the direction from whence the spear had come. There stood a slender and graceful figure, black hands on hips, dark cape fluttering out in the night wind behind him.

"You will not need it," the dark elf explained.

"Huh?" both orcs said together.

"Whatcha seeing?" asked a third sentry, Oonta's cousin Broos. He came in from the side, to Oonta and Figgle's left, the dark elf's right. He looked to the two and followed their frozen gazes back to the drow, and he, too, froze in place. "Who that be?"

"A friend," the dark elf said.

"Friend of Oonta's?" Oonta asked, poking himself in the chest.

"A friend of those you murdered in the town with the tower," the dark elf explained, and before the orcs could even truly register those telling words, the dark elf's scimitars appeared in his hands. He might have reached for them, so quickly and fluidly that they hadn't followed the movement, but to them, all three, it simply seemed as if the weapons had appeared there.

Broos looked to Oonta and Figgle for clarification and asked, "Huh?"

And the dark form rushed past him.

And Broos was dead.

The dark elf came in hard for the other two orcs. Oonta yanked the spear free, while Figgle drew out a pair of small blades, one with a forked, duel tip, the other greatly curving.

Oonta deftly brought the spear in an overhand spin, its tip coming over and down hard to block the charging drow.

6

But the drow slid down below that dipping spear, skidding right in between the orcs. Oonta fumbled with the spear, and Figgle brought his two weapons down hard.

But the drow wasn't there, for he had leaped straight up, rising in the air between the orcs. Both of the veteran orc warriors altered their weapons skillfully, coming in hard at either side of the nimble creature.

The scimitars were there, though, one intercepting the spear, the other neatly picking off Figgle's strikes with a quick double parry. Even as the dark elf's blades blocked the attack, his feet kicked out, one behind, one ahead, both scoring direct and stunning hits on orc faces.

Figgle fell back, snapping his blades back and forth before him to ward any attacks while he was so disoriented and dazed. Oonta similarly retreated, brandishing the spear in the air before him. They regained their senses together, and found themselves staring at nothing but each other.

"Huh?" Oonta asked, for the drow was nowhere to be seen.

Figgle jerked and the tip of a curved blade erupted from the center of his chest. It disappeared almost immediately, the dark elf coming around the orc's side, his second scimitar taking out the creature's throat as he passed.

Wanting no part of this enemy, Oonta threw the spear, turned, and fled, running flat out for the encampment and crying out in fear. Orcs leaped up all around the terrified Oonta, spilling their foul food—mostly raw, rotting meat—and scrambling for their weapons.

"What'd you do?" one cried.

"Who got the killing?" yelled another.

"Drow elf! Drow elf!" Oonta cried. "Drow elf kilt Figgle and Broos! Drow elf kilt Bellig!"

The Lone Drow

THE KNIGHTS
OF MYTH DRANNOR

A brand new trilogy by master storyteller

ED GREENWOOD

Join the creator of the FORGOTTEN REALMS® world as he explores the early adventures of his original and most celebrated characters from the moment they earn the name "Swords of Eveningstar" to the day they prove themselves worthy of it.

BOOK I
SWORDS OF EVENINGSTAR

Florin Falconhand has always dreamed of adventure. When he saves the life of the king of Cormyr, his dream comes true and he earns an adventuring charter for himself and his friends. Unfortunately for Florin, he has also earned the enmity of several nobles and the attention of some of Cormyr's most dangerous denizens.

Now available in paperback!

BOOK II
SWORDS OF DRAGONFIRE

Victory never comes without sacrifice. Florin Falconhand and the Swords of Eveningstar have lost friends in their adventures, but in true heroic fashion, they press on. Unfortunately, there are those who would see the Swords of Eveningstar pay for lives lost and damage wrecked, regardless of where the true blame lies.

Available in paperback in April 2008!

BOOK III
THE SWORD NEVER SLEEPS

Fame has found the Swords of Eveningstar, but with fame comes danger. Nefarious forces have dark designs on these adventurers who seem to overturn the most clever of plots. And if the Swords will not be made into their tools, they will be destroyed.

August 2008